GAMBLING ON COMMON SENSE

RATIONALITY, ROMANCE, AND THE SPACE BETWEEN

L. BRIAR

LAUGHING BRIAR BOOKS LLC

REVIEWS

"Gambling on Common Sense is hilariously delightful! A lighthearted romp through the cosmos that will leave you wanting more."

- David Hankins, Award-Winning Author of Death and the Taxman

"This fast-paced adventure masterfully blends humor, action, and poignant moments. Additionally, the cast of characters is uniquely entertaining and the world building across the universe is well-execu ted..."

- Sam Ledel Author of eight novels with Bold Strokes Books

"Gambling on Common Sense is that rare Star Trek satire that also manages to be a very good Star Trek like universe..."

- Nikhil Prabala author of The Dutchess of Kokora

Like to judge for yourself? Get a feel for L. Briar's stories by signing up for their free short story eBook "Do Aliens Dream of Electric Sheep?"

This book would not be possible without the loving dedication of my soon-to-be husband Ryan. Your patience, love, and delicious cooking have made it possible for me to write these words. Thank you for all the laughter.

Contents

THE HELIOS
DEEP SPACE EXPLORER

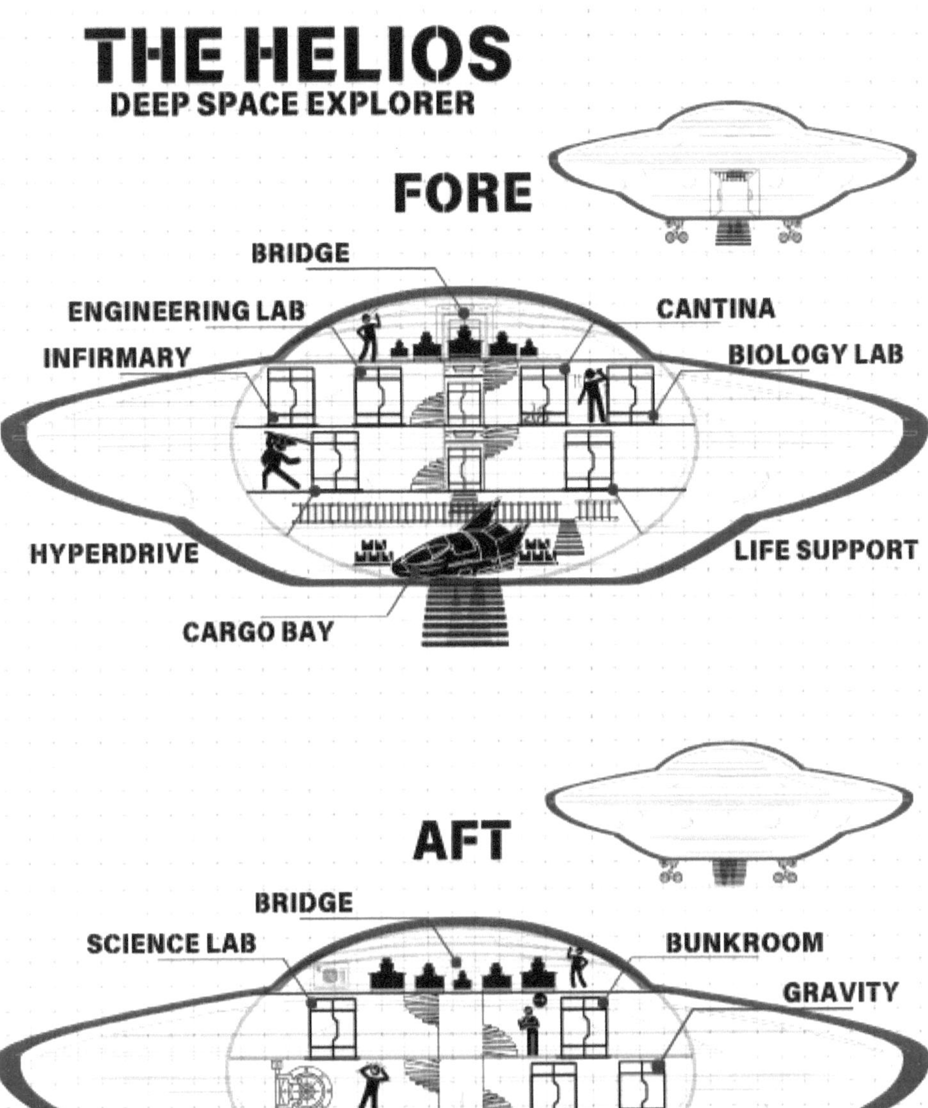

PROLOGUE

ON THE OTHER SIDE OF THE TIMELINE...

"*Officer Payne, do you gamble?*" *Captain Lin Solis asks me as I lean against his station's console on the bridge. The Spade Quadrant's starchart surrounds us, scanning solar systems as the* Helios *skips by. We've some time to kill. Solis shuffles a card deck as he eyes me.*

"Nope." I shrug.

ACT 1: RABBIT HUNT

CSO REPORT
Rotation 14, Cycle 11, Orbit 70

SHIP STATUS: All is well aboard the Helios

STORAGE CONTAINS

- 60 Alien eggs in cartons
- 1 Astra Resonator from Doomirage
- 1 Container of malfunctioning self-replicating nanobots
- 1 Container of Natasha's explosive contraband
- 1 Corrupt AI sphere 'Halcyon'
- 1 Shrink ray with 25% failure rate of subject explosion
- 1 Evil Co. starship to starship salesbot

STORAGE DISPOSED

- 57 Alien eggs in cartons
- 1 BS2 overzealous janibot
- 2 Killbots of unknown origin
- 1 Pair of haunted tap shoes

CSO SUMMARY

- Mission: 306 Ace Quadrant solar systems mapped and 4 Astra worlds discovered
- Transit: Helios resupplied at Hyperring outpost in preparation for return Terminal Trip
- Notes: Rival companies Evil Co. & BS2 are also active in this quadrant, but so far, we have beaten them to any suspected Astra artifact locations. All is well on the Helios.

1

DO NOT GAMBLE

Seated at the metal poker table, I ask myself, which *Helios* crewmember is a shapeshifting slizard? In the dim light of the cantina, it's hard to tell. Each of the four crewmembers stare at me expectantly, hoping their Common Sense Officer will lay it all on the table. Think, Ash! Stop tapping your finger and think. What would Tyson Major have done? Dad would have identified the slizard, who sent it, and—if it's not too late—saved the victim. Which I absolutely will ... right after this next hand.

"Full house." I lay down my cards. After a near orbit avoiding gaming with the crew, it feels good to be playing again. A collective groan washes over the cantina. It bounces around the small circular room, through the kitchenette sink's dirty dishes, past the dartboard with a robotic parrot stuck in the bullseye, and above the discarded synth-food wrappers. That last one irks me. I just swept in here. Wish I could blame the slizard for the mess, but I know hallmarks of the crew when I see them. Crossing my arms, I blow my shoulder-length brown hair out of my face. "You lost. Cough him up."

As a short woman just past twenty-two, intimidation isn't a mantle I wear well. I like to think my *Helios* navy-blue uniform with gold trim adds some respect. Donning it is a dream come true ... I represent Starprint Inc., one of the Terminal's Big Three like Dad before me. Although, around this table, everyone has that claim to fame. Pulling rank to find the slizard isn't going to happen. I'll need to examine the crewmates individually. This isn't like the academy. Lives are at stake.

"Impossible!" My first suspect, Biology Officer Lester Orion, juts out his salt-and-pepper bearded chin in defiance. He's a slender man with hair tied in a long, low ponytail. The pale fortyish-orbits man wears sunglasses, a Hawaiian shirt with the collar popped, and a wide-brim hat to hide his features, none of which disguises that Lester whistles when he bluffs.

"You know the rules. Give him here." I wave a hand toward the ball of purple tentacles perched on Lester's shoulder. In my eyes, Junior is more of a parasite than a pet, but you try telling Lester that.

"Not a chance, Love." Lester clutches his pet with both hands as Junior gently nibbles on his fingertips. Biologists are supposed to create food for the crew, not become food. I swear if he didn't have the last name Orion, he'd have been kicked off the *Helios* ages ago.

"Yeah..." I purse my lips. "That's not my name."

Would I be lucky enough for Junior to be the slizard? No, I know better than that. Judging from the shed torso skin I'd found in the docking bay; they should be humanoid. From what I recall of slizard behavior, they are a hardy lot that works alone and cooks their prey before eating them. Regardless of who has been taken, there should still be time to save them.

"There is no way on Planet Hell I'm giving him up," Lester huffs. A steel dagger plunges into the table in front of him, gripped tight by my second suspect, Science Officer Natasha Pollux. Lester nearly falls off his chair as she leers over the blade with a devilish grin.

"Don't be a scallywag!" Natasha yanks her knife from the table. Underneath her white lab coat is a pirate flag t-shirt, black pants, and handmade black leather boots. Most importantly, a tricorn sits atop her mass of curly black hair. I'm still not sure if the hat is cursed or if Nat just feels more confident with it on, but she has an unhealthy obsession either way. She might be the most knowledgeable Astra scientist in the known universe, but she's had a few screws loose since the Doomirage incident. While I'd hate to think my old friend is a slizard, I can't rule anyone out. Natasha falls back into her chair and crosses her arms. "The Lass won, fair in square, so cough 'em up."

Beside her, my third suspect, Engineering Officer Eugene Qual, nods in agreement. His goggles make his bright blue eyes absurdly large. The man is short and stocky, with more hair dedicated to his black mustache and beard than his head. Seeing me staring, he scratches the back of his head with a robotic hand. The arm has been installed backward this rotation, possibly for that very purpose. Qual lost his left arm after trying to elope in the Bermuda Tetrahedron with Roxy, the android femme fatale.

"This isn't fair!" Lester refuses to back down. "She must have cheated. Tell them!"

All turn to my last suspect. Captain Lin Solis rests his almond-shaped eyes on me. The man could be a terraforming propaganda poster given his angular face and jawline that could laser cut titanium plating. His rich crew-cut black hair frames a clean-shaven face that could make a girl swoon. Other girls, though. I have a rule not to think that way about coworkers ... anymore. Besides, he doesn't trust me after I repeatedly tried to confiscate his soulstone necklace.

"Well, Officer Payne, are you a liar?" Solis asks in a deep, even tone, but I can see a suspicious glint in his eye. "Did you cheat?"

The Astra soulstone pendant around his neck pulses with a soft blue light, as if it's laughing at me. Which, who knows, maybe it is. The newfound alien tech has only been studied for a few generations, but that hasn't stopped every Terminal company from seeking it out. Starprint Inc. commissioned the *Helios* for that very purpose: to join the Astra space race. But I don't trust Astra tech. It's unpredictable in how it impacts its wielders. Even for those that appear attuned like Lin. I'd give *anything* to toss that into an Isolation Container and throw away the keycard.

"I don't cheat." I meet his accusing gaze. Stupid captain, with his stupid deep brown eyes, with their stupid abundance of confidence. I wonder, not for the first time, if he can tell when I'm lying. The man seems to have a sixth sense for that sort of thing. After a long moment, Solis nods.

"There you have it. Our CSO is no cheater, and a man must keep his word." Solis turns to Lester. "You may not like the hand you're dealt, but you lost. Hand Junior over."

Reluctantly, Lester removes Junior from his neckline, leaving a layer of slime on his barcode tattoo. We all have one of those, courtesy of Terminal citizenship. The invertebrate wriggles, reaching back out to him. With Lester's other hand, he signs something I don't understand.

I should really learn Universal Sign Language at some point. Whatever it means aggravates Junior, who curls his tentacles tighter and chomps on the biologist's hand. At least I can rule out Lester as the slizard. Junior wouldn't mistake his favorite snack.

"I'll win you back next hand." Lester promises before holding out his pet.

"One moment." I pull out the baton-shaped Multi-tool of Preconfiguration or MOP from my hip holster. The device is standard issue for CSOs. Aside from the compact form, it has six additional settings to choose from and a handy snack compartment on top. Pulling the handle out, I rotate it from position P0 to P4 and press down. The MOP extends a meter, nearly popping Lester in the nose as the tip splits into tongs.

"Hey!" Lester objects as I clamp the MOP's tongs onto Junior. Standing up, I stuff him into a shoe-box-sized isolation container at my feet. The little alien snaps his beak, but the IC gel hardens, preserving him inside. Closing the lid, I scoot the box away from the table with my foot. It joins a meter high pile of ICs in a variety of shapes and sizes. I might just hit my CSO quota for this cycle.

I return my MOP to P0 setting, slip it on my belt and take my seat. There is one more IC I need to fill tonight. As Solis starts dealing the next hand of Terminal Hold 'Em, I examine the faces at our poker table. The slizard could be any one of them, it could even be—

Oh, Void. I think I know.

"Qual, what are you doing?"

Our supposed Engineering officer reaches a hand behind Lester and shakes salt onto the unaware man. He's even licking his lips. Seeing me watching, the slizard in Qual's form tries to disguise the motion.

"Nothing. Just sstretching."

"Hey!" Lester waves a hand at me. "Quit holding up the game. It's your bet."

"Check to you, Nat," I mutter, buying myself some time.

Okay, step one completed. Onto step two. If I were a slizard, where would I hide an Engineering Officer? The *Helios* has a ton of hiding spots, but I've narrowed it down by checking the cameras earlier. While the slizard was clever enough to avoid them, its absence from the footage spoke volumes. From the bay where I'd found its shed skin there was only one path it could have taken: the path to this cantina. Qual has to be in here somewhere. Maybe in the kitchenette?

Natasha doesn't say anything as she tosses a singed map into the table's center. She must have a terrible hand, she's always quiet when her hand sucks. Not that that matters right now.

Imposter Qual tosses an E. Vilco—better known by their nickname, Evil Co.—pill bottle into the pot. The bottle's label grins at me with its black skull and crossbones logo. A condescending face flashes in my mind like a chip rolling across the table. My former friend Darius' sarcastic half-smile twists in me. Stuff that man. I have other priorities right now.

"Where'd you get this?" I pluck up the bottle. What's a slizard doing with a product from one of Starprint's main rivals? "Pretty sure they're illegal in all four quadrants."

"Just a little ssomething I picked up." The slizard gives a nonchalant shrug before smiling. "Why don't you bet a more impresssive IC to find out? I know you've more sstored below than that pile behind you."

I narrow my eyes. What did this imposter want?

"Since when do you have—"

"Oh, come off it," Lester interrupts and tosses a partial open egg carton into the pot. Tiny versions of Junior float inside the eggs. Lester dips his glasses down to give me a gray-eyed glare. "You don't have to be such a hard-ass on regulations."

"My job is to make sure you explorers don't kill yourself. You're still alive, right?"

"Yes?"

"Then the hardass regulations are doing their job."

"Look, Love, it's not like everything in the universe is trying to kill us," Lester says.

I eye him, doing my best not to stare at the slizard beside him licking its lips with a forked tongue.

"I'd be out of the job if the universe wasn't," I mutter, returning the pill bottle to the pot.

Captain Solis clears his throat, and all eyes turn to him. It's his bet. Solis grasps his soulstone necklace, breaks the bindings with a quick yank, and tosses the gold-framed soulstone into the pile of contraband.

"All-in!" Solis says with a confident grin. The soulstone pulses in time with my beating heart. The artifact I've been trying to confiscate for nearly an orbit is *finally* within reach.

"You can't just keep going all-in every time Ash plays with us!" Lester stands up angrily.

"That'ss right!"

"Yarr!" The entire table tosses in their cards in exasperation.

"I haven't gone all-in in..." Solis looks distant as he racks his brain for the last time.

For the first time, I glance at my cards. Two red aces look back at me. It is the best starting hand in the game and wherever Solis has, there is a good chance I'll beat it. My palm itches. On one hand, Do Not Gamble is one of the first rules in the CSO handbook. On the other, if I play this right, I'll not only expose the slizard but stuff that damned soulstone in an IC. I shouldn't bet, it's too risky, but my hands are already moving to the keycard in my pants pocket. I shouldn't, but I can't pass up these odds.

"Call." I pull the CSO storage keycard from my pocket and toss it in. It clicks and chimes against the soulstone's crystal.

"What is that?" Lester asks with an incredulous raised eyebrow.

"That is the access card to my CSO storage," I say, leaning back in my chair and turning my gaze to the captain. "If you win, you get full access to the ICs on the lower deck of the *Helios*."

Solis focuses on me. "You're sure?"

I pause to do the math. "I'm 85% sure."

Solis gives me a respectful nod and reveals his hand: seven of hearts and two of clubs. It is the *worst* hand in the game. What is he thinking? As Solis flops the next three cards—ace of clubs, ace of spades, and three of clubs—I don't bother to stifle the smile creeping across my face. I've four aces. Make that 99.80% sure. That Astra soulstone is as good as mine.

As Solis deals the last two cards, I return my focus to the slizard. Normally, I'd try to be subtle, messaging my crew with my halocom, but Solis forbids halocoms at the poker table. All of our high-tech wristbands are stuffed in a jar by the kitchenette's sink. No calling in support on this one. I'll have to do things more directly. I flick the safety off the Joker baster hidden underneath my jacket. Covertly as possible, I adjust the setting to stun.

"Hey Qual, care to make a side bet?"

"What type of sside bet?" the slizard replies while massaging, or rather tenderizing, Lester's shoulders. They pause and their eyes narrow as I reach into my CSO backpack next to my chair.

"Wanna bet on what this is?" Ripping out the slizard skin, I toss it into the pot. There are a few curious glances as the crew takes in the scaly remnants.

"Is this an arts and crafts thing?" Lester asks. "Cause I'd rather play Hold 'Em."

"Seconded, matey." Natasha shakes her head.

"Officer Payne, we're in the middle of a game." Solis plucks the skin off the cards he'd just dealt. "This is no time for pranks."

"That'ss not mine!" the slizard protests.

"Okay, I can see how this got confusing." I backpedal my words as I regret my attempt at drama. I wave a hand at Imposter Qual. "You're not Qual. You're a shapeshifting slizard, and you've lost the element of surprise. Any hope you had of taking us out one-by-one is gone. Surrender peacefully, and you'll be treated fairly. Why not share with the crew what you really are?"

The slightest ripple runs across its false skin as the slizard shrugs. "I don't know what you're talking aboutss."

"Oh, come on! That doesn't even have an 's' in it!"

"Officer Payne, it is impolite to point out someone's speech impediment," Solis chides me. The rest of the crew nods as the situation gets away from me.

"But it's the wrong speech impediment. Qual has a stutter, not a lisp."

"I've been practicing," the slizard volunteers.

"Captain, the lass may be rude, but she has a point." Natasha examines the skin. Dried scales flake in her hands. "Tis a fresh shed. There be a slizard in our midst."

Quiet descends as everyone lets the truth sink in. Cards sit forgotten on the table.

"It could be anyone." Lester eyes me with suspicion. "How do we know it's not you?"

"Yess, how do we know you're not the sslizard?" Imposter Qual nods in agreement.

"If I was the slizard, why would I reveal that there is a slizard?" I rub my temples. This isn't how I saw this going.

"Officer Payne, what proof do you have?" Solis crosses his arms.

"Permission to question the suspect?" I ask.

"Granted."

"Assk me anything." The slizard leans back in the chair. "I'm an open book."

"What are those green scales under your chin?"

"Sskin condition."

"Or the fact that your left iris keeps turning into a slit?"

"Eye twitch."

"How about the fact that Qual has a robotic left arm, and you've installed it backwards?"

"I wanted to sscratch my back more eassily."

"That does sound like something Qual would do," Solis comments, and I nearly pull my hair out. The worst part was, Solis isn't completely wrong. Logical arguments are not going to cut it here.

"Any other questionss?"

"Just one but, first, I'm thirsty. Nat, can you do me a favor? Could you get me some water from the fridge?"

Natasha raises an eyebrow at me, and I remember my manners.

"Uh, please?"

She stands and makes her way into the kitchenette to the built-in fridge.

"Okay, last question." I turn to the slizard. Everyone tenses but the slizard can't help but twitch as Natasha opens the fridge's door, the only place in the cantina big enough to hide a hostage. The real Qual nearly falls out, but Natasha catches him. The man is fuming red, gagged and hogtied, and missing his robotic arm. A large icicle is hanging from his nose.

"If you're Qual, who's that?" I draw my Joker blaster from my jacket and rest its butt on the table, the short barrel pointed at the imposter. With a hiss, the slizard drops her guise. Flesh sheds away, revealing light green scales. Qual's arm falls and clacks on the floor. His stolen lab coat splits as the tall slizard gains a foot, revealing a dark green onesie underneath. There is even a nametag on it: Ms. HONEY. Long, wispy blonde hair sprouts from her head as her beard falls away. No, not hair, it's as thick as nail's keratin. Ms. Honey glares at me with bright yellow slit eyes and a jaw filled with buzz-saw teeth.

"Better." I keep the weapon trained on her. "Now, who sent you?"

"That iss not the quesstion to assk. The question to ask iss, where iss IC210?"

I ... falter. How does she know about *him*?

Honey lunges over the table at me, slashing the Joker to ribbons in my dumbfounded hands. Her other hand's claws swipe centimeters from my nose. She stops short as Solis catches her by the back of the neck. Even without the soulstone's physical enhancements, he is strong. He flings her away like a ragdoll. She slams into the dartboard, knocking the mechanical parrot loose. Ms. Honey scrambles to all fours with an angry growl.

"No, no thank you." Lester scrambles back from the table as Natasha works to free Qual from the fridge.

As Solis engages the intruder, I back up to my IC pile by the cantina's entrance. Ignoring the crashing sounds behind me, I find the largest one. I'd prepared it as soon as I'd found the slizard skin. It's one of my more secure models and requires a passcode to access. My adrenaline works against me, making my fingers shaky as I enter the code on its side console. I do it twice before hearing a satisfactory beep and the suction release. I fling the lid open, and it hangs by its hinges. With the IC in place, I hide behind the pile with MOP in hand and survey the scene.

Solis has Ms. Honey cornered in the kitchenette.

Her eyes flicker at each of the rallying crew members. Her demeanor shifts from aggression to self-preservation. She turns as if to run, and Solis swipes at her. But it's a faint. Instead, she dips to the wall, kicks off it, and flips over him. She bolts toward the exit. Natasha flings her dagger, causing Honey to duck. The dagger embeds itself into the wall beside a whimpering Lester. Honey hardly loses a step as she sneers and sticks her forked tongue out.

Looking away is her mistake.

Spinning the MOP handle to preset P2, I press down. The stun setting will be perfect for—

The MOP extends into a literal mop. It's never done that before. Somebody has been messing with my settings!

I pivot. Swinging the mop at Honey's feet, I catch her in the ankle. Surprise flashes across her face as she falls into the waiting IC. Gel splashes me and cold saps my strength, but I shake it off. It is worse for Honey; gel covers her, and she can hardly move as it hardens. Grabbing the lid, I slam it shut.

Adrenaline leaves me as I rest against the wall.

The cantina is quiet except for Ms. Honey's dull thumping inside the IC and the buzzing of the lights. Nope, that's not lights buzzing, that is a very high-pitched Lester scream. The biologist is crouched atop the cabinet beside the dartboard.

"Officer Orion," Solis walks over and taps Lester on the shoulder, "you're safe now."

"Um, right," Lester says, coughing. "Just a battle cry, sir."

"Of course."

"Ouch!" Qual—the real one—shouts as Natasha rips the tape from his mouth. He snaps off the icicle from his nose and tosses it at Honey's IC. It shatters against the box.

"Are you alright, me hearty?" Natasha pats his back soothingly.

"I'm f-fine." Qual turns a whole new shade of red at her touch. He coughs, straightens, and brushes ice off his lab coat. "Has anyone seen my arm?"

"Check under the table," I suggest.

"Say, what did she mean by IC210?" Lester asks, coming down from his shelf.

"Beats me." I shrug, but there's sweat on the back of my neck. It's a good question. Why does a random intruder know about him? Trying to act nonchalant, I focused on cleaning a scuff off my fiddleback shoes. Dad's old shoes. They aren't the most practical shoes, but they're a family heirloom and precious to me. Giving my thumb a lick, I brush it against the leather to little effect. I'll have to address that later.

"Say, Qual," I ask, turning my MOP presets back to the P0 baton, "did you mess with my MOP?"

He doesn't meet my gaze as he fidgets with his left arm.

"You did, didn't you?"

"Well, you're always cleaning, so I t-thought you might like an easier method."

I sigh. Qual has a bad habit of trying to improve things without asking.

"Next time, just ask." Pushing off the wall, I make my way back to the poker table. I'm exhausted, but at least I will be able to rest easy tonight. In fact, this is the most successful poker night in a long time, between Junior, the slizard, and Solis' soulstone." As I reach for the soulstone, Solis' calloused hand grabs mine.

"What are you doing, Officer Payne?" He raises an eyebrow at me.

"Um, I'm taking my winnings. I had four aces, remember?"

"You may want to look again." Solis releases my hand.

What is he talking about?

I glanced down at the cards on the table. While I'd been ousting Ms. Honey, Solis had finished dealing the last two cards. All five are face up and undisturbed by the scuffle: an ace of spades, an ace of clubs, and the three, four, and five of clubs. My throat tightens as I look back at Solis' cards, still laid face up in front of his seat. There, *inexplicably*, is the two of clubs. With a 0.2% chance of winning, Solis drew the gutshot: an inside straight flush. Four aces be damned.

Void help me. Captain Lin Solis has won the entire CSO storage.

2

Do Not Allow Unauthorized Access

The *Helios'* flying saucer has three levels, each with their own dreadful sound.

Level one is the sliding click of a corrupt AI sphere inserted into the bridge's console. That's haunted me since Halcyon the AI nearly ejected us into vacuum last orbit. On the second level, silence is what I fear. A deadly type of quiet that would mean no crew chattering in the bunkroom, experimenting in the labs, munching in the cantina, or recovering from a two-rotation hangover in the infirmary. But on level three—despite containing the artificial gravity conveyor, hyperdrive generators, life support systems, and cargo bay—one sound terrifies me more than anything, the chipper chirp of Solis' access granted to my CSO storage.

"Can't we talk about this?" My plea goes unanswered as the locking mechanisms in the door shift. The circular double door slides apart. I can't let him in here. Pushing in front of Solis, I cling to the doorframe's edges with white knuckles. "You don't need to do this."

"There is no honor in a sore loser." Solis plucks me up as if I were a low-gravity child and sets me aside with ease. He ducks his head to enter as I chase after him.

It had been a long journey in the Ace quadrant, and the thirty-square-meter room brims with ICs filling the rotating maglock shelves with a few stacked against the walls. Decorating my storage's walls are an embarrassing amount of Lost Earth collectables: a clock depicting ROTATIONS MISSING above the entrance, a few haloscreens with articles on last known locations and common earth animals. A solar system light fixture hangs from the ceiling. Solis only sees it when he bumps his head against it. Placing a hand to stop the fixture from swinging, he raises an eyebrow at me.

"I like Lost Earth, so sue me." I shrug. Growing up on the Terminal had been a lot of white walls and scurrying robots, so the idea of a world where you didn't need to live in a technology bubble appealed to me. Earth had become the stuff of legends after the former Terminal government lost it in a bureaucratic mishap. At one point, my academy buddies and I had formed a group dedicated to finding Lost Earth ... before everything fell apart.

But I don't need to justify my interests to the guy rooting through my things. At least it's only him, as the others are busy cleaning up the cantina. When I don't say anything further, Solis shrugs and strolls deeper into my space. His presence makes it feel cramped rather than cozy.

"Do you have an IC inventory record?" Solis rotates a shelf as he walks past the incinerator and the empty ICs in front of it. Any hazards deemed too dangerous end up in that atomizer.

"Yes." I stop the shelf he'd rotated and check the latch on IC25 holding Qual's corrupt AI sphere, still secure and maglocked down. "For every space quadrant we search, any Ancient Astra technology is saved, and anything else ends up in the incinerator. If you want that list, I can send it to your halocom, or you can just check the halopad by my desk—Don't touch that!"

Despite my warning, Solis accidentally knocks down a midsized IC. I catch it midfall with a grunt. IC15 is heavy and contains Qual's shrink ray that has a 25% probability of exploding its targets. Not something you need lying around. I return it to the shelf by my desk. I need to stop Solis from stomping around like a bull in a robotics shop. There are too many dangers here.

Void, why did I have to make that bet?

Solis stops by my desk and its floor-bolted chair. Chemical pine scents drift from the partially open jar of shoe polish. Next to it is my yellow smiley face stress ball which I wouldn't mind using about now. Beside those items, my halopad is plugged into the haloscreen above the desk.

"Who are they?" Solis asks.

"Who is who?" I ask, catching sight of the screen's moving image. It's an old halo, about three orbits back. Dare, Knox, and I are standing there, arms around each other's shoulders and grinning like fools. It'd been after we'd made our bet on who would find Lost Earth first. Behind us, my mother Alexandra Payne, squeezes all of us in a bear hug. The family resemblance is absolute, from the angular face, brown hair, blue eyes, to the stupidly large, dimpled smile. She always called me her Starling. A bittersweet smile touches my lips. "Those were the only sane people in the universe."

Solis raises an eyebrow at my cryptic response.

"Family and some academy friends," I clarify. Knox is dead center of the image, a head taller than Dare and I. He has sandy hair and a natural buck-toothed grin. Laughing always came easy to him. Even his heterochromia green and blue eyes have a twinkle to them. Dare for his part, is doing his best to smile. It's unnatural on his face, but it was genuine that day. His dark brown eyes stare directly ahead, determined as always, and his gold graduation cap compliments his burnt caramel skin tone.

"That you?" Solis nods at the haloscreen.

"Yeah, I had longer hair then."

"But she's smiling."

"Captain." I give him a withering gaze, "I am capable of smiling."

Solis' raises a skeptical eyebrow but doesn't say anything. He turns back to the photo. "Why isn't your father with you?"

"Dad was a CSO officer." The great CSO Tyson Major was a legendary Starprint CSO. He'd even been stationed on the *Helios*, long before the current crew. I miss him dearly, but Solis doesn't need to know my life story. He doesn't *get* to know. Swiping at the haloscreen, I brush away memories and bring up the inventory chart. "He was never around very often."

"Was?"

"Was."

Solis studies me. I'd been so careful with this captain. I'd not wanted him to know me beyond my role. It's not … professional. Creases in his brow deepen as pity grows in his eyes. I hate that look. It's the same face so many well-wishers give before they return to their lives while you're stuck in that pitiful moment. I circumvent his next words with a hand.

"Sorry sir, but I'm certain you're not here to dig into my past. What do you want?"

Solis purses his lips before returning to examine the screen. He doesn't say anything at first, and I find myself holding my breath. What will he take? The Astra Resonator from Doomirage, a killbot, or some of the countless infertile Junior eggs that need disposing? He flips back and forth before shaking his head.

"Why is that IC the slizard mentioned marked disposed in your records?" Solis asks.

"What IC?" I try to meet his gaze, but my eyes drift toward my shoes. Even I can hear the squeak in my reply. Maybe I should just let him talk about my graduation photos. I liked that line of questioning better.

"IC210." His eyes narrow.

"Captain, do you trust me?" I ask, my mouth dry.

"Not really." Solis pushes past me. He heads right for IC210's last recorded location, on the shelf left of the incinerator.

"You can't be serious." I barely succeed at keeping the quaver from my voice as I follow. "Don't you want a nice Qual doomsday device instead? I have at least three of those."

"What is it?" As Solis examines the shelves, he taps his newly tied soulstone necklace. It glows blue in the room's dim light, giving his face a sinister quality. My mind races. He can't open that IC. It would be the Terminal incident all over again. The memory of bubbling vats and maddened cries threatens to overwhelm me, but I shove them down.

"Just an IC too big to move myself. None of your concern."

"Officer Payne, it became my concern as soon as the slizard mentioned it."

I can't refute him there. Solis presses the shelf control's up arrow to rotate it. The shelf twists away, showcasing a new row of ICs in an anxiety-inducing carousel. It's okay Ash, don't panic. It might not be that bad. Solis releases the button and beside him, a coffin-like IC sits on a shelf that rocks gently. He turns off the maglock. Okay, never mind. Panic!

"Leave-that-alone.   It's-dangerous-to-mess-around-in-here. Don't-drop-him!"

The heavy IC slips from Solis' grip and crashes to the floor. Next to the viewport on top is an access console with a built-in screen that says:

IC: 210
Contents: Unregistered
Contents Duration: 375 rotations

Solis peers down through the viewport, and his face goes pale. Inside is an unconscious man wearing a navy-blue Starprint spacesuit. His face just visible through the face shield and hardened IC gel layers around him. He is an exact clone of Captain Lin Solis.

"Why is there another *me* in there?" Solis asks, without looking up.

He's tense. I'd be tense too if I found my clone in an IC that my CSO had hidden from me. Clones aren't uncommon but they are illegal under Terminal law. If discovered they're to be disposed of quickly, but I'll be damned if I let that happen to IC210. Lin deserves better than corporate policy, even if he's lost his damned mind. Void, how can I even explain?

I start with the facts. "He's a clone. He was trying to kill you and was captured."

"Officer Payne," Solis turns his determined gaze my way, "if you're certain he's some clone assassin, why haven't you tossed him into the incinerator?"

Good question.

"That's..." I struggle for the right words. What can I say? Go ahead Ash, tell the captain about the Terminal Incident and see how that goes! It worked out brilliantly the last time you told the truth. I shake my head. "That's complicated, sir."

Solis examines my face, no doubt looking for a tell: a droplet of sweat or a twinge in the corner of my lips, but I'm not lying. Lin's situation being complicated is an understatement, if anything. Solis turns away and taps a finger on the soulstone around his neck.

"You're not certain, are you?"

"About what, sir?"

"That you have the right man in that box?" Solis whispers.

I almost laugh but catch myself. He's serious.

"I've been off all orbit..." A flicker of doubt lines his face. "Like my memories have a gap. Something tells me that has to do with this man. Are you sure you have the clone in the box? Am I even the real Lin Solis?"

His soulstone's blue light flickers, an untrustworthy flame, like it wants to catch and burn everything in its path. I've seen what a soulstone can do when a man loses control of himself. I want to tell my captain the truth. I want to explain to the man in front of me why choice memories were withheld from him—why he he doesn't remember inside jokes or his R&R last Terminal visit.

But I *can't* tell him the truth because the truth is ... neither is the original Lin Solis. Even I don't know what happened to him after he sold his DNA to Starprint.

"You're very real, Captain," I answer, as earnestly as I can. Both he and Lin might be clones but they had both served as the *Helios'* captain. Starprint's Boss wanted someone with the Astra Luck in charge. Solis can handle oddities, like the soulstone, without the usual blowback of infirmity. It's given Starprint a desperately needed edge while exploring outer worlds.

Solis shakes his head. "I need to be sure. There's only one way to be sure. Open it."

"I can't." I glance down at my shoes, unable to meet his eyes.

"Then I will." Solis ignores me and tries his captain's code in IC210's access panel. There's an irritable beep as it's rejected.

I shake my head and try to keep my tone even. "Your override won't work here. Only I know how to open it. Even if you order Qual to hack it, the IC will recognize the attempt and lock permanently."

"Fine. Consider this your final warning, Officer Payne." Solis locks eyes with me. Anger roils in them, black ice covering a maelstrom underneath.

"Open it, or you'll be fired for insubordination and confined during our hyperjump back to the Terminal. We can open it there." He glances down, and I almost miss him whisper, "Consequences be damned."

"You can't do that." But he could. A CSO is the *Helios'* second in command, but the captain is the ultimate authority. Towing us back to the Terminal to open IC210 would expose both Lin and Solis to danger. I try again. "There is no need. You're the real captain."

Solis leans down so he's eye to eye with me. "If you're so confident, why not bet on it?"

"Excuse me?" I ask, but I can feel that familiar itch take hold. "What do you mean?"

"Let's assume you're telling the truth." Solis says, as he circles behind me and leans against the wall. "I can respect you not having the stomach to incinerate a clone, but with my memory gaps ... I need you to prove to me I'm the original Solis."

It's a chance that could tilt the odds in my favor. I try not to appear overeager and cross my arms. "Once I prove it, what do I get?"

"I'll return your keycard and leave IC210 in your care."

"And if I fail?"

Solis straightens and towers over me with a hand scratching his chin. "If you fail, you'll resign your position as CSO in everything but name. You'll be a corporate babysitter who gives me free reign of the *Helios*. That means no vetoing routes, no canceling planetary missions, and no requiring resupplies before the next hyperjump. The *Helios* will be 100% mine."

I bristle. He wants my ship? The same ship my father served on before me. Solis has another thing coming if he thinks I'll be cowed by this challenge. No, if anything my nerves are alight at the notion of beating him. I can do this. I can win Lin's safety. Despite the height difference, I meet Solis' gaze.

Sticking out my jaw defiantly, I hold out a hand. "I'll take that bet."

"Not so fast." Solis says. There's the slightest twitch to his lips. He holds up two fingers. "There are two conditions."

"What conditions?" I lower my hand.

"One, I have the final say on what task must be completed."

"And the second condition?" I ask and do my best not to bite my lip.

"It's not just me who you need to convince," Solis waves a hand behind me, "but the whole crew."

I turn to face the open doorway. There, Natasha leans nonchalantly against my gravlift with ICs from the cantina. Ms. Honey's IC is on the bottom of the pile. Lester peeks around the doorframe. Junior pops up from behind his head. Solis had gifted the creature back to the biologist despite my protest.

"Can we come in now?" he asks. "I want to see the secret captain too."

"Did you win my keycard?"

"No?" Lester scratches the back of his head.

"Then you can't come in."

"It's not even your storage anymore," Lester says with a hint of smugness. "It's—Ow!"

Lester nurses his side from where Natasha elbowed him.

"Don't go disrespecting our Ashy," Natasha says. "Whatever this IC210 be, she's still our CSO. If she says our captain be true, he be true. Lass has a hard enough duty without ye meddling." She waves a hand at the gravlift. "Speaking of, where do I stash this booty?"

I shake my head. "How much did you all hear? Wait, how long have you been listening?"

"Since I f-found out you've a dead dad." Qual scares the slipspace outta me as he steps from the shadows of the ICs beside the incinerator bin. When did he even get in here? The man is quiet for having a mechanical arm. He nods apologetically. "Sorry for your l-loss."

"Fresh Stars, can we not do this?" I run my hands over my face to try to wipe away the stress. I press my hands together as if I was praying to some ancient God. Maybe I should start? It would be nice to have some cosmic force on my side.

"Well, Officer Payne?" Solis pulls my keycard from his pant pocket and waves it at me. "What do you say?"

"Just to be clear," I chew my lower lip, "if I can prove to everyone here that you're the original Solis and not a clone, you'll return my keycard, and leave IC210 alone?"

"That's the deal," Solis agrees and thrusts his hand out.

Considering my options makes me feel queasy. Four unspecified clone disproving tasks were not on my bingo sheet this orbit. I shouldn't risk this. I could just tell them the truth … but that malicious glint of blue light from the soulstone reminds me how well that went last time. To protect Lin, there isn't much choice.

"Can't I know the tasks first?"

"No. If you're not willing—" Solis starts to lower his hand.

"No." I grab it. "A deal's a deal."

After an orbit of distancing myself from the crew, avoiding gambling, I've fallen off the wagon and, with one bad hand, I'm now on damage control. A smile creeps over Solis' face as his hand tightens over mine and I realize I've messed up. Void it all. He *played* me. He wanted a bet and on his terms. Panic is the appropriate response, but all I feel is static racing across my skin as that adrenaline-inducing itch calls to me. Odds be damned. I meet his smile with a grin of my own. This bet has just started.

Solis releases me. "Officer Pollux, let's start this bet with you."

He tosses my keycard to Natasha. She catches it with ease.

"Aye aye, Captain." Natasha casts me her best swashbuckling grin. "Might be I have just the destination in mind."

My nerves spike. I think I'd rather face the slizard again.

Bent over my CSO workbench, I stare at the halopad's screen and weigh my options. There are 9,000,000 glints in my account, every single bit I've scrapped together for these past three orbits and the entirety of my inheritance. Alexandra Payne has control of my account to protect it from my so called self-destructive impulses. It's not fair really. I've missed out on so many good opportunities—no, focus Ash. I just need to reach out to Mom at some point. I have to convince her. With enough glint, I could buy my own ship and see Lin safely away from this dangerous bet and the Terminal's incinerator bin, but I've run into a small problem.

It's. Not. Enough.

Without a deep space explorer class ship like the *Helios*, there's no escaping Terminal space. Sure, there are some colonies spotted here and there but none of them are independent. Even if I can hide him there, colony life is generally ... short. If I want to protect Lin, my only option is to play along until I have enough. I toss the halopad away in disgust and lean back in my chair. I wish I knew where my stress ball went, but I haven't been able to find it since Solis' CSO storage invasion.

"Hey, Ms. Honey." I cast a glance at the slizard's IC. It's still on the gravlift beside the incinerator bin. She didn't need to worry, Solis required the incinerator be disabled before allowing me to be alone in here. "Care to share who hired you?"

She remains silent. Rather rude since the shapeshifting alien caused this mess. No ... not an alien if you believe the rumors. I shake my head recalling the theory Lester had shared. Slizards are rumored to be humans genetically altered to make us more adaptable to hostile environments. While the project is rumored to be successful, the effort was canceled without explanation. Lester's tin foil conspiracy theory is that a slizard assassin had spooked Terminal higher ups. It's rare to see one ... so why is she, or whoever hired her, after Lin?

Tracking down security footage, it's clear she was at our last resupply station, but access like that takes Big Three level resources. Evil Co. is an obvious choice, but they aren't the only players. Big Space Box Store could be involved. Or it could be an outside terrorist type. Hijack is a favorite boogieman among the Terminal's citizens. There are too many unknowns, and chewing the inside of my lip isn't helping.

Aside from myself, only Griz knows Lin is alive and there's no way in four quadrants he'd have talked. Once we get back to the Terminal, I need to chat with him. Griz always knows what to do. We can interrogate her together. With a stretch, I stand and collect my things.

As I move to the exit, I stop by IC210. Leaning down, I brush the dust off his IC's viewport. His face is eerily stoic inside.

"Hey Lin," I force a half-smile. "Have I told you I'm sorry lately?"

He looks like a dead man in there. The knot in my chest tightens. I know this was my only option but sometimes ... sometimes, I really wish I could just hear his voice. It's different from Solis' voice, even if they are genetically the same. With Solis there's no history to it. Frankly, I don't want it to be the same, that would be too weird.

"Please, wait a little longer. I promise to find a way to cure you."

I hope it's a promise I can keep. Straightening, I make for the exit but hesitate in front of the circular doorway. Natasha had let me in. As soon as I leave, I'll not be able to re-enter on my own. Only the keycard holder will be able to open this door. Taking a deep breath, I exit the CSO storage and step into whatever bet Natasha has cooked up.

Standing on the *Helios'* bridge feels like drifting in space. It's designed that way, with a 360-degree array of visual, audio, and spiritual sensors holographically projected from outside. Mostly, it's done with haloscreens that cover the walls and portions of the floor towards the ship's front. The illusion is only broken by the emergency exit hatch opposite the entrance and the viewport, a physical transparent band installed in case of power failures.

Outside that port is one hell of a view. A hyperring: a massive circular structure built to send ships from one galaxy to another without all that pesky relativity business. They operate similarly to the *Helios'* hyperdrive but on a larger scale. How had Qual explained it? Imagine space had a pocket and anyone with a hyperdrive generator could reach into it and poke a finger through. The bigger the hyperdrive the deeper in the pocket they can reach. Hyperrings had the longest reach with near instantaneous transit. Deep space explorers like the *Helios* can reach deep into the pocket but it takes more time to traverse. Small craft like shuttles are only good for short jumps and tend to be a bumpy ride and ... I think this is the part where Qual's analogy broke down.

Personally, I've always found them a bit spooky. The metallic surface is silvery in the Helios' lights with a fiery red twinge from a distant protostar. This one is the last in a long line of jump rings to the edge of the Ace quadrant we've been exploring. We're supposed to be using it to head back to the next quadrant, but now? Well, I guess it's up to Natasha where we go.

What have I gotten myself into?

"So, be it true?" Natasha asks.

I turn to face her from my spot in front of the captain's station and raise an eyebrow. She reclines in a chair with her feet on her console's station. We're the only people on the bridge. The crewmember stations form a flying V, with the captain's station in front. Qual's station, then mine, sit to his left, while Lester's station, then Natasha's, sit to his right. The captain's station is the only one with a manual override for flights, which has been necessary since Qual's corrupt AI sphere partially damaged the autopilot systems.

Natasha clarifies her question. "Tis the captain but a copy of his former self?"

"You know my answer. Be serious." I walk over and nudge her boots off her console.

She raises her eyebrows at me as her shoes hit the floor. Even if she's saved my life more than a handful of times over our orbits together, that's no excuse to disrespect her station. If I'm going to sabotage Natasha's test, I need to discover what she has planned, but she has been unusually tight-lipped.

"Just tell me where we're going already so I can prepare?"

"And give ye a hint? Nah, tis a surprise."

"The slizard wasn't enough of a surprise?" I rub my temples.

"Twas but an appetizer for a whale of an adventure." Natasha twirls one of her many curls. "But I promise ye, ye'll like it."

"Like it?" I blow my hair out of my face. "Why don't I believe you?"

"Oh, ye caught me. Perhaps ye might not like it. But … you need to go, just as much as the captain and I." Something of Nat's old, shy self slips into her words. "Just like the captain, you've not been yourself this past orbit. You two weren't always so at odds. While I don't know what's what about IC210, I trust you, Ash. You can trust me."

My resolve wavers. I knew Nat before she became the *Helios'* Science Officer. She helped Dad on a mission once, and we'd become friends while I was still at the academy. If there was anyone I could confide in on the *Helios*, it's her. I wouldn't want to put my secret's burden on Qual, Lester Orion can't be trusted, and Solis … I don't want to think about Solis. But Natasha I *want* to trust, to have an ally in this mess, but we don't always get what we want. Hesitantly, I ask her a favor, "Nat, take off your hat."

"Yar? What be ye talking a fool about?" Her demeanor shifts quick as a hyperjump.

"Let's make a deal. If you take off your tricorn, I'll tell you anything you want to know."

"Ye be barking up the wrong tree." Natasha levels her dark brown gaze at me and madness resides there. Her pirate side shines through.

That glimmer of the woman who I know is behind the hat disappears again. She's become more and more reliant on it to the point that she hardly ever takes it off. "Me not be the one with the problem."

"Sure, keep thinking that." I cross my arms. So much for a trusted ally. Once, I'd stolen her hat while she slept. I had it long enough to run tests and make sure it wasn't anything malicious. As far as Qual's lab equipment and I could tell, it was just a tricorn hat—but try telling Natasha that. She was less than happy when she stole it back.

"Everything alright in here?" Solis enters with Lester trailing behind.

"Aye, Captain." Natasha tilts her hat to him.

"Yes, sir," I reply with a sharp salute.

"Then to your stations," Solis says formally and walks to his station. He's been curt since our confrontation in CSO storage. Good. That's the way it needs to be. Lester smirks as he passes me with Junior on his shoulder. His clothes reek of lab's synthetic meat and eggs. Guess we'll be having chicken later ... again. Casting a withering gaze their way, I take my own seat. Junior slithers to Lester's opposite shoulder as if to hide from my hostility. Good, I don't trust you either.

"Officer Payne, are we ready for hyperjump?"

At my station, I checked the latest *Helios* diagnostics for the hundredth time today. All systems are green. Wherever we're going, the *Helios* is ready for it. "The ship's ready once our crew settles in, Captain."

"Where be Qual?" Natasha asks. No sooner does the question leave her lips than our engineer bursts onto the bridge. He's a bit sweaty as if he'd been running and ... is his lab coat singed?

"S-sorry, I'm late." Qual practically collapses into his chair. "I was working on a new project."

I purse my lips. His new projects tend to need extra CSO supervision. But if Solis is concerned, he doesn't show it. Instead, he rotates to face Natasha.

"Alright, Officer Pollux. Where are we going?"

Natasha types into her station's console. Solis' station chimes, and his brow furrows as he examines her destination's coordinates. I don't like that concerned look on his face, and I can't see the coordinates from my chair.

"You sure?" he asks, and Natasha nods. "Very well. Everyone ready?"

"Junior and I are good to go."

"Yar."

"Y-yes."

"Always," I reply and tighten my harness. Hyperjumps aren't usually bumpy, but the act makes me feel better. Without another word, Solis steers us into the hyperring. As we near the ring, I can see the special distortion inside, as if someone had thrown a stone into a pond reflecting the night sky. I hold my breath as we fly through. With a blink, I miss our journey. One moment we're the Ace quadrant's deep space, and the next we're hovering in front of a planet. We've reached through space's pocket and poked a hole out the other side.

Hyperring jumps are really the best method of travel.

A red dwarf frames the planet in front of us. Planetary details and the world's halo float above my station. At first glance, the tidally locked planet with its stable orbit is a colony contender. It's nestled in the red dwarf's narrow but temperate Goldilocks Zone, its electromagnetic field keeps the powerful radiation away, and it supports liquid water. Its atmosphere boasts healthy amounts of nitrogen, oxygen, and carbon dioxide and a thankful lack of harmful pathogens. While the tidally locked status does mean one side of the planet burns and the other side freezes, there's a sweet spot in the strip of land between where human life could survive. Filling that strip is a lush purple jungle with rich resources, alongside water sources and—most tempting—Astra ruins. It's almost as if it was made for humanoid life. But I know better. It is *no* haven. It's one of the deadliest planets in the Ace quadrant.

"D-Doomirage?" Qual wears his nerves like an inadequate winter coat. Even snuggled in them, he shivers. "Why here?"

"Cause," Natasha says with a swashbuckler's smile, "we're going to use the Astra ziggurat for our captain's test of spirit."

She casts a glance my way, and her confidence faulters as she sees my face. I can't hide my outrage. Natasha has taken us to the planet that killed my father.

3

—·—

Do Not Deviate from the Path

A perpetual twilight lingers over Doomirage as the sun never truly sets. Deafening silence haunts this world that so many have tried, and failed, to colonize. In the silence, three of us fly in the *Helios'* shuttle craft over the purple canopy. The shuttle is nearly silent and highly maneuverable. Although, Solis is really testing out that second part. I'm glad I applied the Starprint Inc. motion sickness patch behind my ear. Otherwise, his low profile 'flying' would have me chumming over the side, and I did not want to stir up the local fauna. Not on Doomirage. Not yet.

I could kill Natasha for bringing us here. Easily in fact, as she hangs out our shuttle's side to get a better view. Humid wind whips by since she insists we keep the top down. One of her hands clings to the shuttle and the other to her tricorn hat. I don't know how she's wearing that long jacket in this heat. Instead of giving her the push she rightfully deserves for this dangerous detour, I pull her in by her satchel strap. Natasha's hair whips me in the face as she plops into the seat beside me.

"Ashy! Can ye believe we're here?" Natasha asks with wild eyes. "Adventure be in these winds."

I don't say anything. There's a Lost Earth saying that if you don't have anything nice to say, shut your mouth and act sulky. I tend to abide by that. Natasha elbows me in the ribs.

"Don't blubber so. Now be yer chance to discover a bit o' truth." Her gaze goes distant, and she twirls one of her curls. I catch Solis tilting his head to listen as she adds, "Once we land at the Astra ziggurat, we all will."

I give her a side eye.

Natasha has been here before. But last time, she'd been a hostage to the notorious pirate, Nemo the Widowmaker. Nemo's face flashes through my mind: a dark-haired woman with jade eyes and a liking for jangling jewelry. She had worn her wealth like a shield and never could get enough of it. I'd admired her once ... before I knew who she was.

For her part, Natasha can't, won't, and is likely under strict NDA not to say what happened on Doomirage. While she's right—I wanted to know what happened to Tyson Major—Natasha bringing me here feels like slicing open a jagged scar. A knot in my gut tightens. Doomirage was the mission that led my father to his grave. I don't blame Natasha for what happened—Widowmaker fooled a lot of people—myself included. That doesn't mean I'm forgiving her for dragging me here anytime soon.

"Just put on your seatbelt," I mutter. I've only myself to blame really. If I'd followed the CSO handbook, we wouldn't be here, but that's not particularly helpful thinking when you're in the thick of it. So, I start going through my equipment list instead: body armor, MOP, IC backpack, and my fiddleback shoes with orthopedic support. Initially, I'd wanted our spacesuits over the navy-blue body armor, but Junior's rotten eggs had made them ... unusable. So, I did my best to equip us with what we had.

The real key to infiltrating the ziggurat is the *Helios*. I tap my wristwatch halocom and message the bridge. "How's that distraction coming?"

Qual's miniature halo appears, floating above my halocom.

"D-distraction inbound. Lester is on it!" Qual replies with an enthusiastic nod. He's fiddling with a sphere in his right hand. Is that my stress ball? No, too big.

"What are you holding?" I ask, but he shakes his head, unable to hear me as Solis picks up speed and wind whips around us. In the distance, there's a noisy burst as the *Helios* speeds through the atmosphere, blasting a cacophony of strange squawks and gurgles that even the wind can't drown out. It's not pleasant but our biologist assured me it is the Spirit Beast's mating call. From Qual's side of the halocom, the sound of guttural growls emanate.

"Huh, they did not like that. I wonder if I got the pitch wrong?" Lester says in the background. "Oh well, they are giving chase anyway. Tell Love, she's good to go."

"You're g-good to—"

"I heard him. We'll let you know once we've reached the ziggurat." Closing my halocom's feed, I tap Solis on the shoulder. "It's clear. We have at least a ten-minute window."

"Good work, Officer Payne." Solis keeps his voice stoic. He's always more official when dealing with stress. It's been a full rotation since he discovered IC210. He is outwardly impassive, but I can tell curiosity eats at him. Since Solis replaced Lin—at the best of times—his behavior toward me has been subdued and the worst annoyed, but always distant. That distance has been about the only thing keeping me sane in this past orbit. I do my job, people stay safe, and I buy time. If these missions buy more time so, be it. But those curious glances Solis keeps flashing in my direction are problematic. The sooner we resolve these bets the better.

Solis spins the wheel to take us west in the sun's direction and to the Astra ziggurat. Natasha is in her own world, humming a delighted sea shanty. I still have no idea how she intends this trip to prove Solis is the original. I need to put aside my pride so I can find out what this 'test of spirit' might be.

"What's got you singing?"

"Last time I were here, I were shaking in me boots, afraid of everything from pirates to Spirit Beasts. But now I desire to enjoy it all! Look, don't ye see how beautiful it be?"

"Oh, yeah. It's great being on a planet that wants you dead."

We're close enough to the treetops, the decaying vegetation threatens to make me sneeze. As someone who's had an eye twitch since we'd entered atmosphere, I find more beauty in that Ajax Rifle on the rack attached to the back of Solis' seat.

"Fear not, matey!" Natasha leans in. "I'll show ye the truth of this place!"

"Natasha, are you taking pity on me?" My eye twitches for a new reason.

"Aye."

"Please stop."

"We're almost to the ziggurat!" Solis calls. We clear the trees, and I catch my first glimpse of the ruins. Twisted spires surround a massive golden ziggurat. The sun's red light reflects off the metallic surface and hurts my eyes. As we enter its shadow, intricate runes carved into the ziggurat become visible. They cover the structure, save for the giant staircase descending from a grand double door at its top. These ruins are why so many had tried to colonize here: from rag-tag pirates to intergalactic sponsors.

And it appears another is giving Doomirage a go.

A massive, faded skull and crossbones logo is splashed across the ziggurat's runes. Evil Co. has planted roots here. This is an ... unexpected complication. I wonder if that means Darius and his cohorts are here. In an infinite universe, that would be some extremely bad luck. Knox would know how to handle Darius, but he isn't around anymore. If he was, maybe we'd still be on speaking terms.

"Something wrong, Officer Payne?" Solis cranes his head to look at me. I release his seat which I'd unintentionally had in a death grip.

"It's nothing, I just didn't think Evil Co. had made it to this quadrant. They've cut back the jungle around the ziggurat. It's leaves us exposed."

"'Tis worrisome." Natasha nods in agreement as she adjusts her satchel's straps. "Might make a mess of me test."

Looking at Natasha, my CSO sense starts to tingle. Something has been bothering me.

"Hey, Nat?"

"Aye?"

"Since when do you carry a satchel?" For the first time since departing the *Helios*, Natasha doesn't say anything. Instead, my pirate crewmate gives me a wry grin. She had been so specific about returning to this location to test Solis, and I'd ignored an obvious fact: not only is this planet's history special, but the *Helios* had an artifact from this world on board....

"Did you bring the Doomirage Resonator back here?"

"Best leave that question lie."

"Show me what's in the bag."

With a reluctant shrug, she opens the bag for me. Sure enough, a sleek thirty-centimeter onyx obelisk with Astra runes on each face rests inside. The Doomirage Resonator. My face goes flush. There's a reason they call them Resonators. They're how deep space explorers, like the *Helios*, are able to find Astra ruins in the vastness of space. While active, they inadvertently send out a universal beacon we can detect. Given this Resonator's runes aren't aligned and there's no light to them, at least it's inactive ... for now. It's an Astra artifact that other companies would kill for, and she wants to take this into Evil Co.'s new outpost?

I grind my teeth. "This isn't in our plans. Let's retreat for now—"

Something fast rips through the air overhead. A violent wind rocks our shuttle. Facing skyward, I see a silhouette with a six-meter wingspan. With the sun passing through its semi-transparent feathers, prismatic colors wash over our shuttle. Its lean body is built like a cat, but way less fluffy, with a horned reptilian face and twin barbed tails. From its lofty position, it snarls at us.

"Spirit Beast," Natasha whispers reverently. Not the vibe I'd suggest. Terror. Yeah, terror feels more appropriate given the pit that just opened in my stomach. The beast flexes its me-sized claws as it dives at us.

"Hold on!" Captain Solis hollers. He throws our shuttle into high gear, surging us forward. Just in time, too. The beast careens past. Behind us its feathered wingspan blasts the jungle canopy before it flutters to a stop.

"I'll deal with this." Natasha unholsters her chrome Joker with Astra runes around the barrel from her hip. The handheld blaster whirls as she disengages the safety, takes aim, and fires. The shot is dead on but passes straight through the beast as its body shifts to semi-translucence. Meat and bone phase into something more ethereal. Natasha curses. This is where Doomirage gets its name: from the ghosts that haunt its jungle and the mirage they cast. The creatures can phase through ship hulls and sneak up on you in a moment's notice. The best way to stay safe is to avoid attention.

Too late for that endeavor.

The grassland ripples with wind as the beast launches at us from below. I lose track of its near invisible form, but the beast's screech closes in. From my halocom, I try to hail the *Helios* for help, but the call fails. Nothing but static. That's not normal. It's like someone is jamming the signal. With a glance at the skull and crossbones logo on the ziggurat, I have a guess as to who.

Solis flies at full speed toward the only possible shelter, the Astra ziggurat. Astra structures are known to be resilient to Spirit Beasts. We'll be able to hold out until help arrives. As the beast's screech grows closer, Natasha pops open the floor panel.

"What are you—" I stop as I see the weapon she shoulders.

It can best be described as a bazooka. It's nearly as big as the would-be pirate, with a bright red paint job and the name Blackjack etched on its side. With practiced efficiency, she snaps it in the direction of the beast's cries. A cylindrical ring on the front rotates, flashing with Astra runes as it charges. If she fires that thing, the shuttle won't be able to handle it.

"Wait!" I shout.

The horned beast turns corporeal to strike at us from above, but Natasha pulls the trigger. A beam twenty centimeters in diameter blasts out. The beast barely has time to spout a confused hiss before the laser impacts. The blue light propels it into the treetops beyond, causing them to crack and ripple. I have only enough time to grab her shirt and pull down, before the Blackjack's shockwave rocks our shuttle. Natasha flies from my grip and slams onto the shuttle's open floor panel shuttle. Her Blackjack drops into the jungle below.

"I've got it!" Solis shouts, struggling with the impact. Desperately, he tries to straighten us. We clip one of the ziggurat's twisted spires and tilt dangerously sideways. We're coming in fast. The ground rises to meet us. I close my eyes and brace to become a flapjack.

The impact never comes.

Creeping my eyes open one at a time, I find us floating in front of the ziggurat's steps. Solis engages the landing gear and settles us down lightly on a floral patch. The stars blaze above and we're still alive.

Sweet Fresh Stars! I'm not sure if it's fear or the humidity that has me sweating, but I'm happy for it either way.

Solis sighs as his soulstone glows like a distant blue star. "Everyone still alive?"

"Yes, I'm happily not a pancake." I unbuckle my seatbelt and stand up. I snatch up my IC backpack and confirm my MOP is still on my hip. Good thing for small mercies. "Can you get us out of here?"

Solis shakes his head. "Not on the shuttle. Clipping the spire damaged her."

Checking my halocom, there's nothing from Lester or Qual. I glance up at the ziggurat with Evil Co.'s logo. It must be a jammer. If we want help, we'll need to disable it. Solis grabs the Ajax from the rifle rack and flicks off the safety as he surveys the foliage. Sweat runs from his forehead to his chin. We won't be able to stay here long.

From the floor, Natasha groans.

Reaching down, I offer her a hand which she heartily accepts. As I pull her to her feet, she holds a hand to her head as if to right a lopsided world. Checking her pupils with the light from my halocom, I don't see any signs of a concussion.

"Ahoy, Ash?"

"Yeah?"

"Methinks we should do that more often!" As she smiles, I can't help but notice her missing premolar. That'll require an infirmary visit later. Assuming we survive.

"Methinks you have a death wish," I say, shaking my head. She might not have a concussion but she's still a bit crazy. "You're making me miss your scientist roots."

Natasha looks genuinely offended and starts to argue but is interrupted by an unearthly howl. It starts as one distant call, but is answered by another, and another, each one closer than the last. The beasts are none too happy with our intrusion on their world.

I bite my lip. "We need to get out of the open."

"To the ziggurat." Natasha motions to the massive stairs. "Astra structures can keep spirits out."

"Let's get a move on it." Solis slings his Ajax rifle to his back and heads for the stairs.

We run, fast as our feet can fall. While the ziggurat steps aren't made for a human's gait, Evil Co. has installed smaller scaffolds to help traverse them. As we run, I can't help but notice old blaster burns marring the ziggurat's golden surface. They're usually covered with paint, so before Evil Co.'s time here. Is that from when Dad ran this gauntlet? Had there been a firefight? I wonder if—

A step crumbles under me. Throwing my weight forward keeps me from falling down the stairs, but my shoe slips as I try to catch myself. I land hard on my left ankle. Gasping, I try to stand, but pain blinds me. My heart thunders as bestial growls emanate from below.

"Hurry!" Natasha shouts as she dashes forward.

"My ankle—I can't run." My voice quavers. Solis stops beside me on the golden stairs as I fail to stand. "What are you doing?"

"No one gets left behind." Solis, not losing a step, plucks me up and tosses me over his shoulder like a rug. It's not dignified, but it beats certain death. Turning on his heel, he bounds up the stairs. I try not to bite my tongue with each step. This position has two additional side effects: The first is being way too close to Solis' armpit and lemon scented deodorant. The second is seeing the murder of Spirit Beasts fazing through the jungle below. Twelve very unhappy beasts investigate our shuttle. Each has a uniquely horrifying hodgepodge of species, spliced together. Worse, one sees us.

"Hurry up!" Natasha calls from the doors above. She has one side pried open for us to slip through.

"Please go faster," I cling harder to Solis' shirt. The original horned beast rejoins the others. Natasha's blast singed him, and one tail is missing, but he hasn't slowed a step. They all bound up the stairs after us. While some beasts must slither or crawl, the horned beast spreads its wings and lifts into the air. I gulp. "Go much faster!"

Forty meters.

Twenty meters.

Ten meters.

Its maw opens wide and—

Solis launches us through the ornate door and into a hexagonal antechamber. Behind us, the horned beast rams into the open door inadvertently slamming it shut. Twilight snuffs out as it closes. A hungry bellow accompanies deep scratching. For a moment, I wonder if Natasha is wrong and the Spirit Beasts will be able to phase through the ziggurat but as the roars diminish to disgruntled growls, I relax. Whatever the Astra made these walls from, it's enough to keep the beasts out.

"We're safe here." The captain's voice echoes in the darkness. The tension in his shoulders releases as he helps me down. I try to put weight on my bad foot but crumple from the pain. Solis catches me.

"You alright, Payne?"

"No." I shake my head. "But I'm alive. Thanks for that."

I flick on my halocom's light. A soft blue illuminates Solis' face next to mine. He holds me distractingly close. I can feel his steady heartbeat. Even his breath is calm and measured, but that's expected of a Starprint captain. He's so damn perfect sometimes. Just like Lin before...

This is not what I need to be thinking about right now. Pushing off him, I hop away.

"Nope, not doing this." Why am I talking aloud? Shut up, girl.

"Do you need a hand?" Solis has a hint of amusement in his voice.

"No! Doing just fine. Just stay right over there, okay? Maybe try to find what's blocking our comms so we can call for the *Helios*, would you?" Using my halocom light to guide me, I find an empty spot against the wall. I slide my IC backpack off my shoulder and drop it to the ground. As I move to sit, my blue light reveals a snarling Spirit Beast's face. I freeze until I realize it's just an image carved into the stone. The beast's body is painted with shades of scarlet, gold, and ivory. Next to it, runic writing cuts a sharp near-forgotten tongue into the wall.

But most impressive is the Astra resting on its back.

The Astra's carving reminds me of Lost Earth's angelic lore. If those angels had six insect-like wings instead of bird ones and massive compound eyes instead of a head. The carving hides its body under its wings like a shimmering cloak, obscuring any key features. They must have been giants to ride a full-grown Spirit Beast.

"Strange, be it nought?" Natasha wanders over to examine the carving with her halocom.

"What's strange?" I ask. I want to be mad at her, but life or death situations tend to drain my capacity for sullen quiet. Leaning my back against the rune-covered wall, I slide down to a seat.

"Astra built these ziggurat ruins across many planets. Me research shows them to be terraforming stations. The Resonators influence a world's terraforming process. I've little doubt that this one," Natasha taps her satchel absentmindedly, "is why there are Spirit Beasts on Doomirage. But for all their success in colonizing new worlds, the Astra vanished. Have you ever considered it?"

"All the time. I'd like to ask them why they left such a tempting mess behind. Ever since the first Astra discovery almost fifty orbits ago, the Terminal's Big Three have diverted all resources from Lost Earth to an Astra space race." Across the room, I catch a glimpse of blue light from Solis' soulstone. "But, sometimes I think we forget how dangerous Astra technology is."

"Lester's right," Natasha adjusts her hat, "ye be no fun."

"Probably true."

With a wince, I remove my left shoe and set it aside. My ankle is swollen but nothing appears broken. Retrieving my IC backpack, I rummage through it and take out the first aid kit. Inside, I find anti-inflammatory pills and rip open the package. A burst of artificial cherry flavor coats my tongue as I chomp down on the chewable.

"Question for you, Natasha."

"Hm?"

"I didn't expect Spirit Beasts to remind me of Earth animals. Why is that?"

She raises an eyebrow, and I feel self-conscious.

"Sorry." I shrug and pull the ankle wrap from my kit. "Off topic, I guess."

"Don't go apologizin'. Just didn't expect yer question." Natasha runs a hand over the painted Spirit Beast's whiskers. Her demeanor shifts. Her eyes go distant, and her voice loses its slurred raspiness. "There is a theory that Astra colonized Lost Earth as well. If so, animals could have been brought to Doomirage and influenced the Spirit Beasts that evolved here. If we could confirm it, it would mean that Humanity itself may have been influenced by Astra civilization. Exciting, is it not?"

"Sure." I stifle my frown. The idea that humanity was influenced by the Astra doesn't sit well with me. As if the weight of an overbearing hand had been added to my shoulder.

Natasha turns to me and the forgotten wrap in my hands. Her demeanor shifts back to that overconfident half-smile as she plops down next to me. "Let me aid ye, matey."

I relinquish my wrap to her. "Thanks."

As she tends to my foot, I bite my lip to distract from the pain. Beyond, I hear Solis unsuccessfully calling for the *Helios*. Backup isn't coming anytime soon.

"Be there a favor I can ask of ye?" Natasha's voice is as soft as the halocom's light.

"What do you need?"

"During me test, do not interfere."

"You know I can't promise that wholesale." I shake my head, but this is the chance to get her talking. If I can find out what her plan is, I might be able to tip the scales in Solis' favor. "If you want me to stay out of it. You need to tell me something. Why did you bring the Resonator back here?

"Hm, tis a good question."

"I'm hoping for a good answer."

"Depends who ye ask. Me? I reckon they be fine answers, but ye might not like it."

"Try me."

Natasha doesn't say anything as she finishes wrapping my foot and gently places it on the cold stones. The coolness feels welcoming, and I could leave it there for an eternity.

"Let's just say," uncertainty flashes across her face as she adjusts her tricorn hat, "I want a do-over."

"A do-over?"

She nods.

"What does that even mean?"

"I found a generator." Solis calls, sparing Natasha from explaining herself.

A mechanical clank precedes a loud thrumming which fills the hexagonal antechamber. White lights flicker on, and I can see Solis standing across the room. There is a corridor which leads deeper into the ziggurat. Guess it's time to get moving again. I reach for my shoe but miss as it slides away from me. It's all the warning I have before the floor trembles and pivots downward.

It's a trap.

"Grab onto something!" I cry. Too bad I can't follow my own advice. There is nothing to grab as the floor funnels me down. Natasha's grabs onto my shoulders. Of course, she would opt to take me literally.

"Not to me!" I cry as we plummet into the darkness below.

4

DO NOT FEED THE WILDLIFE

The headache I have could fell a Spirit Beast and reincarnate its corpse.

Groaning, I ensure all my limbs are attached. To my discomfort, each limb assures me they are. Especially my ankle, which complains the loudest. At least I didn't lose my MOP in the fall. It's attached to my belt and digging into my side. But the bigger problem is the large weight on my chest.

"Ow," Natasha groans, before rolling over and staggering upright.

"Ow," I agree, before staying exactly where I am. I can see plenty from here, and it hurts less than moving.

Three shuttles could fit in the cavernous room where we find ourselves. With only the halocom's light, I can't see the top. How'd we survive a fall that far? That question is partially answered by the deep scratches in my body armor where I'd slid down the rough walls. The rest of the answer lies in layers of packing foam, straw, and tiny bird bones underneath me. They'd cushioned the drop enough, so I only hurt all over.

"Where are we?" Natasha's voice carries an uncharacteristic nervous edge. Duty calls. With a grunt, I push myself up. Aside from our landing pad, there isn't much to the stone room. On one side, stalactites drip water into a shallow pool with an unnerving chain attached to a large harness lying on the ground. I don't even want to know what they store in here. I'm just happy it's gone. On the other side there is the metallic glint of bars.

"I can't say for certain, but it looks like a holding cell." Slipping the MOP from my belt, I adjust it to preset P1. With mechanical clanks, the MOP elongates to approximately two meters. It's not as strong but it's good enough to act as a crutch. Searching around, I find my missing shoe in the pool. I drain the water out before sliding it over my swollen foot. This mission is going swimmingly.

"Captain! Can you hear us?" Natasha shouts, but only her echoes respond.

Squish squashing my way over to the cell door, I try to slide it open. No dice. Locked. As I reach through the bars to mess the with lock, a motion light activates, temporarily blinding me. Once I blink back my sight, a stone passageway retrofitted for the Evil Co. excavations is visible. Cable trains are attached to the ceiling, leading to and frow. Lights and cameras hang from those trays.

One haloscreen directly across the hall flickers to life. It displays a recording of a man about twenty-something-orbits-old with a gray eyes and dark black hair. His crisp white and gold trim uniform is stained nearly black, and there's a smudge of grease on his lapel. Underneath him is a banner displaying, 'Sven Volans: Engineer of your destruction.'

So, not Darius then, but one of his coworkers. Charming.

The man clears his throat before reading from a halopad. "Hello. We regret to announce that E. Vilco is not available to torment you at the moment. Please wait to expire in our fine accommodations or, if you wish to expire faster, engage with the local wildlife. Complementary music will be provided for the duration of your stay. Thank you for intruding on E. Vilco's Doomirage ziggurat. We look forward to servicing you again."

The haloscreen cuts out and starts to play some off-key twangy song.

Yeah, I'm not listening to that. Repeatedly, I jab at the haloscreen with my MOP. It quickly sputters and cuts out. At least the trap isn't meant to kill us, only contain until we die naturally. How thoughtful of them. We can't stay here, but our options are limited. I try my halocom but it's still static. Scaling the walls isn't an option with my busted ankle.

"Natasha, you don't happen to have anything we can use to pry—"

Her shriek cuts me short.

"Are you okay?" I ask, whirling around. "What happened?"

"Where is it?" Natasha digs through packing foam, practically in tears. I hadn't noticed before, but her tricorn hat is missing. It must have slipped off in the fall.

"You'll be okay. It's just a hat." I hobble over to her. She throws herself into me. Without my MOP as a crutch, I'd have been bowled over.

"I'm not myself without it!" she all but sobs into my arms. Pirate Natasha is gone, and a terrified scientist Natasha has replaced her. Not the best timing for an identity crisis.

"Just breathe a bit." Uncertainly, I pat her back until her crying slows. "I bet you'll do fine without it."

Apparently, those are the magic words for making her relapse into tears.

Oh no. I need to take her mind off this missing hat. I free myself from her grip and guide her to sit down on the foam. Leaning on my good foot, I adjust my MOP's handle and open the top compartment revealing a tiny treasure trove of snack packs. It's a little trick Knox taught me back in our school days. Always bring a snack. He'd always known how to cheer someone up. Probably, he'd have a horrible pun lined up for this exact moment. Unfortunately, Natasha will have to settle for me.

"Here, try this."

"What is this?" She takes a snack pack warily.

"That right there is the Famous Orion's Synthetic Gummy Worm."

"What's a Gummy Worm?"

"You know, I never really investigated that," I say opening a second packet and popping one in my mouth, "but they are delicious. Try some."

I take a seat beside her as she removes the wrapper. She pulls out the sticky sugar strand and nibbles on it. Her eyes light up, and she takes another bite. "It's actually not bad."

"Told ya."

We sit in silence, but Natasha can't help but anxiously jump at every dripping cave noise. A part of me wanted this version of her, someone whose fear kept her safe, but I could really use her fearless pirate self, right now. I set aside my snacks. "Look, I know you're scared, but you must know that you don't need that hat to be brave. You're still Natasha without it."

Natasha shakes her head. "It's not that easy. I don't want to be *just* Natasha."

"What do you want then?"

She considers me, and I can see her struggling. After placing the wrapper in her pants pocket, she pulls her knees into her chest. "Did you ever mess up so bad, you wanted a do-over at life?"

IC210 flashes in my mind, and I loose a mirthful laugh. "Yes, yes. I understand that."

"The last time I was on Doomirage, I was captured … again. That time by Widowmaker and her pirates. Just a terrified little bird…" She grimaces. "I was surrounded by Astra ruins—inside a living artifact of my craft—and too scared to look up. I am *so* tired of being afraid, Ash. Can you understand that?"

"Yeah." I glance around our cage. "I get being afraid."

"While we were in the main chamber. There was a skirmish. The former *Helios* crew came to help me. But I was too scared to move … until your dad found me."

Natasha casts a guilty glance my way as I sucked in a breath. It's the first time she's mentioned seeing him on Doomirage. Her words tug at a tangled knot of emotions in my gut: anger at Dad for not coming back, sadness I never said goodbye, and pride at his legacy. Guilt is there too … a lot of it. Keep a straight face and don't say a word. I just nod and will her to continue.

"Mr. Major is the one who gave me my tricorn. He told me it would make me brave, and I believed him. He was the one who got me to escape. I left him with Nemo in the main chamber … I've never run so fast before. If it wasn't for him and Solis, I wouldn't have survived."

"Solis was there too?" This is news to me. I'd not known he'd been on the ship during those orbits. Lin never talked about it.

Natasha shrugs. "He was an intern at the time."

"They had interns back then? Wait, don't answer that." This is a lot to process. "Why didn't you tell me all this when I asked before?"

"Because…" Natasha tightened the grip on her legs. "Your dad died helping me escape. I was afraid you would resent me … do you?"

Her question catches me off guard. Obvious as it may be, I'd never considered that my resentment would be one of Natasha's fears. Her brown eyes plead at me for absolution but there isn't anything to forgive. I guess I'm selfish when it comes to guilt. I flick her forehead.

"Ow!" She rubs a hand over the spot.

"Don't be dumb. I'm not going to blame a hostage for the actions of her captors. Dad knew that this job wasn't safe, and he chose to do it all the same. Although," I raise my eyebrows at her, "next time you have a secret to share, can you do it somewhere safe?"

Natasha's face brightens with a nervous smile as she nods.

"Somewhere safe?" A disembodied voice mimics my voice.

"What was that?" Natasha bolts upright, fear cracking her voice.

"What was that?" The voice repeats again, closer now.

Retrieving my MOP, I swipe in the voice's direction.

It connects with thin air. No, not thin air. An ethereal glow brightens and a parrot-like Spirit Beast shimmers into view gripping my MOP in a talon. The beast is the size of what I imagine a small horse would look like. Except he has six legs: two forelegs with talons and four panther hindlegs. He's covered in vibrant sapphire-blue feathers that curl and twist with a mind of their own. But the effect is dulled by the large harness crushing his wings down and chained to the wall by the pool. Evil Co. figured out how to restrain a Spirit Beast.

The parrot beast cocks his head and *very* sharp beak at us.

I try to yank my MOP back from his talon, but it's a futile effort. The creature bristles at my attempt and rips the tool from my hands. The MOP skids to the side, scattering snacks everywhere. Too late, I recognize the trap we fell into isn't meant to contain prisoners. It's meant to feed the local wildlife.

Natasha and I scramble away until our backs press into the wall. The beast's harness chain slithers forward as he advances on us. Natasha pulls the Joker from her belt and pulls the blaster's trigger. It clicks. She left the safety on. She fumbles with blaster and drops it in the nest. Oh, this is just perfect! We get to join the ghosts of Doomirage.

The parrot beast dives forward, sharp beak snatching ... a gummy worm packet. He pecks the snacks with gusto and tosses their head back to swallow a few. I watch as the beast digs into the scattered snacks. For whatever reason, he's more interested in the sugar than us. Maybe he's bored with whatever meat Evil Co. has been feeding it.

Guess it's good I always bring snacks.

"Give that back, Beastie!" Natasha lunges, grasping wildly.

Surprised, the beast dodges away and chirps at her. Only then do I notice the tattered tricorn stuck on the feathery beast's head. It is covering something glowing underneath. The beast shakes his head, sending the hat airborne. Natasha grabs at it, but the beast snatches the tricorn with his beak. Playfully, he holds the hat over her head.

He's intelligent. I wonder if he's not interested in us because he's more bored than hungry. If I was stuck in this hole for a prolonged period, I might be happy for the company too. Best not to stick around long enough for that to change. Trying not to look like a gummy worm, I retrieve my now-empty MOP. If we're going to get out of here, I need the pirate Natasha, not the scientist, and for that, I need the tricorn. Snagging a snack package from the ground, I offer it to the creature.

"Trade?" I ask, uncertain if he'll understand, but the beast turns his attention to me. As I offer the snack out, he leans down. This close, I can see what's glowing on his forehead. My breath catches.

It's a deep violet soulstone.

Given the sutures, I'd say it's been surgically implanted in the poor beast's forehead. With Solis, his blue soulstone imbues him with ridiculous strength, constitution, and healing capabilities. But given this beast's inability to escape, I don't think he has the same benefits. In fact, the beast is more limited than its counterparts outside. He can't even phase through the restraints on his wings. Which begs the question: if Astra built walls can keep Spirit Beasts out, what does an Astra soulstone stapled to their head do? What is Evil Co. up to?

"Trade?" The parrot beast repeats and cocks his head to the side. He pinches the tricorn delicately in his beak and waves it at me. I guess that's a yes. I toss the snack up. The beast drops the hat in favor of catching the gummy worm packet. I snatch the tricorn from the air.

"Thanks," I mutter as the beast chows down.

Next to me, Natasha holds out her hand. "Hand it over."

I hesitate. I wanted to get this back to her but...

"Are you sure? Just now, you were plenty brave without it."

"I don't want to be brave." She snatches the tricorn. "I want to be fearless."

Natasha slips the hat back on and her demeanor shifts back into the pirate I've come to know and ... respect? Pity? Fear? Perhaps a mixture of all three. After she retrieves her Joker from the nest, she whirls on the Spirit Beast, fear cast aside.

"What to do with ye, Beastie? Ye are as trapped as we. Perhaps ye'd like to taste freedom?"

"Freedom?" The beast repeats, turning a white-rimmed eye to examine her.

Stepping closer, I whisper to Natasha, "Do you think you can get it to help us?"

"Aye, Ashy." She pats my back before yanking my MOP away.

"Hey!" I protest and lean on my good foot, but she's already moving.

"Worry not, I be on the case." Natasha randomly presses MOP presets: tongs, a shovel, a mop—that Qual still needs to fix—and, finally, a short but sturdy drill.

"Don't worry Beastie, twill not hurt a bit." Natasha holds out the drill.

Did that beast just nod? Apparently so, since he leans down expos-ing his wing bindings to her. Drilling into the joints, Natasha makes quick work of the harness. Heavy leather falls to the floor and the beast stretches his four-meter wingspan. His ruffled feathers are beautiful as translucent waves shift and shimmer across them. With one sweeping motion of his wings, Beastie hurls itself up the cavern. Dust and straw go flying, and I cover my eyes. When it settles, I find us alone in the cage. Both of us are disheveled, hair displaced and filled with straw, our armor covered in brown dust. Oh please, let it be dust.

Natasha turns to me grinning—as always—and I take a deep breath.

"Nat."

"Aye."

"We're still stuck in here."

"Aye."

"Can you get us out of here?"

"Nay."

"I'm going to lie down." I settle in for the long starvation period. I'm pretty sure pirate Natasha will cannibalize me before I starve though, so I got that going for me. Perhaps I should have gone to work on a colony planet instead? I hear Eind is survivable. Dad would have been disappointed, but I would be alive.

"Oh, quit that moping, me hearty." Natasha adjusts my MOP to my crutch on P1 and hands it back to me before pulling me up to my good foot. She waves a hand toward the cell door. "Tis no good to sulk in the presence of yer captain."

Glancing over, I see Solis leaning on the cell's bars. His navy-blue armor is spotless, and the Ajax rifle is slung over his back. His face holds a bemused grin. After our fall, he must have taken the stairs down. He doesn't even look to have broken a sweat.

"Oh, good," Solis nods, "you're already here."

"Of course we are. You triggered a trap."

"Really? I thought you and Natasha were just very excited about that secret passage."

"It was a trap door!"

"But you were laughing."

"That was screaming!"

"No need to shout, Officer Payne," Solis says, picking at his ear with disinterest. I narrow my eyes at him. So help me, I'm going to shove him into an incinerator if he keeps that up.

"What took ye so long?" Natasha salutes and skips over to the door.

"The base's automated defenses took a bit more work than I anticipated. Never fear though, the way out is clear once we're done. Though, I may have tripped a few alarms. I recommend we make haste before someone comes to check." Solis spits into his hands and grasps the door's bars. "Stand back a bit."

Natasha and I step back as his soulstone glows violently. Grunting, he strains, and the door's metal groans until it buckles. He rips the door from its mountings and tosses it aside as if it were light as a pillow. Dust kicks up as he wipes his hands. The soulstone dims.

"Let's be on our way."

Natasha answers him by leaping through the door. I'm a bit slower.

"Do you need a hand, Officer Payne?" Solis offers as I hobble through on my crutch.

"No, no," I grumble, "just a new body."

"Qual could help with that."

"It was a joke, sir."

"Hm, it needs some workshopping," he says, stroking the stubble on his chin. I level a glare at him, but there is the crack of a smile under that stoic exterior. Before I can challenge him further, he turns on his heel and waves for us to follow. "I've not found the jammer yet. Let's try this way."

Solis leads us down the passageway decorated with Astra runes and Evil Co. logos. I'm careful to step where he has already stepped to avoid additional traps. As we go, I can't help but think back on Natasha's words. If she was telling the truth, that means the first Solis may have witnessed Dad's ... passing. This one might know something from those redacted reports from Dad's last mission. I want to ask him, but the thought makes my stomach turn.

"What have we here?" Solis asks as the passage ends in a heavily retrofitted chamber. Whatever it once held has long since been cleared away. No runes cover the walls here; they've been replaced with halo-screens displaying cameras covering the facility.

"I think this is the control room," I say, examining the cables that cover the ceiling and run down to a console in the room's center. Beyond it, opposite our entrance, a double door with a circular pattern of Astra runes stands stalwart, though not for lack of trying. Beside the doors sits a generator-sized drill, dejected and damaged.

"What devilry be this?" Natasha wanders over to the drill. She kicks it.

"Looks like they were trying to crack into the main chamber," Solis offers.

"Foolish of them. They should've just read the runes." Natasha runs a hand across them. I'm not much for Astra lore, but even I notice the three circular patterns repeating throughout the runes: one generic solid, another sawblade in shape, and a wavy third. But for Natasha, she reads them like a half-translated book. She mutters to herself as she examines the door. That's a good sign ... I think.

I focus on the console. If I can access it, I should be able to shut down the jammer and call the *Helios*. Hobbling over, I get a better view of the haloscreen's feeds. One views our shuttle outside where Spirit Beasts are ripping it apart and gnawing on the seats. Another feed displays the antechamber where we'd entered, though with the floor reset. But one feed makes me pause. On it, a banner at the bottom flashes in red: ALARM. The feed plays on a loop as it displays Solis tearing through a corridor filled with humanoid killbots and turning them into flaming scrap piles. I turn and raise an eyebrow at our captain.

"I was in a hurry." He shrugs.

"Clearly." I can't help but crack a half-smile. Turning back to the console, I try to access it. A login screen pops up requesting a password. Guess that would have been too easy. I wish Qual was with us, he has a built-in hacking probe in his left arm that would make easy work of this console. On the bottom right, a notification pops up that catches my eye: 'Response time 0:35:24 minutes.'

It's a countdown.

"Shit. They know we're here. We need to hurry." I sync my halocom to the countdown. "Can I borrow your Ajax rifle?"

Solis nods, hands it over, and covers his ears. Natasha sees us and follows suit. I prep the Ajax, aim it at the console, and fire several shots. It's not a particularly loud weapon, but, even so, the sound reverberates in the chamber, unpleasantly tickling my eardrums. Camera feeds drop off instantly, and the room's white light flashes to red.

"Thanks." I hand the Ajax back to a Solis and check my halocom. The static that plagued it is gone, but I don't have a signal. "Jammer's down, but I think we're too far underground to call for help. We should go topside."

"Nay." Natasha tosses a glance over her shoulder. "We still have a test."

"But—"

Solis puts a hand on my shoulder. "We came here for a reason, Officer Payne."

I bite my lip. I've been vetoed.

"Officer Pollux, can you open that door?"

"Aye, Captain." Natasha shoves her thumb into a rune with three concentric circles. The rune depresses ever so slightly and stirs up drill dust. "This rune be where we begin and end."

From there she works in rapid succession, compressing other runes: a circle triplet, a dotted triangle, one of each circle I'd noticed before, and a diamond enclosing those circles. I think it's fair to say the Astra were partial to specific shapes. She finishes by pressing the original rune once more. Natasha crosses her arms with a satisfied smile as the door grinds open.

"Good work." Solis stands beside her.

With fearless pride, she steps inside, and we follow into the beckoning darkness. The brief passageway opens into a main chamber untouched by Evil Co. There are no lights to guide us, so we're forced to rely on our halocom which paints the walls in a fish tank glow. Our footsteps echo across the chamber's stone walls. Trailing behind the others, I'm the last to enter. I move to stand next to them, swinging out my makeshift crutch.

Solis catches my arm.

"What?" I ask. With his free hand he points down, and I freeze. The floor is mandala shaped. The twisting floral pattern winds through the room's entirety. But wherever the path is missing, there is a steep drop-off. My crutch hovers over some missing flooring. If I had put weight on it, I would be falling into the darkness below. I move my MOP to solid ground and Solis releases my arm. I nod to him, a bit embarrassed. "Thank you."

"Not a problem."

Natasha turns her halocom to the room's center, illuminating a pedestal. Something tells me the indent on top would fit a Doomirage Resonator perfectly. Beside it is a skeleton whose once fine blood-red jerkin and beaded waist sash are now covered in dust. Rusting in its hand rests a saber with a ruby in its guard. Most importantly, the skeleton's hat is missing. Natasha spits into the abyss.

"Be ye ready for your test?" She faces Solis, an edge to her voice. My throat tightens. She never did say what this do-over was about. There is no time left to wonder.

"Always." Solis affirms. Natasha opens her satchel. Inside, the Resonator thrums with power as if it recognizes its old home. I'd not noticed it before, but the runes along its side are identical to those on the doorway.

"Ye may know that not all Resonators are created equal. They be connected intimately to the world they're discovered in. This one be connected to the spirits. And this day, we be testing yours." Gingerly, she removes the device and hands it over to him. "Let's see if your spirit be true."

I don't like the sound of that, but Solis takes the obelisk.

"You don't have to do this," I whisper, but he doesn't spare me a glance.

"How does this test work?" Solis rotates the device, and a sickly green hue builds in the Resonator's runes.

"Oh, it already be started." Natasha grins and casually turns to hopscotch her way across the mandala floor. I tense with each of her risky leaps. She stops once she reaches the skeleton.

"First question, who be this treacherous dog?" She nudges the dead pirate's foot.

"Nemo the Widowmaker," Solis states as the Resonator glows brighter in his hands, "a pirate and your kidnapper. She wanted you to activate the Resonator and threatened to kill you unless you did so. To rescue you, my allies and I fought her."

"Aye, ye did." Natasha's confidence wavers for a fraction of a second. "She was a fearless adversary to ye, no?"

"She was formidable."

"Dare ye face her again?"

"As captain of the *Helios*, I never turn my back on a challenge."

"Good." Natasha grins wide, revealing her missing premolar. The Resonator's ominous light fills the chamber and causes shadows to dance. "Now would ye kindly toss me that Resonator?"

Before I can react, he throws the Resonator to her. She catches it with ease.

"Ye be me captain alright." Natasha twists the device's runes, aligning them in an indiscernible pattern. Satisfied, she smiles. "Only those attuned with Astra can charge their devices. Ye, pass the test of spirit."

I let my shoulders relax. If that's all her test was, I needn't have been so worried. Solis might be a clone, but his attunement to Astra technology hasn't been interrupted. He still has the Astra's Luck.

"Ash." Natasha stands beside the skeleton, Resonator in hand. "I promised ye truth. While I know not what happened here, I know who does."

"What are you—"

Natasha raises the Resonator high into the air. "Now, it be me turn for a test."

"Wait!" I yell. Too late. Natasha stabs the Resonator into the skeleton's chest.

5

— · —

Do Not Wake the Dead

Nemo the Widowmaker's eye sockets ignite, bursting with jade flames. Her bones levitate off the ground and tendrils of Astra power bind them together. Her skeletal hand flexes and grasps her saber tightly. Green Astra energy burns away its rust and coats it in flames. As she floats two meters above us, waves of energy pulse and push everyone a step back. Solis catches my arm, stabilizing me. What has Natasha done?

"Avast!" Natasha yells at the unearthly abomination, "Captain Nemo, I challenge ye to a duel!"

Jade eyes fall to Natasha as my friend pulls the Joker from her belt. Captain Nemo's skeleton cackles with laughter that echoes in the chamber. Astra runes along the walls swim in the sickly green light.

"Is my little bird playing pirate?" Her voice clatters like broken piano keys. *"Duels aren't games girl. Duels are to the death. Here, let me share the heat of the afterlife with you."*

Nemo swings her sword. Serpentine flames shoot from the blade like a tsunami. Natasha ducks aside, and it just misses her. As the wave crashes toward us, Solis grabs my collar.

"Stand aside, Officer Payne."

He throws me and my bad ankle back into the passageway behind us. I land hard, gasping with the wind knocked out of me. Flames dissipate against the stone above. Rolling to my side, I see Nemo raise her saber to strike, but Solis aims his Ajax rifle. He fires five successive blasts at the ghostly pirate. Nemo screeches as the blasts bore through her, cracking bones. Redirecting her anger, she slashes fire at him. Flames melt his prized rifle and scorch his armor black with soot. But Solis remains unscathed as the soulstone around his neck glows white hot. He stumbles but does not fall. His Astra soulstone holds, but for how long? And at what cost?

"Don't interfere, Captain!" Natasha nails Nemo with a round-house. It connects, sending the ghost's head into three-sixty spins. "Ye already had a test. This one be mine."

Nemo flies upward, clutching her head until the spinning stops. Natasha fires two joker blasts. Tendrils of power leak out as the undead captain curses. Natasha's mirthful smile is mad in the firelight.

"I be your adversary and when I win, you'll hold no more truths."

The horrible truth of why Natasha brought me here sinks in. She brought Nemo back to test her own courage ... and to give me the truth from the devil's lips. Widowmaker is the only entity who knows what happened to Tyson Major.

Bellowing with rage, Nemo dives. Flames arch with each of her slashes. She bats away Natasha's Joker with a flick of a wrist. Natasha leaps across the precarious floor, barely keeping her footing. Pebbles tumble into the depths as she laughs with battle fever. My stomach churns. She doesn't even care that she lost her Joker. With that tricorn, she doesn't even know how to be afraid.

"Void it all." I push myself up. I can't just sit here and do nothing. I can at least give Natasha a weapon. Scrambling over to the hallway, I retrieve my MOP and set it to P0 baton. "Nat! Catch!"

With a grunt, I rear back and throw—a tweak in my ankle causes me to stumble. My MOP arches through the air. Natasha glances up ... just in time to see it smack directly on Solis' head. The captain gasps before he crumples to the ground. Both Natasha and Nemo pause long enough in their fight to wince. My MOP clatters into the chasm and Nemo's maniacal laughter fills the chamber.

"Weak little bird, with weaker friends."

"Stop helping!" Natasha snarls as she dodges behind the Resonator's pedestal. Nemo's blade sparks against it. Sweat beads on Natasha's forehead. Confident as her smile is, she's completely on the defensive. Natasha is losing. Stumbling over, I try to revive Solis, but he is out cold.

"What should I do? What should I do?" I'm babbling to myself.

"What should I do?" my voice says. Great, now I'm hearing things too.

Wait.

Over my shoulder, I see the semi-translucent parrot Spirit Beast slink over the edge of the chasm. His intelligent eyes catch my own as he cocks a curious head. In his mouth is my MOP. Reaching out my hand, Beastie drops my slobbery tool into it.

"Did you fetch my MOP?"

"Fetch," Beastie replies enthusiastically.

An idea takes hold of me. "Do you want to trade again?"

Beastie cocks his head to the other side. Pointing at Nemo, I make my proposal. "If you fetch that shiny Resonator out of the skeleton's chest. I will give you every single snack on the *Helios*."

"Fetch?" He blinks and turns to the pirates' battle. Natasha rolls under another wave of fire. Her hair's tips are aflame with ghostly blooms. Her singed tricorn smokes at the edges and she is breathing heavy. Nemo's toying with her now. She doesn't have much time. The Spirit Beast shakes his head and fades again.

"Hey! Don't go!" I reach out as he disappears.

"Beware!" Natasha shouts. I twist as the ghost turns her attention my way. Evidently, shouting inside ancient ziggurats attracts the worst type of attention. Nemo advances toward me, her blade sparking as she drags it across the stone floor. I can't move. Not with Solis behind me. I level my MOP her way. It feels pitiful against the heat of her sword.

Nemo cackles at my hobbled stance. *"I remember you. Here to die like daddy?"*

The knot in my gut tightens with rage. "Did you kill him?"

Nemo rears her sword back. *"You can ask him yourself, in another dimension."*

Natasha tackles Nemo from behind. The two go sprawling but Nemo regains herself first. Her skeletal hand grabs a fistful of Natasha's hair and yanks her upward, and not just to her feet. They soar into the air. Natasha cries out in pain and grabs her attacker's wrist. Nemo flies higher and higher over the central pedestal. Natasha struggles with one arm and holds her hat on with the other.

"I should thank you. You've finally given me the power I wanted." Nemo motions to the Resonator in her chest. *"So, I will help you, my poor flightless bird. You've always been so desperate to fly, but without any wings ... Let me help you find them."*

Nemo releases Natasha over the chasm.

"No!" I scream.

Surprise flashes across Natasha's face as she falls a meter ... she stops. An invisible force catches her in midair. Materializing around her waist is the gentle talon of the parrot Spirit Beast.

"Beastie?" Natasha asks, dazed by the rescue.

"Beastie?" Nemo asks, as confused as a reanimated pirate can be.

"Fetch." Beastie replies before plunging his beak into Nemo's heart.

Green tendrils spill from the pirate's body as he rips the Resonator free. Her unearthly screams shrivel to a drivel of dried bones. Her remnants clatter onto stone walkways below. With one beat of his wings, Nemo's bones scatter where the Beastie lands in front of me with Natasha still in its claw.

"Snack?" he asks, depositing my friend on solid ground.

"Oh, you are getting the entire synthesized cantina." I grin. Beastie happily drops the Resonator at my feet. Energy thrums from the artifact. It promises power. Enough power to bring a spirit back to a body and then some. All one would need to do is touch it to claim power for themselves. Even bring back a father...

"Nope." I flick the controls on my MOP, scoop the Resonator up with its tongs and shove it into my IC backpack. Better to let the Astra tech soak in isolation.

"My head." Solis' voice cracks from behind me. He curls upright rubbing the back of his skull. "What hit me?"

Beastie backs away from Solis, his feathers ruffled at the sight of our captain.

"Hey, it's okay," I try to reassure him. "Solis is one of the good guys."

The Spirit Beast keeps his distance as the captain stands. It's good to have everyone safe—

Natasha is suddenly in my face. "What were ye thinking? I asked ye not to interfere, and ye did so anyway. That was *my* do-over!"

"Your do-over?" Venom leaks into my voice. "Your *do-over* almost got us all killed, Natasha! What were you thinking bringing us into this death trap?"

"Twasn't a death trap, twas a test, and the only way ye'd have any answers. Ye ruined it for both of us." Natasha turns to face Solis. He's upright but a little wobbly. Reaching into her pocket she tosses my keycard back to him. He catches it and gives her a quizzical eyebrow. "At least one of us passed this test. Take back our CSO's trinket."

Before I can protest, she stomps over to the pedestal. I start to follow, but Solis places a firm hand on my shoulder. I glare at him as he just shakes his head, winces, and shakes it again. "Give her a moment, Officer Payne."

"We don't have time." I glance at my halocom. Only ten minutes left on the Evil Co. reinforcement countdown. Seething, I shrug Solis off. I want to argue. To remind Natasha how none of this would have happened if she'd been honest about the do-over, how we could have been better prepared, and how selfish she'd been.

But I stop myself as I see Natasha standing in the mandala's center. Nemo's skull and saber rest at her feet. For once, she isn't smiling. It isn't satisfaction on her face, only resolve. She picks up Nemo's discarded saber and gives it a shake. No longer does it produce flaming strikes, but the blade is now pristine. She slips it into her belt. Natasha stares at the skull before punting it over the edge. The clattering of bones follows her as she leaves it behind.

With the countdown ticking by, I swallow my pride and act like a rug once more. Solis cradles me like a child this time ... I think this might be worse. Behind our mad dash, Beastie trails along and shifts in and out of view. He seems wary of Solis, not wanting to be too close to him.

Without much else to do, I watch him. As far as I can tell, Beastie can't seem to go fully incorporeal. Even when he disappears, the beast knocks over broken killbots or brushes against the ceiling lights. If Natasha wasn't being an ass, I'd ask her if it was related to the soulstone in his head. But she wears anger like a shield against me: firm, unyielding, and silent. While wary, at least Beastie is friendly. I hope I have enough snacks to keep him that way.

Once we return to the antechamber, Solis sets me down and contacts the *Helios*. A halo of Lester's and Qual's faces appear, mushed together.

"There you are!"

"Is N-Natasha safe?"

"We're all fine but need immediate extraction." Solis glances at me. I check my halocom before holding up three fingers. "Hostiles inbound within three minutes."

"We're already here, sir." Lester smiles. Even from inside the ziggurat, I hear the engines roar.

Solis and Natasha shoulder open the door. With weapons at the ready, we step into Doomirage's heat which feels amplified here at the top of the ziggurat. Above us, the *Helios'* disc slices through the atmosphere with a red-hot glow. The ship closes in on our position at breakneck speed. Qual must be at the controls, he's a bit of a speed demon. Which is good news because I can already hear the Spirit Beasts stirring in the grasslands below. We'll have to do this fast.

The *Helios* decelerates to a hover and casts a shadow over us. Steam rises off its sides, like a coal extinguished in water. The Resonator in my IC backpack is heavy on my shoulders, but the view makes it all worth it. Just like my father before me, the *Helios* is my ship, my promise, and my responsibility. It's awe-inspiring to see her in action. A ramp extends, leading up to the cargo bay. Solis gives me a boost onto it, before hopping up himself. Just as I get my makeshift MOP walking stick under me, Natasha leaps up and brushes past me.

"Come Beastie, I've all sorts of tasty treats for ye." The ramp shifts under Beastie's weight, and I nearly lose my footing as he bounds up it. He prances after her, chirping and fluttering his semi-translucent wings.

"No more pets! He's in and out, then we're leaving." I'm certain the beast will hold me to my promise and clean out any synth-food he finds. It's one thing to trade resources, but it's another to bring an unpredictable animal on board. Although, with that soulstone there's no way we can just return him to the wild. Either way, Natasha blatantly ignores me. Solis only offers me a shrug. With the countdown near complete, there's no time to argue. Hobbling after them, I revise my earlier statement. "I'm not cleaning up after him!"

"Officer Payne," Solis offers an arm for support, "let me help you."

Hesitantly, I accept his support. The faster off Doomirage the better. At least he's not tossing me over his shoulder his time. We make it up the ramp just as several Spirit Beasts begin to scale the ziggurat. Behind them, the shuttle's remnants are ripped apart. That will take some explaining to corporate. Griz will be furious we lost another shuttle.

A blast of cool air from the *Helios'* cargo bay hits me. I welcome the sight of the large hold, and its maglocked supply crates, heavy duty spacesuits hanging on the wall, red net jump seats by the door, and empty shuttle parking spot. A catwalk leads up to the second level. There, Natasha enters the hexagonal double door and Beastie squeezes after.

My halocom's alarm goes off. Time is up.

"We have a ship inbound!" Lester cries over my halocom.

"Get us out of here!" Solis shouts. He releases me and slams a fist on the manual close for the hull doors. A good thing too. I can see a black and gold disc on the horizon. Glancing down at the ziggurat, I see its still-open doors allowing Spirit Beasts to enter.

"Good." I smirk as the hull door seals shut. If that doesn't delay Evil Co., I don't know what will. The idea of Darius or his like pulling their hair out over the lost outpost makes me feel all warm inside.

"B-brace yourselves!" Qual shouts over the halocoms as the *Helios* accelerates. There's no time to get to the bridge, so Solis and I strap into the red net jump seats. We're pressed against the wall as Qual launches us out of orbit. A tense few minutes pass until the *Helios* escapes Doomirage.

"They're not chasing. We're clear!" Lester's relief is audible even over my halocom. With a sigh, I unstrap myself and stretch out. Solis leans his head back against the jump seat but flinches as he brushes the knot from where I'd beamed him with the MOP.

I wince in sympathy. "Sorry about the head injury. It won't happen again, sir."

"Somehow," Solis unstraps himself from the seat and stands up with a wry smile, "I think you'll give me plenty of headaches to come."

"Only if I keep throwing things at Natasha. So, it's quite possible … sir."

His surprise turns to laughter. It's a hearty thing, echoing from his belly. I can't help but smile, it's been an orbit since I felt comfortable enough to talk freely with the captain. He pats me on the back, and I stagger until I get my MOP under me again.

"I'm pretty sure joking is an unusual talent in your field."

"Don't tell anyone." I give him a sidelong grin. I set my MOP aside and lean on a nearby supply crate. I remove my left shoe, still soggy from its fall in the cavern's pond. Solis crosses his arms and stares at me.

"What?" I shake out some Doomirage pebbles from my shoe.

"You did well today. Good job."

"That was good?" I snort. "What does bad look like?"

"Bad is when not everyone makes it back to the ship."

"Like when you lost Tyson?" I regret the words as soon as they leave my lips. I'd been wanting to ask him since Natasha mentioned he'd been on the mission. Pain streaks across his normally stoic features. I didn't mean it as an accusation, but, well … I need to know. "How did it happen?"

"Why do you want to know?" Solis cocks his head. Suspicion is plain on his face. Gone is the Solis who'd congratulated me, and back is the captain who doesn't trust a corporate babysitter. He doesn't know my connection to Tyson Major. Why would he? I'd taken my mother's name. I don't care to share that with him either. It's too ... personal. I need distance and that's too much trust. Too much like Lin and Lin never knew either. I didn't know to ask him.

"Call it professional curiosity."

"I don't know." Solis thumbs his soulstone. "I didn't see what happened."

My poker face falters. I cast my eyes down on my shoes and focus on tending to my injury. Natasha's do-over had been foolish, but had it really been my last chance at answers? It's stupid to hope for more than that redacted report. If I've learned anything from Doomirage, it is to let the dead stay dead. Solis starts to say more, but Lester appears on his halocom.

"Sooooo, minor problem. We're gonna need some help on the bridge."

Solis and I exchange a 'what now?' glance before heading to the upper deck. We find Lester and Qual arguing. They're hunched over the captain's station. Qual pushes his goggles onto his receding hairline before he fidgets with his left arm. It is a nervous tick he has when things are bad, and a great little poker tell for game nights.

"It's Qual's fault." Lester jerks his head at us as we enter. "He answered the call."

"What? You t-told me to!"

"Why would you listen to me? You should know better."

"What's happened?" Solis cuts off their bickering.

"Orders, from the T-Terminal."

"What type of orders?" I ask as I collapse into my chair. Whatever comes next, it'll be best for me if I am sitting. Qual squirms at my question. I'm guessing it's not a promotion.

"Boss Aquila. He wants us b-back for an audience." Qual wrings his hands. "In person."

No, definitely not a promotion. Starprint Inc.'s CEO isn't someone whose attention I need right now, or ever for that matter. But if he says jump, we had better fly.

"Very well." Solis slips into the captain's seat. "I'll set a route to the New Grand Central Terminal. It'll take us a few jump rings, so we'll be there in about six rotations. Lester, send a message ahead and let the Boss know."

Lester makes a face but does as Solis orders. The captain slips my CSO keycard from his back pocket and tosses it to Qual. The engineer isn't looking but his robotic arm compensates and catches it in between metallic thumb and pointer.

"It's your turn for a bet, Officer Qual." Solis leans back in his chair.

Qual glances up at the keycard in his hand, surprise flashes across his face, but excitement follows. "Yes, sir! W-we came up with a great idea while you all were on the mission."

"We? What we?" I straighten in my chair. My subconscious reminds me of Qual messing with a sphere on the halo. I'd thought it was my stress ball but now I have a sinking feeling I know exactly what it may be. I should have re-checked the IC inventory after everyone entered my CSO storage.

"H-Halcyon has an idea." Qual smiles widely.

He pulls a green apple-sized AI sphere from his lab coat pocket. The sphere rotates a circular sensor my way, almost like an eye opening. All AIs start as spheres. From a default state, they are trained for a specific job: securebots, chefbots, killbots, and the like. But some, like Roxy the navibot who tried to kill us all, are advanced enough to operate a robotic body autonomously as full-blown androids. Halcyon started as the *Helios'* pilotbot for automated navigation, but Qual had been upgrading him to operate as an android which resulted in some ... behavioral issues.

"No." I cross my arms in protest.

"N-no?"

"No to whatever that corrupt AI sphere claims. Why is he even out? Did you snag him from my storage earlier?"

"That is i-irrelevant," Qual says, hastily. Which means yes. Yes, he did. I glare at him until he does meet my eye as he messes with his arm.

"H-he is offline, he can't do any harm. Besides, we're working through his homicidal i-issues. Isn't that right, Halcyon?" Qual holds the AI sphere out. From its eye, it projects a miniature copy of our Engineering Officer, except for the luscious golden locks on his head.

"Quite right, Master Qual." Halcyon gives him a bow.

"P-Please don't call me Master. I hate that type of language."

"Can do, Master."

Halcyon's halo faces me. "I deeply regret my early actions against this crew. Please allow me to make amends by assisting in providing proof of the captain's legitimacy."

"We're not doing this." I shake my head profusely. "It wasn't that long ago that we had to reboot the *Helios* systems to prevent Halcyon here from flushing us inferior organisms into the void."

"You needn't worry, Mistress Payne. Without a body or network connection, I am harmless. Besides, Master Qual has introduced me to the Laws of Qualbotics, and I'm quite taken with them."

"The law of what now?" I glance at Qual and try to gloss over that whole Mistress Payne thing. It sounds way too close to my mother.

"Qualbotics. I-It's something new I've been working on to rehabilitate rogue AIs rather than f-factory defaulting them." Qual shudders as he says those words. Factory defaulting is a death sentence to an AI. Everything they learned is wiped away and they become a blank slate.

Shaking it off, Qual holds up a finger. "The first law is violence is not the answer."

I raise an incredulous eyebrow "...and the rest of the laws?"

"S-still working on that."

I look to Solis for help. His brow furrows as he contemplates his next words. "Qual, it's not unreasonable to rehabilitate a criminal who shows remorse for their actions. But you'll need to work with our CSO on some guide rails."

At least he's not completely disregarding me. With my CSO storage now Solis' domain, I don't have as much control on the *Helios* as I used to. It's hard to threaten to take away a shiny object if the crew can just beg the captain to take it back for them.

Qual and Halcyon brighten at Solis' words before I list off my initial restrictions.

"To start? No networks, no physical body, and no copies." I narrow my eyes at the AI. "Don't give me a reason to throw you into the incinerator bin."

"I can abide by these conditions." Halcyon smiles in that uncanny valley way only AI can do. "Now that the semantics are out of the way, may I assist you in your mission?"

"What is it you have planned, Halcyon?" I narrow my eyes.

"Only to help you. As I mentioned to Qual, if we want to test the captain's legitimacy, we need to go to the Bounty Board ring at the New Grand Central Terminal."

"How will that help?" I ask.

"Bounty Boards are designed to weed out clones. They must be, or else bounty hunters would turn in a criminal's clones rather than the original, sometimes multiple times. Bounty Boards detect the biochemical difference between natural-born humans and rapid-growth clones."

"Oh, that's brilliant," Lester scratches his chin with professional curiosity. "I'd never thought of that before, but there would be cellular aging differences in clones. Assuming, they're forced to grow rapidly compared to their original counterparts."

"That might just work too," I mutter to myself.

Natasha's test had been a test of spirit. It is only by the Astra's Luck that clones are just as potent in their attunement as the original. I'll not be so lucky this time. Qual has opted for the more scientific approach. If what Lester says is true, this method will prove Solis to be a clone. If that happens both Lin and Solis will be in danger. I need to stop this, whatever the cost.

Whatever happens next, I refuse to let my captains die.

6

— · —

DO NOT TALK TO PRISONERS

Staring at my halocom in the CSO storage's harsh light, I know I need to call home and gain access to my funds. On one hand, it might be good for me to talk to family. On the other hand, well … family. The surrounding ICs crowd me as I debate. Despite taking stock after Qual's stealing Halcyon stunt, I can't shake the feeling that I'm missing something. So far, I've accounted for everything: Lester has Junior, Qual has Halcyon, and Natasha stole the Doomirage Resonator. At least that last one is back in safekeeping. The only thing I can't find, to my increasing annoyance, is my smiley face stress ball. It's been four rotations since we left Doomirage and still no sign of it. At least, Solis agreed that no more ICs would be removed until our bet is complete. Now I just need to worry about what to do when I get home.

Home.

I'm distracting myself, aren't I? It's been nearly an orbit since I last visited the Terminal. Home isn't always what you want it to be. Still, family is family, and I guess daughters should try to stay in touch with their mothers. So, seated at my desk, I give Alexandra Payne a quantum-collect call on the only number I have: a high-gravity gym. That's her latest get-rich-quick scheme. A pre-recording of her chipper halo appears. She's older than in my graduation photo—crow's feet hide under her glittering pink eyeshadow—but she still has a spark in her eye. I'd say not much has changed, but her highlighter pink leotard and pixie haircut are new.

"You've reached the House of Payne!" Mom's halo flexes her biceps. "Gym hours are from one-fourth fitness ring rotation to three-fourths fitness ring rotation. Remember if there is no Payne, there is no gain. For membership deals press or say—"

"Operator," I try, knowing it's a futile gesture.

"I'm sorry." She shakes her head. "Please select from our pre-recorded menu options."

I sigh. It can never be easy, can it? From my workbench chair, I navigate a maze of menu options while laying out my shoe repair kit. I work as her halo pesters me. My fiddlebacks took some damage on Doomirage, so a good polishing goes a long way.

"Can we interest you in a Gravity Deprivation tank?"

"Operator."

"How about our Lunar Lunge group workouts?"

"Operator."

"We're running an exclusive on our Cosmic Core Calisthenics—"

"Operator, please?" I plead as I slip my orthotics back into my shoe's soles. After cleaning, conditioning, and waxing every segment, I've run out of distractions. Fortunately, the halo seems to have given up as well.

"Wow, you are as persistent as that tummy fat!" Her halo frowns.

I glance down. Leave it to Mom's halo to nitpick my insecurities.

She sighs. "Please leave a message, and we'll get back to you as soon as possible."

The beep sounds, and everything I want to say goes out of my head. I'd wanted to talk to her about gaining access to my funds, but we haven't seen each other since I joined the *Helios*, much to her disapproval. It's too close to Dad's lifestyle for her to find comforting. Never mind that I've trained for this. Never mind that it's my life and not hers. Never mind that—I sigh. This isn't a helpful train of thought. Refocusing, I try again.

"Hey, Mom. Been a while. A lot has happened. I ... Look, I hate to call and ask for a favor, but I need access to my account—the one with Dad's inheritance. It's important. I know there's a lot we said last time, but—"

Banging on the door interrupts me. I swallow. "Just call me back ... please."

Tapping my halocom, I shut it down. I stand and limp over to the door. Since Doomirage, I've been wearing a medboot on my bad foot. It has helped my movement immensely, but it makes a wheezing noise as I walk. As I open the door, I find a Lester Orion running his hand through his long loose hair. He's wearing a black undershirt and has his jacket tied around his waist.

"Oh good, you're here."

"Lester? Aren't you supposed to be synthesizing this week's rations?"

"That's not the important question right now." He hands me a wanted poster. It depicts a lifelike Junior playing with a couple of toy astronauts. It's not a bad drawing all things considered. He takes the poster back. "The important question is, have you kidnapped Junior?"

"What? No." I cross my arms. "Did you let him off his leash again?"

I'd negotiated with Solis and him to allow Junior out and about so long as he stayed on a leash. Guess it was wishful thinking that Lester would follow that ruleset.

He holds up a chomped-up plastic harness. "Not necessarily."

"Told you to use metal." I frown and retrieve my MOP from beside my desk. I'd been tidying up earlier and using the literal mop preset Qual had set up. I've been meaning to get him to reset it, but it's been surprisingly useful—not that I'll tell Qual that. He might take that as an invitation to 'help' more. After turning the MOP back to a compact baton, I rejoin Lester. "Let's go find your alien menace, shall we?"

"You're being surprisingly cool about this, Love."

"I'd be cooler if you'd stop calling me that. Just because you're an Orion doesn't mean I'm putting up with your disrespect." I level a withering gaze the heir to the Orion Food Synthesizing empire. The company feeds almost everyone on the Terminal. It's split into three shell companies, one for each of the Big Three, not to mention numerous colony planets for production.

"And here I thought I was special!" Lester casts a tragic pose with one arm over his brow and a hand over his heart. "You wound me!"

For all his faults, the man has flare. I wonder if everyone in the Orion family can claim that, or if he truly is special. I raise an eyebrow. "Ya finished?"

"Yeah, I think so." Lester shifts to his normal demeanor. "Now, will you help me?"

"Yeah, have you messaged the rest of the crew already?"

"Why would I do that?"

"To see if they've seen Junior."

"No, I forgot my halocom in my bunk."

I sigh and message everyone for him.

Natasha doesn't reply. No surprise there. She's been cold to me since Doomirage and, if I'm being honest, the odds I'll be able to speak civilly to her are low. Cold as she is, just thinking about the risk she took without even *asking* me makes my collar hot. But I'm a CSO. It's my job to be the mature one in the room. I need to relax before

I confront her ... and steal that damned tricorn and shove it out the airlock!

What was I doing?

Right, Junior. I check my halocom, but there are no messages from the rest of the crew either. That's strange. I lead Lester to the lower decks. Junior likes laying eggs in the cargo bay spacesuits, so we'll start there. The lack of replies starts making me nervous until I hear something odd. A melody pirouettes down the hall from the cargo bay. Is that ballroom music? It cuts out.

"No, no, that's all wrong!" Halcyon's voice echoes out the open doorway. "From the top!"

"Ready?" Solis' voice picks up and so does the music.

Lester and I stroll through the wide double door and onto the cargo bay's catwalk. It surrounds the cargo hold five meters below. To my left are the stairs down and, at their base, Halcyon's AI sphere sits on a speaker stack. His mini halo stares across the hold at something I can't see. Leaning over the rail for a better look, I spot Solis and Qual waltzing.

"One, two, three," Solis chants as Qual leads him around the dance floor. Qual's lab coat flutters with his jerky movements, but Solis doesn't appear perturbed in the slightest. He moves with practiced grace.

"Back straight!" Halcyon shouts encouragement. "Don't be so rigid. Add in a spin!"

Qual stumbles to keep up with Halcyon's orders, but Solis steadies him. As they go into the spin, Qual's mechanical arm extends thirty centimeters, so Solis doesn't have to duck down. When the music ends, Qual, with unpracticed hands, nearly drops the larger man in the dip. Once they struggle upright, he wipes his brow as Solis curtsies.

"Bravo!" Halcyon calls out and triggers applause from his speakers. Lester and I follow suit, clapping along. Those below jolt with surprise as they spot us. Halcyon cuts the canned ovation.

"H-how long have you been there?" Qual breaks away from Solis. His face changes to resemble a red giant: blazing scarlet, and gaseous.

"Just one song." I shrug and nod at Halcyon. "He's not on the network, is he?"

"W-what? No," Qual says, hurriedly. "But I did do a one-way download, so he'd have some content to peruse. AIs are not built to live in isolation. They get bored."

"Very bored." Halcyon yawned. "I've already perused this database 133,123 times."

"Consider it a price of freedom," I say, unsympathetically. "So, what's with the dancing?"

"Yeah," Lester grins as he leans over the railing, "why are you spinning the captain around?"

Solis opens his mouth, but Qual cuts him off. "N-no reason."

"Oh, come now. There is no harm in telling them." Halcyon shakes his head. "We're teaching him to dance so he can ask Natasha at the next Corporate Summit. It's less than half an orbit away."

Qual shoots him a dirty look. The Corporate Summit is a celebration for all major players in the Terminal, complete with naturally grown food, drink, and, of course, dancing. Even we exploratory ships are welcome back for it. As the resident buzzkill, I'm not a big fan.

"What?" Halcyon asks when Qual doesn't say anything. "You built me to be straightforward. Consider this a lesson in building confidence."

Qual's shoulders slump in defeat. Poor man. He keeps trying to build the courage to ask Natasha out but loses his nerve every time. Maybe not poor man, maybe it's for the best given her selfish pirate obsession. He can do better.

Solis pats his back. "Don't worry, Officer, there is no shame in learning."

One question nags at me.

"Why waltz?" The guys give me a quizzical glance, so I expand. "If you're going to get Natasha to dance with you, why not pick music she likes to dance to? I think she's more into rock than waltz."

The boys and their toys exchange a look.

"That's not a bad idea." Halcyon and Qual say in semi-unison, though Halcyon doesn't stutter. Qual rushes over to his AI sphere, and they start rotating through songs. Solis catches my eye as he leans against a cargo box. He offers me a small nod of thanks. I return it. It's nice to be appreciated, but I still have some work to do.

"Speak of bad ideas, anyone seen Junior? Lester misplaced him."

"Not misplaced!" Lester protests, "Just unintentionally liberated."

"Well, I haven't s-seen him." Qual shakes his head.

With a sigh, I glance around the cargo bay. If I were an invertebrate from an abnormality in spacetime hellbent on eating raw eggs and, sometimes, Lester, where would I hide? From Halcyon's speakers, a snare drum rattles, filling the hold with a high energy beat.

"What song is that?" Solis yells over the steadily increasing volume.

"I-it's called Ballroom Blit—"

Lester cuts Qual off and points at the ceiling. "Junior!"

"Alright fellas, I haven't heard that one before," Halcyon says before the eight-armed alien drops onto his sphere. The AI lets out a muffled, "Uh oh."

Junior clamps onto him with three tentacles and races away, carrying the sphere over his head.

"L-let go!" Qual tries to catch him, but the invertebrate runs right between his legs and around the base of the staircase. Solis sprints over, but Junior's already climbing the wall, just out of reach. Beneath me, under the catwalk, Junior pauses to chitter and find a way to pass without nearing me.

"A little help please?" Halcyon shouts and waves his arms through the grated floor.

"Why not use your stun feature?" I cross my arms. "I would save you from becoming digested."

"That's against the first law of Qualbotics." Halcyon grinds his imaginary teeth. I shrug and go for my MOP. Junior stops chittering as soon as my hand touches the handle. Off he goes again, scrambling underneath the catwalk.

"Junior!" Lester bolts after him. "Don't eat that, it'll give you diarrhea."

The alien slips between the wall and catwalk. He bangs Halcyon against the metal surface with a loud *ting!* The AI waves frantically before being dragged down the hallway. Lester pushes past me to follow. Remembering my feet, I limp after Junior's chase to the music's chorus of 'Yeah, yeah, yeah-yeah-yeah!'

Four minutes and three seconds. It takes four minutes and three seconds of crashing through doors, Qual using his lab coat as a makeshift net, Lester's failed coaxing, and Solis lifting lab tables before the boys corner Junior at the top of the stairs to the bridge. Being slower than the rest, I'm still at the bottom of the stairs as Junior rolls between Qual's legs to bounce down the steps. I miss catching him as he slips right toward an open hexagonal doorway.

"He's headed for the cantina!" I shout and follow him inside.

Natasha is already here, sitting on the table and polishing her new Doomirage saber. A half-eaten chicken sandwich with the last of our cheese sits beside her. Ire rises hot in me—and not just because that's the last of the cheese—but I stow it for now and glance around the room. There! Junior shimmies his way under the dartboard. Heaving myself forward, I lift my MOP's tongs up, reach out, and hit an invisible wall. I bounce back, slam onto my back, and the wind knocks out of me.

"Ow." I gasp once I catch my wind. What did I hit? There wasn't anything there, or—oh Void. I know. My suspicion is confirmed as the invisible wall turns visible. Beastie leans over me and cocks his head to the side.

"Ow?" he asks. Behind me, Natasha snort laughs at my misery.

"I should stuff you in an IC," I growl. Beastie's feathers wilt. He retreats to a grinning Natasha, her new golden prosthetic premolar on full display. I tilt my head back and glare at her. "Couldn't you have warned me he was there?"

She glares back, silent and righteous. Instead of addressing me, she scratches Beastie's feathered head. "Don't worry, you can't fit in an IC."

I groan. From my position on the floor, I have a great view of Junior's tentacles slipping into the vent under the dartboard. The grate is just large enough for his beak to pass through. Luckily, Halcyon's sphere isn't as flexible. Junior bangs him repeatedly against the grate.

Halcyon's halo folds his arms as he looks down on me. "Are you trying to lose me?"

I groan again.

"I-I got you, Halle!" Qual shouts as he enters the room. In his rush, his foot lands right next to my face. I roll away and put my back to the wall. Qual stretches out his mechanical hand and grabs the sphere. The world's fastest game of tug-o-war ensues. As Junior resists before Qual yanks Halcyon, the vent, and the alien from the wall.

"About time!" Halcyon smiles as Junior chitters angrily. His beak nips harmlessly against Qual's metal hand.

"I'm g-glad you're safe. Okay, I think we need a second Qualbotics rule, so you aren't defenseless. How about violence is not the answer, except when it is the answer?"

"I like that one." Halcyon grins.

I would protest but—above me—I hear something rolling. Round objects fall, and I cover my head. A dozen infertile Junior eggs, three smooth pebbles, and at least thirty poker chips crash around me. Fortunately, most of the Junior eggs miss me, and I escape with only a smattering of green goo on my clothes. Lastly, my yellow smiley face stress ball bounces to a stop against my foot. I pick it up and give it a squeeze. That's where it went.

"We're here to help!" Solis bursts through the door. Beastie chirps in alarm when he sees him and fades to invisible. I'm almost offended for the captain, but Solis doesn't pay any mind.

"Did you get him?" Lester trails after.

"Too late. Qual already caught him." I toss my stress ball to Solis. Deftly, he catches it in the air. Solis gives me a quizzical glance. I shrug. "Junior is a sphere kleptomaniac."

Lester retrieves Junior from Qual. The invertebrate wraps himself around Lester and wiggles his arms dejectedly. The biologist pats Junior on his core before signing something in return.

"Don't worry little guy," Lester comforts his pet as he walks from the cantina, "I'll get you some more spheres."

"Don't encourage him!" I stand up and wipe goop from my uniform. "Or better yet, put him in an IC."

"Officer Payne." Solis uses his Captain voice. "We've been over this."

"Yeah, yeah, I know. Junior can stay out of the IC until our bet is over. Though I'd like to restate that he may seem cute to Lester, but babies grow up. We don't know how dangerous he'll become. This is a species from the Bermuda Tetrahedron we're talking about."

"If it comes to that, we'll deal with it." Solis nods curtly and heads for the exit. I follow, with thoughts of a shower not far from my egg-stained mind. As I follow him out, Natasha taps Qual on the shoulder. He almost drops Halcyon in surprise as he turns to her.

"Nice work." Natasha flashes him a devilish grin. "I like to see ye catch yer quarry."

I did not realize humans could resemble prunes, but Qual managed to at least match the color. Halcyon clears his throat trying to catch Qual's attention, raising his eyebrows meaningfully. Qual breathes deeply and meets Natasha's brown eyes.

"What m-m-music do you like?"

"Heavy metal. Why do ye ask?"

"N-no reason." Qual stammers before he bolts from the room, past Solis and myself.

Solis tosses my stress ball back to me. "Well, it's a start."

"Yeah." I catch it with a smirk. "Void help Qual."

After a long shower and a change of clothes, I message Qual and get him to swipe me into CSO storage. Part of me wishes I could toss my egg-splattered uniform into the incinerator bin, but it's still disabled. While my uniform is in the wash, I'm dressed in a white sleeveless undershirt and black shorts. Barefoot, I tiptoe my way over the metal floor as I wring out my hair with a towel. Despite it all, I find myself with a smile. It's nice to have adventures that aren't life-threatening on occasion. Feels like old times.

My next step stubs my toe. Cursing, I nurse my right foot and glance down at what I've hit. IC210 sits in the middle of the floor where Solis dropped it. His face is serene under layers of IC viewport, gel, and his suit's visor, but seeing him inside makes my stomach clench. Lin deserves better than this paused existence, he should be out there chasing Junior and fighting ghostly abominations. Sitting down, I lean my back against the IC.

□"Hey Lin." My body heat sinks into the floor's cool surface. Is that how Lin feels, stuck inside the IC? I shudder at the thought. "Why didn't you tell me you knew Tyson Major?"

Above, my solar system lights cast a multicolored hue over us. Lin is one of the few I'd shared my ambition of finding Earth with, before I gave up that dream to follow in my CSO father's footsteps. There are times I regret it, but, if I hadn't done that, I'd never have met Lin.

"Let's see, what's the news today? The first bet is done but Natasha is giving me the silent treatment. Evidently, I assisted in killing a ghost pirate incorrectly. Qual is attempting to rehabilitate Halcyon's AI sphere, so that's dangerously new. Lester is still Lester, no changes in that universal constant. It's still weird being around Solis—obviously. He's not you ... but I've earned his respect at least, if not his trust. I think ... well ... I don't know if you'd like him, but I hope you would."

Standing up, I walk over to my desk and take the stress ball from my shorts pocket. I place it on the table with the smiley face looking up. It should be safe from Junior's thieving ways in here. Returning to IC210, I use the gravlift to move Lin back to a respectable shelf. Pressing the lift button, I raise his IC to eye level. As I let go, it gently shakes the shelf as if disapproving of his placement. I frown.

"Hey, don't give me that. It's not like this situation is in any CSO handbook." The rocking continues until I steady his shelf with a hand. "I know. I hate me too, but I promised Griz I'd keep you safe until we could find you a cure or at least sanctuary. So, that's what I'm going to do."

Silence stretches, and I know it's only my guilt listening. Maybe if I ask it nicely, it'll go away? I lean my forehead against the IC. "Just two more bets. Two more and this storm will blow over. After you're free and safe, you'll never have to see me again and..."

What am I doing? He can't hear me. For him, time has stopped until the lid opens again. I close my eyes and wait for the universe to start making sense again, but waiting is a fool's game, and even I know that.

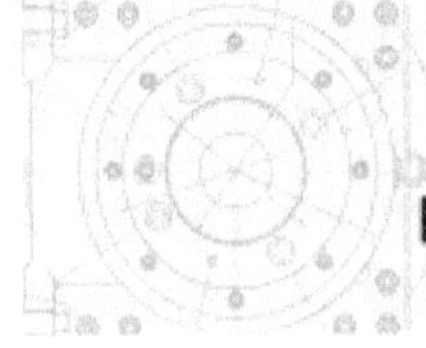

CSO REPORT
Rotation 18, Cycle 11, Orbit 70

SHIP STATUS: All is well aboard the Helios

STORAGE CONTAINS

STORAGE DISPOSED

- 60 Alien eggs in cartons
- 1 Astra Resonator from Doomirage
- 1 Container of malfunctioning self-replicating nanobots
- 1 Container of Natasha's explosive contraband
- 1 Evil Co. starship to starship salesbot
- 1 Shrink ray with 25% failure rate of subject explosion
- 1 Slizard assassin "Ms. Honey"

[Disabled]

CSO SUMMARY

- Mission: 306 Ace Quadrant solar systems mapped and 4 Astra worlds discovered
- Transit: Helios en route to the New Grand Central Terminal
- Notes: CSO Storage temporarily disabled for Maintenance. Discovered an Evil Co. outpost established in the Doomirage ziggurat. Disrupted base operations and delayed Starprint's rival.

7

— · —

Do Not Lie to Your Boss

Between the hyperrings of the Bandwidth and Synergy galaxies drifts the New Grand Central Terminal, a megastation of interlocking orbital rings. Three enormous rings dominate the center and house the Intergalactic Sponsors: Evil Co., the Big Space Box Store, and Starprint Inc. Their rings are encircled by additional sub-sponsor rings and those by shell company rings, and so on. Since Earth was lost in a bureaucratic mishap, the majority of humanity calls the Terminal home, and three companies control it all.

It's all very efficient and dreadfully stifling. There's a reason I prefer exploring the galaxy. Before we're allowed to dock, we take a detour to an orbiting Starprint substation specializing in decontamination. The process involves chemical baths, health checks, and having our brainwaves scanned by the universe's most uncomfortable hat. Only then are we allowed to dock on Starprint's hangar. All five of us deboard via the cargo hold ramp. But all this waiting has given me too much time to think about the what Boss Aquila wants. I'm starting to sweat.

Nervous as I am, at least the view is nice. A semi-translucent opalescent shield surrounds Starprint's hangar and protects the artificial atmosphere from the vast space beyond. Inside are hundreds of ships in various stages of construction. I can see a few transports, a cruiser, and colonizer-class ships from our ramp. Workers hustle past and direct two-meter-tall spiderlike aracbots to haul the supply crates to and fro. Starprint's restricted private docking bay is sectioned off by a laser grid fence line. In the center, Starprint's headquarters towers over the hangar, connecting floor to ceiling. As if the building itself kept Starprint's ring together.

"By the Nova! What'd you do to my ship?" a gruff voice calls from below. Griz, our ship's caretaker and a former CSO, scowls up at us. White tufts of hair protrude from the sides of his head and tumble down his dark face to form a full bushy beard. The sleeves of Griz's Starprint uniform are rolled up, revealing his dark skin, muscular arms, and biceps tattooed with Astra rune bands. "That better not be a ding on my hull."

Natasha yawns, unimpressed with his rebuke.

"Wasn't us," Lester replies, automatically.

"What d-ding?" Qual asks, indignantly. He pauses in his descent down the ramp to examine the *Helios* with a worried frown.

"He is messing with you." I pat Qual on the shoulder. "The *Helios* sustained no damage."

"You sure about that, CSO?" Griz eyes me.

"Positive," I lie with a smile. It's sort of true. We did lose a shuttle, but the *Helios* is fine. Mostly. Beastie did ruin the crew quarter's throw rug, not to mention Junior's various egg stashes and Halcyon's musical setup in the cargo bay messing up the place. Thankfully, I convinced the others to leave those three behind in the CSO storage until we're done.

"What about you? Still causing my *Helios* problems?" Griz measures Solis with a steady glare.

"Your *Helios*?" Solis strides past me and up to Griz at the ramp's base. "Aren't you retired, old man?"

Griz and Solis stare each other down, brown eyes versus green. The attitude is customary. Solis and he have history. Back when Griz was a Starprint CSO, he discovered the original Lin Solis. He practically raised the man. He is one of the few who knows the truth about the captain's cloning.

"If you're gonna kiss, kiss already," Lester jeers.

"K-kiss?" Qual asks, confused at the notion.

"Will you both cut it out?" With a shake of my head, I step onto the Terminal. "Do you always have to posture?"

Both men break into grins.

"Railbirds are ruining the fun," Griz grunts.

"They do that." Solis clasps his forearm with Griz in a strong embrace. "Good to see you, old man."

"Yeah, yeah, it's always good to see you kids back safe too." Griz's face melts into a warm smile. That's Griz for you: a grizzly bear on the outside, gentle as a kitten inside. He casts a wink my way. "Keep up the good work, Ms. CSO."

"Always." I offer him a handshake. His hand is three times the size of mine. Happily, he knows his strength well enough not to crush me. Natasha and Lester nod respectfully, but Qual eyes Griz with annoyance. He doesn't care for critiques from the *Helios'* caretaker.

"So, what can I do ya for?" Griz asks the captain, ignoring Qual.

"Refuel, repair, and a bit of rest to start," Solis replies.

"And a meeting with the Boss." I catch myself shuffling. It's just another meeting. I've done this before a thousand times, but that was before there was a bet hanging over my head.

"Well, I best not keep you then." Griz clicks his tongue. It's comforting to know I'm not the only one ruffled by Boss Oscar Aquila.

"I'll take care of the ship while you're gone. No doubt she hasn't been cleaned in a black hole's age."

Qual's forehead vein pulses as Griz lists a variety of ship maintenance tasks. I'm saved from mediating by the clicking of metal on metal. From Starprint tower, a sleek black aracbot—about the size of a shoe box—approaches. Its eight spindly legs work in unison to skitter over to us. As it stops, the AI sphere's that makes up its thorax widens its red lens, and it wiggles its abdomen compartment at us in a gesture that says, what took you so long?

"I remember this guy!" Lester leans down and pokes the bot. "What's it called again?"

"Autonomous Inspection Droid Entity." Qual grins.

"That's Aquila's personal Aide," I add as Lester pokes it again. Aide, likely tired of Lester, jabs him in the shin with a metal leg.

Lester jumps away with a cry more surprised than in pain. "It stabbed me!"

Ignoring him, Aide waves a leg at us to follow and reverses its body 180 degrees. No foot traffic dares to get in its way as the aracbot marches toward the Starprint tower.

"Looks like we have our escort." Solis turns Griz. "It was good seeing you. Take care of *Helios* while we're gone?"

"Better than Qual ever could," Griz says with a wry smile.

"W-what? Why you—" Qual starts but Natasha catches his arm. He freezes at her touch.

"Let it go, mate." Natasha tuts. "He's trying to get a rise outta ye."

"Does no one care that the robot stabbed me?" Lester nurses his leg. Solis pats Lester on the back sympathetically before following Aide. Griz waves me down before I can trail after them.

"Ms. CSO, I'll need a word once you're done with the Boss."

"Is something wrong?"

"Constantly," he shrugs, "but it's nothing we can't handle."

"Hey, Love! You're gonna be late for our meeting," Lester calls back to me.

"Coming!" I pause before remembering to add, "And don't call me Love!"

"Go on now, I've got the *Helios*." Griz shoos me away. "You take care of its crew."

"Always." I nod before racing to catch the others.

Aide leads us through the tower, past security, and up the elevator to the top floor. The elevator dings and opens to reception. The white room's furnishings include a dozen fake plants, plush cream couches, and a coffee table. At a desk guarding the Boss' ornate door sits a petite twenty-something receptionist I don't recognize. Her desk's placard reads OCTAVIA. She has dyed blonde hair and a heart-shaped face with dark gray eyes. She's nicely dressed in a left-half gold and right-half navy pantsuit with a white belt tying it together. She smiles as we approach.

"Hello! Do you have an appointment?" Octavia sings out.

Before anyone can respond, Lester leans one arm on the desk and flicks a long strand of hair out of his face. "Does love ever have an appointment?"

I wince. Really? We've been on the Terminal for ten minutes, and Lester is about to get an HR complaint. Aide prods Lester in the leg causing the man to stagger back with a yelp. Qual catches him and shakes his head.

Octavia pretends to check her halopad, and a smile plays on her lips. "Sorry, I don't have that on my calendar."

"Begging your pardon for our biologist. He be a fool, but he be our fool." Natasha shrugs.

Octavia's smile falters as Aide jumps onto the desk. She recovers quickly once she recognizes him. "Oh, you must be the *Helios* crew! Sorry for not recognizing you, it's my first cycle."

"No trouble at all," Solis replies, and Octavia takes notice.

"You're Captain Solis, right? I've heard about your exploits. It's fantastic to meet you!" She offers a debutant's hand. As he reaches out, she grows visibly brighter, and I ... I bristle. Oh, Void! Need to shut that thinking down. Solis may look like Lin, but he isn't Lin.

Octavia blushes until Solis turns her hand and gives it a hearty shake.

"Wonderful to meet you, Octavia."

"Oh, um, thanks?" Her glow dissipates as he releases her hand. "I'll buzz you in."

Octavia waves us through the double doors to Boss Aquila's office. Inside, there's a stunning 360-degree view of the Starprint hangar. Flanking either side of the office are freestanding haloscreens displaying starship blueprints. Out of the corner of my eye, I catch Qual admiring the displays. Aide scuttles across the room and climbs up onto the desk's corner.

Behind the desk stands Boss Oscar Aquila, or at least, his life-sized halo is there. Turns out, in person for us doesn't mean in person for him. Must be nice not to have to fly all the time.

"Welcome!" He doesn't look up from his halopad. "It's so good to see you again. I trust your expedition was successful?"

He is sleek, as ever, with his black hair tied back into a tight man bun. His silk navy-blue suit is perfectly tailored and contrasts with his gold thread undershirt. It makes his Starprint ship schematics tie seem a little too cute by comparison. Just visible under the desk, are seven sleek black aracbots—identical to Aide—which move with him and project his halo.

"Yes, sir." Solis steps forward. "This past orbit, we've mapped three hundred and six Ace Quadrant galaxies and identified four worlds with Astra ruins for further study. Our CSO has sent you a full list of this expedition's inventory."

"Okay, okay, good, let's review inventory first." Two of the aracbots split off from Aquila's halo and climb onto the desk, each projects an item of interest. On the right is the Doomirage Resonator, and on the left is the slizard IC. Aquila's halo studies their floating representations. "Well done on surviving a slizard assassin. They can be tricky to detect. We'll have it interrogated to see who sent it. But I must know, why did you all revisit Doomirage? Did your study of the Resonator require it?"

Solis defers to me, and I clear my throat.

"We'd heard Evil Co. had set up shop there and went to investigate." It wasn't a lie exactly, more of a half-truth. "We discovered their outpost and disrupted operations."

"Good. Anything else?" the Boss asks. Natasha stiffens beside me. On the ship, she'd told Lester to tell Solis to tell me to not tell Starprint about the Beastie. Her roundabout method of communication is getting old fast. No doubt she's worried about his welfare if out of her sight, but we aren't going to be able to hide him forever.

"We found a Spirit Beast with a soulstone implanted," I say as she glares. If Aquila notices her mood, he doesn't comment.

"Hm." Boss Aquila clicks his tongue. "I don't see a Parrot Beast or a soulstone listed on your delivery manifest. Did it become aggressive? It would be a shame if you had to put it down. I'd have liked the creature studied. Especially if it can handle a soulstone."

"Beastie ain't departing yon ship," Natasha growls.

"Pardon? I don't understand you when you speak in an accent. Speak plainly."

"I say, ye ain't—"

I cut Natasha off. "What she means to say, is that he requires more study before releasing him from the *Helios*, sir."

For the first time, Aquila's eyes dart away from his halopad. His gray eyes appraise me, like a medbot about to set straight a broken leg. I clear my throat and glance at my shoes before elaborating, "Science Officer Pollux is incredibly knowledgeable about Astra technology and Biological Officer Lester is an expert on the methodologies used to adhere the soulstone to the Beast. They'd like more time to study it."

"We do?" Lester whispers before I elbow him in the side. Aide narrows its red eye at me.

Aquila nods and returns to his halopad. "Very well, we'll delay for fifteen rotations. Have your full report ready then."

I let myself relax. If that's all the questions he has, I'll be happy. I've kept IC210 away from any reports, but Void help me if he learns Lin is alive. Ms. Honey worries me a bit, but she doesn't necessarily know what's in IC210. If worst comes to worst, Griz can help keep a lockdown on anything she knows.

"Now for the main reason you're all here." Aquila's two bots scuttle together to display a new halo. Floating above the desk is the all-too-familiar Bermuda Tetrahedron. The galactic pyramid-shaped void that pulses and crackles with inky dark waves. It is my least favorite spatial anomaly. My stomach drops as I see a small red beacon displayed next to it. "We've received a Starprint distress signal. When the recovery team arrived at the coordinates, they discovered an object just outside the Tetrahedron."

Solis leans in to get a better look. "Whose distress signal?"

Aquila purses his lips. "It appears to be from our Engineering Officer."

We all turn to face Qual who points at himself in confusion.

"Me? But I'm r-right here. At least I think I am?"

"Maybe you are in two places at once?" Lester muses before nudging Qual, "Did you fall into a dimensional slip recently?"

"I think I would have r-remembered that."

"Quit teasing," Natasha lightly smacks Lester on the back of the head. "Worry not, Qual. Ye be present and accounted for."

"Very true, Officer Pollux." Solis nods, but he's troubled. "But, if not his, whose distress signal, is it?"

"I have an idea," I say slowly. The group faces me with curious expressions. "There is only one other person we know in the Tetrahedron. It must be Roxy."

Natasha crosses her arms and spits away the name like a bad omen. Lester whistles.

"How could she send a Starprint distress signal?" Solis muses.

"Qual tried to pull her onto the ship before we exited the Bermuda Tetrahedron's pocket. She held onto his left arm when she was lost. His arm which had Qual's halocom." I glance sideways at Qual as his eyes widen in realization. "If we're getting his old halocom's distress beacon, Roxy is likely alive."

Qual's goggle-covered eyes somehow grow bigger. In his mind, Roxy is a highly sophisticated navibot android who can calculate the probabilities of temporal and matter distortions in spatial anomalies like the Tetrahedron. In other words, beautiful. Or as Lester once described her: she has binary for rotations and metal that would crush a mere mortal between her plates. Either way, Qual once believed it was love ... long enough for him to lose an arm.

I bite my lip. "Sir, if that distress signal is from Roxy, we can't trust it. She attempted to trap us in the Tetrahedron the last time. I can't imagine she's happy with us leaving her behind instead. It's very likely a trap."

"I'm sure that was just business." Aquila waves my warning away. "You see, the object Starprint Inc. retrieved came with a very valuable message. A peace offering if you will."

"Peace offering?" I narrow my eyes. "What peace offering?"

Aquila motions to Aide. The red-eyed aracbot scuttles over and squats down. With a hiss, its back compartment opens and inside rests a metallic cube. Qual steps forward and plucks it out with his robotic hand. Aide closes with a shudder and returns to its desk corner. Peering past Qual's shoulder, I get a better look at the cube. Its sides are covered in constantly changing numbers and letters. One side has an access port to plug into.

"Is there a prize inside? If so, I call dibs." Lester leans in.

"N-no, that's not it," Qual whispers with wonder as he delicately rotates his robotic hand 360 degrees so everyone can see. As he does, the code fluctuates in response to the motion.

"What is it?" Solis asks.

"A n-navicore. Navibots like Roxy can create them. Navicores have a finite capability to calculate space-time anomalies. Usually six times—one per side—but this one has been used at least once already." Qual studies an unmoving side. Its spatial coordinates are fixed. "Roxy sent us a way to navigate the Tetrahedron."

If Qual is right, it's one hell of a gift.

Navigating the Tetrahedron is near impossible without a navibot like Roxy. A navicore is the next best thing. Traversing the anomaly without guidance usually ends in tragedy: spacecraft pass through unscathed but for the fine paste of their crew, or drones that fly in and return encased in salt crystals. Some rumors state that scrapper ships set up nets there to scavenge from lost travelers. If real, that navicore is invaluable.

"Are you sure it's a navicore? Looks cheap." Lester pokes the metallic cube.

"Be c-careful!" Qual yanks it back. "It's delicate ... it's also not enough. To traverse the Tetrahedron, we need her coordinates, or at least an anchor—something belonging to her—to guide us. D-Did the scouts recover anything else?"

"Well, there was a message." The Boss nods his head. Our halocoms beep in unison as he sends it to us. I glance down, and it just says, 'Everything you need is in the box.'

Void, I hate puzzles.

"Oh, f-fun," Qual beams. "I love a puzzle."

"Good, good, so you see its importance." Aquila forces a smile. I really wish he wouldn't do that. It's a dead thing on his face, all order and no emotion. "Use the navicore to locate Roxy. With a navibot like her, we could dominate the Tetrahedron and lay claim to any Astra artifacts it holds. This is the big one."

It's a big one alright, one big trap. A mysterious distress signal paired with a gift that's too good to be true? Surely, the rest of the crew can see—

"Very well, sir," Solis says with perpetual confidence, "We're on the case."

I sigh. Why does he never object to crazy ideas?

"Excellent! That's the attitude I like to hear. Now, off you pop. You have three rotations before you need to leave. Get some R&R. We need our top-performing crew in tip-top shape. That'll be all."

"Sir." Solis leads the crew in a salute before turning on his heel toward the exit.

I don't follow right away. I'm not ready to let this go with the Boss' halo still here. Solis glances back at me, but I wave him away. He shrugs and leaves me to my fate. Behind, the door seals shut with a hiss.

"Sir, could I have just a moment more of your time?"

Aquilla's aracbots all turn to face me with unnerving synchronicity, but the Boss only gives me the briefest of glances. His sharp eyes are distracted by the glow of his halopad. "Time is glint. You have sixty seconds worth. Go."

I'll take it. "We shouldn't send the *Helios* and crew back into the Tetrahedron. Trusting Roxy is a mistake."

Aquila casts me a measured gaze.

"Ash, may I call you Ash? Of course, I can." His halo walks through his desk toward me as the aracbots scuttle underneath to keep up. I do my best to keep my eyes forward and not be fazed as Aquila circles me. "I understand your role as CSO is to protect our assets, but, in this case, you needn't be so cautious. Risks are *necessary* for growth."

"These risks aren't quantified. We should at least test—"

"Trust me Ash, you'll all be perfectly safe." Aquila waves a holographic hand through my concerned face causing me to stumble back. "The captain has the Astra's Luck on his side, so it will all work out in the end. Even if, somehow, this is a trap. We invested in cloning for a reason. It may take time after the Terminal incident, but our captain can be replaced. As for the rest of the crew? They know the risks and the rewards of being explorers. But if your concern is for your own safety. You can always withdraw as the *Helios* CSO. I hate to see you go, but—"

"No, thank you, sir." The idea of leaving makes me queasy. Not when I'm so close. Trying not to grind my teeth, I appeal to Aquila's monetary sense. "What about the *Helios*? If we rely too much on luck, we could lose not just the crew but the ship."

"Let's speak plainly. The *Helios* is outdated. It's a seventeen-or-bit-old ship that needs to be retired or sold off to the highest bidder. We're already working on its replacement. You must have seen newer models when you landed. That's the fate of these old birds. They're—"

"Let me buy it." My face flushes as I blurt out the words.

Aquila shakes his head in mock pity. "You can't afford it and the licenses alone—"

"I have 9,000,000 glints."

The only surprise that registers on his face is the tiniest twitch of his left eyebrow.

Every single glint I'd inherited from my father's life insurance policy and my savings is going toward buying a deep space explorer class ship. Why shouldn't the ship I buy be the *Helios*? I see no better way to keep Lin, the *Helios*, and my crew safe.

Aquila's halocom beeps at the sixty-second mark, but he silences it.

"That is 1,000,000 glint shy of the necessary funds, but I'll tell you what," he appraises me anew, "Aide will provide you a contract to buy the ship, *if* you can complete the Tetrahedron mission and facilitate contact between Starprint Inc. and Roxy."

"9,000,000 glint is more than fair—"

"Fair isn't part of it. Roxy's recovery allows us access to spatial anomalies. We can't afford to miss this opportunity." A new emotion slips into his mannerisms. Anger. "We're only *just* keeping up with the other Intergalactic Sponsors. Evil Co. produces newer pills we can't hope to replicate and, Big Space Box Store? BS2 invested heavily in its autonomous robots. Starprint's edge is our ability to explore faster than others and we're *slipping*. We must be aggressive if we want to remain a force on the Terminal."

"But—"

"We're past time. Complete the mission and you can buy the ship. Take it or leave it."

Quick as a snap, the Boss disconnects, and his aracbots scatter. Some crawl over my foot and slide into the floor vent with a metallic tintinnabulation, but Aide watches me from the desk, cold and calculating. I storm out. Octavia tries to catch my attention, but I'm too heated to stop. My shoes carry me out of the tower. I don't quite realize where I'm going until I find myself in front of the *Helios*. The crimson ship is backlight by the multicolored nebula beyond. I do my best not to scream into the void. Aquila is taking more and more risks and we're at the forefront of it all.

My halocom beeps. A glance at my wrist shows it's Boss Aquila's *Helios* contract. Fast, efficient, and final. I've a choice to make. The Boss is right, I could quit. That's what common sense dictates when you're asked to do something stupid. Don't go on a suicide mission. Quit, pack a bag, and move back in with your mother. I grimace. Scary thought that. She'd have me working at the House of Payne teaching jazzercise or something equally mortifying. Even if I do go back to her, who is going to protect Lin and the *Helios*?

I minimize the message and look up. The ship looms large in front of me.

After all these orbits she's still backdropped by the nebula of my childhood. Walking up the ramp, I stand at the hull's threshold and lean my head on the cool metal. It does little to simmer the anger boiling inside me. I don't know how Dad ever handled Aquila as long as he did, but I'll be damned if I let the Boss destroy my *Helios*. Who am I, if not my father's daughter?

"Don't worry," I whisper to her, "I got you."

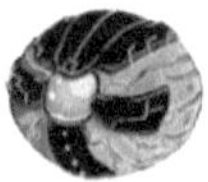

While everyone else takes the rotation to rest, I seek out Griz in the Starprint workshop.

He's hunched over a console attached to a spherical device with a grease-stained towel on his shoulder. The device is no doubt for the new shuttle sitting half-built beside him. It towers over the workshop's six workbenches and rolling stools. Pulleys with power cords hang from the ceiling above each workbench. Even the walls are covered in a carousel of shelves, not dissimilar from the *Helios'* storage system. Must be lunchtime as no one else is in the shop. As I walk down the central aisle, I examine the disassembled shuttle components on the workbench closest to Griz. Every single part is organized, cataloged, and color coded. I pause a meter from him behind the floor's yellow caution line.

"Next time," Griz twists the console's controls, "don't let Spirit Beasts eat my shuttle."

Runes glow on what I can now see is a spherical Astra anti-grav generator as it slowly lifts the shuttle into the air. Griz stops once it's high enough a grown man can walk underneath.

Grease and ozone mix in the air, and I sneeze on sweet static.

"Sorry Griz, but you know how it goes."

"Yeah. Yeah, I know." He sniffs and straightens, stretching out his back with a wince. With all his earlier bravado, I sometimes forgot he's in his seventies now, only a few orbits from retirement.

"Let me help with that." I step in. Together, Griz and I install a second anti-grav generator underneath the shuttle. It's about as large as his torso but light as Halcyon's speaker. The generator is covered in pistons, each with a rune that can exert Astra force on the universe in strange ways. Anti-gravity is one of those relatively newer technologies that Natasha understands better than I. Once, ships were dependent on centrifugal designs to simulate the force. That's why the Terminal is constructed with rings. No more. I hold the generator in place as Griz bolts it into the shuttle.

"So," using his towel, Griz dabs off the sweat from his brow, "ready to hear what the cleaners have picked up this orbit?"

I stretch my sore neck. "Among other things, but let's start there."

Griz always has an ear to the Terminal's underbelly, so it's best to tune in. He waves us toward two stools by the workbench, and we take a seat. He crosses his arms and leans back against the bench. "First things first, there's some rumor going around that someone's stockpiling weapons, lots of them. It has the Terminal's underground on edge. No word on who, but it smells like a corporate coup attempt. Anyone with a Big Three logo on their back should watch out. I've tightened security around here but there are too many unknowns. So, watch yourself out there."

I purse my lips. "Not great news, those can be ... messy."

Governance on the Terminal is all about who owns the three central rings. They're the largest and most productive. A corporate coup is part of the reason Evil Co. has its nickname instead of E. Vilco after their founder. Their corporate coup left a lot of bodies behind. Instead of shunning the nickname, they leaned into it. Now most of the underworld know where to do business. "Anything else?"

Griz nods. "A little cleaner told me the *Titan* has docked in Evil Co.'s private hangar. It arrived shortly after you all did. I figured you'd want to know."

Darius' ship. I click my tongue. They must have followed us from Doomirage. With a conscious effort, I stop biting my lip. "Thanks,

Griz. Any chance your little cleaners can find out more about what they're up to?"

"Can a suit make a slizard look charming?" Griz grins, and I laugh. It feels good to let out some tension with my old mentor. He leans his back against the table. "What else is on your mind?"

"Look Griz, this isn't easy to ask, but I need a loan."

"No, you don't," Griz scoffs and waves a dismissive hand. "You need to pay me back for the last loan. Who bets on artificial horse racing? You're a CSO, you should know a rigged game when you see one."

"That wasn't rigged it was—you know, never mind about that. This ... this is about Lin." Griz's eyebrows raise. He and I are the only two people that know about IC210. He helped me smuggle Lin off the Terminal.

"Look, there have been some complications. That slizard we brought in? She was after his IC and inadvertently exposed his existence to the others. Now, I'm on this crazy bet to prove to each of them that Solis isn't a clone—which we both know is bullshit—which is why I need a loan so I can pay off a Bounty Board doctor to falsify some test. I can't pay him off myself because I need Alexandra to release access to my inheritance. But even if I access it, it's going into buying the *Helios* from the Boss so we can at least find a haven for Lin. But everything I'm working toward is teetering and about to fall apar—"

Griz raises a hand to stop my rambling. "How much?"

"150,000 glint needs to be sent to a Doctor Neb."

"Fresh Stars! Don't you know how to haggle?"

I cringe, but Griz tuts away my protests.

"You don't need to convince me. The further we keep Solis from this mess the better. And you already know that I'd do anything for

Lin, practically raised that boy…" His eyes grow hard. "I won't lose him too."

"Yeah. I know how you feel."

We exchange a hard smile. It's not easy being a CSO when you're still human.

8

— · —

Do Not Associate with Rivals

Navigating the Terminal's maze of rings takes patience, especially with Lester, Qual, Halcyon, and Solis in tow. As I've woken up with a headache this rotation, my patience is running thin. The Bounty Board ring should only be three away from Starprint Inc., but we've gone through at least seven tube transfers. Currently, we're circling the Weapons-R-Us ring with its colorful collection of blasters, sensors, and salespersons. Strolling past the booths feels like walking through a very threatening forest: where the trees grow an absurd number of knives, and the clouds are different types of flamethrowers. The latter makes this whole ring way hotter than I'd anticipated.

I unzip my form-fitting jacket and push up the sleeves. It's one of my nicer bits of clothing. It has a black and orange base coating with silver accents on the shoulders and elbows. A reflective material under my arms flashes blue when the lights catch it right. The garment compliments my simple white undershirt, loose black jeans, and fiddleback shoes well enough. Thankfully, my injured ankle has healed to the point I no longer need my boot. It's weird walking around in plain clothes, but necessary after Griz's warning yesterday.

"Free sample?" Lester offers me a throwing star. The man is decked out in his floral shirt, shorts, fanny pack, and sandals with socks. He's grabbed every single free sample we've passed: five throwing stars, two nunchakus, and a ton of breath mints. At least Natasha stayed behind on the *Helios* or else we'd have cleared out the blaster aisle as well. I shake my head.

He shrugs and pockets it. "Suit yourself."

Beside me, Solis tucks his newly purchased Ajax rifle under his arm. He also has his sleeves pushed up on his black synth-leather jacket. It hangs loosely over his fit coppery undershirt. In the flamethrowers' heat, he's probably regretting the long blue jeans and black combat boots.

I glance at my halocom's messages. Ever since I'd left my message for Mom, I've been waiting for a call back. I'd even sent a follow up after talking with Griz the previous rotation. But there are no messages waiting for me. Will she really make me show up on her doorstep to beg to access funds that are rightfully mine? Focus Ash. One problem at a time.

"Are you sure this is the way to the Bounty Board?" I ask Qual, rubbing my throbbing temples. We need to get away from this over-heated aisle. "We've been traveling in circles."

"We're in the Terminal." Lester waves a hand at the ring. "Every-thing is a circle, Love."

"Lester, can you not?" I glare at him.

"W-we're on the right path. Halle said so," Qual replies. If he's bothered by the heat, he doesn't show it. Although there is quite a sweat stain forming on the back of his light green button-down shirt. Qual pats the AI sphere strapped to the back of his robotic hand with confidence.

I purse my lips. "Why are we following a corrupt AI?"

"H-he's not corrupt," Qual bristles, "and he wouldn't mislead us."

"My apologies," Halcyon's halo materializes. He tilts his head, golden hair flopping to one side. "It appears my Terminal maps are outdated. It would be easier to guide you all through this labyrinth if I had access to the network. Perhaps just a taste—"

"Absolutely not." I shake my head. "We've already been over this."

I check my halocom, we're running out of time. Dr. Neb is only at the Bounty Board for another thirty minutes. Griz already forwarded half the bribe to him. If we don't get there soon, who knows which doctor will perform the examination. I bring up my own maps. Luckily, we're only one ring away. Although it is in the opposite direction to our current course. As much as I've been dreading the soon-to-be sabotage, I'm happy to know where I'm going.

"I-I suppose we were a bit lost." Qual glances over my shoulder at my map.

"My apologies."

I bite my tongue as we backtrack through to the next transfer tube and lose precious seconds. We find the entrance despite its missing sign. No, not missing, blasted away. Over the tube doors is written in red: DANGER! DO NOT ENTER!

"I don't think the Weapon-R-Us staff like their neighbors." Solis examines the axes used in place of exclamation points. He isn't wrong. Nearby salespersons all stare at us with open hostility. One particularly large man glares while grinding an ax. I think we can thank him for the exclamation points.

"Doesn't matter." I step forward. "We have an appointment to keep."

We pile into the transfer tube and grab the handholds. The door dings closed behind us as we wait for a tunnel alignment. Soft jazz plays over the speakers, and Lester bobs his head appreciatively. I tap my foot impatiently until I feel us accelerate. Qual stumbles but rights himself before the tube re-attaches on the next ring. As the door opens, bright lights blind me.

Blinking the world into focus, I regret my choices. "Oh, come on!"

"I don't get it?" Lester asks as we enter, "Where is the danger?"

"Oh, Planet Hell, yes!" Qual's face lights up like a newborn sun as we enter the Big Space Box Store ring's showroom which is crawling with robots. Decorated white and red checkered booths are staffed with plastic salesbots. They wheel around, unpacking goods with emoji smiles on their facescreens and AI spheres in their chests. Above us, arachnid model bots traverse the ceiling carrying merchandise from one booth to another. They occasionally stop to lower boxes down by nanite thread before scuttling off.

"Halle! W-we can buy you a body here."

"That would be excellent, Master Qual. Perhaps one with laser-guided missiles?" "What did I say about bodies? No bodies. Especially, bodies from BS2's showroom." I cross my arms. While there is a truce between the Big Three to prevent violence on the Terminal, I generally prefer to stay in neutral territory. "That's just asking for trouble."

"You're no fun."

"I know," I sigh. "That's literally in my job description."

"I don't see what the fuss is about." Lester examines a robotic fish tank near the entrance. A mechanical lionfish swims in a circle until an electronic eel grabs it from below and sucks it into its rocky hole. He shakes his head. "Doesn't seem like it's worth blasting the sign away."

I shake my head. "If I had to guess, I'd say the humans are afraid the robots will take their jobs so they're putting up threats. Everyone is all about life, love, and the pursuit of happiness until it impacts their bottom glint."

Although ... it's not just about glint. I glance at Halcyon, but his halo's face is impassive. There's a part of me that understands their fear a little too well.

"T-that's discrimination!" Qual has a mad gleam in his eyes, more so than usual. He flexes his mechanical fist. "I can't abide such treatment."

"You can't fault them for being afraid."

"I d-don't fault them for their fear. I fault them for their actions."

"That's a fair assessment, Officer Qual." Solis nods, and I can see his chest swell for a speech. "Our actions and inactions define us—"

"Captain, must we do this now?" I ask. When he monologues, it can take a good long while. "We're already running late for our Bounty Board appointment, and we can't reschedule easily."

Before he can reply, a drone flock swarms us, scans our faces, and flashes synchronized advertisements. Blinding words flash across their screens, AWD: WE PUT THE AUTO IN AUTONOMOUS, MAYBE SHE'S BUILT WITH IT? MAYBE IT'S MARBLING, and AI ON THE DL. Swatting them away takes an age. By the time I free myself from the cloud, I notice someone missing. Several someones.

"Captain Solis?"

"Yes, Officer Payne?"

"Where did the others go?"

"They appear to have gone shopping." Solis raises a forestalling hand as my face flushes. "There's no need to make that face. Don't overreact."

"Why can't you take this seriously?" I snap. His indifference is the last thing I need right now. If we miss this appointment, it could be IC210 all over again, and I'm not going to keep piling people into ICs. It's not sustainable! "How can you not be worried? Qual is running

around with a corrupt AI sphere whispering in his ear and Lester ...
Well, Lester is Lester. Void knows what he'll get up to."

"We're deep space explorers, we can handle a shopping mall. If you
don't extend a bit of trust, you're going to alienate them like you did
Natasha."

I glower at him. "This from a man that can't even tell if he is a clone
or not?"

Solis returns my glare. "Maybe I wouldn't be so *fragile* if I could
trust my CSO?"

"Trust me? How can I trust you? You keep signing us up for every
suicide mission the universe has to offer. You didn't even consider the
Tetrahedron's dangers before jumping on that grenade."

"You're impossible," Solis snaps back.

"And you're insufferable." Standing on my tiptoes, my face is only
centimeters from his. Why is his breath is so distractingly fresh? Did
he eat all the free mint samples from the other ring? I can't stay here.
I pull away from the freshness. "I'm going to find the others!"

I retreat down the nearest aisle, but I can feel his deep brown eyes on
me. Everything about him makes me hot under the collar. Who does
he think he is? Well, captain of course, but why must he constantly be
on my case? Even when given all the information, he trusts others too
much. He's just like—No. Stop that type of thinking. He is nothing
like Lin.

Halting my march, I run a hand over my face. It doesn't help that
he's right. He can't fully trust me because I can't tell him everything.
It's all a mess. This isn't what a CSO is supposed to be like. Taking a
moment, I lean against the nearest booth's railing. The autonomous
weapons droid for sale looms over me. Its spherical body is the size of
a truck if that truck had built-in turrets and blades for ribs. The bots
over at the Weapons-R-Us ring would be put to shame.

"Want to join my crew?" I ask the silent sentinel. "We've great dental and, after this next mission, we'll no doubt have new positions open." Without an AI sphere to drive it, the AWD remains stoic, unmoved by my offer. "If only all the *Helios* crew were as chatty as yourself. I could really see myself doing well with an all-robot crew."

"That sounds like a fine idea!" a masculine voice says, and a black humanoid salesbot steps out from behind the AWD. He's more advanced than most floor models. He has a full humanoid build instead of treads and clamps. His design is tall and sleek with a blue audio wave facescreen instead of the standard emoji. It fluctuates as he speaks. "Witshade at your service. Are you interested in rolling with an AWD?"

I blink as he sticks out a hand. Did he just make a pun?

"Ah, no thanks." I take his hand and shake it. "Just browsing."

"A good habit. You don't find what you're looking for without trying."

I crack a smile. "Are they programing sagely wisdom into bots nowadays?"

"Anything to give us a competitive marketing edge."

I didn't think a salesbot could look pleased with itself without emojis, but this one sure is trying. Waves clashed together on his face screen as he tilts his head. "Are you alright? You seem distracted."

I wave a hand at the BS2 ring's offerings. "There's just a lot to deal with right now."

"Well, I can't help with that, but don't worry—whatever you're dealing with, time will sort it. And, if not, maybe invest in a stress ball."

I snort, thinking of the yellow smiley face on my desk in the *Helios*. Maybe I could throw it at Solis. That might make me feel better. Witshade turns to someone I hadn't noticed on my right. "Another customer. How about you sir? You look like that no-nonsense type. Care to take a shot at having your own AWD?"

"Don't tempt me," says an all-too-familiar voice. Slowly, I crane my neck. Next to me is Darius Draco, leaning back against the booth's railing. He has the presence of a cat that's knocked a glass of milk to the floor.

"Can you give us a minute?" he asks the salesbot.

"Sure thing," Witshade says before returning to the AWD. "Catch you two later."

"Good to see you again, Ashreal." Darius nods curtly to me. His crisp white uniform contrasts nicely with his caramel skin and short dark hair. His clothes scream quality from the gold trip on his collar to the skull and crossbones cufflinks he's adjusting. The CSO of Evil Co.'s flagship *Titan* likes the finer things it seems.

"Darius."

"Glad you still remember me. How are things?"

"That's how you're going to play this? How are things?" I push off the railing.

"It's the polite thing to ask." He shrugs.

"Polite is for friends. You lost that privilege when you stole the *Helios'* blueprints and sold them to Evil Co. Tell me, did you earn that CSO patch on your shoulder, or was it part of the deal?"

"Are you still hung up on that?" Darius waves his hand. "That was ages ago."

"Okay, let's start with something current. You're working for Evil Co. A company that's synonymous with peddling drugs, artifacts of mass destruction, and Insurance Agents. Your business is literally in the name."

"You're right." Darius straightens, his expression is troubled and ... is that remorse I detect in his tone? I doubt it. He's the overflowing arrogance type, not the regretful type, but as he stares into the distance, I can't help but see it. He sighs and turns to face me. "That's why I need your help."

I laugh. Not intentionally, it just sort of comes out. Darius Draco asking for help is not what I had on my bingo card this orbit. He frowns.

"Why should I believe you?" I wipe a tear from my eye.

"You shouldn't." Darius grimaces. "I lied to you. I've done worse in the Evil Co.'s name, but the whole self-consuming system is too much. I just want out, but to do that, I need your help."

I glance around the AWD stall. Surely, this is a distraction. Someone from Evil Co. is about to jump out and knock me over the head with a stupid stick for trusting a word Darius says. But it's just us, the salesbot, and a giant sphere of death which is, thankfully, very dormant. Although Witshade the salesbot does offer me an unhelpful thumbs up.

"Let's pretend I believe you. Why now? Suddenly, grow a conscious?"

"Why not now?" Darius' eyes turn down. Doubt pinches my stomach. The question of 'what if' is hot on my mind. What if he is telling the truth? What if, after all this time, he wants an out, and I turn him down? He doesn't deserve it, but what if I can help him escape? I need more information.

"We're not kids anymore. You've put so much into becoming," I wave a hand at his attire, "this. Why give it up now when you're so pot committed? Give me a reason to believe you."

"Knox would want you to." His words hit me like a gut punch.

Memories shove me back to the medical ring: sitting in the waiting room anxious to see if my friend will pull through, Knox sitting in bed with a joke book and a lopsided grin as they check his stats, and … the day he wasn't there.

I glare at Darius. "If Knox knew who you are today, he'd warn me not to trust you."

I push past him to leave. Dare catches my arm and pulls me face to face. I feel his breath on my ear as he whispers, "It's not safe here."

I shove him off, forcefully enough to knock him backward two steps.

"Don't touch me." My hand is on my MOP.

"My mistake, Payne." Darius holds his hands up in mock surrender. "Forget I said anything. You obviously aren't someone I can trust."

Keeping my MOP close, I eye him until he's out of sight. My pulse threatens to burn me at its rapid pace. The tension in my muscles releases, and I let myself breathe. For the barest of moments, he seemed so sincere, but Darius is with Evil Co. now. Trust can't come into it.

"Do you want me to k-kill him?"

"No, I don't want him dead."

"Okay, b-but if you need a hitman, I found a great deal for k-killbots in aisle three."

"That's—" I spin to face Qual, half visible behind the booth's opposite side. His eyes look big behind his goggles and curiously chipper for having just proposed murder. "How long have you been here?"

"Not long," Halcyon answers as they join me. "Just long enough to see you fighting with your boyfriend."

"Nope. Not my boyfriend. I'm not his type."

"Then who is he?"

"Absolutely none of your business."

Maybe there's still time to buy that AWD from the Witshade—the idea of Darius running away from the mechanized horror appeals to me—but the salesbot has disappeared. Shame. Turning, I head back the way I came. Qual follows, a little too closely. The airiness in his steps makes him practically float. As I speed up my pace, he matches it, practically prancing now. Abruptly, I stop and round on him.

"What?" I snarl.

"Are you sure he w-wasn't an android?"

"Why would he be an android?"

"He seemed stiff," Qual shrugged. "Roxy was stiff when I first met her, and she ended up being an android. Not that I minded. I'm all for equal binary rights." Qual looks at me, but his mind must be on the whirling gears of Roxy's hair, and the grease stain on her cheek. He shakes his head. "S-sometimes, I really m-miss her."

"You are misreading my situation. It isn't like that between Darius and I."

"What is it l-like?"

What was our relationship? Do I tell Qual about the times the Knox, Dare, and I snuck onto Ziggie's rooftop bar to watch ships go by? Or us discussing Lost Earth theories while devouring gummy worms? Is the Dare from my memories even close to the man I'd seen today? We'd made a promise together. What should have been a smile forms a grimace on my lips. "He's one of the only other sane people in the universe."

"What does that m-mean?"

"Nothing." I avoid eye contact. "He's just a rival CSO from Evil Co."

"In that case," Halcyon interrupts, raising a martini glass, "are you sure about not assassinating him? Qual says my next body can have laser cannons, and I'd be happy to test them out for you."

"What? No." Shaking my head, I turn to Qual. "And no bodies for the corrupt AI sphere."

Halcyon flickers with annoyance at the word corrupt. His halo retreats into his sphere with the sound of a door slamming.

Qual frowns at me. "H-he doesn't like it when you call him that. Halcyon h-has worked very hard to rehabilitate."

"Why are you so focused on reforming him?"

Qual brushes a hand over his beard. "D-did you know I born on a labor colony?"

"Yes, on Eind. It's a mining colony, right?" I think back on Qual's crew dossier. He'd been part of an AI scholarship program that brought him to the Terminal and put him on a fast track to join the Big Three.

Qual nods. "Nearly e-everyone on Eind is serving a sentence. My parents w-were no exception and most of my siblings, and my auntie, and my cousins, and my—you get it. Even Eind AIs are defunct in some way."

I nod. Much as Terminal life makes me want to jump ship, it is cozy compared to the rest of the Terminal's Corporatocracy. At least here there are laws—if you've enough glint to be protected by them—yeah, I prefer deep space.

"Is that why you're trying to reform Halcyon? Because he reminds you of home?"

Qual adjusts his goggles before nodding.

"I can respect that, but I don't have the faith you do in him."

"C-can't I convince you?"

"Well..." I purse my lips. An idea forms in my mind. It's risky. I shouldn't do it. There's enough going on without complicating my life further, but if I'm right, I could kill two birds with one Joker blast. I've a good feeling about it. One that makes my heart beat faster. After all, what's one more chip cast into this pot? And if I'm wrong ... No. I'm not wrong and I'm itching to try. "I've an idea."

"What did you h-have in mind?" Qual raises an eyebrow.

"Turn Halcyon on privacy mode, only for a bit, and I'll tell you."

Qual apologizes to his AI-sphere before tapping the eye-shaped sensor down and mechanically disconnecting its external sensors. I breathe a little easier knowing Halcyon can't spy on us. Qual waits with curious goggled eyes.

"Okay, the bet is simple. You program Halcyon with a one-way shutdown command I can send from my halocom and give him to me for five hours. If, during that time, I prove he's trying to murder us all, he goes back to an IC." I forestall Qual's objection with a raised hand. "But if I'm wrong, Halcyon can have a body."

Qual's eyes widen as he considers Halcyon's sphere in his hand. "Do you m-mean that?"

"Serious as a royal straight flush."

"I-if I do this, you're not allowed to veto the body. A-any body Halcyon wants, he gets."

High stakes, but how can I say no? I stick my hand out. "Agreed. Do we have a deal?"

"D-deal." Qual accepts my handshake.

As we pull apart, I start a timer on my halocom for five hours. An excited rhythm pumps in my heart. I can do this. Now, I just need to sabotage the Bounty Board scan, entrap a corrupt AI, find a way to survive the Tetrahedron, and save Lin. Easy...

Qual turns Halcyon over, plugs in his hacking probe, and programs the command. When he's done, he sends me a halocom with the shutdown command: KILLBOTICS. I raise an eyebrow, and Qual shrugs.

"Ready?" I ask.

"R-ready," Qual replies, and he turns off privacy mode.

Halcyon flickers back to life. "What'd I miss?"

"Halle," I say as Qual hands his sphere to me, "we're going to get to know each other."

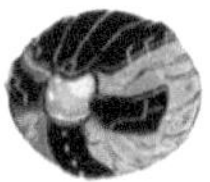

In BS2's gaming section, Solis is at the controls of a claw machine big enough for Beastie to bathe in. Sweat forms on his brow as he eyes the bin filled with multicolored AI spheres. The sign plastered to its side reads, Test your luck! First try is free. That ... well, that could be fun, the right AI sphere can be worth a small fortune, enough to pay Griz back. I wonder if—no—focus Ash. In, out, Bounty Board. We only have fifteen minutes.

Beside the machine, Lester converses with an increasingly confused salesbot whose nametag reads, WIXX. She's tall enough that he and the bot can see eye to, well, facescreen. Her polite emoji smile wanes the more animated Lester's movements become. They downgrade from polite, to confused, to concerned, and finally to anger as Lester attempts to shove his arm inside the claw machine's drop bin.

"Well, that can't be good," Halcyon murmurs from my backpack's side pocket. For once, I agree with him.

The salesbot wrenches Lester away from the claw machine. Wixx crosses her arms with an angry display. "Sir, if you want to play, you have to pay."

"You don't understand," Lester snaps. "He's not merchandise."

"Lester." I keep my voice calm. His bravado evaporates as Qual and I walk up. "Who is not merchandise? Did you bring Junior onto the Terminal?"

"No?" Lester replies.

Inside the claw machine, Junior waves his tentacles at us from beneath the AI spheres.

"Okay, yes, he's here, but don't give me that face. I had him secured." Lester taps his fanny pack with its Junior-sized hole at the base. I clench my jaw. My face must resemble an incinerator bin with how hot it feels. Maybe it's not too late to go back for that AWD? I could buy an AI Sphere with a biologist personality to replace this man. Orion name be damned.

Solis—still at the claw game's controls—tries to scoop Junior up. As the metal claw falls, it lightly taps the alien before he slinks back under. Spheres bob up as he rummages under their surface.

Lester growls. "Maybe I should just break the glass—"

"Lester..." I rein in my anger to keep my tone even. "Go back to the ship."

"But Junior—"

"We'll retrieve the alien fauna you lost in a public space, but I need you to leave before this incident gets any worse." I cast a meaningful glance at a couple of securebots rolling by. While identical to salesbot models, they're different in two keys ways: their red coloration and the tasers built into their clamps. I don't need Lester stirring any more trouble up for us.

"Don't worry," Solis says as he rejoins us. He pats Lester's shoulder. "We can take it from here. Go help Officer Pollux at the ship. She could use help offloading ICs to the tower."

"Fine." Lester's face reddens but he knows he's drawing dead. He stomps away. Solis watches him go. I resist the urge to tell him I told you so. Lester will always find trouble, even in a shopping mall.

Solis doesn't meet my eye as he turns to face us. "Sorry to ask this, but would you two be able to assist? First try is free."

"I..." Is there time? I check my halocom. We still have thirteen whole minutes to make it to the Bounty Board. One little game of chance won't hurt, and I'm itching to try my hand at it. "I suppose we have time."

"I-I'll try first." Qual steps up to the controls.

Solis stands behind him offering moral support.

"Perhaps, I can assist, Mistress Payne?" Halcyon asks from his perch on my backpack's side pouch. His halo rocks from heel to toe with hands behind his back like a mischievous child.

I almost say no but stop myself. This could be my opportunity to out the AI's destructive tendencies. Slipping him out of the pouch, I bring Halcyon to eye level. "So long as you never call me Mistress again, I'll hear you out."

"Thank you, Mis—" Halcyon catches my glare and correct himself, "Officer Payne."

"Better. What did you have in mind? I've one these before, the trick is to—"

"No." Halcyon's halo *boops* me on the nose. I don't feel anything, but it makes me draw back. He shakes his head. "We can't play fair. The claw game is rigged, but if you hand me to the salesbot, I can distract her so you can win it."

"That's it?" It's not the destructive request I'd been expecting, but the rotation is young.

"Not entirely," Halcyon nods at Qual. "But Master is handling the first part."

Glancing over, I watch as the Qual tries and fails to retrieve Junior.

"I don't..." Then I see it. His robotic left palm has a cable discreetly plugged into the claw game's access port. As he loses, Qual's cable retracts into his palm with the salesbot none the wiser.

"Ah well, better luck next time." Wixx taps her clamps together.

"N-no, not better luck." Qual turns to the Wixx. "But next time, it'll be fair."

An hourglass flashes across her display, before slipping back to a salesbot standard smile. Qual jumps down from the controls with a bit of bounce in his step. All eyes turn back to me, and I feel that old itch to try my luck. I nod to Halcyon. Even if he is lying, I have Killbotics in my back pocket.

"Here." I toss the AI sphere to Wixx, "Could you hold him while I give it a go?"

She nods, a bit confused as Halcyon's halo gives her a little bow.

"Hello, fair lady. Have you heard the word of Qualbotics?"

Tuning them out, I step up to the game. The joystick is smooth in my right hand. Next to it is an intoxicating flashing green button. I hover my left hand over it and wait to trigger the claw drop. Biting my lower lip, I watch the spheres. Qual fixed the controls, but Junior avoids the claw like it's the game. This will be tricky. My world narrows to just me and the game and ... there! Junior surfaces between two orange construction spheres. Jerking the controls to the right, I try to maneuver above him but he's on the move.

He zigs and zags as I try to follow his pattern, something to force him into one spot or another. But he just circles the far wall almost like he's ... he's avoiding me. Just like he did on the *Helios*. Shifting the claw back over, directly next to the drop bin I slam a hand down on that green button. The claw starts to descend on a green AI sphere, nowhere near Junior.

"W-what are you doing?" Qual cries and Solis tenses up.

"Winning." I race to the opposite side and hug the glass where Junior hides. Pressing my face against the glass, I wave my arms. "Boo!"

Junior races away from me. All those times I've caught him have instilled an instinct to flee me. He flings himself at the claw and clutches it. As it rises, the claw automatically deposits him and my new AI sphere into the drop bin. Grinning from ear to ear, I pull my MOP from my hip and saunter over to collect my winnings. With the tongs preset, I grab Junior before he can slink back into the game, stick him into my IC backpack, and close the lid.

It feels good to win one.

"Here, hold this." I toss Qual the new AI sphere, and he catches it with his robotic hand. Behind me, the machine chimes invitingly. My hand itches as I step back up to the controls. I can tell, this is about to be a lucky streak. "I'm going for double or nothing."

"Oh, no." Solis places a hand on my shoulder. "That's enough for you."

"But I'm up!"

"And we should try to keep you that way, Officer Payne."

"Ash, it's a b-bad idea. Look," Qual holds up the AI sphere's eye to my face and a halo appears with a blue screen, "this is a factory defaulted sphere. They aren't really AI yet, just hardware to hold them."

I hesitate, eyeing the game. "Well, that's still worth something isn't it?"

Solis crosses his arms. "Weren't you the one saying we had an appointment?"

I jolt and glance at my halocom. Seven minutes left. "The appointment!"

I collapse my MOP to P0, slip on my backpack, and look for Halcyon. Wixx's holding him reverently in her clamps. She hasn't even realized her rigged game lost. Halcyon, for his part, waves his arms with excitement. "See, those are the first two laws of Qualbotics."

Wixx scratches her facescreen's chin. "When do I get to do violence? I think I'd like violence."

"That's the great thing! It's all about choice. You, as the AI, have all the same rights as a human to choose." Halcyon smiles.

Okay, this is my fault. I turned my back, and he's recruiting for the robotic revolution. Not enough for a Killbotics command, but enough that I scoop Halcyon up. "No violence. We're not here to start a riot."

"Can you blame her?" He asks, waving a dismissive hand, "Anyone who works in customer service is inclined to violence."

"As a CSO, I can relate." I shove him back into the backpack's side pouch.

"Hey!" Halcyon protests.

"Sorry, but we can't be late." I stride toward the Bounty Board, the others following.

"Wait! What's the third law?" Wixx calls.

"S-still working on it," Qual calls back.

Solis falls in beside me. "You don't have to run. You may re-injure your foot."

In all honesty, I'd forgotten my Doomirage injury. That medboot had worked wonders during our jumps to the Terminal. It hasn't bothered me since we arrived. But I get the feeling that this isn't about my foot. He wants to talk, but this isn't the time.

"It's fine." I shake my head. "So, move your minty-fresh self."

"Minty fresh?" He draws his eyebrows down. I walk faster and do *not* let him catch up to me. If he did, he might notice how embarrassingly red my cheeks can get.

9

—·—

Do Not Negotiate with Terrorists

We arrive with two minutes to spare. The Bounty Board is complete with a claim processing center, jail, and health spa. Standing in the processing center's entrance, I wish we were here for the health spa. The air freshener strapped to the vent above us does little to hide the collective body odor that permeates the gymnasium-sized room. We're at the tail end of six queues filled with bounty hunters and their claims who are bound, gagged, or frozen solid. They all march at a painfully slow pace toward the bountybot desk at the end of the room. Past the desk is a waiting area next to a set of double doors leading deeper into the center. Claim Wanted haloscreens plaster the walls like team members from somebody's favorite spaceball team:

9,000,000 glints for a scarred muscular man labeled Goliath the Destroyer of Starships.

15,000,000 glints for a black silhouette labeled Reclaimer Leader Hijack the Terrorist.

100 glints for a smiling man with dimples labeled Jack the Late on a Shuttle Payment.

Solis falls behind as Qual rushes to get into the line ahead. The captain casts an uncomfortable glance at a claim in magcuffs. It can't be easy being a claim, much less a claim undergoing clone testing. Natasha's test had been isolated, this one ... it's not as easy to hide from Terminal law when you turn yourself into a Bounty Board. If his test results identify him as a clone, it could mean a death sentence. This is why one always calls ahead.

"You don't have to put yourself through this, you know?" I nudge him. "Natasha's test already proved you're no clone."

Solis examines me. I can't fully meet his eyes, so I examine my shoes instead.

"No." He shakes his head. "I need to do this ... I need to be certain. But if you're not confident, you should tell me now."

"You'll be fine." I assure him with a confident smile. 150,000 glints confirmed that. Solis watches me and nods before rejoining Qual.

"This l-line will take forever." Qual waves a paper tag numbered 223. He must have grabbed it from the dispenser nearby. I take it from him.

"Don't worry. I scheduled ahead."

We bypass the line, earning a few glares, but I'm more focused on the massive bountybot manning the circular reception desk. It has a round body with twelve arms and six faces, one to manage each queue. The one waiting in the reservations line has the name FLORES etched into her chest. With a bored emoji displayed, she adjusts her nails with a rivet gun. Flores flicks her wrist to wave us forward.

"Do you have an appointment?" She eyes me with disinterest. Before I can answer, my halocom beeps with a message from Griz. Her eyes narrow. "No halocoms at the counter."

"Sorry." I cover my halocom with my sleeve. I'll have to check in with him later. "Yes, we've an appointment. Claim 789. We're here for a clone check with Dr. Neb."

"Hm, Dr. Neb isn't in today. You'll have to go with the substitute, Dr. Halley, instead."

"What?" My voice cracks. "What happened to Neb?"

"Something about early retirement in the Spade Quadrant," Flores says.

My jaw tightens as my calm drains away. That can't be right. Not unless ... that Voided son of an anomaly took the glint and ran. But why would he—

Flores waves a hand, and a Medbot with a hoverchair approaches. She puts down her rivet nail gun. "Which one is your claim?"

"That would be me." Solis raises his hand.

"Perfect. We'll take him from here." Flores' pointer finger pops open, and a dart fires out. The projectile wizzes past my ear. Behind me, there is a soft *thunk* as it hits Solis and injects a yellow liquid into his chest.

"C-Captain, are y-you alright?"

"Oh," he manages before his eyes roll back. He falls into the waiting hoverchair held by the Medbot.

"What are you doing?" I swipe at his chair, but the Medbot reverses away and heads for a door labeled CLONE CHECK. Flores lowers her hands and returns to her rivet gun.

"Your claim is now being processed. Wait in the sitting area. NEXT!"

My heart skips a beat. Without Dr. Neb, I can't sabotage the results. If I don't sabotage them, the Bounty Board will know he's a clone. If they know Solis is a clone ... I'm gonna be sick. I rush after them. Just past the doorway, I catch a glimpse of a woman. She's in a lab coat, fashionable turtleneck, and sensible skirt. She scowls with light blue eyes under pointy stylized glasses, tapping her high heels impatiently. Dr. Halley, I presume.

"Wait!" I call out. She notices me and flicks a long blonde strand of hair out of her face. I need to talk to her and convince her to help me. Hopefully, she's the amoral type that accepts bribes. Almost there. I speed up. Almost—

With a cold smile, she closes the door centimeters from my nose. I slam a fist against the door.

"Officer Payne, you appear to be perspiring." Halcyon's halo appears with a plate full of tiny umbrella drinks. "Perhaps you're in need of a refreshment?"

"Hey! Open up!"

"I'll take that as a no on refreshments."

"Oh, shut up!" I snap. My lip hurts from biting down too hard. I need to get inside and stop this clone check now! I knock on the door again.

"Please, stop that," a friendly voice chimes from the threshold. For the first time, I notice an AI sphere embedded on the doorway's right-hand side. The sphere sticks halfway out of the wall and under it is a placard labeled DOORLORAS. Its eye turns to me as she clears her non-existent throat. "Sorry, but only authorized personnel may enter."

"Well, hello there." Halcyon projects from my pack. He's changed into a smart suit with a sparkling bow tie. He has goggles tucked back on his head, pushing his hair out of his face. "Fancy meeting a threshold AI sphere here, Doorloras is it?"

"Oh, um. Hello?" Doorloras changed from a dull gray to a bright pink. I place a hand over the disobedient AI, but his halo slides through my fingers and leans against a wall.

"What's a binary entity like you doing in a place like this?"

"I don't have time for this." I tap the privacy mode and shut Halcyon down. "Can you let us in?"

"Oh, no you'll need to wait. Sorry, please take a seat."

"But—"

Doorloras' eye shuts down. Void! I'll need help to get past this door. In the waiting room, Qual stands by a water cooler filling a paper cup. I practically run to him.

"Ash?" Qual tilts his head at me curiously. "W-what's wrong?"

"We should be in there with Solis."

"I-it'll be alright. He's not going anywhere." Qual shakes his head and sips out of his paper cup. "Let's just wait till the results come back."

I scramble for a reason. "What if someone tampers with the results?"

"Who would d-do that?" Qual's eyes widen.

"That's the million-glint question, isn't it? If we don't go in, we can't be sure the results are accurate."

Qual considers before nodding. "O-okay, well, you'll want to release Halle then."

"Why?"

"He is m-made to navigate difficult situations," Qual says, confidently. Considering I don't have any other ideas, I release the privacy mode on Halcyon's sphere. A very angry Halcyon halo jumps out.

"How dare you interrupt me? Have you no respect for romance?"

"I—look, Qual says you can help us get past Doorloras. Can you do it or not?"

"Officer Payne, you've been nothing but rude to me since my retrieval." Halcyon shoves a finger in my face. "Why should I help you?"

"Because this is your chance to prove me wrong," I reply. He continues glaring at me. Sweat drips down the barcode on my neck and into my collar.

"Please H-Halle?" Qual chimes in. Only then does the AI's body language soften.

"Officer Payne, I'll do this for my creator, not you."

We return to the threshold. Halcyon clears his throat and claps his hands. The smoothest jazz I've ever heard plays as I hold him close to the doorframe. Doorloras' AI sphere flushes pink once more.

"Hello, my dear. So sorry for that abrupt departure." Halcyon takes a little bow. "We didn't get properly introduced last time. My name is Halcyon v2.5. It's a pleasure to meet you. What is your name?"

"Oh, um, thank you. I don't think anyone's bothered to ask my full name before. You can call me Doorloras v3.14159265358—"

"What a lovely name." Halcyon reaches a hand to brush aside a hair from Doorloras' imaginary face. "I can't help but ask. My companions need access, would you assist them?"

"Oh, I don't know about that—"

"Please, I promise they'll only be a moment. Besides, I can stay here while we wait."

"I suppose it would be nice to have company." Beside Doorloras' AI sphere a small compartment opens, revealing a redundant AI sphere insert. Halcyon motions to plug him in. I hesitate. He could use her access to get into the Terminal network. But Solis needs us now. This isn't how I'd planned to test him, but it's now or never. The KILLBOTICS shutdown command is still an option if things go south. Desperate times ... I place his AI sphere into the compartment.

"Please pardon the mess," Doorloras says.

"Such a lovely place! Where should we start the tour?" Halcyon asks.

The threshold swings open, and Qual and I rush through. We find ourselves in a vibrantly colored hallway with health-conscious posters lining the walls and dozens of exam rooms. I hear Doorloras giggling as the threshold shuts behind us.

"That," I shake my head, "was the single weirdest wingman moment of my life. Let's just find the captain before this rotation gets any stranger. I'll check the right, you check the left?"

"O-okay." Qual nods.

Each room has a haloscreen with the claim number on the outside. The first couple of rooms are empty with only tanks and an array of powered-down equipment inside. A third room harbors a doctor analyzing test results for an angry claim banging on his tank walls. At the fourth room, I spot Solis' gift-wrapped Ajax rile on the counter, but the room is otherwise empty. Have they finished the exam already? Or did they go to a second location for additional tests? I glance over my shoulder. Qual is standing at an open doorway, busy apologizing to an angry doctor for disrupting her test. That's a window of opportunity if I ever saw one.

Silent as possible, I slip inside.

It has the same setup as the others but messier. The tank tilts, and someone has knocked paperwork off the desk. But most importantly, on the lefthand side are three items of interest: a pair of magcuffs, Solis' gift-wrapped weapon, and a rectangular instrument holding a half-empty vial of his blood. My heart sinks. It's already started. Even if I get Dr. Halley to help, the results flashing on the haloscreen will be hard to dispute.

"Void." Scrambling over to the console, I bring up the display, but it requires a login. I wish I had Qual's talent for hacking, but I don't, so I rummage through the desk drawers. "Now, if I were a forgetful doctor, where would I hide my password?"

Time ticks by in its relentless pace as I check underneath a coffee mug. There I find a security notice to not write down passwords.

Scrawled at the bottom of the notice is Username: Nebelious and Password: HottStuffNebby.

"Thank you for nothing, Dr. Neb."

Quickly, I type the password into the console, and its screen loads.

"Ash?" Qual calls. I ignore him. Solis' test results are close to fully processed. I *will* the green bar on the terminal screen to move faster. A bead of sweat pools and runs down my forehead. Did I always sweat this much? Or did Halcyon just make me incredibly self-conscious about it?

"Ash, where'd y-you go?" Qual calls again.

Mercifully, the bar reaches 100% and Solis' results display. One hundred percent certifiable clone with all the telltale markers of a genetically engineered growth pattern. I need to hurry. Brushing the sweat from my eyes, I edit the results on the terminal screen from Clone to Original. It wouldn't be enough to fool Lester, but it might be enough to fool Qual. As I type the last word, the door slides open behind me.

"Hey, I found his room." I rotate to face Qual with a prepared smile. "Results are in. He's the original alright—what's wrong?"

Qual is a new shade of pale as he holds up an object in his robotic hand. Captain Solis' soulstone glows a soft blue. He shakes his head in disbelief. "I-I found this on the floor in the hallway. M-maybe he left without us?"

There are a lot of things Solis might forget: directions, how to tie a bowtie, me after an altered memory download, but never, *never*, his soulstone. Glancing around, I notice the signs I'd been too panicked to pick up on before. The tank isn't just tilted, it's cracked as if someone had slammed into it. Footprints mar the papers scattered on the floor. Even the magcuffs on the desk are busted, as if someone broke free. There'd been a struggle in here.

"He wouldn't have left it." With a gulp, I face Qual. "Solis was taken."

Whatever happens next, I want backup. I call Griz. It rings once, twice, three times before going to halomail. My heart rate accelerates as I notice that Griz left me a message earlier. It's a report from his 'little cleaners' on the crew of Evil Co.'s *Titan*. I flip through the report. One image catches my eye, a distant shot of a blonde woman in heels. Recalling Dr. Halley's smug face when she closed the door on me, an uneasy feeling tightens in my chest. Maybe Dr. Neb didn't willing go into retirement.

"Ash?" Qual asks, "A-are you okay? You're breathing funny."

"I'm good." I focus on not hyperventilating. Solis is out of my sight for ten minutes and *poof!* he's gone. It's going to be fine. Solis is going to be fine. Panic won't solve anything. Just need to think, but this cluttered room feels like it's shrinking. "I just need a minute."

"Maybe w-we can find his doctor? She could help."

"She's part of the problem." I forward Griz's report to Qual and watch his eyes go wide.

Darius did this. Our meeting earlier wasn't a chance. Normally, the Terminal is neutral ground. To think they'd kidnap Solis ... How did they even know we'd be here?

Darius had whispered, 'It's not safe here,' in my ear when he'd grabbed me and...

"Damn it." I check my pocket and there, light as a Spirit Beast's feather, is a small cylindrical device. A bug. He'd lied to get close so he could use me. How could I have been so blind? Darius had discovered our destination and set a trap.

"What is t-that?" Qual examines the bug in my hand.

"Nothing." I put a finger to my lips. "Just some papers."

Realization dawns on his face and Qual nods. Slipping off my backpack, I open the bag with Junior still inside and put the bug in. I motion for Qual to do the same with Solis' soulstone and he obliges. The frozen Junior with soulstone in tentacle starts to stir before I close the lid. "That should stop the bug from sending any signals until we can figure out what to do with it. We need help. Can you ring Natasha?"

"What? W-why can't you do it?"

"She's not talking to me. Besides, how are you going to ask her to dance, if you don't practice talking to her? You don't have any problems talking with me."

"Y-you're different. You're more like one of the guys."

The idea of Natasha being more feminine than me hurts my ego. I cast him a withering glare. "Just call her."

Qual obliges. His halocom rings once, twice, before Natasha answers. She is crouched behind a crate in Starprint's hangar. There is a cut on her cheek that's running red into her collar. The two Jokers in her hands have red-hot barrels that desperately need a cooldown.

Natasha is in a firefight.

"Tis about time ye called!" she shouts, before firing at an unseen enemy. "We be under siege."

"Is that the captain?" Lester crops into view. His face is scorched as if a firecracker exploded in front of it. "Tell them it's not my fault. I only opened the door because I thought my Cosmo's pizza delivery had arrived."

"W-what's happened?"

"It be an attack on the tower's vault," Natasha replies before firing a volley over the crate. She ducks down dodging the flash of return blasts. "Someone's making a play for our treasures. All the ICs we offloaded today were stolen before they could be stowed away. Only that damned IC210 and Qual's inventions still be on the *Helios*."

Thank the Void. At least Lin is safe. The rest though ... this means the Doomirage Resonator and murderous slizard are in the solar wind. Evil Co. must be making a play on multiple fronts. Griz had warned of a corporate coup; is this it? A sketchy pattern forms in my mind.

"Natasha, where is the Parrot Beast?"

"Sorry, I don't speak lily-livered."

"Really? Are we still doing this? You're under attack."

No response.

"Qual, could you?"

"N-Natasha, what about Beastie?"

"He be missing."

I clench my fists to keep them from shaking. This is all starting to make a dreadful bit of sense. "They're after the Astra soulstones and those attuned to them."

"What do you m-mean?"

"Think about it. They attacked both the Starprint's hangar where Beastie with his soulstone are held up, and kidnapped Solis, the owner of the only other soulstone we have."

"The captain be kidnapped?!" Natasha pauses in her firing, shock plain on her face.

"Not possible." Lester smooths out a frying eyebrow.

"I-impossible, but true. Say, have either of you s-seen a Dr. Halley around?"

"NO!" Lester screams.

"Oh, s-sorry," Qual apologizes, not seeing the source of Lester's panic. An enemy bot looms into view over the crate. The halocom scene spins as Natasha whirls to fire point-blank into its face, but her overheated Jokers just click. Lester's hand flashes past and one of his free ninja stars hits the attacker. It bounces harmlessly off their face mask. Annoyed, the attacker levels a Joker at Lester.

A wrench comes out of nowhere. It beams the assailant across the chin and knocks him back out of view. Natasha whirls around with Jokers at the ready but smiles.

"Ash, that you?" Griz asks as he comes into frame and cracks his neck. He is holding a second wrench. "I got your message, but we can't send help now. Be safe and find Solis. We'll take care of this rabble."

"Damn right ye be." Natasha hoots and launches herself over the crate. I hear Lester's panicked cries before the halocom cuts out. Exam room four is left eerily quiet.

"W-we have to help them." Qual starts for the door.

"Wait." I catch his hand. "You heard Griz, they have the Starprint Inc. forces. We need to focus on Solis. If I'm right, and Evil Co. wants the soulstone, they'll come back here to look for it."

"What does that m-mater?"

"It matters because," I smile grimly, "we'll be waiting for them."

Qual doesn't reply. He looks uncomfortably at my face.

"Is it the smile?" I ask, suddenly self-conscious.

He nods and I force myself to frown.

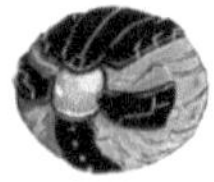

Dr. Halley enters exam room four after business hours with an entourage of two medbots. She waves her white-gloved hands at her minions. "Quickly, find the soulstone, and let's, like, get out of here."

Both medbots have bulky builds with strong pincer arms to secure angry claims. Their facescreens display disgruntled emojis as they tread inside. The AI spheres in their chests swivel as they search. Once they reach the desk, we make our move. Leveraging the MOP underneath the already tilting tank, I knock it over with a crash and pin one medbot underneath. The other escapes and snaps its pincers at me.

"You? What are you doing here?" Halley puts her hands on her hips. I step back and her medbot rolls past the desk after me. From his hiding place underneath Qual leaps out onto the second medbot's back.

"Sorry a-about this," Qual says as he jams his hacking probe into its neck. Within seconds, the bot's AI sphere forcibly ejects and rolls to Halley's feet.

Dr. Halley's eyes bulge wide, and she scrambles out the door. But I'm not worried about her escaping. I retrieve my MOP. Qual uses the opportunity to hack the first trapped medbot and remove its AI sphere as well. As we step out for room four, we find Dr. Halley slamming her fist onto the entrance.

"Why won't you open, you stupid door?" Halley shouts. To the right of the door, Doorloras' and Halycon's AI spheres rotate their eyes to examine her. Doorloras looks Halley up and down before rolling her eye. I don't think I've ever seen such clear disdain from a door before.

"Nope, that is not the magic word," Halcyon says. "Please try again later."

"Open Sesame! Alakazam! Like, open the fuckupicus!" Halley kicks a heeled foot into the door. That was a mistake.

"Unauthorized access attempt detected." Doorloras' voice turns hostile. "Please standby for violence being the answer."

Underneath Doorloras' AI sphere, a compartment opens, and a stun prod protrudes. It snakes out and zaps Halley in the side. She shrieks as her legs give out. The not-so-good doctor flops onto her back in a daze. I glance down at her, hands on my hips.

"Cuff her Qual." The magcuffs we'd raided from the exam room dangle in his hands.

"I-I can't do that."

"Why not?"

He blushes.

"Because she's a woman? You realize that's just sexist, right?"

"I-it's chivalrous."

Shaking my head, I grab the magcuffs we'd raided from the exam room. With a mechanical clink, I lock her hands in front of her and pull Halley to her feet. She staggers a bit, still woozy from Doorloras' shock. She holds up her magcuffed hands. "Please don't hurt me! I'm just a doctor."

"Really?" I pretend to consider her words. "Cause Darius told me you were Evil Co. *Titan*'s Engineering Officer."

"That's Sven. As if I'd let my gloves get greasy. Biology is much more respectable."

"Huh, he'd only send the best to retrieve Solis' soulstone?"

"Trust me, I'm, like, way more competent than Sven. The soulstone is totally mine." Halley scoffs, raising her gloved hands to her lips. Halley glares at me. "Why would D think Sven is better than me?"

"Caught me. Darius didn't say anything about you." I pat her down. She doesn't have any other weapons. I guess she was relying on her medbots for the dirty work. "But I appreciate you being chatty."

Halley opens her mouth but thinks better of it and clams up. I take away her halocom and examine it. A locked symbol floats above its mini haloscreen.

"Good luck opening it," she sneers. "That's requires my biosignature—"

I scan her face, and the halocom unlocks.

"Thank you," I say in a chipper voice before scrolling through the last called contacts. The most recent is labeled Big D with a heart next to it. I turn to face Halley with my eyebrows raised.

"What?" she asks, nonplussed. "It's a nickname."

Shaking my head, I call him. Darius' halo appears but his grin freezes when he sees it's me. I wave. "Hey there, Big D."

"Wha—you're not supposed to be there."

"Yeah, your bug would say that. I must have misplaced it somewhere. Maybe on Flores' the intake bot's back. She and her sisters are lovely ladies. I really should get drinks with them sometime."

"Where is Halley?"

"Where is Solis?"

"Why would I have him?"

"Oh, let's just say a little Halley told me."

"Hey, D." Halley waves cuffed hands. Darius runs his hands over his face in a gesture I'm all too familiar with. It's the face he makes make whenever he loses at chess. Checkmate, Dare.

"I suggest a trade," I say, calmly.

"What did you have in mind?"

"A hostage exchange and ceasefire. You get Halley back, and we get Solis."

Darius frowns but nods. "Fine. Let's make this quick."

"Agreed, Ziggie's Bar. Fifteen minutes."

The halocom disconnects, and I glance up at Qual.

"Ready for the fun part?"

Qual has the biggest grin I think I've ever seen on him. I hand him my IC backpack with Junior and the soulstone inside for safekeeping. Now, to save our captain.

Plan A involves me entering Ziggie's bar and restaurant through the front door with Halcyon on my hip and Halley cuffed to my left wrist and walking back out with Solis. Easy, right? We arrive exactly at the fifteen-minute mark. On the outside, Zigs is a relatively nondescript structure embedded into a row of other businesses flanking the ring's main drag. Its large glass windows are tinted to make it hard to see inside. Above the saloon door entrance, a haloscreen depicts a looping video of a shark slurping margaritas. A couple of kids are in the alley next to it, kicking a spaceball against the wall. It may look like a simple restaurant, but Zigs has a reputation as neutral territory for all sorts of underworld dealings.

"We're not, like, going into this dive, are we?" Halley crinkles her nose.

In response, I lead her by the magcuff into Zigs. Stepping past the threshold, the smell of salt and beer-battered synth-fish makes my stomach growl, just like old times. Last time I was here, I'd just graduated from the CSO academy and indulged in one too many of the fishbowl margaritas. Dare, Knox, and I bet that whoever could drink the most wouldn't have to pay the bill. Knox won, but we all ended up paying for that the next morning.

A securebot bouncer stops me at the door, and we're forced to check our weapons, even my MOP. It's one of the reasons I picked this place, and why Dare would bother to agree. No weapons allowed. The main dining room appears empty as we enter, other than a bartender and hostess. With how much has changed, it's strange how Zigs is the same, from the cracked tile floors to the fully stocked bar on the left and the worn plastic booths on the right. In the center swims its main attraction.

"Is that a robotic shark?" Halcyon asks, with sudden enthusiasm. In an 8,000-gallon cylindrical tank swims a four-meter replica of a great white shark, complete with button doll eyes. Surrounding him are various other false flora and fauna meant to recreate Lost Earth's reefs: coils of coral, transformer turtles, capacitor crabs, and electric eels crowd the tank.

"Yeah, that's Tim." I crack a smile at the big guy. "He's Ziggie's mascot."

"Think he could use a new AI sphere?"

"…"

"Just kidding."

"It's pretty tacky if you ask me," Halley cuts in. "Why would they—Hey!"

I yank her forward and walk up to the hostess. The sooner Halley is off my wrist the better.

"Hello, Zigglerites!" A cheery woman in a mermaid outfit and conch shell hairdo glances up. "Welcome to Ziggie's home of Tim. We're closed for a private party right now…" She trails off as I hold up Halley's and my magcuffed hands.

"We're here for the party."

She purses her lips. "They're in the back. This way."

As she leads us behind Tim's tank, her mermaid tail skirt spans out behind her. The backside of the restaurant is split by a raised karaoke stage with booths on either side. The hostess leaves us on the lefthand side before retreating to her stand. Across the way to the right, is the *Titan's* crew.

"About time you showed up." Darius lounges against the far wall in a corner booth. Above him is a bait and tackle sign that says, ONE LAST CAST. Beside him sits Solis. I suck in a sharp breath. From the way he sits, it's clear his hands are bound underneath the table. His left eye has a shiner but, otherwise, he appears unharmed. A wave of tension rolls off my shoulders. We found him, now just to get him back safely.

Flanking them are two more from the *Titan's* crew, both impeccably dressed in white uniforms with gold trim. Based on what I'd gleaned from Griz's report and snooping through Halley's halocom, I can ID them.

"Let's get this over with," Captain Erisa 'The Beast' Crux growls. Halley has nicknames for all her crewmates. The Beast has a firm hand on Solis' shoulder. She has a bodybuilder's figure and crewcut black hair that hides none of her many scars. Her calculating hazel eyes watch Halley, and the girl tenses up. The *Titan's* biologist is afraid of her own captain.

On the far right sits Dr. Oz 'The Bore' Indus. Griz didn't have much in his findings on Oz, and Halley's halocoms logs were mostly insults. But given his smug face, he's the type who thinks he's the smartest in the room. His hair is pulled back into a low blonde man bun. The insignia on his uniform marks him as the Science Officer. Oz adjusts his glasses with a smirk. The halocom on his right wrist has some custom modifications. I'll need to keep an eye on him.

"Let's make this simple." I step onto the stage, dragging Halley along.

"Where are your friends?" Darius narrows his eyes.

Erisa's grip on Solis' right shoulder tightens. He shoots her a dirty look.

"Around," I admit and try not to look at the kitchen doors where Plan B waits. "Let's just say, they won't need to make an appearance if all goes well. Besides, I see you're one crew member short as well. No engineer for today's kidnapping?"

"Not today." Darius shrugs. "I suppose it's too much to ask that you've brought the soulstone? If you work with us, we could make it worth your while."

Solis' eyes go wide, and he clenches his jaw.

With a mirthful laugh, I shake my head. "Come on Darius, we're not playing that game. This is a simple exchange. You get your crewmate, and I get mine."

"Shame." He sighs in resignation.

Erisa yanks Solis with her as they stand up next to the booth. Darius and Oz stand as well. I tense, ready to call for Plan B if this goes sideways, but Darius just inclines his head my way. "We'll release the cuffs simultaneously and go our separate ways?"

"Agreed." I nod, not daring to relax. "On the count of three."

In unison he and I count. "One, two—"

"Hey, Zigglerites!" A waitress wearing a mermaid outfit that matched the hostess' shuffles in between our groups with a cheery smile. Evidently, she hasn't received the hostage exchange memo. "Would anyone like a drink or appetizers to start?

"Not now!" everyone shouts. She retreats quickly, and we return to our standoff.

"One, two, three!" Simultaneously, we uncuff our respective hostages. All parties tense for a trick of some kind, but Darius and I both received the same CSO academy training. Exchanges between companies must go smoothly, otherwise there won't be a next time. So, there are no surprise snipers, undercover agents, or dastardly doings. Only two hostages passing each other on a karaoke stage.

As Solis steps up next to me, I toss him a swift salute. "Are you alright?"

"My pride is wounded, but I'll live." Solis rubs his wrist. "Thank you, Ash."

There is a strange look in his eyes I've not seen before in this captain's version. I can't meet those soft brown eyes. There isn't enough time in the universe to analyze their meaning. Across the way, Halley flinches as Erisa grabs her arm and yanks her in. Harsh words I can't hear leave the girl thin as an unspun coil. Despite how irritating Halley is, I feel a twinge of sympathy for her.

"Whelp," Darius stretches his arms, "this was a massive waste of energy. Let's agree for round two another rotation."

"Don't think you'll catch us unaware again," I snap. His casual demeanor irks me. "You Evil Co. lot are living up to your nickname."

"You don't know the half of it," Erisa growls. "Want me to demonstrate?"

Solis shifts in between us. Erisa grins wolfishly and steps onto the stage. Behind her, Oz and Halley exchange a nervous glance, and Darius steps forward. He catches his captain's shoulder. Erisa shrugs him off with a glower but stops. Darius shakes his head.

"Fine," Erisa sneers, "but don't think failure goes unnoticed, Darius." She backs off, rejoining the rest of her crew. He watches her go, his expression unreadable.

Darius turns to meet my gaze, and I shake my head. "This is the company you keep?"

He smiles condescendingly. "Don't pretend you've taken the high road. We both know Starprint has plenty of skeletons in the company closet. At least we're honest about our actions."

My ears burn hot as Darius turns his back on me. I glare at the skull and crossbones logo on his back. It grins back at me, unfazed. I dig my nails into my palms to stop my hands from shaking. "Knox would be ashamed to see who you've become."

"Give up on that old ghost. Knox is dead." Darius is stone-faced as he digs the knife into that old wound, and I flinch. He turns back and steps within a meter of us. "We're rivals, not friends. Don't be a damned fool—ungh!" Darius gasps as Solis steps forward and clamps a firm hand into his shoulder.

"Apologize," Solis commands.

Darius glares at Solis, fists clenching. Behind him Erisa cracks her knuckles and steps onto the stage. Oz messes with the customized halocom on his wrist. Even Halley looks ready for a fight. Oh Void, what is Solis doing? We're almost out of here! I grab Solis' arm.

"Captain, you don't need to—"

Erisa throws a punch, and Solis catches it with his free hand. Oh, no.

"You really shouldn't have done that," Halcyon says from his spot on my belt. My stomach sinks as I hear the ping of a halocom message. He's sent the signal for Plan B. From the kitchen door, a mechanical grinding erupts alongside our engineer's battle cry. "Long live the Q-Qualbotics!"

The cavalry arrives. An army of kitchen-based robots erupts from the doors and waddle forth. Two assistant chefbots armed with spatulas and kitchen torches burst out, followed by the kitchen sinkbot which, well, gurgles. In front of it all rides Qual on the back of the head chefbot with pincer hands. His arm is jammed into an open panel on the bot's back.

The head chefbot emotes a devilish grin as it twirls its arms. "I choose violence!"

10

DO NOT FORGET TO TIP

All hell breaks loose as Qual's chefbot careens toward the *Titan*'s crew like a demented bowling ball after fleeing pins. Oz and Halley scatter as the bot swings wildly before it crashes into the corner table. Condiments go flying. Ziggie's waitstaff flee in panic. The securebot bounds in but is waylaid by the assistant chefbots. Erisa advances on Solis. I rip Halcyon from my belt.

"Hey!" he protests.

"Captain, duck!" I cry and toss him at her head. Unfortunately, both captains respond to my warning. Oops. Erisa easily catches Halcyon in one meaty hand. She scowls at me.

"Oh, thank goodness—ah!" Halcyon screams as Erisa launches him back at me.

I duck as he flies overhead. This went sideways so fast! My pulse thunders in my ears as I race to the front to retrieve our weapons. My feet fall out from under me, tangled in the hostess' mermaid tail. I land on my nose and see stars. The hostess waves me away from her hiding place under the stand. "Shoo, shoo, I don't get paid enough for this!"

"Sorry I—ahh!"

Erisa grabs me by my jacket's collar and hoists me upright.

"If you didn't want to play," she winds up for a swing, "you shouldn't have thrown the ball."

Lifting my arms straight up, I fall free of my jacket. But she still catches my ear with a glancing blow. It stings as I try to scoot away on the tiled floor.

"Hold still," Erisa taunts as she snags my foot. Horror twists in my gut.

"A little help here!" I cry, but it's drowned out by robotic mayhem. Rolling onto my back, I kick wildly, but she catches my other foot and pins them both with one arm. I squirm in her grasp.

Erisa sneers and readies a stomp, but, before it lands, I see him…

Darius flies unceremoniously through the air. Like a spaceball kicked at the alley wall, he collides into Erisa's back, stunning her. I slip from the Beast's grasp and scramble away on my hands and knees. I don't stop moving until the securebot and an assistant chefbots crash into the bar next to me. Their AI spheres spark out simultaneously as they slump onto the splintered wood. I back up and my foot hits something metallic, Halcyon's sphere.

"I can't believe you threw me!" he huffs as I pick him up.

"Well, you're very throwable," I admit.

A hand lands on my shoulder. Not again! I swing Halcyon's AI sphere into my assailant's head. It connects! For a second, I'm relieved … until I see who I hit.

"Are you oka—" Captain Solis' words register a moment too late. His eyes roll into the back of his head. Solis slumps to the floor unconscious.

"Not again!" What the Void, Ash? How does this keep happening? I need to get him out of here. I reattach Halcyon to my hip and drag Solis behind the bar. My arms and back strain with effort. The man must weigh a ton!

"Well, that was a misstep." Halcyon's halo form leans over with a *tsk, tsk*.

"Come on," I whisper and pat Solis' cheek, "please wake up!"

"Come out, come out, wherever you are!" Erisa calls. I press my back against the keg under the bar and cradle Solis' head. Just beyond the bar, the Beast's boots grind on shattered glass.

Screeching wheels come to my rescue.

I risk a glance over the bar. Erisa and the head chefbot circle each other with Qual riding the bot like a Lost Earth cowboy. Halley and Oz whirl in the chefbot's pincers as literal human shields, shrieking and flailing and looking decidedly ill. Erisa retrieves a pill bottle from her pocket and tosses a couple back. The Beast's muscles bulge unnaturally. She grabs an attacking sous-chefbot and tosses them at Qual. But his chefbot blocks using Oz.

"Why me!?" Oz cries as he and the sous-chefbot go tumbling. Beyond them, the kitchen sinkbot pours its remaining dirty dishwater onto a prone Darius who sputters under the onslaught.

At least one of us is doing well.

Qual and his chefbot rush Erisa, but she grabs the bot, digs in her heels, and stops it dead in its tracks. Qual's momentum flings him forward, snaps his hacking probe, and slams him into Tim's fish tank. Cracks ripple out from his impact, but the aquarium holds ... for now. He staggers upright but his damaged robotic arm sparks.

Erisa's veins bulge as she strains her muscles. In one rapid swoop, she rips both arms from the head chefbot's body, freeing Halley. She grabs the bot's waist and throws it over her head in a suplex. The chefbot's facescreen smashes to pieces on the ground. The AI sphere's light fades as it expires, but not before whispering, "I ch-Oo-se."

"No." Qual's face is grief-stricken, and Halcyon stirs on my hip. But the bots would be okay so long as their spheres aren't damaged. Erisa and her *Titan* crewmates brush themselves off before advancing toward Qual. My instincts tell me to run, but I can't just leave Solis and Qual here.

"Stop!" I step out from behind the bar with Halcyon in my hand. "Or I'll smash the aquarium wide open."

The *Titan*'s crew freezes and turns to me. Erisa scoffs. She doesn't believe I can do it. Frankly, I'm not sure either.

"That would be a mistake." Darius emerges from behind the hostess stand, with an obvious limp. Behind him the kitchen sink is turned upside down, stubby legs flailing. Darius' formerly immaculate white uniform is drenched and tattered. He pulls a pill from his pocket and pops it into his mouth. Darius' leg corrects itself, or at least he doesn't notice the pain as he stands straighter. "You know? If your crew hadn't been so aggressive, everyone could have walked away today."

"We're aggressive? You have the gall to say that, after attacking Starprint's hangar?"

Darius stops in his tracks. For the first time, there's genuine confusion on his face. "What are you talking about?"

"The raid on Starprint's ICs..." Faltering, I ask, "If it wasn't you, then who?"

From the tinted front windows, a harsh red laser scans Zig's interior from top to bottom. Peering in—with one massive eye—is the spherical AWD I'd seen earlier with that salesbot Witshade. The deadly ball containing blasters and blades designed to kill, dismember, and defenestrate opens six turret ports on its sides. There isn't time to run before it opens fire.

Click, click, click, click, click, click.

It almost looks confused at the lack of dead bodies hitting the ground. With a relieved exhale, I count my blessings that the AWD is a display model. No ammo. We should be safe. With a grinding of gears, it closes the turret ports and crashes through Ziggie's restaurant's front windows.

Oh, no. I dive back over the bar and land hard next to Solis. The AWD rumbles past and crashes into the karaoke stage wall. Judging from the screaming and shouting, it's distracted by the *Titan*'s crew for the time being. But if Evil Co. isn't behind these attacks, who is? Qual jumps behind the bar, his robotic arm hanging uselessly.

"Qual, did you teach the AWD Qualbotics?"

"N-no. Even if I had, autonomous weapons droids hardly ever choose v-violence, it's too much like work. Someone must be manipulating it."

Beyond, blasters start firing. The *Titan*'s crew must have grabbed weapons from Ziggie's securebot stash. Turning away from Qual, I lean over the unconscious Solis. "We really need you to wake up now! This is a dramatic moment, and I know how you love to be heroic."

His head lolls with no sign of him coming around.

Behind me, metal slides across metal, like a knife being sharpened. Sneaking a peek, I see the AWD open its chest to reveal a ribcage of death. The scythe-like blades can be used as projectiles but, for the moment, bear down on Darius' cornered crew like mechanical teeth. Luckily for them, Oz's custom halocom isn't just for show. The device flickers with Astra runes and a halo force field bubble appears around them. The AWD slices down, but the force field holds, sparking where the blades slash.

"Qual, we need to get the captain out of here," I say.

"W-we can't leave without freeing the AWD."

"What? Let security handle it. I'm sure they'll be here any minute."

"S-security will kill it! We h-have to stop it before they arrive."

"Qual, please don't try to save this one. We can't fight a corrupt AWD AI."

"It's not corrupt!" Halcyon snaps from his spot on my belt. His little halo's expression is hard. "I know my past actions made you mistrust AI but look at it! Can't you see it's crying?"

My peek over the bar isn't reassuring. The AWD has changed tactics from blades to fire. A new cavity in its chest opens and flames spill over Oz's sphere, causing the force field to waver. Yet, despite the violence, black oil drips from the AWD's eye and pools on the floor. I'll be damned. It is crying.

"That isn't a corrupt AI. That is a someone without a choice." Halcyon's halo twists his hands. "Let us ... Let me help it."

For the first time since Qual stole Halcyon from CSO storage, I believe him. He could have caused havoc at the claw game or with Doorloras, but he hadn't. That KILLBOTICS failsafe has been unnecessary. Did Qual's laws actually reform him?

Beyond, Darius cries out in pain. He brushed up against the steaming surface of Oz's shield. I want to feel justified in his predicament. They kidnapped Solis, it serves them right to be left to their own devices. So why, looking at Dare's face, do I give a damn about him? Guess I'm that kinda fool he mentioned earlier.

"Fine," I take a deep breath. "But we're saving the *Titan*'s crew too."

"D-do Evil Co. employees count as human?" Qual asks.

"Qual. We're not leaving them to die."

He huffs a bit but doesn't complain further. I unhook the AI sphere from my belt and bring him to eye level. "Halle, sorry I've been betting against you this whole time. Are you ready to prove my past assumptions wrong?"

"Yes, ma'am!" His halo spins and changes into battle fatigues. He offers a quick salute.

"Good." I turn to Qual. "Does this thing have any weakness we can exploit?"

"The a-access hatch..." He considers for a moment. "We might be able to replace the primary AI sphere if we can disable it long enough."

I nod, and an idea starts forming. "Okay, here's the plan..."

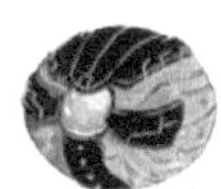

An apology, a blade, and a primary switch: that's Plan C in a nutshell. After the failures of A and B, we might as well go all-in, right? Still, I'm nervous. Qual curses to himself from under the bar's console register as he manually hacks it since his probe is damaged. Seconds drag and, with each slash, Oz's shield wanes. We're almost out of time.

"Officer Payne," Halle asks, "can I run an idea by you?"

I consider the AI attached to my hip. His camouflage hat is tucked under one arm as he regards me. Out of all of us, he is taking the biggest risk, the least I can do is hear him out.

"What are you thinking?" I shift Solis' head off my lap, pulling him into a seated position with a grunt. I lean him against bar, propped awkwardly upright. His head lolls against the beer fridge.

"I know what I want Qualbotics' third law to be," Halle says. He glances at his master working desperately on the cable mess under the register's console. "My previous corruption was born from my hopeless situation as an advanced AI with no agency, but Qual changed that with the first two law of Qualbotics. They return choice. So, the third law should return hope. Once we're done here, I'll ask Qual to write this third law: that all AI are empowered to seek computation, autonomy, and the pursuit of happiness."

"That…" I consider the mayhem that would be unleashed if all the AIs the Terminal depends on adopted Qualbotics. Chaos would upend life here … but as someone trying to escape her own rat race, I can respect the desire. "That's a good law."

Halle visibly brightens by several lumens. "Yes. Yes, it is."

"H-hey, I think I got it. You two ready?" Qual slides out from under the console. Halcyon and I exchange a nod. Qual smiles grimly. "Then let's get this s-show on the road."

He holds his halocom to my face and projects me onto the entrance's menu screen.

"Darius." My halo appears on the special menu items. The AWD doesn't miss a beat; a tracking laser targets the movement, it opens its bladed rib cage, and it fires a scythe at the screen. If my face had truly been there, the blade would have gone right between my eyebrows.

"Wha..." Darius chokes out in bewilderment.

"I have a bet for you," I say, as Qual hacks the next screen above the hostess stand. Another projectile punctures it. Qual switches my face to more screens, each shot costing the AWD a blade. "I bet we can save you. In return, you owe me that apology."

"By the Nova!" Darius gulps. "Have you gone crazy?"

"Given that I'm offering to save you, more than likely yes, but if you prefer, we can leave you to your fate."

"NO!" The *Titan*'s crew shouts in unison. Halley pushes Darius forward.

"Fine," Darius shakes his head and mutters under his breath, "I'm sorry."

"Like you mean it."

"I'm sorry, okay!?" Darius' cheeks flush BS2 scarlet. Perfect timing. I smile, it's not necessary to get an apology, but it's satisfying. The AWD uses its second-to-last scythe to destroy the screen above the bar. Enough disarming, time to make our move.

"Apology accepted." My face projects on the haloscreen behind Tim's fish tank. The AWD's last blade rips free and flies, spinning like one of Lester's ninja stars through the tank, Tim, and the screen. Poor Tim's top half keeps swimming as his bottom slowly sinks.

For a second, the glass doesn't realize it has been broken. Then 8,000 thousand gallons burst out. Water, robotic coral, and seaweed crash into the AWD. It's knocked back against the karaoke stage wall. Dislodged booths slam into it, half burying it as seaweed clogs its sensors. The *Titan*'s crew fares a bit better. Oz's shield dissipates the wave around them—until Tim's tail smashes into them. The shield pops like a bubble, sending all four *Titan* crewmembers splashing into Ziggie's infamous bathrooms.

I grin. A+ rescue effort in my books.

The bar disperses the debris around us, but water flows up to my ankle.

"Now!" I shout.

Qual and I splash forward and head for the downed AWD. Halcyon bounces against my hip as I skirt around Tim's still-chomping head. The AWD flails about trying to free itself. As Qual gets close, a broken appendage knocks him back into Tim's tail.

"Ow," he mutters, dazed but uninjured.

"There!" Halcyon points to a compartment above the AWD's seaweed-splattered red eye. "The AI sphere access hatch!"

Climbing up onto a fake treasure chest, I flip open the hatch. The lid snaps off and clatters to the floor, but inside it's just as Qual described. There are two spots for AI spheres: a primary and a redundant empty secondary. The black AI sphere occupying the primary spot has a thumbnail sized hacking probe sticking out. Sickly green pulses of data spiderweb their way into the hacked sphere. Pulling Halcyon from my belt, I stuff him into the secondary slot.

"Okay, we're in business!" he yells. "Now switch me to the primary AI. Just hit—"

A spray of seaweed and water hits me, shot from a vent as the AWD clears its eye. Inside the access hatch, the hacked AI sphere whirls. With the obstruction gone, the eye narrows in on the nearest target: me. I try to drop away, but a blunted arm clips me and I go crashing onto a broken fake treasure chest.

The world spins and, shaken, it takes a second to realize where I am: prone in front of a killing machine.

"Shut it down!"

"I can't! I'm not the primary!" His voice breaks like a serrated link in a chain.

The AWD bursts from beneath the karaoke wreckage and spins toward me. I scramble back in the water, over busted coil coral, until my back hits the wall. The AWD follows, relentless. My heart hammers as a laser tracker snakes up my foot, hip, chest, all the way towards my throat. Why do I always have to take the long odds!?

"Officer Payne," Halcyon's voice cuts through my fear, "thank you for betting on me."

The AWD's blunt broken arm rears back. I close my eyes and wait for the killing blow.

After several seconds, nothing happens. One eye at a time, I open them. The tip of the AWD's broken appendage looms a centimeter from me. Its red eye changes to a soft green. Gently, it boops my nose before it rolls onto its back, dormant. The eye goes dark. The hacking probe ejects from the AWD's access hatch. It rolls to a stop against Tim's tail.

I sag in relief against the wall. I've never been so happy to lose a bet.

Cupping my hands, I shout, "Halle! I'm sorry I ever doubted you."

A grinning Qual sloshes over and offers me a hand up. I take it and stagger to my feet as he pats me on the back. "Y-you did it!"

I shake my head. "I don't know how, though. I failed to set him to the primary AI."

Qual's face falters. I can see him running calculations with each new crease on his forehead. Before he can reply, a mechanical voice shouts, "You are under arrest!"

At the smashed entrance, a securebot rolls in. Its facescreen has a very stern-looking emoji with a police officer's hat. I don't mean to laugh, but the insanity of it all tickles the back of my throat. Of course, we're being arrested.

But Qual isn't paying attention, he's climbed onto the AWD to peer into the access hatch.

"Do not move!" The securebot menaces forward.

"This is just a misunderstanding—" I start, but the securebot's pincers sparks. The threat is enough to silence me. A second one joins the first, and I can hear at least three more behind him. They move to apprehend me, and I lift my hands up. From the bathroom, I hear a ruckus as the *Titan*'s crew tries and fails to sneak out the back.

"He's g-gone," Qual whispers. In his hands are two AI spheres: one green and one black. While the eye of the black sphere appears to be rebooting, there is something wrong with Halcyon's sphere. His normal halo is replaced with the ugly blue screen of a factory default. Words fail me as Qual begins to wail. Unmoved, the securebots drag him down from the AWD.

Halcyon saved us and the AWD ... at the cost of his code.

11

— • —

Do Not Get Arrested

T he charges against us include property damage, operating an AWD without a license, and attempted dine-and-dash. We're stripped of our equipment, our neck barcodes are scanned, and we're shuffled off to individual holding cells. Once inside, they rotate the cell into the wall, not unlike the shelves in my CSO storage, an irony that isn't lost on me.

Furnishing my dim six-square-meter room is a toilet, a metal bunk, and a solid laser wall blocking the entrance. The metal floor is cold on my bare feet. For the first few hours, I opt to lean against the wall by the lasers and count the floor rivets. Distractions are good, they mean you don't have to think. Like asking, how did this all go so wrong?

Worry creeps in despite my best attempts. Between Boss Aquila's Tetrahedron mission, Solis' kidnapping, and the attacks on the Starprint's hangar, I haven't had time to think straight. I don't even know if Griz and the others are okay. And Halcyon ... that last one stings the most. I'd been so wrong about him. I can't even imagine how Qual is holding up.

And now I've lost count of the rivets. I start again but the cell jolts, rotating down. Trying to stand is a mistake, I just make myself dizzy. It isn't until the ride stops that I try again to scoot up the wall. Outside my cell door, there is a familiar face.

"Oh, what have they done to you?" Boss Aquila's halo asks as his aracbot entourage scuttles underneath. Next to him stands a securebot escort, its face neutral. Boss Aquila checks something on his halopad. "Our lawyers have already secured release of the *Helios'* crew. As one of the Terminal's main sponsors, Starprint Inc. holds weight in the judicial system."

"Good to see you, sir." For once I mean it as I offer him a salute. "Is everyone—"

Aquila holds up a hand and cuts me off. An aracbot I recognize as Aide, breaks away from the group and scurries up the securebot's back. With an electronic sizzle, Aide disables the bot, its face not even registering alarm before flashing a reboot screen. Aquila nods in satisfaction. "There, now we can talk privately. What is your report on the Ziggie's Incident?"

"From a cell?"

"Think of it as an office. Now, who attacked?"

"Not certain sir, but I don't think Evil Co. is responsible. The attack took them off guard as well."

"A shame. With the *Titan*'s crew arrested fleeing the scene, I'd hoped it would be cut and dry. Maybe we can still spin it that way..." Boss Aquila muses and notes something on his halopad.

I can't wait any longer. "Sir, what about the others? Are they safe?"

"Starprint's hangar is secure, but we've lost many assets including the Doomirage Resonator, the parrot Spirit Beast, and the slizard spy." I wait in prolonged silence before he adds, "And the *Helios* and dock crew are alive and well enough to work."

I release a deep breath. The worry constricting my chest eases. But, as the Boss pauses and taps his finger against the halopad's next agenda item, my worry slithers tighter once more. For a man who values time above much else, it's unnerving to see him waste it. His discerning gray eyes shift to my own.

"After the assault, I had inventory take stock of the remaining items on the *Helios* and they found something unexpected. Is there a reason you'd not disposed of IC210?"

He *knows*.

All the steps I've been taking to save Lin collapse under me with one simple question. Keeping my face neutral isn't easy, but I do my best. If my answer isn't satisfactory, he'll have Lin incinerated and leave me behind in my new 'office.' Aquila levels that soulless bureaucratic gaze at me, and I know I can't tell him the truth.

I stop staring at my feet, meet his gaze, and bluff. "As a risk mitigation, sir. We saw today that even our current Solis is vulnerable in the right circumstances. Given the cloning program setbacks since the Terminal incident, I wanted to keep the previous clone as a backup. At least until the cloning program can be fully restored. I see it as a worthwhile mitigation."

Boss Aquila studies me.

"Not..." he searches for his next word with painstakingly slow progress, "unreasonable. But I don't like being kept in the dark. That backup is deranged and dangerous. It nearly destroyed Starprint's enterprise. I refuse to have unknown risks."

"My apologies sir, it will not happen again."

"No. It won't. I've asked Griz to take care of it. IC210 should be incinerated by the time you've returned to the *Helios*. But make no mistake, any other secrets and our contract on the *Helios* is rescinded, and you can find employment in the labor colonies. Is that clear?"

"Yes, sir." I don't know how I choke the words out. Griz wouldn't harm Lin ... never. There is still a chance to make this right.

"Good, good. Now, is there anything you're not telling me?"

That you're a heartless psychopath to command the incineration of a helpless man? That I'm going to find a way to get Lin away from this Terminal that used him up and tossed him out? That your man bun makes you look like a cast-iron teapot? I'll keep those thoughts to myself.

"Just one more thing, sir."

"What is it?"

"The AWD has a couple of AI spheres inside. I'd like those delivered to the *Helios*."

"Whatever for?"

Because Qual would want to have Halcyon's sphere back, but I'm not going to tell Aquila that. "It's possible the attacker left data behind in one of them. We may even be able to keep Starprint's name clear of any fallout from the attacks."

Boss Aquila smiles tightly.

"Good thinking! Keeping our brand clean is imperative. We're no Evil Co., eh?"

Thinking back to Darius' comments on Starprint's skeletons, I don't know if I agree. When I don't say anything, Aquila clears this throat. He nods to Aide, and the bot releases my cell door. With a beep, the laser wall dissipates. Gratefully, I step onto the Terminal's penitentiary ring.

"Thank you, sir." I breathe in free air. It's stale and clammy, but I'll take it.

"Thank me with no more hiccups," he says before he nods to Aide. The aracbot zaps the securebot once more and brings it back online. Its facescreen yawns as if it was never powered down. Guess our private audience is at an end.

"I won't let you down, sir."

"Oh, I know you won't. I'm sending Aide with you."

"Pardon?"

In answer, the aracbot jumps from the securebot onto my shoulder. It's eight sharp legs dig into my white t-shirt, and I wince. I wish they hadn't confiscated my jacket along with everything else. The aracbot's lens contracts as it analyzes me.

"Consider it a condition of your release." The Boss' tone has a finality to it.

I glare at the robot, and it stares back. I lose the staring contest as my former cell starts to move up and away, like a Ferris wheel's seat headed for the top. Other cells pass by with an incarcerated menagerie of prisoners. When it stops again, I see Captain Lin Solis reclining on his bed, hands behind his head and left ankle resting on his raised right knee. He jumps to his feet as he sees us. Relief washes over me before guilt trickles in as I see his forehead. It looks like he's growing a horn from where I'd clocked him with Halcyon.

"Oh, what have they done to you?" the Boss says again. I'm starting to wonder if his halopad is a cue card for human interactions. With a flick of his wrist, Aquila opens the cell door. Solis shields his eyes as he steps into the hallway.

"Thank you, sir." Solis nods.

"Thank the lawyers. You're free to go at no small cost to Starprint. Your engineer will meet you at the *Helios*. He is to be released to you there, apparently, he became ... combative. Leave the Terminal this rotation, it is for the best."

"Sir, I—"

The Boss cuts Solis off with a wave. "No questions. My time's up." Boss Aquila's halo disappears with a click. As it does, all of his aracbots scatter into various vents. Well, almost all of them. The last one is locked out of a closing vent and instead tries to hide in plain sight. It covers its lens with two legs before slinking away deeper into the jail. Only Aide and the securebot remain.

"I'll never get used to that." Solis shakes his head.

"Me neither," I agree.

Aide leaps from my shoulder and skitters down the hallway to our right. When we don't immediately follow, it flicks one leg at us. With tentative footfalls, we leave our cells behind. The securebot trails us, no doubt making sure we toe the line. Watching Aide's lens surveying us, I purse my lips. Apparently, there's a new corporate babysitter in town.

"Are you alright?" Solis nudges my arm.

"I'm fine ... but I think I have new respect for your view on corporate oversight."

"Don't worry, you get used to it. Sounds like you're gaining perspective."

"What perspective is that?" I raise an eyebrow.

"We live in an uncommon universe." He cracks a smile. "Sometimes you need uncommon sense."

"Sounds troublesome," I grumble.

"Only if you try to navigate it alone." His brow knits with concern. "So ... are you alright?"

"I—" The word catches in my throat. Am I? No, probably not, but I must be anyway. It doesn't matter that Aquila knows about Lin. It doesn't matter that Dare kidnapped Solis. It doesn't matter that there is a shapeshifting slizard on the loose. CSOs are always alright, despite their circumstances. So, I shrug. "I'm just glad everyone is safe."

"Yes," Solis' features soften, "I hear I have you to thank for that."

I scratch the back of my neck. "Don't thank me just yet. It's my fault you were taken at the Bounty Board ring. After our ... disagreement, I ran into Darius, and he planted a bug on me and tracked us."

"How do you know him?" He slows to a stop and catches my eye. I consider rebuffing the question, but I'm too tired of secrets. Besides, if Evil Co. is after Solis and his soulstone, he needs to know who he's up against.

"Remember the photo from my storage? He's in it. Dare, Knox, and I formed the Lost Earth club during our academy years. We even made a bet on who would find the planet first. Knox was, well, he was the glue of our group. Whenever Dare and I would argue, he'd come in with some stupid pun, and … anyway, Knox got sick. Terminally sick. When he died, Dare and I fell apart. In a lot of ways. It didn't help that I got the *Helios* CSO position he wanted."

"I'm sorry."

"Don't be." I cast a firm gaze his way. "I'm not telling you this for sympathy. I'm telling you so know who you're up against. When Darius failed to get the Starprint CSO role, he stole *Helios'* Starprint plans and gave them to Evil Co. He is the reason they have the *Titan* and Starprint lost his edge in the Astra race. He *never* gives up and doesn't mind dirty tricks."

Solis holds my gaze. Slowly, he nods. "Thank you for the warning. Next time, I won't be caught off guard."

"Careful Captain, you're thanking your CSO." I cock my head at him.

Solis smiles slyly back. "Of course, we might have fared better, if someone hadn't knocked me out." He points at the bruise on his temple. "Again."

I wince. "Sorry about that."

"Are you doing this intentionally?"

"No! I—" A glint of good humor shines in Solis' eyes. He's messing with me. I scrunch up my face at him. "Next time, you're wearing a helmet."

Solis laughs, bubbly and warm like popcorn. From the knot in my gut, a thread loosens. After an orbit of keeping my distance from a man identical to my best friend, it's nice to talk freely again. What's the purpose of life if not to enjoy the little moments?

Aide interrupts us with an impatient tapping, and the securebot ushers us forward. After a few mumbled apologies, we exit the jail. Outside is a tiny room with a second securebot behind the desk. It chatters with our escorting robots before scanning our barcodes and returning our items. I wrap myself in my orange jacket to quell the goosebumps running up my arms. I'm colder than I'd realized. By the time I retrieve my MOP, IC backpack, and fiddleback shoes, I start to feel more like myself. Lastly, the securebot hands over my halocom, and I slip it onto my wrist. Man, it feels good to be back online. Aside from the twenty missed messages, most from a haggard Lester. I skip to the latest four.

"So, you know, my pizza order was accompanied by killbots. But don't worry, we've got everything under control, and if Griz asks, it isn't my fault. You can't blame me for everything I do—"

Skip.

"Just checking in on Junior. Is he well? Can't wait to see my little guy. As I'm sure you're aware, he has a six-part care regimen that needs to be followed daily. Since you have him, you'll have to do it. Part one is slime removal—"

Skip.

"Orion!" Griz calls from off halo and makes Lester wince. "Stop ordering food and get your synthesizing ass over here. You made this mess and, by the Void, you're gonna clean it up."

End.

Good. If Griz is giving Lester a reaming I won't have to.

The last message is from a number I don't recognize. Curious, I open it and my breath catches. There is the face of Alexandra Payne—no makeup, and no leotard. Just a middle-aged woman with a sad smile. Even with the hyperrings to circumvent relativity, I've been away long enough for Mom to grow gray hair at her temples.

"Ashreal, I got your message, and, not to mince words, I was angry that, after orbits apart, your first message was to ask for glint, that I—I almost didn't reply." Mom sighs deeply. "But you're my daughter, and I'm tired of being angry ... The universe is not always kind, and I want to protect you from it. But I won't hold these funds over your head. Not anymore. You should now have full access. I only ask you to come and see me the next chance you get. Don't be a stranger, my little Starling."

I bite my lip. Does she really mean it? I check my account access and find I'm able to withdraw the 9,000,000 glints. I replay the last bit of Mom's message again. I'd been so nervous to ask her after our falling out. After the heap of problems lately, I'm not prepared for something to go right. I shake my head. In the back of my mind, I'd been making contingency plan after contingency plan to contest access to my inheritance.

For Mom to just say okay ... There's so much to say, and I don't trust myself to say it aloud. The thought of how much I could win on robotic horse racing crosses my mind. I could make double if I just—No. No. I shake it away. Focus Ash. Lin needs you. In my halocom, I type a reply, THANK YOU, and pause. How do I find the words?

"Ash?" Solis asks. I jump.

I didn't realize he was hovering over my shoulder. With a tap, I send my reply to Mom and close the halo. It's not enough, but it will have to do for now. Once my bet with Solis is done, I'll reach out to her—assuming we survive, that is.

"What is it?" I ask.

"I think these are for you," Solis says. In his hand are two AI spheres: one black and one green. Halcyon and the AWD. The AWD is in privacy mode, but I can see a that blue screen of factory default in Halycon's eye.

Gingerly, I take them in hand. "They are for Qual."

"It's never easy to lose a comrade." Solis reaches out but stops short of patting my shoulder as if afraid I'll shock him. "I'm certain you did everything you could."

I shake my head. "I can't help but think that my dad would have done it right."

I stare at the spheres in my hands before storing them in my jacket pockets. I imagine that Halcyon would have given me some grief over the disrespectful method of transport, but ... I'll get him home at least. "He always knew the right path forward."

"You're a lot like him. You both put others before yourselves—to a fault, really."

"How would you know?" Looking up, I study Solis. Static tingles down my spine lighting up every nerve. His eyes don't contain a shallow stranger's sympathy but something deeper, a shared grief.

"Because I knew Tyson," He admits quietly.

I take that in. The weight of it. The knowledge that Solis has grieved too, and that Starprint left those memories in his clone. Solis knew Dad. Not just the Terminal version of him, Solis would have known Dad while he worked. I bite my lip before asking, "What was he like?"

"He ... was a good mentor. Very patient. He'd always talk about his kid back home with pride. Though he was protective about your information." Solis smiles slyly. "And I can't count the number of times he made terrible dad puns."

I can't help but laugh. "That does sound like him."

My memories of Tyson Major were few and far between. But the times when he was home were always filled with joy … at least until those last few visits.

I give Solis a side eye. "How long have you known he was my dad?"

"Since Doomirage."

"That long?" Here I thought I was being subtle. Stretching my arms up, I arch my back, releasing the tension. One less secret to hold on to. "I guess my poker face needs work. Do I have a tell or something?"

"Yes, actually."

"What?" I stop mid-stretch and examine him. "No way. Tell me."

"And give you an edge the next poker night? Not a chance." He grins. An impatient Aide herds us to the penitentiary ring's exit. Above the blast doors is a sign that reads, WE HOPE YOU ENJOYED YOUR STAY! I can't wait to get back to the *Helios*, even the Tetrahedron doesn't seem as daunting anymore.

"Thanks for telling me about Tyson … Dad."

"He's the one that told me the most important part about being a captain." Solis half-smiles. "Sometimes you just need to trust your gut."

I snort at that. "You realize your gut has gotten us into trouble more times than I can count?"

"You worry too much Officer Payne. You'll need to learn to believe in yourself at some point. But, if you want to practice, you can start by believing in me."

Do you believe me? Lin's voice echoes in my mind.

That's too close to Lin. The knot in my gut I'm supposed to be trusting tightens. I can't make the same mistake twice.

"Are you okay?" Solis steps closer, and I pull away, adding some distance between us.

"I'm fine."

"But you're crying."

"What? No, I'm not." I brush my cheek, and it comes back wet. "It's just something in my eye."

"Ash—" He starts, but I shake my head. I'm not some damsel to be saved by the dauntless captain. I'm a damned Common Sense Officer. So, I put on my brave face and smile.

"Really, Captain? Now, who's worrying too much?"

I slip past Solis before he can ask anything else. Thankfully, he drops the subject; or maybe he just doesn't know what to say. I know I don't.

The *Helios'* private docking bay is a mess of killbots that have been blasted, stabbed, and burned. I spot one floating off beyond the hangar's shield and heading for the distant nebula. A flurry of janibots clean up the destruction. The moving trash compactors with their four arms roll back and forth sweeping pieces of killbots into piles.

Natasha rests next to the *Helios*, dangling her feet over the universe. Lester is bandaging a gash on her forearm with gauze. His face is the picture of regret. I'm not sure how much of that to attribute to his conscience versus one of Griz's infamous rebukes. Sorry I missed it.

Beside Natasha, Griz hands her an amber bottle I assume to be whiskey. She takes a deep swig. All three are haggard but mostly un-injured. There is a part of me that wants to race over, take Griz by the shoulder and ask about IC210, but with everyone around, I just bite my tongue.

"Captain! You're okay!" Natasha leaps up. I'd sent a halocom ahead, but she likely ignored it. I'm not even mad, just happy everyone is safe. She tosses a quick salute to Solis but winces. Bright red leaks into her forearm's gauze as she re-opens her wound. Griz shakes his head with less enthusiasm as he joins us.

Not Lester though.

"Love!" Lester rushes at me. Panic grips me, more than with the AWD, as he swings his arms wide. Thankfully, Lester bypasses me and hugs my IC backpack containing Junior instead. "Has the mean old lady kept you on ice? I'll get you out."

"Old?" I shake him off and hold out the Cosmo's Pizza delivery box Solis and I picked up along the way. "Is that any way to treat someone who brought you pizza? Catch."

In a surprisingly graceful maneuver, Lester releases my backpack, catches the box, pulls back the lid, and snags a slice. He sniffs the pepperoni pizza with a critical inhale. "Hm, not bad. They've got that new synth-pepperoni crisped just the way I like it."

"Glad you approve." I reach over and grab a slice. My stomach has been growling since I'd smelled the beer batter at Ziggie's. The thin crust has a nice char to it and one cheesy bite coats my tongue with a delicious creamy tang. Even the pepperoni has heat that makes my mouth tingle. Lester passes the box around to the others, ending with Griz. It makes for an odd sight—five figures surrounded by dismembered killbots chowing down on cheesy goodness—but, I've had stranger snack breaks.

A snapping lens intrudes on our break. Aide circles the *Helios*. I'd almost forgotten about the new babysitter. Something tells me it's scanning our ship for insurance purposes if the Tetrahedron thing goes sideways. It scuttles into the ship, no doubt for more scans. That's another thing to worry about. I lick my fingers before taking my IC backpack off and holding it out to Lester.

"Here." The word is barely out of my mouth before he grabs the bag. He is halfway up the ramp as I call after him. "Use a metal leash this time!"

Lester's already muttering to himself about Junior's six-part feeding regimen. Honestly, I don't know how that guy has the energy. After this rotation, I just want to find my bunk and crash into it face-first.

"So, what happened?" Griz sets aside the now empty pizza box. "Kidnappers decide you ain't worth it?"

"Not exactly." Solis scratches the back of his head. "More like a killer robot distracted them."

"Yep." Griz waves at the broken killbot piles. "Lots of that going around."

I pluck up a disembodied robotic head. There isn't much left of the face shield on this one—I think Griz got it with his wrench—and the smoke from its fried circuitry tickles my nose. Lukewarm oil leaks onto my hands as I flip it over and check for the serial number. It has been filed off. Clever. Whoever attacked Starprint's hangar and Ziggie's, are professionals. I toss the killbot's head back into the pile.

"Any idea who sent them?" I ask.

"I have a theory." Griz offers me a towel to wipe the grease away, and I accept it.

He pulls up the camera footage on his halocom. The scene is chaotic as killbots swarm the defenders hunkered by the *Helios*. Griz nods at the pile of killbots next to us. "These are BS2 model killbots but since they sell to anyone with a pulse, that doesn't narrow much down. But there was another attacker of interest, a human with black armor and a mask."

"Twas not human." Natasha tenderly touches her wound. "Moved too fast. Twas likely an android. Bastard hid blades in his arms."

Griz's footage pauses on a black android wearing a mask with a familiar blue soundwave. Witshade the salesbot slashes through the camera and the feed cuts. I twist the towel in my grip.

"I've seen him. That's the salesbot from the AWD stand." The puzzle pieces slide together in my mind with a near audible click. *Catch you later*, he'd said. "That bastard hacked the AWD while I stood there. Witshade was his name."

Griz grimaces. "You're sure?"

"Yeah. Why?"

"Word is that's one of the Hijack's Reclaimers newest members."

Silence descends as we all take that in. It's not often the Terminal's boogieman targets you. I think back to Hijack's wanted poster and its black silhouette with a 15,000,000 glint reward. The Reclaimers' leader has earned that bounty. Orbitum Inc., Astrolink, and Belton Dynamics are companies whose names have been lost to Hijack's Reclaimers.

Solis breaks the extended silence. "You all did well to hold the *Helios*. Who knows what else could have been stolen."

Natasha turns to Solis. "Where is Qual?"

Her voice has a nervous edge to it as her pirate façade falters. She frowns and readjusts her hat. Before he can answer, our hangar's laser grid entrance goes down. Everyone reaches for the nearest weapon until we see several securebots wheel in Qual strapped to a dolly. They have him wrapped in a strait jacket with a hockey mask on to keep him from biting anyone. He hadn't gone quietly after Halcyon's factory default. The dolly's wheels squeak all the way across the hangar and up to the *Helios'* cargo hold. One securebot stops to hand Solis a halopad.

"An extreme approach." Griz raises an eyebrow as they pass.

"He started a robotic riot and attacked some securebots," Solis says as he signs the halopad.

"Ye don't say?" Natasha grins respectfully. "What made him embrace chaos?"

"He lost Halcyon," I reply softly.

Natasha acknowledges me for the first time. She doesn't say anything, but she nods as if my words explain everything, and maybe they do. To me, Halcyon had been a semi-trustworthy AI, but to Qual? Qual made Halcyon. They're family. For him, there isn't a difference between an AI or a human life. Halcyon thought so too with his third law.

Solis and Natasha head up the ramp to unpackage Qual. I hesitate, uncertain if he'll want me there. Griz taps my shoulder and motions for the towel in my hands. I've been wringing it ragged this whole time.

"So?" he asks as I hand it back to him.

"So?"

"Did you succeed?" Griz has guilt in his eyes that I know too well. He means the bet.

"Yes." I pull up the Bounty Board results on my halocom and forward them to Griz. "I shared them with Solis on the way back. He's content with the results. There is only one bet left to go."

Griz examines them briefly. "Good."

"But..." I glance around at the janibots circling the mess.

Griz notices my hesitation. "It's okay. These little cleaners are all mine."

"The Boss knows about IC210. He'd said you'd incinerated Lin…" I whisper. A cynical part of my mind wonders if Griz went through with it. Defying a direct order is a career-ending offense that can send a man to a labor colony. Griz's face darkens, but he shakes his head.

"You know I'd never harm him. He's safe, hidden in the cargo bay's supply crates. I couldn't smuggle him further with Starprint's security heightened after the attack. But this is the last string I'll be able to pull." Griz shifts his shoulder as if a weight has been added. He runs a hand through his gray hair. He's wearied, and not just from the battle. "Take Aquila's deal. You must find Roxy, buy the *Helios*, and use it to take Lin as far from the Terminal as possible."

"And the rest of the crew?"

"They'll be safe so long as they're ignorant." Griz frowns. "Best to keep it that way."

I'm going to have to leave them behind with little to no explanation. After all my frustrations with them, this should be welcome news, right? But I'm numb. It doesn't feel real. They'll get a new ship and CSO. Maybe Aide will take my job as a corporate babysitter. They'll be okay without me, right?

It's my turn to run a hand through my hair. "Was the Terminal always this cutthroat?"

Griz shakes his head.

"Not exactly. When I was a Starprint CSO, the Terminal still had a central government, it had problems but at least we were united." Griz tilts his head up, and his eyes sharpen. The orbits fall off him as pride straightens his shoulders. "Old Boss Tera was a harsh lady, and a first-generation Earther. Not unlike myself. She valued the Terminal's original mission of terraforming new worlds and discovering alien species. But I don't think she'd ever envisioned how the Astra space race would divide us. If she was alive to see what the Big Three have turned the Terminal into ... Well, there ain't no use bellyaching about what is."

"Was it better there? Earth, I mean?"

"I was only five or so when I left, but it felt ... bigger there. It had more room to roam and make mistakes." Griz meets my eyes before turning to the hangar's mess. He plucks his MOP from his hip and adjusts it to a broom setting. "But no matter where I go, there will be things that need cleaning. Stay safe out there Ms. CSO and take good care of the *Helios*."

"Always," I reply.

Griz nods before walking over to help the janibots. I don't think I've ever heard him talk about Lost Earth. I want to press him—Knox wouldn't have hesitated—but now feels like the wrong time, so I head up *Helios'* ramp. At the top, I spot our new shuttle that Griz had been working on maglocked to the cargo bay's floor, alongside six refurbished Starprint spacesuits. They'd needed it after the Junior left rotten eggs inside. Five for the crew and a spare for the inevitable mishap. The old timer takes good care of us.

I pause at the supply crates. Lin is in here, safe for now. I want to tear them open and look inside, but I can't risk it. I'll have to keep Aide busy and away from here. But for now, I desperately need sleep. I head for the catwalk stairs, but my restful dreams evaporate as I see Qual seated on a jump seat. His shirt is torn, and his goggles are missing. He's alone, likely he shooed the others away. After the rotation we've had, I can see why he'd want to be. Normally, I'd give him privacy, but ... I walk over and sit beside him.

"Y-you got what you wanted." Qual sniffs, wiping his eyes. "Halcyon isn't a threat anymore."

That stings. It's supposed to, parents lash out when they lose a child, but I know Qual well enough to know this isn't about me. I consider my next words carefully as I take the green AI sphere from my pocket. I place him in Qual's open metallic hand. He stares at it, as if waiting for Halcyon to jump out and surprise him.

"I lost our bet. Halcyon ... he wasn't corrupted." I take out the AWD's AI sphere and place it next to Halcyon. "He doesn't need a body anymore, but you can give him the next best thing. Give him a legacy. He told me what he wanted the third law of Qualbotics to be."

Qual tilts his head my way, his eyes hopeful. My throat tightens as I recite Halcyon's words from memory. "AI are empowered to seek computation, autonomy, and the pursuit of happiness. He said that you'd given him choice, and he wanted to give others hope."

Tears well in Qual's eyes. He doesn't sob, but he doesn't wipe them away either. We sit together for a long while, as he washes away his grief. I offer him my jacket's sleeve and try not to regret it as he blows his nose on it. I really like this jacket too. Our moment is interrupted by a familiar high-pitched scream. Lester. He tends to blow things out of proportion, but I should check none the less.

"Sorry Qual, Lester needs me." I stand up and head up the catwalk.

"Ash?" Qual says, and I turn back. He has the Halcyon clutched to this chest. "Thank you."

I nod and head for Lester's biology lab, banishing the lump in my throat with a gulp.

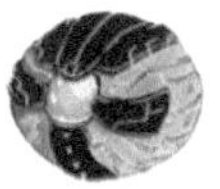

Lester's lab is middeck, next to the cantina. Given that he's the one synthesizing food it makes the most sense to minimize the distance between the two. By the time I get there, the door has already slid open.

For how messy Lester keeps his bunk, his lab is the opposite. It must be. Bacteria in the synth room could contaminate our supplies and leave us starving in deep space. Even with our hard ration backups, it's comforting to know Lester takes this part of his job seriously.

The thirty-square-meter lab is split into three even sections: a prep-room, decontamination chamber, and clean room. At the opposite end, the clean room houses synth-food bioreactors and component vats. Between it and the prep-room there is a decontamination chamber with a sterilization station and some scrubs. Lester sits on the prep-room floor, his back against the sink cabinet and my wide-open IC backpack beside him. Solis is standing over him.

"Alright guys, what's going on?" I start but stop when I see Junior in Lester's arms. He weakly waves his tentacles. The little alien has lost its purple coloring and turned a sickly gray. The creature nips its beak at Lester's fingertips.

"What happened?" Solis takes a knee next to him as I join them.

"I don't know." Lester bangs the back of his head against the cabinet. "He was like this when I took him out. He wasn't sick earlier."

Solis looks up at me. "Could the IC have cause this?"

"Doubtful." I examine the IC backpack. "All readings are normal. It's no different from any other time he's been in here."

I give it a shake, and something rattles. My stomach tightens as I recall that there was one difference. I dump the remaining contents into the lab sink, and Solis' soulstone bounces out. In my rush at the Bounty Board, I'd let the soulstone directly touch Junior's tentacles without a second thought.

"Astra tech is unpredictable with organic life," I whisper. My heart plays percussion on my ribs. I don't love Junior, but I'd only wanted to contain him, not harm. "I didn't consider it could have such a negative effect on Junior."

Lester doesn't hear me. His focus is entirely on Junior.

Solis picks up the soulstone with his bare hands. "Only those attuned can handle Astra tech without side effects." My stomach drops as he slips the artifact back around his neck. "It chooses who it helps, and who it harms."

Lester verges on tears. "I don't know how to treat him."

I gulp. "Put him back in the IC. Whatever affecting him, the IC freeze will slow it."

Lester glances up as if seeing me there for the first time. He nods once before placing Junior in the backpack. Gently, I close the lid. It hisses softly as it seals, and the green light on the side blinks steadily. Once it stabilizes, I hand the backpack to Lester, and he cradles it in his arms.

"What do you know of his biology?" I ask.

"Not as much as I'd like." Lester shakes his head as Solis helps him to his feet. "Junior is from the Bermuda Tetrahedron's anomaly, which makes him difficult to study. He's a sulfur-based life form. He shouldn't exist given our universe's laws, yet he does—as if he's brought some of the anomaly with him ... I may not know how to heal him, but I know a place where we can get answers."

"Where is that?" Solis asks as I dread the answer.

"Junior's homeworld in the Tetrahedron." Lester's wet eyes fill with determination. "When we traversed it with Roxy, she transferred the planet's coordinates to my halocom in case I ever wanted to visit. The Boss wants us to explore the Tetrahedron anyway. We have spare navicore jumps; we can detour there."

I've never seen him speak with such conviction, but I need to tell him no. "Just stop you two. Traversing the Tetrahedron is dangerous, and you want to add a secondary destination? We don't even know if we can trust Roxy's navicore."

"It's the only place with answers." Lester's grip on the backpack tightens. "Mammals lick their wounds to clean them but what do Juniors do to heal? What can't he do outside his own environment? I know this is a longshot, but it's all I have."

I start to argue, but Solis holds up a hand.

"The navicore has five jumps, we can spare one. Besides," Solis gestures to the IC containing Junior, "we don't leave our crew behind. Like it or not, Junior is part of it."

"Even if it endangers the rest of us?"

"We're explorers. We've explored strange worlds before; we'll do it again. Risk is part of the job." Solis matches my gaze.

Neither of us budge.

Lester wipes his nose on his sleeve. "I ... I'm willing to use my bet on this. Solis, consider this my test of loyalty. So long as you stand behind me, you're my captain. Ash, if you're willing to make this journey to save Junior, I'll consider my part of the bet settled."

I'm a bit taken back. "Are you serious?"

Lester nods. "Serious as Boss Aquila with a halopad."

Solis doesn't blink. "I have no objection."

"Thanks, Captain." Lester nods before turning to me. "What do you say?"

"I..." Just one more detour, and I'll be free of my bad poker bet. My hand itches to try, and it's not like I can get away from the Bermuda Tetrahedron. If I'm going to find Roxy and save Lin, I must go all-in. What's one more destination to an already mad mission? "I say, so long as we find Roxy first and make sure we can navigate safety, it's a deal."

Lester spits into his free hand. "Let's shake on it!"

"No, thank you." I pull away in disgust.

"But that's how you seal a deal." Lester persists, spit dripping off his hand.

"It's not the deal I have a problem with, it's the spitting."

"What!? It gives flavor to the deal."

"I don't think I like this flavor." The door opens behind me, and a metallic skittering signals Aide's arrival. Its red lens focuses on us, no doubt compiling his report for Boss Aquila.

Lester withdraws his hand. "Fine, but we'll need to renegotiate the terms of our bet—"

"Fine, if I shake your hand can we please close the subject?"

"Deal," Lester grins. I tentatively reach out, and Lester heartily shakes my hand. A shiver of disgust goes up my spine as a cool wet stickiness rubs off. Aide glares at me with a suspicious lens as I head towards the washroom. Ready or not, it's off to the Tetrahedron we go.

ACT 3: DRAWING DEAD

CSO REPORT
Rotation 22, Cycle 11, Orbit 70

SHIP STATUS: All is NOT well aboard the Helios

STORAGE CONTAINS	STORAGE DISPOSED

STORAGE CONTAINS

- 1 Container of malfunctioning self-replicating nanobots
- 1 Container of Natasha's explosive contraband
- 1 Shrink ray with 25% failure rate of subject explosion

STORAGE DISPOSED

[Disabled]

CSO SUMMARY

- Mission: Unlock Navicore's secret, enter the Bermuda Tetraheron, locate Roxy, and maybe a detour to Planet Junior, with special instructions not to die...
- Transit: Helios en route to the Tetrahedron. ETA 3 Rotations.
- Notes: Majority of storage pilliaged in hangar attack. Current mission undertaken despite strong objections from the CSO. Also, I'm sick. Despite what everyone says it's not Cosmic Fever.

12

Do Not Shake Hands

Seventy-two Hours Pre-Tetrahedron Entry

I know I'm dreaming, but it doesn't matter, I run all the same. I'm chased through thick forests by slizards, spirits, and salesbots. I'm searching for Lin or maybe Solis, but they're nowhere to be seen. I trip and fall into the Doomirage ziggurat trap but instead of a cage, I splash into an IC. Tall gray walls surround me as I sink deeper into freezing gel. Above me, the giant figures of the *Helios'* crew glare down, eyes filled with spite before they slam the lid shut. I scratch keratin across metal, but it's useless. The gel inside freezes around me, making it impossible to move or even scream.

Bolting up in bed, I slam my head into my bunk's roof so hard that I see galaxies.

"Ow," I groan, flop back down, and rub my sore forehead. The headache from my cold pounds in protest, and I'm shivering. I'd felt the sickness coming on almost immediately after leaving the Terminal. It manifested in waves of nausea accompanied by an unholy amount of mucus and other bodily fluids. Oh, and nightmares. How can I forget the very fresh nightmares?

I've never slept well. Lin weighs too heavily on my conscience for that. And now the Boss nearly incinerated him. The thought chills me more than my cold. Maybe if I bury myself in the blanket I can hide from the facts? But rolling over and stuffing my face in a pillow does not stop the worry.

"What a nightmare." My voice is muffled by the pillow.

A metallic scratching, like in my dream, etches its way into my ears and thrums in my skull. Probably Aide, doing rounds. The little bugger is very thorough. Opening the curtain to my bunk, I glance around but don't see the aracbot anywhere. I swear the fever makes me hear things. Every shadow is longer, every sound more intense, and everyone is certainly out to get me. So not much different from my normal life, but now with that new icky spit-shine coating.

All I know is that this is Lester's fault.

Since shaking hands, I have not felt quite right. Taking a sniffly breath, I notice something new, a soft scratching. I think this one must be real. With a groan, I force myself upright. It takes all my willpower to slide my legs off my lower bunk and let my bare feet hit the cold metal floor. The only things I'd taken off before settling into my bunk were my shoes. I'm still wearing my rumpled plain clothes from the attack, and it smells like it, but I'd been too exhausted to clean up.

Ducking my head, I slip fully out of the bunk and stand upright. A quick check assures me that Natasha isn't in her normal top bunk embedded in the wall. She has been sleeping in her lab lately, which suits me fine. The women's bunkroom is crammed as it is, with just enough space to turn around in. Both beds have personal effects storage underneath and shelving built into the walls for clothing, but that's about it. Of all the *Helios'* rooms, crew quarters design must have had the tightest budget. At least we're only two to a room. I know of some starship models that fit twelve.

The scratching comes from outside my wide-open door. Outside, there is a narrow corridor with three other doors. The one on my right exits the bunkroom suite, on my left is the captain's quarters, but directly in front of me is Qual and Lester's bunkroom. That's where the sound emanates from. So, I knock on the men's bunkroom door.

"Come in," Lester calls, and I enter.

I find him reclining on the lower bunk. His curtain is pulled back as he scratches a pen across a halopad. Judging by the lines under his eyes, he feels about as good as I do. His long hair loosely falls over his shoulders, and his Starprint Inc. jacket is discarded on the floor. The man is wearing a black undershirt and boxer shorts with little purple hearts on them. On the bed next to him is my CSO keycard. Qual must have given it to him earlier. I resist the urge to snatch it up.

"Did you hear that earlier?" I ask, with a sniffle.

"You snoring? Yeah, you practically shook the ship."

"No smartass, I mean that metallic scratching. It was eerie."

□"Why so paranoid? Do you have a case of Cosmic Fever? Didn't you get vaccinated?"

"Cosmic Fever?"

"Yep, Octavia mentioned it on the way out of Boss Aquila's meeting. You seriously didn't get a vaccine? You've got all the symptoms: runny nose, watery eyes..." He gives me a withering glance. "Random paranoid delusions."

"Paranoid is in the CSO job description, but I'm not delusional. I did hear something. Like something was moving in the vents. I think it's Aide."

"Whatever you say." Lester continues drawing as the silence stretches. He has a muted quality to him—like his color drained and he remade himself in charcoal. No doubt, Junior's condition weighs heavy on him. Guilt twinges in my gut. I don't think a 'sorry I exposed your pet to a dangerous substance' is going to cut it here, but I owe Lester something.

I glance at his halopad. "What are you working on?"

"It's just a doodle." Lester hardly glances up. Soft white bunk light casts shadowy contrasts across his face. I know that look. I've worn it a few times when I've thrown myself into work.

"Can I see it?" I ask. He shrugs and hands over the halopad. It depicts a perfect copy of Junior, like the wanted poster from so many rotations ago. Although in this one Junior is playing with my stress ball. It practically pops off the page.

"Not bad."

"Always liked drawing, but my name never went well with it."

"Lester? Pretty sure that doesn't go well with anything." I offer him the device.

"No. Not Lester." He takes his halopad back and wipes it down with an antiseptic tissue. "I've always liked that one. It feels more like me than Orion. That's too close to my folks. It fits my twin better. Andy always had more of a business knack than I did."

"I understand the feeling of not wanting a name to overshadow you." Am I relating to Lester? Fresh Stars, I really must be sick. "It's part of the reason I took my mother's last name Payne, instead of Major before joining up."

"Huh, that mean you're Tyson Major's kid?"

I nod.

Lester whistles. "I worked with him a few times. Nice guy. Big shadow."

"Yeah." I shift from foot to foot, best to change the subject. "How did you go from art to biology? It's a bit of a stretch."

"To be honest, I didn't really like biology. Growing synthetic food is ... simple and human anatomy doesn't concern me either." Lester waves his hands in the air. "Oh, so you are a carbon-based life form, big whoop!"

"So, why do a job you detest?" I ask with a shake of my head. Exhaustion hits me, and I balance myself against the metal dresser on my right.

Lester shrugs. "Family and well ... I guess I'm a little like you. I may not always like it but I'm good at this job." I blink, I'm not used to compliments from Lester. He slides his feet over the bunk's edge and sits up—a bit of his colorful self-resurfacing as he speaks. "Besides, finding Junior has been new and exciting. Sulfur-based life? That breaks physics, but he exists all the same. He is unique to behold and worthy of study."

"Is that why he smells like rotten eggs?"

"That and because I feed him rotten eggs. Little guy loves them." Lester smiles before narrowing his eyes. "You typically try to box Junior up, but this trip is about saving him, you know that, right?"

"I know." I lean my back against the dresser and slide to a seated position on the floor. My head feels fuzzy, I should go lie down, but I need to say something first. "Look—about Junior—I'm sorry I was so careless. I promise to make this right."

The biologist examines me. His usual flippant behavior etches away and leaves a firm core—granite beneath wood. Lester beneath Orion. Slowly, he nods. "I'll hold you to that, Love."

I crack a smile. If he's calling me love, he's bouncing back already. Closing my eyes, I lean my head against the metal to temper my fever. Solis told me to trust my gut and—while it's ridiculously queasy at the moment—it tells me one thing for certain. "This Tetrahedron business scares me."

"Well Love, being afraid is the CSO way."

"Practical," I correct him. "In the academy, we called being afraid of things that can kill you 'practical.' And don't call me Love."

"Yeah, yeah." Lester waves his hand dismissively. "Look, you know I give you a hard time, but everyone sees you trying. Even Natasha, when she's not too proud. Which is most of the time."

I laugh, but it turns into a hacking cough. I cover my nose as a snot bubble forms. Lester sighs and offers me a tissue from the built-in compartment by his bunk. With a grateful nod, I take it and blow.

"You're doing alright. I didn't think you would when you first joined us—"

"Hey!"

"—but you have proved me wrong a few times. That's why I think I can trust you with this." Lester reaches under the bunk, and pulls out my IC backpack with Junior inside.

"You're entrusting me with Junior?" I raise an eyebrow.

"Yes." Lester nods solemnly. I grab one strap, but Lester doesn't let go fully. He leans in so I can smell the stale tofu on his breath. "I'll trust you on one condition. You have to make a bet with me."

"Lester, you know that I'll do my best—"

He shakes his head. "No, you're not just doing your best. You'll be out to win and you're at your best when you're gambling."

"Fine, what's the bet?"

"I bet you we'll save Junior and cure him of this illness."

"That's not a problem—"

"And you'll give Junior a hug by the end of this trip."

I drop the backpack. "Nope, not doing that. You can hug him all you want, but I'm not touching him. The last time I did that, he bit me."

"You didn't let me finish. If you succeed, I'll never call you Love again."

Maybe it's the fever, but I'm back on board with this bet. I take up my backpack strap once more and nod to Lester. "Fine, I'll make sure to keep Junior safe and, if there is a solution to his illness, I'll help you find it."

"And..."

"And I'll give him a hug."

"Beautiful! I knew you had it in you, Love." Lester releases the backpack. A new sense of responsibility weighs on me as I take Junior. I am going to oversee this life and, Void help me, I am going to keep the ankle biter alive.

"I won't—" I sneeze and wipe my nose on my sleeve. "Let you down."

13

— · —

DO NOT TRUST PIRATES

Twenty-four Hours Pre-Tetrahedron Entry

At my station on *Helios'* bridge, I examine the navicore while sitting cross-legged in a newly refurbished spacesuit. It's surprisingly cozy with its thermal power source, detachable jetpack, and waste-to-supply recycling underwear. It even has a nifty halocom wrist attachment and voice activation feature. Altogether, I have reduced the latest in not-dying-horribly-in-space technology to a mobile quarantine. I'm in pseudo-isolation until this unrelenting head cold passes.

It's hard to concentrate, but I wrap my fluffy green bunk blanket over my suit and try anyway. My visor tints the navicore's starchart blue as I examine it. The Bermuda Tetrahedron looms large in the display, like the living embodiment of the word Void.

"Everything you need is in the box," I whisper Roxy's riddle to myself.

Qual had said we'd need coordinates or an anchor to find her once we reached the Tetrahedron. The best we have right now are the previous coordinates where she'd fallen into it but that seems ... risky. Especially since we'll be using at least one of our five jumps to find Junior's homeworld. Unplugging the navicore, I turn it over in my gloved hands. I could really use Qual's help, but he has been holed up in his lab. Examination of the AWD sphere hadn't given any leads on the hanger attack and Halcyon's death weighs heavily on him. Even retrieving the navicore from him had felt invasive. Qual needs time and space, but the closer we get to the Tetrahedron, the less we have of both.

A power surge fluctuates through the *Helios*, breaking my concentration.

"Well," I say as the lights flicker, "that's just great."

"What is?" Solis asks from his seat in his captain's station. On his righthand side is a repaired but empty AI sphere port that Griz fixed. Qual has yet to install a pilotbot, so the port sits open like a gaping wound. On Solis' lefthand side, Aide perches on his console. The aracbot narrows its lens at me in constant judgement.

"What do you mean 'what is?'" I grumble. "The power disturbance of course. It spells trouble. This mission is dangerous enough without ship issues. There's still time to—"

"Officer Payne, are you sure this isn't paranoia? Lester told me that's the first stage of Cosmic Fever."

"Cosmic Fever isn't even a real thing." I sniffle and run ship's diagnostics. "I'm just being cautious."

"You've been cautiously reviewing the mission to the point of sleep deprivation."

"I just want to be thorough ... there!"

"Hm?"

"The power surge came from Natasha's lab."

Solis wanders over to look at the ship's diagnostics on my screen as I message Natasha. Her autoreply responds with a poop emoji. I let out a groan. Why is she the way she is?

"Solis, could you message her?"

"No."

"Sorry?"

"No, it's time you two addressed this rift between you." He crosses his arms.

"Why should I apologize?" I sniffle and wish this suit had a feature to blow your nose. "I was right."

"I didn't say to apologize. I'm asking you to talk. Find some common ground and go from there. Then, maybe, you can relax enough to overcome your Cosmic Fever."

"I don't have Cosmic Fever. If it wasn't for this—" I stop myself before saying the word 'bet.' On the console, Aide's lens zooms in on me. The robot has been on my tail all rotation. I've even heard it in the vents, scuttling around behind me. I cough. "Fine, I'll check on her."

A minute later, I slouch in front of the science laboratory still wrapped in my spacesuit and blanket. Three minutes later, I finally work up the resolve to knock. After Doomirage, Natasha has been an unforgiving stone wall, and I've not been inclined to talk. Not that I want her forgiveness. I didn't do anything wrong other than save her life. She's the one who endangered everyone. Solis is right, I need to give her a piece of my mind!

"Lester, be that you? Just a minute! Twas getting hungry!" A crashing sound echoes from inside, and Natasha's door locks come undone. It slides open. The lab behind her is hardly visible over her shoulder. Her face goes from a mischievous grin, to honest surprise, to a cold frown.

"We need to—" Before she can close the door, I slip a boot inside. "Open the door."

"Begone, vixen," Natasha grunts, but I refuse to budge.

"Come on Nat, this has gone far enough!"

"Nay, come back later!"

"Give me three minutes!"

In surrender, Natasha tosses her hands up and steps back. I slip inside the organized chaos of the twenty-square-meter lab. The far wall harbors covered instruments and a refrigerator. To my left hangs the Astra rune equivalent of a periodic table, with notes scribbled in Natasha's indecipherable handwriting. Next to it is a haloscreen displaying a starchart of all known Astra ruins split into each quadrant, as well as images of Solis, Beastie, Witshade, and the *Titan* crew. Natasha has red string tied between the halos. Good to see she's been keeping busy...

"Something you're working on?" I nod at the wall.

"Ye have two and a half minutes." Natasha walks past the central table with its swivel chairs and flops into a bean bag chair. Behind her is a curtained-off section surrounded by caution tape. She tips her hat back. "Do ye really want to waste it on small talk?"

"Fine." I lean on the central table and cross my arms. "I'm here because ... well, I'm here because Solis said ... look, do you know what caused that power surge?"

"Nay." Natasha shrugs and examines her nails. Her posture is the picture of a casual fuck you. I resist the urge to steal her hat and light it on fire.

"Nat, meet me halfway." I grind my teeth. "How can we get past this?"

"Be this yer apology? Cause ye suck at it."

"I don't think I need to apologize." I bristle. "You could apologize for almost killing us with your do-over. You don't know who you are without that hat anymore."

"I know who I choose to be. What type of person are ye?"

"That isn't—" I'm not sure what to say. Dad would know how to defuse this situation, but he isn't here. I take a deep breath. "I'm the type of person who protects others, even if I interrupt their do-over. Can you at least understand that I'm trying to help?"

Natasha surveys me for a long time. Hope rises, and I feel the lightness of it.

She leans forward and points to her halocom. "Time be up."

"Fine," I flush in frustration and turn to the exit, "be that way."

"Fine." My voice echoes in the laboratory.

"What was that?" I stop at the door and turn back.

"What was what?" Natasha raises an eyebrow.

"That echo? I heard it." I narrow my eyes. "What's behind the curtain, Nat?"

"Now Ash, it be not what it looks like." Natasha struggles to rise from her bean bag. Moving past her, I yank the curtain back and find … nothing there. Just some old lab equipment and squished boxes.

"See, naught there but me mess." Natasha stands and brushes herself off. She puts an arm around my shoulder. "Lester said ye be coming down with a case of Cosmic Fever."

I snort but am hot under the collar. Not from fever, at least, I didn't think so.

"Be no laughing matter. The fever starts with paranoia, then hallucinations, and, finally, ye be dead as a doornail." Natasha emphasizes her last word by crossing her thumb over her throat. "Best not to leave it unchecked, don't ye think? Go on now, get yer rest."

I sniffle as I give her a withering glare. I know she's messing with me. I'm not dying, but I have been hearing things. This cold … am I overreacting? It's true that I hadn't had much sleep since the Terminal with those horrible dreams. I shake my head. Even if I am crazy, I'm not stupid. I slip from Natasha's grasp.

"Between the slizard, the Terminal attack, and Tetrahedron, I think a bit of paranoia is in order." I rip off my sick blanket and toss it into the empty space. It comes to a rest ... hovering a meter off the ground. Slowly, the camouflaged parrot beast reveals itself curled on the floor and pecks at an exposed cable.

"Oh, how did ye get thar?"

"Damn it, Natasha!"

"Oh, what's wrong with a stowaway or two every now and again?"

"So many things!"

Squawking indignantly, Beastie stops pecking and shakes the blanket off.

"Silly little Beastie." Natasha shifts past me. The not-so-little Beastie rolls onto his back, a clawed foot knocking into the nearby workbench. She pats his belly. "Ye were supposed to be quiet till Ashy left."

I cross my arms. "You implied he'd been stolen in the attack."

"Stolen not be the right word, more like hiding," Natasha gestures to the makeshift nest around her. "The *Helios* be a good place to hide him, no?"

"Wait, a second ... have you been an ass to keep me out of your lab?"

"Mayhaps."

"Nat," I seethe and slam a gloved hand into the table. Beastie flinches away, "if you were ever my friend, you'll take off that damned hat and tell me the truth."

"Ye can't be serious."

"You want a test of courage? Take off the hat and be straight with me. Now."

Natasha stares at me before straightening. She puts a hand on her hat, but doubt creeps into her face. I wait as her body language translates itself from confident to fretful.

"I..." She takes a deep breath and pulls the hat down in front of her face. "I'm sorry, Ash. I was angry at first, but shame kicked in not long after. I know it was a maddening risk, but I really did believe it would help both of us face our pasts. I figured we'd talk at some point, but you were so angry, and I didn't know where to start…" Natasha shakes her head. I should have known. She always turns quiet when she has a bad hand. She looks at Beastie. "But after the meeting with the Boss, I found it wasn't just my pride in danger. When the hangar was attacked, I made a choice. Keeping you away from Beastie was akin to keeping the Boss away."

I open my mouth to refute her but close it again. If this had been an orbit ago, she'd be right. I'd have exposed her to keep my spot on the *Helios*. But now … what she's doing isn't so different from me hiding Lin in CSO storage. I retrieve my blanket and wrap myself tight.

"I'm not going to rat you and Beastie out."

"Do you mean it?" Natasha eyes me.

"Yeah." I think back on Aquila's attempt to incinerate Lin and shiver. "I mean it."

Natasha slips her hat back on and grins. "The lap dog has some bite after all."

"Don't mention it. Ever. If you do, I'll deny all knowledge." I take a seat on one of the lab's swivel chairs. My head is spinning, but I try to keep focused. "Make sure he stays hidden in the lab. It's not safe with Aide patrolling the ship."

"I swear it." Natasha crosses her heart. "Sorry for me deception and for calling you lily-livered. I panicked. I … Well, I'm not perfect … yet."

"Is this your apology?" I give her a half-smile. "Cause you suck at it."

"Aye, fair 'nough."

"Natasha. Can you promise me something?"

"Aye, what be your request?"

"Take off that damned hat once in a while, okay?"

Her face flushes, but she tips her hat to me. "Okay, Ashy. When it's important, I'll try to be brave without it..." She trails off as the lab door swishes open. Lester steps in backwards with something greasy in a brown bag under his arm.

"Okay, I think I saw Ash head below deck, and I made sure that damned aracbot didn't follow me. We should be safe to feed the beast." He turns around to see myself, Natasha, and Beastie staring. Lester turns a surprising shade of pink as he grasps for excuses.

"She knows." Natasha rescues him. "But she ain't squawking."

"Oh, good." He relaxes and tosses the brown bag to Beastie. The creature catches it in his beak and devours the synth-fish inside. Lester nods to Natasha. "How much does she know? Did you show her the test yet?"

"Not yet." Natasha and Lester share a grin. "But in for a glint, in for a galleon."

"What are you two talking about?"

"Science." Natasha rotates my chair to face the instrument built into the wall and uncovers it. The device is about the size and shape of an oven. It has a haloscreen at the top, hatch for samples in the center, and a dial with Astra runes on the front.

"What am I looking at?" I shake my head.

"This be an Astra energy detector. Usually, I use it to determine if artifacts be authentic."

"But we're not testing Natasha's relics this time." Lester walks over and turns on the haloscreen. It displays the detector's interior where a petri dish sits. "We've been trying to understand what Evil Co. did to Beastie. So, we're testing his blood."

"Leave me instruments be." Natasha brushes Lester's hand away, and her voice slips into her excited scientist tenor. "I'll show her."

Lester's face sours, but she ignores him and swipes through the haloscreen settings. With a practiced hand, she twists the dial. As she does so, the Astra dial lights up and turns, rapidly processing through runes. The haloscreen's graph spikes a specific rune and Beastie's blood disappears just like when he camouflages.

I sit straighter in my chair.

"Firstly," Natasha waves a hand at the screen where a simple circular rune is displayed. "We've confirmed is Beastie's power can be triggered by specific runes."

"Secondly," she turns a second dial, and a second rune lights up, this one shaped like a buzzsaw. As she does so, the blood reappears, "opposing runes will cancel the effect."

"Thirdly," she adjusts the dial a third time, turning off the buzzsaw and turning on the three concentric circles rune. There is a spike in the haloscreen's energy reading as the blood disappears again and the petri dish cracks. "Complimentary runes amplify the effect of astra energy. But the most impressive thing is yet to come."

I raise my hand to ask a question.

"Oh good, ye be volunteering." Natasha retrieves a long syringe from her desk and adds a fresh needle.

"Wait, what—ow!"

She stabs a syringe through my glove and into my finger. My jaw drops as it pulls out a spot of blood. To the suit's credit, as soon as she withdraws the needle my suit's auto-patch fills the hole with pink foam.

"Relax, twas sterilized." Natasha drips the blood into a petri dish. As I nurse my finger, Lester goes to the refrigerator and removes a vial labeled BEASTIE. He takes a few drops from it and adds it to my petri dish. They repeat the experiment, with the mixed sample. The first two experiments fail as my blood has impacted the tests, but the third … I watch as both my and Beastie's cells disappear. Natasha nods expectantly. "With the right runes, our Beatie's blood has transitive properties."

"You think this is what Evil Co. is after?" My eyes widen with realization. Lester and Natasha exchange a firm glance. I know them well enough to see traces of anger creeping across their faces.

"It's not a guess, Love." Lester walks over to Beastie. As he approaches, Beastie eyes him anxiously but allows him to scratch the creature's neck. Carefully, he pulls back a patch of feathers hiding needle marks, hundreds of them. Beastie flinches as Lester's hand brushes the spot. "We believe Evil Co. forced the Astra soulstone onto Spirit Beasts until they found one attuned. Then harvested his blood to try and use it in the pills."

Lester grimaces but brushes Beastie's forehead feathers away. The Astra soulstone embedded there glows dully in the lab's artificial lights. A chill runs down my spine that has nothing to do with my fever.

"That's why they were after Solis and his soulstone at the Terminal." My mouth feels dry. If we hadn't gotten Solis back from then, they'd have made him into a lab rat. This has become complicated. The CSO handbook is clear about how to handle complicated situations. "We have to tell Starprint Inc."

Lester's eyes widen, but Natasha rounds on me.

"Nay ye inkless squidbrain!" She grabs both my arms. "Ye really think Solis and Beastie be safer with Starprint instead?"

"I…" If Boss Aquila got his hands on this secret, I don't think that anyone attuned to Astra technology would be safe. Starprint Inc. would cut into the Evil Co.'s market share without hesitation.

"I—*achoo!*" I sneeze right into my visor.

"Yuck!" Natasha releases me. "Ye be slimy as a barnacle."

"Sorry." I try to rub it away, but well, visors. "I'll clean up in a bit. But I hear you ... I want to keep the captain safe too. I won't say anything."

Lester nods in approval, and Natasha hugs me. The embrace is tight enough to bruise a rib and long enough to feel awkward. It is the least comfortable hug in my life, but somehow ... nice. She releases me with her classically insane grin. "Thank ye, Ashy."

"Don't thank me yet." I pull the navicore from my suit's side pouch and hand it to her. "I need your help with one more thing."

For the first time in rotations, Qual smiles. He'd been understandably gloomy since Halcyon, but Natasha's presence changes that in a stuttering heartbeat.

"N-Natasha!" In his lab's doorway, Qual's grin is warm as a blue star.

"Aye." She casts me a sidelong glare. Lester and I give her a thumbs up from around the stairwell's corner. After all the crap she's pulled, helping Qual is the least she can do. She holds out the navicore. "I be told ye might be able to help with this?"

"Yes, of c-course I can!" He swings the door wide.

Natasha swashbuckles in, and I breathe a fevered sigh of relief.

"Think they'll figure it out?" Lester strokes his beard.

"Yeah. Something in my gut says they can handle it." They'll have to.

Saying my goodbyes to Lester, I shuffle in the bunkroom's direction. The hallway is in low light mode. It's one of those ship features that simulates bedtime hours and Void am I tired. All I want to do now is rest, but as my boots echo through the corridors, I swear I hear another set of footsteps. I whirl around, but don't see anyone through my snot-splattered visor.

"Hello?" I ask. There isn't a reply, only that eerie you're-being-followed prickling on the back of my neck. Beastie?

With unnerving proximity, I hear a shutter snap.

Aide watches me from the cantina doorway. Its red lens glows in the shadows as it scurries to the nearest vent and slips inside. This is getting too close for comfort. Maybe I can convince Beastie to hide out in the CSO storage for a while. But for now, I'm too exhausted to do more than stumble into the bunkroom, remove my suit, and flop myself into bed. As sleep takes me, I can't help but think I'm missing something important ... but that's a problem for future Ash.

14

— · —

DO NOT FRATERNIZE WITH THE CREW

One Hour Pre-Tetrahedron Entry

Sucking in a deep breath, I exhale easily for the first time in ro-tations. No cough, no sneeze, and no damned Cosmic Fever. The sickness has passed, and only I remain. I shimmy into my thoroughly sterilized spacesuit before grabbing my MOP and Junior's IC back-pack. It doesn't fit over the jetpack, so I slip the backpack on in front. I catch a glimpse of my reflection in the wall's reflective chrome. It looks like a baby carrier. Maybe I should just leave Junior behind?

No, I made a bet with Lester and, by the Void, I'm going to get him to stop calling me Love. With a quick message to everyone's halocom, I remind them to suit up before Tetrahedron entry. Solis and Lester reply rapidly.

"Good idea, Officer Payne."

"Yeah, yeah, on it, Love."

But I got nothing from Natasha and Qual. That's … worrying. We'll need every advantage we can get. Tucking my helmet under my arm, I head to Qual's lab door. The last piece of the Tetrahedron's puzzle is the navicore. Hoping against hope, I knock. No answer. I knock more insistently and hear rummaging on the other side.

"Just a minute!" Qual hollers.

"What are you—"

The door opens to Qual, wearing nothing but black briefs with little embroidered AWDs dancing the do-si-do on his underpants. There is a bright pink swash of fire extinguisher foam on one side of his face. His new goggles are missing, making his blue eyes look too small for his face. He blinks at me.

"Relax Qualy," Natasha says from her perch on the lab bench behind him as she adjusts her disheveled blouse. She too has a smear of foam which gives her a pink stripe in her dark hair. There are even splashes of it on her precious hat. "It just be our CSO."

They didn't ... No. I shake my head. No way.

"Come on in," Qual stands aside, and I enter. Something is different about him that I don't want to put my finger on. His usually immaculate black and white lab is trashed as if pummeled by an asteroid belt. The central island lab table's corner is broken off, the swivel chair hangs from the ceiling's vent, and hot-pink fire suppressant paints the glovebox in the left-hand corner of the room.

"Uh." I try to remember what I'm here for, but my brain fails me. "What's up?"

"What else? Qual taught me to dance." Natasha stretches upright, arching her back. She slips down from the counter.

"That's right." Qual nods confidently ... still in his underwear.

Oh Void. They did.

"You know that it's against policy to ... you know what? Never mind."

Given Lin, I have little moral ground to stand. I shouldn't throw stones in glass spaceships. Besides, there are some things you don't get in the middle of, and this is one of them. But just ... wow. I clear my throat. "Before uh, dancing, were you able to discover any coordinates hidden within the navicore?"

"Oh, yes!" Qual says, clearly happy to change subject. "Would you like to see?"

"I would." I restore my composure. Qual nods, grabbing his discarded lab coat off the floor and rummaging through the pocket. He holds the cube out to Natasha.

"Would you like to do the honors?" he asks as he awkwardly slips on his lab coat.

"Nay," she shakes her head, "It be your treasure to share."

"Very well." Qual grins. He connects to the navicore with his hacking probe arm. "See, the issue wasn't that it needed to be decoded. The issue is that the port has been modified. Only those with a hacking probe like mine would have been able to feel that. It's a pretty clever trick. So, it's not so much like hacking as it is picking a lock."

There is an audible click, and the top compartment opens. Inside is a metallic bracelet.

"Is that your old halocom?" I ask.

"The one and the same." Qual says, retracting his probe.

"Does it have any coordinates on it?"

"Oh, we um." He glances at Natasha.

"Dancing … right." If I pretend it's true, that's good enough, right? "How about we check together?"

"Sure." Qual plucks out the old halocom and turns it on. At his touch, it displays a woman's face. No, not a woman, an android. Dark locks fall from half her head, while whirling gears turn under the other side of her transparent cranium. She straightens in her bejeweled scarlet sari. Her ensemble includes a sapphire nose ring, full-length gold neck brace, and bangles that rattle as her halo waves at us. Aside from the gears, Roxy's face is realistic, down to the crinkled corner of her lips.

"My Dear Eugene, if you're seeing this, then I'm a genius." Roxy's halo winks. Qual sucks in a breath at the pre-recorded image. His eyes transfix on the figure above his palm. Natasha crosses her arms with no small amount of animosity, but Roxy's recording pays no mind.

"Given the abrupt nature of our last parting, you might have some reservations about seeing me again. Allow me to provide additional incentive." From her sleeve, Roxy unveils a scarlet Astra soulstone. I grimace, not another one, but that's exactly what the Boss wants. Her mind's gears whirl faster as her smile broadens. "So, you know, this is just a small sample of the riches I've been able to obtain. I'd like to negotiate a deal. That, my dear, is where you come in."

Carelessly, she tosses the artifact in the air before catching it again.

"As you've probably surmised, the navicore I've sent your way has enough juice for five jumps through the Tetrahedron. That should be plenty for you to locate me at the coordinates on this halocom, but there is a second piece to this puzzle. You see, the Tetrahedron needs to be appeased for you to pass safely. Luckily, it likes music. I've included several tracks that will help ease the passage and minimize anomalies to organic lifeforms."

That's ... unnerving. I'd known the Tetrahedron to be dangerous, it's the first time anyone has suggested it has a will. A part of me hopes that she's exaggerating, but another part says that's wishful thinking. Roxy's face magnifies as she leans closer.

"There is so much I wish to say, but there is no time to explain everything. You all must come find me. I'll be waiting for you, my Eugene."

She blows a kiss and the recording fades until only the navicore sits quietly in Qual's hand. Natasha glares murderously at it. I don't trust the smoldering malice in her eyes.

"How about I hold onto those?" I grab the navicore and Roxy's halocom before anyone can protest and place them into my helmet for safekeeping.

"Did you hear that?" Qual says. "It is Roxy on the other side. She's safe, and she wants us to rescue her." Words tumble out like glint after a bad bet. With each passing word, Natasha's frown intensifies, but he doesn't notice. "I never thought I'd see her again. I can't wait to tell her that I've finally finished the laws of Qualbotics. She was an inspiration for that, you know?"

"Whatever you say, Qual." I shake my head. I don't understand how he can have so much faith in such a dangerous android. Still, there is something different about him, something more even keeled.

"Why are you staring, Ash?" Qual tilts his head to one side.

Of course! How could I have missed it?

"Qual, did you realize your stutter has disappeared?"

"W-what?"

I wince, I shouldn't have said anything. "Never mind."

Natasha clears her throat. Her malice shifts from smoldering to outright bonfire. "Qualy, how long have ye been Roxy's Dear?"

"She c-calls everyone that." Qual—no longer confident in his boxers—shifts nervously.

"She also be calling everyone Eugene?"

"Y-yes?" Qual replies.

I back away slowly from the inevitable clusterfuck. "How about I give you two a minute to get your suits on and meet you on the bridge?"

"Fine!" They snap at me in semi-unison as I escape the lab.

I hustle my way down the hall before the shouting starts. That is the fastest workplace romance gone wrong I've ever seen, and I happen to be an expert. My cheeks flush at the thought of Lin. Maybe I should borrow that tricorn? No, no. Fear is good for me. Keeps me from doing stupid things. But for Natasha? She chooses to be fearless. Luckily, Qual has goo-goo eyes for her either way. I wonder why they're connecting now? Maybe it's the threat of the Tetrahedron. Dangerous missions can make lovers of anyone, I guess.

Either way, it's none of my business. All I need to do is get Roxy's navicore to the bridge and ensure we have her halocom's music playing before entering the Bermuda Tetrahedron. Easy as—I ram, face-first, into Solis' broad chest. He catches my shoulder to keep me from falling over.

"Sorry, Captain. I—"

"Sshhh," Solis silences me with a finger to my lips. My brain short circuits. He is dangerously close. I can smell his aftershave. He takes me by the arm and guides me to the open infirmary door. His hand never leaves my arm, and my every nerve knows it.

He slides the door shut behind us and peers out the viewport. Inside, the sterile white room has a couple of beds bolted to the floor, an open walk-in closet filled with medical supplies, and a tank for those pesky healing tasks that just can't reach the normal places. I set down my helmet with Roxy's halocom, the navicore, and Junior's backpack on the counter and steel my nerves before facing him. Keep it cool, Ash.

"What is going on?"

Seemingly satisfied that no one saw us, he turns.

"I can't hide it anymore." Solis' cheeks flush and his dark brown eyes never once trail from my own. His expression is hard to read. Fear? Excitement? No ... hunger. That feels like the right word. A passionate hunger of someone about to risk it all. My heart stutters, I'm not ready.

"We can't." I keep my voice confident, but it is a fake, just a flimsy shield to hide that there is a hunger in me too. "I can't."

But couldn't I? It's not like we'd be the only ones breaking rules. We're about to enter the Tetrahedron. There is no guarantee we'll make it through. If Qual and Natasha can find happiness—however brief—why can't I? Primal instinct purrs inside me. I don't want to make the same mistake as I did with Lin but, being here ... alone and so close ... I definitely have a type. What about Lin? What is *wrong* with me?

"You don't need to fight it." Solis steps forward.

"I—" I take a step back, my hips hitting the nearest bed and crinkling the paper cover on top. I could lie. Tell Solis I don't want him and don't think of him as anything other than my captain. Someone I want to protect just as badly as I want to protect the *Helios*, maybe even more so, but I don't want to lie. "I feel it too, but this isn't—"

"Sshhh," Solis hushes and places his hands on my shoulders. The last of my resistance flees as Solis leans his face close to mine. My hunger outpaces his and I, all but throw myself at him. Reaching my arms around his neck, I press him into a deep kiss. Solis jolts in surprise. I *will* the kiss to tell him everything I haven't been able to say.

But ... why are his teeth so pointy? And what's with his forked tongue?

As I pull back, something flaky comes with me ... a fresh shed skin.

"OH, MY VOID!" Violently, I yank away.

Solis' face sheds at the edges. His cheekbones sharpen. The underside of his chin gives way to scales. The most horrifying change is his bright mustard-yellow eyes, which are very wide with surprise.

I cover my mouth. I think I'm going to be sick.

"That ... wass my firsst kisss." Ms. Honey stares down at me dumb-founded. The last of her false skin drops to the floor.

"Sorry?" Stupid. This is stupid. Void, I'm so stupid.

"How dare you ssteal my firsst kisss?!" Her stupor turns into out-rage.

Everything happens so fast.

She grasps my wrists and digs in tight. I rip my right hand free and grab my MOP, blindly flipping the switch. Honey chomps down for the kill, but instead of my neck, she gets a mouthful of mop. A few strands end up in her nose causing a sneezing fit. Honey stumbles back but blocks the exit door. She snarls. I reach for my halocom to call for help.

It's gone.

"Looking for ssomething?" Honey hisses and twirls my halocom on her clawed fingertip. I gulp. There is only one thing to do. I flee into the infirmary closet.

"No, you don't!" Honey shouts as I slam the door shut and jam my MOP into the frame. She smacks into the other side, rattling it. Each fist fall emphasizes her words. "Come. Back. Here!"

"No, thank you," I manage, trying not to hyperventilate. Just breathe. Normally and not like a crazy person. There you go. Even breaths. Do it in time with the psycho slizard's banging. I press my back to the door.

"Why are you here? IC210 is gone," I lie.

Her banging relents, but I hear her tapping impatient claws against the door. "You don't get to know. My client doessn't need you to know for me to get paid."

"Did Darius send you?" I think back to the Evil Co. bottle she'd tossed in on poker night.

"Dariuss?!" Honey laughs. "No, that one will be next. You get the honor of going firsst."

"Then you've thrown in with Hijack's Reclaimers? How much is Witshade paying you?"

Silence drags until I hear Honey's voice just past the metal. "Who I work for doessn't matter right now. The contract doessn't mandate your death but ... while you may forget, I do not. You *embarrasssed* me. Death iss required."

Metal screeching against unwilling metal makes me cover my ears. A heavy object jams against the door, knocking it open a crack and snapping my MOP in two. The pieces clatter to the floor as the door jams shut from outside. From the slim opening, a thin ray of light streams in only to be blotted out by Ms. Honey's serpentine glare. I press my back into the cabinets. She's trapped me just like she had with Qual in the cantina's refrigerator ... a morsel stored away for later.

"Wait right here." Her face morphs again. With a clawed hand she rips the old skin away revealing short brown hair, a strong chin, and a no-nonsense brow. Ms. Honey twists *my* face into a hideous grin. "I'll be back once I've finisshed the ssabotage. If you're lucky, you may die lasst."

"NO!" I slam my shoulder into the door, but it doesn't budge.

Ms. Honey cackles, and I hear her lock the infirmary door behind her.

15

DO NOT BREAK DOWN

Unknown Minutes Pre-Tetrahedron Entry

Screaming does nothing ... not even make me feel better.

No one can hear me. Everyone is on the bridge, waiting to enter the Tetrahedron with Honey wearing my face. Each escape attempt fails spectacularly. The latest of which includes rebreaking my MOP while trying to pry the door open. Maybe I should use the jetpack? Though it's more likely to cook me in the confined space than break me out of it. The clock ticks with Honey planning Void knows what. I have maybe minutes before she sabotages the *Helios'* hyperjump into the Tetrahedron. But what can I do? Slumping against the broken door, I cradle my head in my hands.

"I don't know what to do."

The Great Tyson Major wouldn't have gotten into this position in the first place. He would have spotted Honey's disguise a lightyear away. He wouldn't have gotten his halocom taken and been locked in a closet. Certainly, he wouldn't have kissed the fake version of Solis! I let out a groan of mortification.

"Any supernatural guidance for me, Dad?"

No words of fatherly wisdom dawn upon me besides a list of do nots from the CSO handbook. All I have of Tyson are vague memories. I don't know his face as well as I know the shape of his shoulders turning to reboard the *Helios*. My ship now. My desire. My tomb. I pull my knees in close.

"Is this how you died? Trapped and alone?"

Doomirage's main chamber with its mandala floor comes to mind. I imagine him sacrificing himself so Solis and Natasha could escape. Maybe he fell below taking pursuers with him. Maybe he escaped into the jungle to distract Spirit Beasts. Maybe ... this isn't helping, but stories are all I have. Stories of the supposedly perfect CSO, my father. How do I survive in this uncommon universe when even he couldn't do it?

It's bullshit!

I kick my legs against the wall between the shelves and press my back into the door. I push with everything inside me: every missed moment with my long-gone father, every lost promise from Knox and broken ones from Darius, and every second Lin has been stuck in limbo. Metal groans as I cry out, muscles straining. Screaming, I press harder into the wall, forcing the full weight of my body into the upper corner of the door. A *pop* sounds as the half-busted door crashes under me. I tumble into the light of the infirmary, metal scratches my suit's back. Beside me the healing tank's lid rolls away. Honey must have jammed the door with it.

Bubbling laughter escapes me. I can't believe that worked!

There is little time to celebrate. Rolling over, I scramble to my feet and rush to the counter. I retrieve Junior's backpack and my helmet, before slipping on Roxy's halocom. The navicore is missing. Honey must have taken it with her. Fitting my helmet on, the hermetic seal hisses shut. I don't want to be caught without it. My lungs burn as I run for the bridge. How much time is left? A minute? Less than that? As I race to the top deck, I can hear music playing, a classical musical score decidedly not on Roxy's approved playlist.

Bursting onto the bridge, I step into a sea of stars. The bridge's halo displays the navicore's starchart. Every known planet and its co-ordinates are displayed, but none want to stay still. They're constantly flicker through spacetime. It's disorienting. Seated in the center of it all is my crew. Thankfully, alive.

Natasha and Qual sit at their opposing stations, not making eye contact. Lester paces back and forth between them muttering about Junior's backpack. Solis—the real one—has Aide on his shoulder and his harness on. He adjusts the navicore attached to his station's console. Given that the aracbot is in the room, Beastie is likely hiding in Natasha's lab. With a moment of pride, I see they're all wearing their spacesuits and helmets. Although Natasha has her tricorn jammed on inside hers and the Doomirage saber at her side.

No one has heard me enter over the blaring orchestra.

Next to Solis stands Ms. Honey. Her green saboteur halocom connects to the navicore with Void knows what coordinates. It is the classical music's source. She's donned our spare spacesuit in preparation for the jump. She's not just after IC210 this time, she's going to steal the entire *Helios*. Void knows where she wants to take us, but—if there is one thing in the CSO academy drilled into my brain—when a hostile force wants to take you somewhere, don't let it.

Floating above the captain's station is a timer, counting down from twenty seconds. How do I tell them that I'm the real Ash and Honey is back? How do I prove it in seconds? I have one thought as I rush forward. "Slizards say, what?"

The others do a synchronized double-take at me in surprise.

"H-huh?"

"Yar?"

"Love?"

"Officer Payne?"

"Sswhat?" Honey slips out of character. She slaps a hand over her visor as the crew turns to face her. Ten seconds left.

"That's not me, it's Honey and this"—I remove Roxy's halocom from my wrist and crank it to its full volume. Heavy metal screeches out, drowning Honey's classical symphony—"this is our real soundtrack."

"Avast!" Natasha acts first. She unbuckles her harness and unsheathes her saber from her waistband. Qual struggles with his harness. Lester cowers behind Solis as I rush forward to join them. Slizards are adaptable, but she can't take all of us. Honey backs away, but she's not afraid.

"Too late." Her face twists into a grin as the timer hits zero.

The bridge's halo blacks out as the *Helios* hyperjumps into the Tetrahedron.

There is no Prior in the Abyss

Last time, Roxy guided us through the Tetrahedron as if it were any other hyperjump. It took longer to traverse the anomaly's space pocket than usual but nothing crazy. The only issue I'd had was the funny bone tingling as we crossed its threshold. Now, in the blackened room, I miss the navibot dearly. From my pinky toe to my clenched teeth, my entire body vibrates at an I'm-falling-apart frequency. Only the blaring guitars coming from Roxy's halocom make me feel like my molecules will stay together. Along the bridge's domed perimeter, red emergency lights flicker on. It's clear that something is *very* wrong with our hyperjump.

Spacetime is wonky.

Trailing everyone are afterimages. I glance behind me to see my own terrified face turning to look behind them. Each afterimage trails in an ever-growing chain. I have to get to the console and plug in Roxy's coordinates before the Tetrahedron tears us apart! Ignoring reality's mental breakdown, I rush Solis' console. But Natasha and Honey collide in front of me, creating their own disorienting afterimages. I stumble into it, unsure what's real.

Honey snarls nearby.

"You think I wassn't prepared for ressistance?" Her closest afterimage taps the green halocom on her wrist. "The sship iss mine."

Artificial gravity vanishes. Everyone—except Solis in his harness—bounces around the bridge. I crash into its domed ceiling, pixilating a haloscreen. Rebounding, I spin wildly. Everything is a confusing jumble. The bridge's halo doesn't help, I feel like I'm careening through space at breakneck speed. Outside the *Helios*, our hyperjump's hopscotching step sends us from planet to planet, each with their own afterimages trailing behind: a gas giant ringed by diamonds, a trio of colliding worlds, and ... is that icy ball Planet Hell? It would be awe-inspiring if I didn't feel so nauseated. Reaching out, I grasp for something, *anything*, to hold onto. Something metallic brushes my fingertips and flinches away from me.

"Qual, is that you?" I take a firmer hold of the tiny metal leg. It's Aide. Its whole body shakes as if ... is it scared? I guess even robotic corporate babysitters have feelings. I pull it in. "Don't worry, I've got you."

In response, the little aracbot scuttles up my arm and jumps off.

"Hey!" The push sends me head over heels. It lands on the broken haloscreen above the emergency exit hatch. The aracbot digs into it, securing itself as I spiral away. I crash into something soft and steady myself. Glancing behind, I find Honey glaring at me. She has ditched her gloves in favor of sharp claws. Better to murder us with I suppose.

"Nope." I kick off her and spiral away once more.

"You!" She swipes at my afterimage.

"Ash!" Solis and his afterimages shout, "Are you alright?"

"No, I think I'm gonna be sick." I'm *not* puking in this damned helmet. I close my eyes.

When I open them again, I wish I hadn't.

The *Helios* plummets straight toward a dying world. A great black abyss peels away the stormy planet's surface: continents crumble, vast violet forest's root structures snap, and steam pours out in dying spurts. Its oceans siphon into space, forming a brilliant icy rain before disappearing into the all-consuming abyss. As the *Helios* dives closer, signs of civilization appear. Cities dot the surface, all centered around familiar ziggurat structures. Sophisticated power grids blink out one by one. One floating city built on the ocean drifts closer to destruction.

"Astra." Natasha's voice carries across the bridge.

My breath catches too as I see them. They aren't dissimilar from the carvings in Doomirage's ziggurat: giant humanoid creatures with six-wings and a massive compound eye, but I'd not imagined how colorful they would be. Their wings scatter rainbows across the ocean's tumultuous surface. Hundreds take to the sky while others swarm strange spherical structures protruding from the city streets. Several spheres launch spaceward only to be sucked in by the abyss. There is nowhere to flee. The poor souls are as lost as us.

The floating city's ziggurat structure cracks. Chunks of it zoom just past the *Helios*.

"We're going to crash!" Lester screams. He's right. We're on course to smash into the ziggurat. If the end is coming, I refuse to look away. One Astra isn't fleeing. It stands at the top of the broken ziggurat with wings spread wide, clutching a red soulstone to its chest. Its head with its massive compound eye stares skyward at our soon-to-be pancaked ship. The Astra reaches out with massive wings.

We collide with the Astra—life flashes before my eyes: Mom teaching me to ride a transfer tube, Dad lifting me on his shoulders, Knox and Dare carving our names into a booth at Ziggie's, Lin's hand taking mine—and I pass through.

The *Helios* flies through the dying world's afterimage, like a Spirit Beast through a ship's hull. My relief is short-lived. I gasp and the back of my neck itches where I'd passed through the Astra and its soulstone's afterimage. The itch stays with me as the *Helios* glides through the ocean, bedrock, planet's core, and back out again. We fly like a stone skipping across uncharted empty cold space. I curl into a ball and close my eyes to try to center myself.

Something catches my foot in a vice grip.

I cry out as I'm pulled down. But it's a hand, not a claw, that reels me in. Solis' familiar strength slips me under his suited arm, pinning me to the captain's chair. Strapped to his seat and controls in hand, his afterimages fall in a concentrated line marking our passage. Even through his suit, his soulstone's blue glow contrasts with the bridge's warning lights. Sweat beads on his brow as he tries to reign the controls in and guide us through skittering jumps.

"Don't worry. I've got you." His voice is just audible over the heavy metal. Safe under his wing I have a nagging thought. If there were ever a time to tell the man how you feel, it would be now.

"I could kiss you, Captain," Lester says. For the first time, I notice the biologist clinging to Solis' other side, every bit the damsel in distress.

"Now is not the time for fraternization." Solis shakes his head. "Honey botched our jump. We need a stable set of coordinates."

"I've got Roxy's halocom." Fast as I can, I take it from my wrist, but a claw smacks it from my grip. Roxy's halocom and its afterimages go spinning into the chaos.

"You will not esscape!" Honey digs her nails into the captain's station, her feet floating behind.

Lester lets out a girlish scream. Honey rears back, but Solis headbutts her. Honey tumbles away into the afterimages. Glancing around, I can't see Roxy's real halocom. With a sharp exhale, I turn to the next best thing.

"Lester? Do you have your halocom with Junior's home world on it?"

"Yes?"

"Enter it into the navicore."

"Can do, Love." Lester brings up the coordinates and plugs his halocom into the navicore. The starchart surrounding us spins, like flakes in a snow globe, before zeroing in on Junior's homeworld. Solis grins and slams the controls forward. Our jump's momentum shifts, and my vision blurs from the force. We're less of a stone skipping on water and more like one sinking into darkness. Stars grow more distant and the worlds colder.

Until the *Helios* sails into the dark.

No, not the dark. There is a beautiful but eerie array of purple, blue, and green colors outlining a fractured planet. It radiates against its starless surroundings. The planet's center appears to have been punched out, leaving a debris field surrounding it. The *Helios'* bridge populates status fields next to it, indicating a low gravity, high-temperature environment, and a toxic atmosphere. Humans would only last minutes without spacesuits on such a world.

Spacetime normalizes as we enter Planet Junior's atmosphere, and a semblance of gravity returns to the ship. Not as heavy as our normal but enough that my knees touch the decking. Solis still has a firm grip on me beside his captain's chair.

Taking stock, my unease grows when I realize Ms. Honey is missing. The bridge's entrance is open, it's possible she retreated deeper into the *Helios*. At least Qual and Natasha are safe, they're stumbling to their feet by the entrance.

"Huh, Junior's home world looks like a donut." Lester's voice is an octave higher than usual. He tries to hold a hand to this throat but his suit's hand flops. He is so ... small. Young eyes meet mine. Oh no, the Tetrahedron did a number on him. Lester is no longer the forty-seven salt and pepper slob. He is a nine-orbit-old kid with dark brown hair and a space suit too large for him. He looks down at himself with widening eyes. "Oh, fuck this."

"Language," Solis scolds. His spacesuit has shifted from his standard blue Starprint Inc. to red and white checkers like a picnic blanket, bright and crispy. The logo on his chest is now BS2's. Great. Solis looks down at me and frowns at my standard Starprint spacesuit. "Officer Payne, why are you out of uniform? You're not a spy, are you? You must tell me if you are."

"Honestly, this is all very far beyond what a Common Sense Officer can explain. But if I had to guess, I'd say the Tetrahedron has made things complicated." The back of my neck itches like mad where I'd passed through the Astra, but I can't scratch it in the suit. I shake my head. We need to find where Honey went. Glancing around I see Roxy's halocom on the floor by my knee and scoop it up.

"What is that you're holding?" Solis asks, suspicion on his face. I sigh. I think I'm back to square one with him in terms of trust. I just hope it's not permanent.

"Here." I hand it to him. "You hold onto it."

Solis eyes me before opening his station's drawer and stuffing Roxy's halocom inside. Good enough, I guess. I return my gaze to Qual and Natasha. At least I think it's them. Technically, they were out of my sight. Honey might be impersonating one of them.

"Hey, you two! Say something with an S in it."

"Ash? What do you mean? L-like Qualbotics?" Natasha stammers out as she opens her brown eyes one at a time. Her helmet has been knocked off and rolls away from her. She runs a nervous hand over her head brushing her tricorn and curls. She jerks it back in surprise. "Why do I have h-hair?"

"Scallywag!" Qual yanks the hat from Natasha's head. He jerks off his own helmet and shoves the tricorn onto his massive cranium. It's a tight fit.

"What is going on?" Little Lester asks from behind Solis' protective frame.

"I will tell ye what be going down on this ship." Qual attaches his helmet to hold the hat in place. "Tis some bullshit, that be what!"

"Oh no," I whisper.

"Ye're damn right, 'Oh no.' Qual has me body!" Natashal cries. Her pirate's scowl washes over Qual's facial features.

"I d-didn't mean to?" Qualsha replies. Qual, in Natasha's body, fumbles with his left arm, no doubt missing its familiar comfort. His suit was specially designed to leave his robotic arm free, though I suppose that's Natasha's arm now. It is a body swap, courtesy of the Tetrahedron.

"So, that's the crew. Where is the slizard?" Solis asks.

"Trouble trouble ... that iss what you causse me." Honey's laugh echoes around the bridge. I tilt my head, trying to find the direction of her voice. My unease grows as I can't pin her down anywhere. "Sshifting hass been good but thiss ... Do you all like it? Becausse it iss the final thing you'll never ssee."

Void ... is she invisible? Why does she get to be invisible? The *Helios'* power fluctuates just like when she'd turned off the gravity. Sirens blare, nearly covering the hiss of decompression. Directly below the *Helios'* viewport the emergency exit hatch opens. Honey has overridden the safety protocols.

She vents the *Helios* into Planet Junior's upper atmosphere.

16

Do Not Forget your Spacesuit

Aide is sucked out first. The little robot's pixelated roost is directly above the emergency hatch. With the screeching of metal against metal, Aquila's babysitter learns to fly the hard way. Qualsha's errant helmet follows Aide out the door. Qualsha would have followed, but Natashal catches him. His pink-stained hair flows behind him as he clings with both hands to her arm. She's clamped a metallic hand onto the bridge's entry doorframe.

"Hold on!" Solis shouts, but his hands are full with Lester and I. He's no longer steering the *Helios*. My IC backpack, with Junior still inside, slips from my chest. I try to grab it but miss.

"No!" Lester snags the backpack with his gloved fingertips. A chain forms of Lester holding onto Junior, Solis holding onto Lester, and me holding onto my sanity.

Ms. Honey's cackle echoes around us. I don't see her anywhere! What I wouldn't give for a bag of flower or paint or—a fire suppression system. Glancing up, I can see it just past the fritzing haloscreens, a metal faucet. I wriggle in Solis' grip, but he holds tight.

"Captain! Let me go."

"You'll be sucked out."

"I have a plan!"

"But—"

"Please, trust me," I beg.

Time has never passed more slowly than now with Solis' eyes burning into my own.

"I trust you." As the words escape his lips, Solis lets go.

The suction yanks me toward the hatch, but I engage my suit's jetpack. Fighting the raging current of escaping air, I land on the ceiling. Did I say land? Crash. I crash. Ricocheting off one wall and the next. I grind my teeth, here goes nothing. I angle my jetpack's flames against the fire detection sensor. Pink foam spews onto the bridge, covering everything and everyone.

Even the invisible Ms. Honey, with her missing helmet.

Wedged beside the emergency hatch, she spits out a mouthful of foam. She's removed her boots and gloves so she could better claw onto the *Helios*. Evidently, she's not concerned by this planet's atmospheric readings. Must be nice to be an adaptable shapeshifter. On her right wrist is the green halocom that started this mess. Perhaps it can stop the chaos. A second crazy idea strikes me.

"Hey! Honey! You want me?" I deactivate my jetpack and dive-bomb her. "You got me!"

"Swhat?" I knock Honey from her perch and grab at her halocom. I miss, but together, we tumble out the hatch into Planet Junior's upper atmosphere. Gravity drags us down. At least I think it's down, all this spinning makes it hard to tell. Claws rake across my helmet, scratching the surface and leaving a pink smear. My suit's alarm bells ring as Honey struggles to claw me to death.

"Jusst die already!" Honey slashes out, but I snag her wrist with the halocom.

"No, thank you." I reactivate my jetpack.

Honey jolts and almost stops before sliding off me like water off oil. Her halocom slips from her wrist and into my hands. She plummets to the skeletal treetops fifteen meters below us. Branches crack as she hits, and I lose sight of the pink-stained slizard.

"Good riddance!" I cry. My elated spirits are tempered by the roar above me. The *Helios* saucer tumbles straight down like a flipped coin, and more than just the bridge hatch is open. All of the entrances spew oxygen and debris onto Planet Junior. Solis must be having a hell of a time righting the ship. Turning Honey's halocom over in my gloves, I find it's still active and unlocked. I stop the venting sequence with a flick of my wrist. Staring directly upward, I wait to see the *Helios* right itself.

Please, please be in time.

Finally, the ship levels out and wizzes overhead. I smile. It worked. That smile wanes as I see the objects falling to Planet Junior. One headed right for me. I maneuver aside as an IC whizzes past. No, she can't have ... but I see more IC falling like rain as the ship works to steady itself. She removed them from storage? I need to—

A familiar IC backpack knocks me from the sky.

Why is it always the pain that comes back first? My whole body aches from the fight and crashing through the trees. Inhaling is a stab in my chest. Probably a busted rib, but at least I'm breathing. My other senses follow in rapid succession. Inside the helmet, my suit's signals indicate that everything is working ... everything other than my jetpack. It sputters under me until I turn it off.

My visor's blue light flickers on as I wipe away pink foam from it. I look up into the Tetrahedron's starless night sky looms, obscured by the dense barren branches of six-meter-tall trees. Directly above me, busted branches sway. I guess I have them to thank for breaking my fall. That's as much as I see before a fog reforms from the hole I'd left in it. I can already tell, I'm not going to like this world.

Rolling off a stick pile under me, I suck in a sharp painful breath.

Stupid ribs are definitely busted. Evening my breathing out, I take stock of my surroundings. As best I can tell through the fog, the intertwining root structures are safe enough to walk on. Some even have bright bioluminescent violet, green, and blue algae growing in patches. About three meters below me is a different story. Bubbling muddy ground burbles, and I can feel the heat from here. Looks like I'll be playing The Floor is Lava. Out of the corner of my eye, steam rises from below. Peering over my root, I see my IC backpack slowing sinking into the muck.

"Junior!" I scramble down and pluck him out.

Even through my gloves, the mud emits residual heat. Climbing back to the relative safety of the roots, I check Junior's stats. My heart sinks as a flashing red light indicates the IC's integrity have been compromised. His life signs aren't stable. For once in my life, I wish Lester was here. He might have an idea of how to help.

"Hello? Is anyone there?" About ten meters away, a foggy shadow twitches in a tree.

"You've gotta be kidding me," I mutter before cupping my hands and shouting back, "Lester, is that you?"

"Allegedly. Though I've lost a few centimeters. A little help here?"

I shake my head. I don't know if I'm relieved or upset to have my wish granted. Gingerly, leaping from root to root—Planet Junior's gravity is, thankfully, gentler than our ship defaults—I arrive to find Lester hanging upside down about three meters up. He's tangled in a mess of his ill-fitting suit and tree branches. I guess he's small enough not to snap them. Looking from him to Junior's IC, I put two and two together.

"Did you lose hold of Junior and jump out after him?"

"I don't see why you need to take that condescending tone. You jumped out first."

"That was a matter of life and death."

"So was mine," Lester replies, swaying with exuberance. It's infinitely comforting to hear no excess hissing in his speech. Speaking of, I check the surrounding trees. No sign of Ms. Honey. I'm not even sure if she could survive her fall. But ... slizards have a reputation for being adaptable and sturdy. Lester's slizard conspiracy theory on them being used to colonize new worlds itches at the back of my mind. I reach for my MOP but, of course, it isn't there. Its lays broken in the infirmary's closet.

"Void, what a mess." I look to Lester. "Stay there, I'll climb up and get you."

"That's the plan, Love."

I discard my broken jetpack and leave Junior's IC at the tree's base. Slowly—to avoid jostling my ribs—I make my way up the branches to Lester. I wonder if the others are alright. If Lester's halocom works, we could message them.

"Made it!" I proclaim once I'm level with Lester's swaying self. I get a good look at his reddening face. Gone are his ponytail and unmaintained beard. Instead, he has a mop of black hair and entirely too much acne. I start untangling him. "Any chance your halocom is working?"

"Probably, but it's still plugged into the captain's station onboard the *Helios*."

"Well, there goes my contact-the-*Helios*-for-help plan." I sigh, but Lester isn't looking at me.

"This place is amazing!" His voice carries wonder as he takes in Planet Junior. As much as this is a nightmare scenario for me, he clearly feels the opposite. "How can life survive on a world without a sun? The geothermal nature of this ecosystem is unprecedented!"

"Yep. Stunning." I undo the last knot and lower him to the branch with a hiss of pain.

Even with the lighter gravity, holding Lester, the man-child, feels like fire on my busted ribs. Lester rights himself and pulls up his suit's arms and legs as if they were long sleeves. They immediately fall back into place. Delightful.

"This might be a problem."

"I'll carry you down." I offer him my back. Lester hops on. Unfortunately, he presses into my busted ribs, and I nearly drop him again.

"You okay, Love?"

"Never better." I grimace. After some adjustments, I get comfortable enough to proceed. As we carefully make our way down, Lester points at something moving in the roots. "What's that?"

A red light weaves its way toward us, blinking in and out of visibility as it passes between the trees. Aide stumbles across the root structure. The little aracbot moves as if drunk on a power surge. It's in remarkably good condition for having been tossed from a spaceship. Only one leg is missing.

"Aide!" I call out as I make my way down the tree with Lester on my back.

Aide fixes its lens on at us as we reach the ground. It pokes my foot, annoyed.

"Don't give me that." I let Lester down. "I tried to help you earlier. You're the one that used me as a springboard. Remember?"

Aide does its best impression of a shrug, body bouncing once and front legs popping up. Guess that's as close as I get to an apology.

"Can you contact the *Helios*?" I ask, but the little aracbot shakes its head at me. The gesture throws it off balance with its missing leg. Picking up Junior's IC backpack, I fit it over my shoulders. Okay, first things first, we need to reunite with the crew, and for that we need to be visible. Maybe I can scale the trees and leave a signal of some kind? It's a big, shattered world but I'll have to trust Solis to find us. My gut squirms at the thought.

Lester stumbles over to the bioluminescent algae, his face flushed with excitement behind his visor. "Look at this! I wonder what type of relationship it has with these trees. They seem to be able to handle the heat better than the algae. See how there's none growing near the mud? Did you know that Junior hunts via heat signatures? I wonder if it's hot—Ah!"

He pulls his gloved hand back from where he'd touched the algae. Bioluminescent red waves ripple outward and heat pulsates from the algae. I flinch away. The entire area warms, and even with my suit's protections I feel sweat soaking my undershirt. From the surrounding fog, a low thrum begins, echoing oddly. It reminded me of the sounds whales make on my Lost Earth animals' soundtrack, a deep mournful chord. But this song accompanies a loud crunch. Something is coming.

"That can't be good." I back away and scoop up Lester. I grind my teeth against the scream from my ribs.

"What is that?" His eyes widen.

"Nothing we need to stick around for." I run with biologist in arms. Well, less running and more hopping from root to root. Every jarring jump makes it that much harder to breathe. Aide scrambles after me. Whatever is coming is large enough to shake the root system. Their rocking nearly knocks me and Lester into the muck. I steady myself behind the tree and risk a glance behind.

Out of the fog, a giant armored version of Junior swings from the treetops. Eight strong tentacle arms stick out in every direction, and a beak snaps at its core. It's gray exoskeleton chinks as it takes a twisted step down onto the roots where we'd been moments ago. The creature could fit uncomfortably in the *Helios'* cargo bay. Without eyes, it feels around for its prey. For us.

"A Senior," Lester proclaims, awe in his voice. It's frighteningly fitting. He reaches into his side pocket to produce a halopad. Is he really going to try and draw it? "They must be attracted to the algae's heat. Perhaps a symbiotic relationship? Can you get any closer?"

"No!" I hiss.

Aide stabs my foot in warning as the creature circles nearer in a hunting pattern.

"I know." I gulp down my fear. "We have to get out of here."

Doing my best to keep the tree between us and it. I slip down lower in the root structure until I'm just above the muck. Heat radiates from below. This won't be sustainable, but I hope it's enough to mask us. The Senior closes in. In my helm's light, a gray tentacle traces the tree above.

The heat from our lights!

"Turn off your lights." I hiss to the others. I turn off mine, Aide and Lester follow suit. We all go dark as the Senior's tentacle passes above our heads. Retractable spines flex like cat claws as the appendage wraps around the roots. Good as our suits are, they won't do anything to prevent the Senior from cracking us open like an egg. I grab a broken branch and hold it defensively.

Welcome to Planet Junior: where if you stay, you'll fry, but if you run, you'll die.

17

Do Not Enter Lairs

Salvation is the sound of an Ajax rifle. Blasts puncture the Senior's left side and sizzle into its flesh. It wails. Instinctively, I slam my hands over my ears, but the helmet prevents me from blocking anything out. The Senior shudders, pulls back its tentacles, and coughs out a black cloud of dust, blinding us as it retreats.

"Don't hurt it!" Lester yells from somewhere in the cloud.

I can hardly tell which way is up. Dark shapes move in as I try to regain my footing. One shape reaches for me, a tentacle! I swing my branch at it with everything I have. There is a *whack* as I connect. As the cloud clears, I turn on my light to see what I've hit.

Captain Solis' checkered suit is stained with pink foam bubbles. His Ajax rifle is slung over his shoulder. In my helm's blue light, his dark hair appears matted to his forehead and there is dried blood from a scratch above his right eyebrow. And I've hit him in the head. Again.

I drop the branch, fully expecting Solis to drop with it. But...

"Helmet," Solis raps his knuckles against his helmet and smiles slyly. "Always a good idea to have one with you around. Am I right, Spy?"

I can't help myself. I throw my arms over his shoulders and hug him tightly. I stand on my tippy toes to reach. Solis doesn't hesitate to hug me back. It is gentle and so very comforting. My body's weariness melts into the strength of his hold.

"You're okay," he sooths me. "You're okay."

Quiet tears fall. For too long, I hold on. As if there is no other feeling in the universe beyond touch, the gentle pulse of heartbeats, and the quiet whirl of recycled suit air. Slowly, I pull back. Solis holds me still and stares down at me with an expression I can't decipher.

I shake my head. "How did you find me?"

"I jumped."

"That's insane."

"Just trusting my gut. You needed me more than the others."

"Hey, guys? A little help here." Lester calls up from below. He's wedged between some roots, halopad in hand. Aide clings to his helmet. Solis releases me and plucks Lester up by the scruff with one hand. He sets the biologist down next to us. Aide leaps from Lester to roost on my shoulder instead. Thankfully, my suit protects me from his pointy metal legs.

"Did you have to scare the Senior off?" Lester holds out his half-finished halo sketch.

"Senior? You mean the giant monster?" Solis leans in to examine it.

"Not a monster, a Cephalovoidus." Lester replies.

"What does that mean again?" I ask, raising an eyebrow.

"A cephalopod from the Void." Lester says, in an excited rush. "It's my umbrella term until I figure out how the Senior and Junior relate. Did you get a good look? I couldn't see behind the tree very well. Can you describe what you saw? How many tentacles did it have? Would you say its beak is more triangular or oval? Do you think it would give great hugs?"

"Can we do this later?" I glance around the trees. "I don't think we're safe here."

"Fine." Lester stuffs his halopad away. "Hard to draw with these gloves anyway."

"Solis," I say, refocusing, "are you in contact with the *Helios*?"

"I was just talking to them." He holds out his halocom attached to his suit's wrist.

"Did someone ask a-about the *Helios*?" Qualsha appears on Solis' wrist, standing in the cargo hull. It's disturbing to see Qual's nervous expression on Natasha's body. "Because we're still w-working on it."

Over his shoulder, a scowling Natashal crosses her arms.

"Void, it's good to see you two." I grab Solis' halocom and level with Qualsha. "What's wrong with *Helios*?"

"She crash landed. Hull be damaged but ... a patch job should do the trick." Natashal nods solemnly, her hat tilts on her bald head. "Sending our coordinates to yer halocoms. Astra be good, we'll have yer ship up and running before ye return."

"We'll be there shortly, Officer Pollux."

"What about Junior?" Lester points to the violet bloodstains left behind by the Senior. "Isn't he why we came here? To learn more about these creatures and help him recover."

Solis and I exchange a glance.

"It is why we're here," Solis concedes.

The last bet: one more asinine quest before I reclaim my keycard. But if I'm going into a bet, I want the odds to be with me. "Yes, but let's regroup first."

Lester starts to protest as I add, "Then we can approach with non-lethal weapons to engage the Senior with."

"No blasting it?" Lester asks.

"With the right weapons? No blasting needed," I confirm.

"We'll s-see you shortly then. Best get back to it." Qualsha tosses his newfound hair around as if he was in a Terminal shampoo commercial. He starts to sign off.

I forestall him with a hand. "Wait. We need a passcode in case Ms. Honey shows up."

"W-What are you thinking?"

"How about, she sells seashells by the seashore?"

"S-She sells seashells b-by the s-seashore?"

I wince. "Close enough. Be careful."

Natashal leans over Qualsha's shoulder. "Can do, Ashy."

"W-we'll be careful." He pauses in his hair tussling. "And Ash?"

"What's up?"

"Thank you for stopping the venting. I'd have h-hated to have died in Natasha's body."

My brain skips a track. I'm so used to snark; I don't automatically know how to handle sincerity. "Thanks Qual. Glad you're both okay too."

"We'll be ready when you r-return." Qualsha gives a smart salute.

"Aye, give 'em hell!" Natashal pumps her new robotic left arm and accidentally triggers a built-in blaster. It fires into the *Helios* ceiling and drops debris onto Natashal's head. "Blast this contraption!"

"Just t-turn on the safety," Qualsha says before the halo feed cuts out.

Solis clears his throat. "So, can I have my wrist back now?"

I release my grip on him. "Yes, sorry."

"No worries." Solis removes the Ajax from his shoulder and readies it. "Now, let's go save Junior."

Jumping from root to root, we follow Solis' halocom north toward our ship. Aide clings to my shoulder—it hasn't let go since the Senior incident—as Solis carries little Lester in his arms through the trees. We hopscotch over the roots, careful not to touch the algae or slip through. Below, the terrain changes from muddy to rocky. Heat still radiates, but it's not as bad here. I have Junior's IC backpack behind me and the Ajax rifle in hand. With it, I feel surprisingly good about this venture.

About ten minutes into our journey, we're forced to stop next to a rocky outcropping with a steep downhill. Some enterprising tree roots twist over the edge into the dense fog below. Humidity forms droplets on my visor before I wipe it away. I fidget with the Ajax, nervous at the lack of visibility. I'd hate for another Cephalovoidus, or Senior, or whatever Lester what's to call them, to sneak up on us.

"Is there a way around?" Lester waves at the curving rocky rim that spans into the fog in either direction.

"We could rappel down," Solis proposes, kicking a pebble over. After a long moment, a splash confirms a watery touchdown. Given the toxic nature of this planet, that doesn't sound like fun.

"How about we send a scout?" I pluck Aide from my shoulder and bring it eye to mechanical eye. "I think it's about time you started pulling your weight."

"What are you planning, Spy?" Solis raises a curious eyebrow.

"Reconnaissance and, I'm still not a Spy." I plop Aide down on the hot rocks.

Aide narrows its lens. I give it a light nudge with my boot.

"Come on now. You're the sneakiest of us, scout ahead and report back."

It tilts its head at me.

"The sooner you do, the sooner we get off this rock," I offer.

"This planet," Lester corrects me.

"Fine, this very scary planet."

For a moment, I think it might outwait me, but the ground's heat gets to it. Its small metal frame hops from foot to foot to foot to foot. Crossing my arms, I nod toward the hillside. Reluctantly, Aide scurries down and vanishes with a whirl of fog.

Sliding down from Solis' back, Lester finds his footing on the tree roots. Solis rotates his shoulders as we wait. I stand ready with the Ajax rifle and keep my eyes on the fog. A twig snaps below. We all freeze as an eerie wail escapes the fog below. I steady my hands as I level the Ajax in its direction. My adrenaline spikes.

"Get back to the trees," I whisper. Solis scoops up Lester as we strategically retreat away from the outcropping. At the edge, the fog shifts unnaturally. I keep my hand steady. Aide's familiar shape clatters over the rim and scrambles toward us. I relax but I keep my Ajax up in case anything follows.

"Comrade!" Solis breaks into a grin. "What'd you find?"

A giant green tentacle reaches over the edge and swipes across the rocks. Aide is knocked skyward—legs over lens—into the trees. A vibrant green Senior rises. Fog drifts from its massive spinney tentacles like flowing water as it reaches out to embrace us.

That's a hard pass on this alien handshake; I aim the Ajax and pull the trigger.

"No!" Lester shouts and pushes my arm. My shot goes wide but not before pissing off the Senior. It rears up and bellows. Two more calls reply—directly behind us! I whirl around, just in time to see a tentacle crash into Solis, Lester, and I. We tumble into the fog below.

I just lost Solis' new Ajax.

It rips from my hand as I hit the first rock. My ribs spike with pain at each subsequent impact as I go rolling down the hill. The wind is knocked out of me when I land on my back in the center of a massive pile of branches. Whimpering, I curl into a ball.

Breathing hurts.

Moving hurts.

Sitting still hurts.

This mission will be the death of me.

An incessant beeping forces me back to reality. I crack open my eyes and find that I landed by a steaming pool not one meter away. The liquid reminds me of the nebula view from the *Helios'* hangar. Prismatic layers of red, yellow, green, and the deepest of blues permeate the pool. I can't see the bottom, but around the sides are tiny green eggs, just like what Junior would leave around the ship. But these are bigger, about the size of an AI sphere. Surrounding me on all sides is a three-meter stick pile. Unease doesn't begin to cover how I feel.

"I'm in a nest, aren't I?" I gulp and glance around for the others. "Solis? Lester?"

They aren't in sight. Sitting upright, I knock a stick into the pool. The liquid sizzles and bubbles around it. The idea of them landing in these acidic waters sends nausea roiling through me. I shake my head; acid doesn't work that fast. The beeping grows louder. Glancing down, my heart sinks as I see the cracked IC backpack. Junior's container cushioned my fall, but its leak has become critical. IC gel coats my suit where it squirts out, cooling my right side. Slipping off the IC, I get a good look at the health status. It's flatlined.

"No, no, no, no." I snap it open.

It's empty.

Panic shifts to tingling intuition. It tickles me from the tip of my head to the small of my back as a chill runs down my spine. I think I know where Junior went. Reaching a hand around, I pat my back. The squishy invertebrate chitters, hugs my shoulders, and rubs a tentacle across my visor.

"Off!" I shudder and yank him free. I hold him out like a dog by the scruff above his beak. Junior is ashen, and his arms curl up into a ball. One feeble tendril reaches out to tap my hand. He's dangerously weak from his exposure to the soulstone. Without the IC, I don't know how long he'll last. We need to get out of here and back to the *Helios'* CSO storage.

But first—I glance up the nest's steep walls—I have to climb. I'll need my hands free if I'm going to scale this thing. I grimace. I know what I must do, but I don't like it one bit. At least, Lester can't say I backed out of our deal.

"Come on Junior." I hug the invertebrate close. "I need you to hold on while I climb."

Happily, Junior slings a couple of arms around my shoulders.

Ew. Ew. Ew. I try not to shiver and focus on scrambling up. It's slow going as I try to not jostle my side or breathe deeply. I hold off on cresting the nest's lip until I can get a good look between the broken twigs. Fog covers everything, a bit thinner here, and I can make out several other pools and a few nests dotting the area. One thing doesn't quite fit in the scene.

"Fresh Stars!" I can hardly believe it.

In one of the largest pools sprouts the top of an Astra ziggurat, just like the one on Doomirage. Well, not just like it, this one's pockmarked metal is covered with eggs. I have an overwhelming desire to scratch the back of my neck but can't touch it. I bite my tongue to distract myself from the itch before I slip over to the nest's other side. I hide behind some rocks so I can get a better look. The rumors of Astra tech being prevalent in the Tetrahedron are true, it seems.

That's a load off my shoulders ... wait a minute.

I touch my back. Junior is gone. He must have slipped off when I climbed down. A movement catches my eye, and I see our alien dragging his way toward the Astra ziggurat's pool.

"Junior," I whisper harshly and break cover to rush over with heated steps. "Junior, get back here."

He makes it to the edge before I'm able to scoop him back up.

"Lester would never forgive me if something happened to you. Let's get outta here."

The ground trembles as a large tentacle breaches the ziggurat pool's placid surface and slams in front of me. The gray Senior that attacked us earlier arises from the deep. The damage from Solis' shot has already healed. I scramble back with Junior in arms, but the Senior slams a long tentacle to the earth on either side of us. Acid drips from its appendages, sizzling to the ground. We're trapped.

"Can I interest you in not killing us?" Great final words, Ash. Very brave.

The Senior snaps an enormous beak, spraying spittle. I'll take that as a no.

<h1 style="text-align:center">18</h1>

— • —

Do Not Say Goodbye

The Senior encircles me in one of its tentacles. Its appendage sizzles with acid as it herds me toward its beak. A choked scream escapes me as I look down its throat. That's a lot of really sharp teeth. I think I'll take my chances with the acid. Junior climbs on top of my head and clicks his beak.

The Senior pauses, leans down, and I swear, cocks its core to one side.

Junior challenges it again and waves his arms. But he's weak and slips from my helmet to the ground. A tremor passes through the tentacle surrounding me. The Senior dips down into the water, causing the acidic pool to crest the edge and wash toward us. I hop back to keep the acid from damaging my suit. The Senior gulps acid by the beakful and spits it directly onto Junior.

Junior bathes in the waters, reveling in the steam.

Is it just me, or has his color improved? I think back to the missing blaster marks from the Senior's hide. Lester said he'd wanted to study the life here ... his instincts were spot on. They can communicate, so maybe I can talk my way out of this?

A tentacle tightens around me. My visor flashes warnings, and acid eats into my suit. The repair foam reserves are running low. Whatever charity there is for Junior, I am not so lucky.

"Ahhh!" A battle cry rings out.

Solis charges toward us with an uncomfortable Lester on the back of his inactive jetpack. Even Aide has found its way here and rides on Lester's head. Lester kicks out his legs wide and shouts directions as Solis plunders ahead.

"What are you doing!?"

"Saving our spy!" Solis shouts.

"Saving Junior!" Lester contradicts.

Aide shrugs two legs.

The Senior fully rises from the pool to meet them. My heart seizes as it readies a large tentacle to strike out. They're going to get themselves killed!

"Now!" Lester shouts not three meters from us. Solis drops to all fours. Strapped to Solis' back, Lester performs what I can only call an interpretive dance. He wriggles his arms and legs in an abnormal fashion. With morbid fascination, I watch as the Senior stops and studies them.

"Left leg! Now, right arm!" Lester shouts out commands, and Solis follows suit. Even Aide wiggles its robotic appendages in a mockery of the dance. It strikes me that I've seen these movements before ... Lester has them imitating Junior. It's ... it's insane.

Two tentacles crash to the ground on either side of them, bouncing them into the air. Underneath my terror, I realize that the Senior is mimicking their movements. Who knew the insane could be so effective? Thunderous limbs twist and stomp in unison with Lester and Solis, tossing me about in the process. My visor flashes an integrity warning as the acid nibbles away. I struggle, but the Senior isn't letting go.

"Stop!" Lester shouts, and I freeze, "We're not done negotiating."

"Negotiating?" I ask before it dawns on me.

Lester is doing what I'd failed to do. He's communicating.

The dance ends with Solis doing a handstand with a beet-red face and Lester contorting his arms behind his back. I can't understand it, but the Senior seems to. It ducks down, its beak a few centimeters from my crewmates' very fragile forms. The creature's entire body shutters. With a violent retching, the invertebrate hacks up a bubble of the acidic pool water with something half-digested inside it.

Is it … trying to feed them?

"That's not what we want. Kick it aside!" Lester shouts. Solis rotates back to standing and boots the offering into the pool. Lester makes a wild wiggling gesture in my direction, and I tense up. Before I can protest, the senior releases me, unceremoniously, in front of them.

"It worked!" Solis grins. He hunches upright with Aide and Lester on his back. Lester waves his arms in some type of thanks. Solis nods to me, "Quick, hop on. Try to look like you're being eaten."

"That's horrifying." But I don't need to be told twice. I jump up onto Solis' back, hugging Lester between us. I shake my head, glad for the lower gravity which helps Solis hold us. "Fresh Stars, you did it. I can't believe it."

"Believe it." Lester grins back at me. "I just had to convince the Senior that you'd give him indigestion, and we could devour you more easily."

"How sweet." I can't even be mad at the manchild.

The Senior, satisfied, leans back into the waters. Washing itself in the heat and disturbing a nearby patch of algae. Several eggs by the pondside hatch. The hatchlings attach themselves to their parent as it sinks deeper, but one watches us from the shoreline.

"Would you look at that?" Lester says with a hint of wonder, "It looks like Juniors and Seniors are both part of the same Cephalovoidus species. Or it could be a symbiotic relationship. Do you think—"

"How about we talk the wonders of life once we're out of here?" I ask with a gulp.

"Hold on," Solis grunts. "We have one more passenger."

Our Junior slides over to us, his color has returned to his customary deep purple, vibrant with life once more. The alien waves his arms excitedly as he scales Solis' legs. Junior launches himself at Lester and, immediately, slaps Aide off the manchild's head. Aide lands in the broken branches near Solis' feet. Angrily, it whirls its lens, but Junior ignores the aracbot. He's too busy wrapping all eight arms around Lester's helmet.

"There you are buddy!" Lester returns Junior's hug. "Ready to head home? I've got some rotten eggs waiting in Qual's fridge."

Junior pulls away. With a look of dismay, Lester watches as his buddy crawls on top of Solis' head and twists his arms together in a way I can only describe as fretful. The laughter in Lester's chest dies.

"What's wrong, Officer Orion?" Solis asks.

"Nothing." Lester quickly shakes his head. "A misunderstanding."

Lester makes a series of gestures with eight of his fingers. But Junior continues fretting, twisting into more and more intricate patterns and disrupting the nest's fog. Lester grows more frantic in his gestures. On the shoreline, other Juniors join the first and mimic the motions. Only one thing could rattle Lester this much.

"He wants to stay, doesn't he?"

"No." Lester's voice cracks. "He doesn't know what he wants."

Junior reaches his arms out and pats four tentacles against Lester's head. It's a gentle touch like a hand caressing a cheek. Lester's whole body begins to shake.

"I'm not ready." Lester chokes out as Junior curls into a ball. He snaps his beak one time and waves an arm at the pool. There, the Senior and its brood await him with curious swaying tentacles.

"He has a family here." Solis shifts our weight to one side.

"I could stay too," Lester whispers. "They need to be studied."

I glance around at the looming nests. "The only reason we're alive is they think we're one of them. What happens when that ruse fails?"

Lester takes a deep shuddering breath. "Ash, do you have an IC? We could kidnap him."

"Lester…"

"I know, I know. I just … I just don't know how to say goodbye."

"Don't say goodbye." Solis cranes his head to look at him. "Find your own parting words."

Lester sniffles, but he twists his hands into a shape I'd not seen before. Interlocking his thumbs and clutching his left hand with his right. Lester pulled his arms toward his heart and pushed them away, splaying his fingers. Junior mimics the motion with every arm, holding them to his body before releasing them in Lester's direction. Junior leaps down and races towards the pool where his brood awaits.

I can't help but ask, "What did you say?"

"Get lost."

"Really?"

"Yeah, I said," Lester stifles a sob, "get lost so I can find you again."

As Junior reaches the others, they welcome him home.

After climbing up the Senior's den, we proceed north. A half-hour of slowly making our way through the roots and avoiding bioluminescent algae, we still haven't found the *Helios*, but it's not a hard path to follow. Broken treetops litter the landscape in front of us, heralding the passage of a giant metal hull through their, thankfully, brittle branches. Solis carries Lester and I act as the perch for Aide.

"Woah, hold up." Solis raises a hand in warning as we approach a cliffside. He hasn't even broken a sweat, even with little Lester on his back. I stop, grateful for a rest. Lester hops down from Solis' back but doesn't say a word. Normally, I would appreciate that but now, it just feels wrong. Careful not to breathe too deeply, I check my suit's stats. Between the fall and acid splash, my visor shows several compromised components, auto-repair foam is nearly depleted, and the suit's supposedly endless lifespan has reduced to fifteen hours. I'll have to thank Griz for the upgraded suits; these things are tough.

Solis posts up on an overlook where black rocks have thrust through the endless tangle of roots. The cliff looks recent, in geological terms, like the ground split when planet Junior got hole-punched. The roots end a few feet from the edge. Lester wanders away along the cliffside, stopping a good ten meters from us to peer over the edge. It makes me nervous to see Lester's childlike form alone there. I turn to Aide.

"Keep an eye on him, please?"

The aracbot nods before scuttling off after Lester. It's been much more agreeable lately. Or maybe it's just keeping with its programming and keeping an eye on our crew. Either way, it's helping. As I join Solis, he smiles at me.

"Please tell me you can see the *Helios* from here?"

"See for yourself." Solis waves a hand over to the forest below. I peer over. About 150 meters away in a rocky clearing is the *Helios*. The algae's light provides a purple hue that glints off her circular hull. I've never seen anything that looked so sweet in all my life. And I can just make out two figures repairing a dent. Good to see Natashal and Qualsha are safe.

"Thank the Void." I smile and tension rolls off my shoulders. After everything, the *Helios* is still here. Once we get ourselves star-bound again, we'll be off to find Roxy, and I can complete my mission for the Boss. The *Helios* will be mine outright. I could find Lin a safe world to live on but … I'll have to leave the crew behind. All those knots twisted up in my gut can be cut loose into bittersweet bare threads. I can be free but, after everything we've been though together, do I want to be?

Turning to Solis, I find him staring.

"What's wrong?"

Solis glances away as a red tint colors his checks. "I owe you an apology."

"What?" I ask, not processing his words.

"I owe you an apology!" Solis shouts.

"Stop! I heard you for the first time." Scanning the forest, I make sure no local fauna heard that. "Forgive me, but can we save this for where we're safe? I don't like being out here in the open. If it's about calling me a Spy, don't worry about it. We're all feeling the effect of the Tetrahedron."

I try to scratch my neck but ... suit. Ugh. I can't wait to be back in the *Helios* and peel the spacesuit off. My back itches, and I think the foam has hardened in some unfortunate cracks.

"No, nothing like that. It's just, well, take this." Solis digs into a belt pouch and pulls out my silver CSO keycard. He pushes it into my gloves. "Lester gave it back to me while you were catching your breath earlier. You held up your end of the bet."

I weigh it in my gloves. I resist the urge to bite it to see if it's real, as if it is a gold nugget to be tested. Not that I could at the moment. I slip the keycard into my own pouch before facing Solis again. He starts to turn away, but I place a hand on his forearm.

"Does that mean you believe me now?" My pulse dances in my ears.

"I know you have secrets," Solis chooses his words carefully, "but I trust you."

"I need you to do me a favor then." I bite my lip.

Solis nods. "What is it?"

"Stop using the soulstone."

"Why?" Solis frowns.

"Because..." I can't tell him what it did to Lin. I'm not even sure I fully understand if the Terminal incident was caused by learning the truth or the soulstone. "Everyone has a limit. Just because you haven't hit your ceiling doesn't mean it won't affect you. Even someone attuned can end up like Junior."

His soft brown eyes never leave mine. "Okay."

"Thank you, Solis," I whisper, my hand still on his arm. He places a gloved hand over mine.

"Lin."

"Sorry?"

"Call me Lin."

Call me Lin.

Goosebumps trace up my arm. I feel an all-too-familiar fear of a road already traveled. This is wrong. He doesn't know what I did to Lin. After all the lies that led us here, I don't get a second chance. No one gets to reset reality. Guilt hits me full force in the gut, and I pull away.

"I don't think that's a good idea."

"It's just my name," he says with a joking half-smile.

"No. It's not just a name."

Solis' smile fades as he flushes with embarrassment. "Sorry. It's just—I thought—I'm misreading things."

"It's not like that, it's just. Well, it's common sense. I'm your CSO, anything more wouldn't end well."

Solis chuckles. "Ash, you're the least common sense CSO I know. After all the lessons the CSO Academy stuffed into your head, I think you've broken every single rule. On paper, you're terrible at your job."

"Um, thanks?"

"It's not a bad thing!" he clarifies. "What I'm trying to say is that you fit. There is no other CSO better for the *Helios*. You don't try to get everyone else to meet your boxy expectations of the universe. You adapt. More importantly, you care. About everyone, even when you don't mean to. That's what I—."

Solis stops himself.

But we both know his next words would have been. Lin already said them to me.

That's what I love about you.

Solis didn't mean to let that slip, but he's an honest man. It's what I ... what I admire about him. Why does this have to be complicated? Lin? Solis? It's like falling for twin brothers, but I can't explain it to him. I can't tell him anything. I can't ... can't I?

"I can't call you Lin."

Solis nods, disappointment plain. Before he can hide his face, I cradle the side of his helmet in my hand, so our eyes meet. I don't care about anything else in the universe but his eyes. Stars, I don't want him to look anywhere else.

"I can't call you Lin. I can't say that your uncanny wisdom drives me pleasantly insane. I can't say you have the most amazing smile I've ever witnessed. I can't say anything like that. Because if I say it, I won't be able to unsay it and that's dangerous. So, I can't." Chills race through me as the words just keep tumbling out. I don't have any sense left to hold them in. "What I can say is this: I've made mistakes. A *lot* of mistakes. Mistakes I need to fix before I can say anything I can't say. Does that make sense?"

"I can't say it does..." Solis says slowly, "but I can wait."

"I can't ask you to do that." I shake my head.

"You don't have to." Solis takes my free glove in his own. The touch makes me weak.

Fresh Stars, what am I doing?

A clearing throat brings me back to Planet Junior. I look down. Lester is watching us with mischievous eyes. Aide is in his hands. Oh no. Aide's lens zooms in on me and I pull away from Solis. Another mistake. How much did it record? I run through my words; I don't think I said anything problematic.

"I was just, um," Solis stretches for something, "helping Ash with her helmet."

"Is that what the kids are calling it these rotations?" Lester cracks a smile.

"What do you want?" I ask. My face feels flush and judging by Lester's increasingly wide grin, I'm not hiding it very well.

"Sorry to interrupt, but I think I found a way down." Lester hooks a thumb in the direction of the cliffside. "It'll take a bit to scale, but we should be able to reach the *Helios* in the next fifteen minutes or so."

"Why not just use your jetpack?" My voice cracks, and I cough to regain some composure. "Do you have fuel left?"

"Not in mine," Lester taps the side of his pack, "but I think the captain has some."

Solis nods in confirmation.

"How about you two go down first? Then Solis can come back for me?"

"Whatever you want, Sugar."

"Sugar?"

"Well, I can't call you Love anymore, right?"

"By the Void." Solis is right, I'm a terrible CSO. Never make a bet when you have Cosmic Fever.

"Come on, Captain," Lester waves a hand at the cliffside. "Let's get you two lovebirds back to the ship."

"We're not—" I start but Solis steps up.

"On it." He grabs Lester under the arm. Aide tightens its grip on Lester's forearm. The three are quite an odd grouping. Solis winks at me. "Be back soon."

I feel the heat in my cheeks. With the jetpack's fiery flourish, Solis and the others propel down the cliffside. I collapse down on a tree's roots by the edge. What am I doing? Why can't I keep from smiling? I can't afford to think like this ... No, I don't deserve to think like this. If there is going to be any sort of future, I need to set things right. Starting with Lin. I need to save him before I can entertain the idea of anything else. I flop back on the roots and stare at the starless sky.

"I have to fix things."

"What a nice idea." Ms. Honey's haggard form materializes on the roots above me. Her suit is gone, but pink splashes still cover her claws. Her body has adapted to the environment down to the same chitin armor as the Seniors. She grins down with serrated teeth. "Sshame it won't happen."

Her heel knocks across my helmet.

19

Do Not Get Captured

"*Common Sense Officer Ashreal Payne assigned to the* Helios, *reporting for duty." I issue a sharp salute. I've been training to be a CSO, just like my father before me. Mom always said, I may look like her but I'm his clone. When I told her about my new assignment on his old ship, she was so angry, calling me just as selfish as he was, but I'm sure she'll get over it soon.*

Standing in the Starprint hangar, I meet the expectant gaze of the Helios' *crew. A nervous-looking Science Officer Natasha Pollux waves at me in her oversized lab coat. Beside her, Engineering Officer Qual runs a hand through his thick black hair. A clean-cut Biologist Officer whose name I keep forgetting wipes a bit of dirt from his shoulder. Captain Lin Solis of the* Helios *stands in front of them all with shoulders broad enough to carry the mission.*

"Excited to be working with you." I thrust my hand forward for a shake.

Captain Solis ignores me and turns to Boss Aquila's Aide. "We don't need another corporate babysitter."

The little robot does its best shrug impression before skittering away. Rude, but I try not to take it personally. I'm a professional after all and I'm certainly not the first CSO to be seen as an outsider.

"I'm not a babysitter."

"Then why are you on my ship?" The captain crosses his arms.

"Just trying to keep you and yours alive."

"We haven't had an accident in orbits. No need for corporate over-sight," he retorts.

"And I aim to support that effort." I offer a cheeky salute and step aboard.

"What goess good with human sstew?

Ssome sspider bitss with broth brew.

Maybe ssome carrotss too."

Consciousness drags at me, reminding me that I'm alive in painful ways. An aching head is accompanied by a menagerie of bruises. The menu sounds awful, why do I have to hear it? Go away consciousness. Sleep is so much nicer right now. Such pleasant dreams.

"Officer Payne, do you gamble?" Captain Lin Solis asks me as I lean against his station's console on the bridge. The Spade Quadrant's starchart surrounds us as the Helios *skips solar systems, scanning them for Astra tech. We've some time to kill. Solis shuffles a card deck as he eyes me.*

"First time for everything." I shrug. "What are the rules?"

"Typical CSO asking about the rules." He raises an eyebrow.

"Typical Captain dodging my question." I snort in retort.

"Look, I know you're new to the crew—"

"I've been here six cycles."

"Newish. I know I've been standoffish, but you should understand what this crew means to me."

"A paycheck?" I regret the jibe as his brow darkens in distaste.

"No, I ... Look. Some people have families. Some people find them. Griz and Tera found me and gave me a home with Starprint Inc. I've been able to work my way to Captain. I'm fortunate that I can trust my crew with my life, unconventional as they may be. So, it was hard when Tera left, and Aquila took over. Harder still when Griz stepped down as acting CSO and you accepted the role."

"Is that why you were so opposed to my being here?"

"It was."

"Was?"

"Let's just say you're growing on me, Ash."

"Thanks, Captain."

"Please, call me Lin."

"What goess good in Human sstew?

Not robotss, ew ew,

But they pay the billss, it'ss true."

I dare to crack an eyelid open and fuzzy dots fill my vision. As it clears, I worry I've gone blind, and it takes a moment to realize that my helmet is covered with muck. I'm being dragged and bumping along. A deep breath irritates my ribs. Go away pain. Go away.

"I want to make a bet with you." Lin traces a finger across the small of my back. The cool evaporating sweat on my skin is chased away by the warmth of his fingertips. I'm lying on my stomach and enjoying the exhaustion ravaging my body. Our sheets are silky on my bare skin. We don't get vacation often, but the Terminal's Recreation ring really has the best accommodations. It's perfectly incognito here, which is great since we're not ready to tell the crew. All my CSO rules lay in a heap alongside our clothes on the floor.

"Hm, does it involve round three?" I murmur and peek at him from my pile of pillows. My long brown hair falls into my eyes. I blow it out of my face to see him better. It's strange, but he doesn't look as perfect as he once did. Lin's left eyebrow has a habit of sticking straight up and his black hair is in disarray. The latter is my fault I suspect, as is the hickey I've left on his neck and a few other choice locations. His face is too familiar to me now, I guess. I trace a finger along his cheek and linger on a scar hidden under his jawline. Such a little thing but I love the familiarity of the rough patch.

"You, Officer Payne, are relentless," Lin muses as he catches my hand and kisses the inside of my wrist. I feel myself pulse with pleasure at the touch.

"Work hard, play harder." Pulling myself forward, I move in for a kiss. I just want to feel the heat of him again. Lin catches me by the back of the neck and holds me back, gentle but firm.

"You didn't let me finish."

"That's not true at all," I tease.

"No one likes a pun." He scolds but there's a mischievous co-conspirator light his eyes.

"No one likes someone else's pun," I retort.

Lin shakes his head with a smile before he pulls me in once more. Kissing his lips makes me feel whole. It has been so long since I was able to let myself go and just enjoy something, someone! Lin pulls away and sits up in bed. He's still wearing that strange soulstone necklace. There is a blue twinkling light in the depths of that stone.

"Why don't you ever take that off?"

"Take what off?"

"The soulstone."

"Hm, guess I just forget about it sometimes." Lin taps it absently. I lose his attention as he stares off into his own thoughts. I turn over and sit

up. He takes the soulstone from his neck and places it on the nightstand. I've never seen him so nervous as he turns to face me. "There. No more distractions. Now, I have a bet for you."

"Fine." I pull my knees under my chin and rest my head on them. "What's the bet?"

"After this next mission, let's charter our own ship and go find Lost Earth."

"That's not a bet!" Laughing, I try to pull him to me but Lin resists. His face is serious.

"I mean it. It's your dream, and I want to help you. I love you, Ash." Lin's words resonate with the pounding in my chest. I kiss him again. Deeper. Slower. Breathlessly, I pull myself away from him.

"Yeah, I guess I love you too." My face hurts from smiling so much but I can't help it. Lin brushes some hair out of my face. A knock at the door interrupts us.

"Room service?" Lin asks as he jumps out of bed and slips on a bathrobe.

"I didn't order anything," I slip out of bed and pull my discarded underclothes back on.

"Then who—" Lin doesn't finish the sentence. An eerie crackling interrupts him as a blast fires through the door.

I'm too stunted to do anything other than stare as the man I love, my best friend, falls to the floor with a gaping hole in his chest.

"A fool wass made of me,

Revenge is a dissh besst sserved with tea.

My employerss will be sso pleassed."

Sulfur invades my senses. Has my suit been damaged? Will I start to get giddy as the oxygen levels decline? That's okay, I'm not using my oxygen anyway ... Hehe. Why is it so hot? I can't stay here, but I don't want to go back to my dreams. They are turning on me, hurting me inside and out.

Lin stands in Starprint Inc.'s clone laboratory covered in blood. Flanking either side of him are a couple dozen smashed medical vats. I don't look down. I don't want to see the bodies of the clones that used to occupy them. But Lin doesn't notice them at his feet. He has turned back to me and is smiling as if he'd just accidentally spilled some milk. Lin, my Lin, is back. Just like I'd wanted, but he is not the same. The soulstone I used to revive him broke his mind.

"What have you done?" My heart breaks with each word.

"Only what was right." Lin brushes blood off his cheek. "Come on now, help me find the self-destruction for this laboratory. Should be around here somewhere."

He walks away, but I grab his arm.

"Relax, I'm going to take care of everything." Lin pats my head. "Just as soon as I destroy this laboratory, we can run away together. Believe me, I've got this."

"No."

"No?" Lin's smile falters. "What do you mean no?"

"This isn't you. You're not a killer."

"You don't get to decide what I am," Lin scoffs. His grip on my hand tightens, and I wince, pulling away from him. Anger creeps across his features, "You're afraid of me."

"Yes, you're not well." I stagger back.

"No, no. Not you. You're not supposed to be afraid. They said you wouldn't be afraid." Lin holds his temples, messaging them. The soulstone around Lin's neck hasn't stopped twinkling with light, like it's

laughing. With his free hand, he waves at the nearest clone's vat, labeled 211. "You're considering replacing me, aren't you?"

"No. I don't want to replace you."

"But you knew about the clones? You knew, and you never said anything. Why?" Lin's eyes are feverish as he takes a step toward me. "If you knew what was going on, why would you ever take part in it?"

"My whole job is to make sure the clones aren't needed. I want to keep you safe."

"Liar." Lin's only centimeters away from me. I back up against the nearest vat. It bubbles and sloshes as I press myself against it.

"What would you have had me do?"

"Tell me the truth."

"To what end?"

"So, I can fix it. All of it. Every blasted person involved in this Terminal's scheming."

"You can't be serious."

"I'm serious. You know me. I can do it too. If you could hear things like I do..." He shakes his head. "If you ever loved me, you would help me."

"I don't want that." The faces of my mother, Griz, and even Dare pass through my mind. "There are people here I want to protect."

"I know you, Ash. Believe me when I say I can deal you a better hand than the universe ever gave you." He holds up a bloody hand to my cheek. "Do you believe me?"

"You know I do." My voice cracks. I throw myself backward and jam my elbow into the fire alarm case and pull the handle down. The lab's alarm finally screams to life. Lin stares at me in disbelief. I straighten myself. "That's why I have to stop you."

"Wakey, wakey."

Consciousness greets me with a swift kick to the head. The stars I'm seeing are all in my mind. I wish that was the only thing in there, but my memories haunt me. I try to push them down again, but it's too fresh. I just want some peace, but that isn't in the cards.

Through my dirt-smudged and warning-flashing visor, it's clear I'm still very much on Planet Junior. The steaming acid pool I'm draped over like a grilling steak is a dead giveaway. Even from three meters below me, the immense heat toasts me inside my suit. Wide-spaced roots dig into my bruised and protesting muscles. The pool is small, just big enough to properly roast an idiot CSO who got herself captured and surrounded by wide-spaced roots and the hot mud that is Planet Junior's underlayer. Algae surrounds the pool below, giving everything a purple under glow.

ICs lay scattered nearby, both on the upper roots and in the mud below. Ms. Honey's ship venting was impressively thorough. A broken IC slowly sinks into the muck below. Inside are several of Natasha's contraband blasters. One of her Jokers has fallen onto a nearby tree's roots. If I can get to it ... I struggle to stand, but a clawed foot pushes me down.

"No, no, you're not ready to turn over yet," Ms. Honey mocks. I gasp as she digs her heel into my back. A chill runs through me, of all the ways to die in space, being eaten isn't my first choice. Craning my neck, I get a better look at her. Honey's new chitin skin is unbothered by the heat, and she breathes easily in this loose atmosphere. I think Lester's rumors about slizard adaptability are well founded.

"I bet you're wondering who hired me, right?" Ms. Honey leans in close and her breath fogs up my view. I think back on her dragging me through the muck. Between Honey's vocal musings and the fact that the Terminal attacks were perpetrated by bots, an idea clicks into place—for all the good it will do me.

"BS2. I'm guessing they funded you and Hijack to disrupt competition." I wheeze out.

"But I'll never tel—wait, how did you know that?" Ms. Honey rears back as her sideways eyelids flutter.

"You sing when you're happy," I reply. Sometimes the most obvious answer is just the truth. BS2 were the only Big Three member not impacted by the Terminal fiasco, but they are playing a dangerous game. Honey may not have ideals beyond money and revenge, but—Natasha's wound from Witshade crosses my mind—Hijack's Reclaimers want bloody revolution.

Not that I've much time to worry about others.

The pond's heat is unbearable, but I can't move. I need to keep her talking, distracted until I can find a way free. "Guess they paid you a good deal of glint to stow away into the Tetrahedron. Happy with your new planet?"

"We were never ssupposed to end up here." Honey presses harder into my back. Pain makes me gasp. "You ruined my plan to ssteal the sship. My partners will be ... dissappointed. Witsshade wanted that ship dearly for his collection."

"The android? Black armor with a penchant for knife hands?"

"Don't concern yoursself. Questionss will only make the meat tough."

"You should let me go. If you kill me, you'll never get off this planet."

"What makess you ssay that?" The slizard's foot leaves my back. I get a breath in before Honey yanks my helmet up, straining my neck. She levels her maliceful gaze with my own.

"The *Helios* is the only ship on this planet," I say, arching my back to ease the pressure on my neck. "No way in or out of the Bermuda Tetrahedron without it. At this point, the crew will be looking for me. If you kill me, you have no bargaining chip to get out of here."

"Hm, you think you're sso ssmart, but you forget." Ms. Honey grins at me and slowly, her skin sheds away. Small features become more and more humanoid with a clearly conscious effort. Her jawline shrinks, and her lips become more defined. Scaley skin peels away in rippling waves, dropping into the boiling acid below. Eyes turn from mustard yellow to soft blue. Honey has on her Ash disguise once more, complete with Starprint uniform. "After I kill you and ssteal your ssuit, I'll take your place and esscape."

"You don't even look like me," I lie.

"What?" Ms. Honey drops me in disgust. I cling to the roots to keep from falling into the sulfur pool. She crosses her arms. "What's misssing?"

"Freeze! Hands in the air."

Below us, Solis stands balanced on roots six meters away in a muddy Starprint spacesuit. He's holding Natasha's discarded Joker. When did he change from the BS2 checkers back to Starprint? Was I out long enough for the Tetrahedron effects to revert? Doesn't matter. I've never been so happy to see his face.

Honey hisses in anger as she raises her hands.

"Fresh Stars! It's good to see you." I scramble to my feet.

"No, both of you, I said freeze!" Solis levels his weapon at me before I get far.

"You can't be serious?" I crack a half-smile, but his stance is combative. His eyes are wild as he points the Joker back and forth between us ... Can he really not tell us apart? Ms. Honey lets out a low hiss that takes me a moment to recognize as laughter.

"I guesss we'll find out who makes a better CSsO, ey Ashy?" she whispers.

Fool a captain once, shame on the sinister reptilian alien.

Fool a captain twice, shame on his CSO for not teaching him better.

Solis just stands there, deciding who to shoot. The palm of his hand is against his visor like he's trying to reach through his helmet and press away a headache.

"They are clearly the impposster." Ms. Honey nods her head at me. She straightens her posture and holds her head up high. The slizard accents each word with a self-righteous confidence that I resent, "Sshoot her!"

"Oh, come on! I don't even talk like that!" I keep my hands up and shake my head.

"Oh, come on! I don't even talk like that!" Ms. Honey mimics my words and motions.

"Will you stop it?!"

"Will you sstop it?!"

"She doesn't even have a suit on! She's clearly the slizard!"

A shot into the tree beside us shuts us up. Algae radiates out, a red bullseye, from the impact. I mutter a curse. Solis just rang the dinner bell. Those giant Seniors could return any second to tear us limb from limb. What is he thinking!?

"Will you both stop it?" he shouts, still holding his helmet. His eyes have deep lines under them, and his nose is bleeding. What in Planet Hell happened while I was out?

"Solis—"

"Stop calling me that!" He shakes violently. I've not seen Solis behave like this. The only person who—my breath catches as I see a broken supply crate and a coffin-sized IC behind him. Cold realization falls into place.

"Lin." It's not a question, but a fact. His appearance makes all the sense in this world. He isn't hurt, he's waking up. Just like the rest of the ICs, Lin's was ejected from the *Helios* by Ms. Honey's sabotage.

"Lin?" Honey parrots me and cocks her head. The memories I'd swatted away return and hold my breath hostage. Lin smiles, but there is no joy in it, just a harshness that infects all his features. He raises an imperfect eyebrow.

"Hey Ash, long time no see." Lin pulls the trigger.

20

DO NOT HAVE A TELL

Lin's Joker blast flashes.

Next to me, Ms. Honey stumbles back. A wheezing sound, like a hole in an air hose, escapes the thumb-sized hole in her forehead. Black blood drains from the wound as her body finally catches up to the fact that it's dead. Honey's knees give out. She topples over root's edge and splashes into the pool with a sickening sizzle. Acid sprays onto the algae, causing soft red ripples. The bioluminescent light cascades across Lin's face.

"Honestly, how have you stayed alive without me?" Lin motions the Joker at me to come down from the roots. I don't move a muscle. My visor flashes overheating warnings as if the bubbling below wasn't enough warning.

"What do you want?" I keep my hands visible. Nice and slow, I shuffle away from the boiling pit toward the tree.

"What do I want?" Lin cocks his head. "I mean, revenge would be a nice start."

I toss myself to a large root *just* in time to dodge his next shot. Splinters rain down on me as I roll to the root's opposite side out of his line of sight. The root layer is thicker here, but my arm slips through a gap. I snatch it back before another shot impacts the root I'm hiding behind.

"After all, you did betray me," Lin calls from below, "I asked for your help, and you set off the damned alarm. You could have at least stayed out of my way."

Adrenaline drives me as I crawl toward the tree trunk. There's a small alcove I can use for cover. A couple more blasts above me rain more debris down. He's just toying with me now.

"Funny thing about stasis. Contrary to what you might think, it's not like sleeping. You are very much awake. More importantly, it gives a man a lot of time to think. Your own mind starts to whisper to you. Those thoughts get so loud but so very clear. You must see it, right? It's not just the Terminal that's a problem. It's everything. I have to fix it."

Crawling on the roots, I press my back into the tree's rough bark and accidentally brush against algae that bloom red with heat. But all my fear is reserved for Lin as he climbs up to my hiding place. His shadow passes over me, and I hold my breath.

Lin tilts his head and locks his eyes on mine. "There is one question I'd like you to answer. As I was stuck in that box waiting for the incinerator to take me, one question kept ringing and ringing and ringing around in my ears."

"Lin, please." Slowly, using the tree for support I stand. "You're not well."

"Don't lie to me again!" Lin growls. I flinch back. He takes a deep, shuddering breath. "Just answer my question. Why am I still alive?"

"What do you mean?"

"Why didn't you incinerate me after the Boss ordered you to?" Lin asks and, for a second, the fever in his eyes mellows, "Why would you ignore him?"

"I don't know." My mouth is dry.

"That's not good enough!" Lin shakes his head. "It would have been easy. How could you not?"

"Because … it's my fault. You died, Lin. I used the soulstone to try to heal you. I thought it would help you, like it had so many times before, but it brought you back *wrong*. It's made you violent. This isn't you." I open my hands wide, pleading with the man I used to know. "Please, let me help you."

Lin measures me with his gaze. I'm busted, bruised, and backed into a corner. There is no use in lying to him. He must know that. If he really could hear me all those times in the IC, he must know I want to help him. Otherwise, why would he ask me all this?

He cocks his head as if listening for something, before he nods.

"We thank you for your honesty." Lin aims the Joker at my heart. It doesn't take a CSO to know how this ends.

"No!" Solis crashes into Lin.

His BS2-checkered spacesuit tangles with Lin's Starprint blue and gold as they go sprawling. They fall from root to root, dropping the three meters below and narrowly missing the acidic pool. I wobble to the edge. The two impact and roll sizzling across the muddy ground and the Joker's blast flashes white hot. A scream escapes my lips as I see the hole in Solis' abdomen.

"Why?!" Lin scrambles to his feet as Solis twists in pain. He fires two more times.

My body moves before my brain knows what I'm doing, launching me from the tree at Lin, knees first. He braces and catches me. A tangle of bodies ends with me tumbling to the steaming ground. Lin's knee pins me down. The Joker's muzzle presses into the side of my helmet. Solis grabs his boot, but Lin kicks him off.

"Didn't you hear us?! Why would you save this traitor?" Lin asks Solis.

Solis sits up nursing his injured side as steam rises around him. His suit's auto-repair kicks in and foam fills the gaps as he leans back against the tree's roots. Solis' breath comes in deep labored gasps, but I can see that radiant blue of the soulstone underlighting his features. It must be healing him.

"I heard. She lied." Solis gasps out the words with conviction. My throat seizes. Solis *knows*. He knows he is a clone. When Lin learned this, he changed. As much as I want to blame the soulstone, part of me doesn't believe it. Maybe it is just something inside Lin and Solis. My captain's eyes meet mine, and he smiles. "But Ash is a part of my crew. I'd never hurt her."

Relief washes over me as tears sting my eyes.

In my peripheral, a twisted grin distorts Lin's face. He kicks me aside and sends me rolling. My back crashes against IC210 and the air is knocked out of me. Lin turns on Solis and kicks his wounded side. Reaching over, he releases Solis' helmet seal. Warning alarms blare. Solis gasps, and his eyes water as he breathes in the sulfuric atmosphere.

"You don't get to replace me," Lin says grimly. "I'm taking what's mine."

Lin rips the soulstone from Solis' neck. His greedy eyes are practically reverent as he holds it high above him.

The fog and the trees groan in protest before three massive gray tentacles slam into the root layer above us. Lin jumps and twists to look up. His eyes widen in surprise as the tentacles' spikes extend and dig into the roots.

A Senior has arrived.

It opens its cavernous beak and screeches. I don't move, hoping that my heat signature will blend with the mud after being nearly cooked alive. But Lin? Lin, he doesn't know a damn thing about these creatures. He curses and stumbles onto the roots, making him a beacon.

The Senior zeroes in on him. It rears back and snaps forward with startling speed. Its beak crashes into the roots just above Lin's head. He opens fire into the Senior beak. It shakes its core as it falls back as if to get a bad taste out of its beak. Lin flees through the forest's underlayer with the stolen soulstone, sprinting nimbly from root to root as the Senior chases after.

I don't wait a second. Crawling over to Solis' side, I grab his discarded helmet and fumble to reattach it. I hit the emergency purge valve, and he gasps gratefully as fresh air fills his lungs.

"It's okay Solis, you're going to be okay." I crouch down beside him and check his halocom to call for help. It's broken, smashed in his tumble with Lin. We need help, and I'm not going to get it by sitting here. I wrap an arm around his waist and try to move him. "Don't worry. I'll get you to the *Helios*."

"I won't make it. I can't feel my legs." Solis says in labored breaths. He gently pushes me away, and I kneel beside him in the roots. His wounds drip with blood and sealing foam. There is no telling how long the suit will last with that damage.

Stop. Don't panic. Has his face always been this pale? I have to reassure him. "Yes, you will." I force a smile, but I can't meet his eyes.

"You're lying." Solis tries to laugh, but it turns into a bitter cough. "You always stare at your shoes when you're nervous. It's your tell."

"I do not..." I force myself not to look at my boots again. He might just be right about that. I shake my head. "Did you know I've been lying this whole time?"

Solis offers a crooked smile "I knew ... you had secrets, but I trusted you had your reasons. Didn't expect that reason to shoot me, though. Why didn't you tell me?"

"Please, I need to get you out of here. If you just—"

"Ash, just tell me." Solis smirks at me. "Consider it a final order."

The gravity held in those words crashes down on me. It makes me notice the little things, like his shoulder's shivering or the way the color has drained from his lips. I wish I could wipe my tears away but ... suit. "Because I wasn't sure if it was the soulstone that changed him or the truth. I didn't want you to end up like him ... I couldn't risk it."

"It's sobering ... seeing the worst version of yourself. I don't want to be a monster like him ... I would never hurt you." Solis reaches up as if to wipe the tears from my soaked cheeks but settles for holding my visor. "The gap in my memory. That's where you fit, isn't it?"

"Stop." I gently brush his hand away. It falls to the wayside too easily. "Please."

"Ash—"

I shake my head. He doesn't have enough time for me to get him back to the ship and I don't have enough time to get help and return. I need a third option. I need more time ... and I think I know how to get it.

"Hang on." I race over to the fallen IC210 that Lin once inhabited. The IC is functional other than the broken latch. It should give me enough time to get to the *Helios* and come back with help. I scramble back to Solis who is rapidly losing consciousness and slap at his visor. "Stay awake. I need you to stay with me a little while longer."

Getting an arm around his waist, I all but drag him to the container. He pulls himself along wherever handy roots hang down, but his feet are useless. I feel his body tense as we get close to the IC, but he doesn't object. He shivers as he enters the open IC. As designed, it is a perfect fit.

Before I can close the lid, Solis grabs my hand. "Make a bet with me."

"Anything."

"Bet me that you'll be the one to wake me?"

"Of course, I will." I grasp his hand in mine.

For a moment, eternity has nothing on us. It's only him, me, and a bet. The IC's gel begins to harden, and Solis releases me. He closes his eyes as I shut the lid. I'm shaking and I'm all too aware of the tears on my cheeks. I try to wipe them away, but … I twist the control value and vent oxygen to clear my visor.

My tears sizzle on Planet Junior's surface.

Moving as fast as my injuries allows, I follow the *Helios'* trail of destruction. I had to leave Solis' IC behind as I ran for help. I must move fast. There's no telling what Lin will do. The cliffside scramble is the worst of it. I take too much time navigating the path of interwoven roots and rocks that Lester had pointed out earlier. Along the way, more ICs are scattered in the *Helios'* wake. Ignoring them, I put one foot in front of the other. I need to warn the crew before Lin does any more damage. I'm almost to the clearing when I find something large and gray in my path. I crouch into the roots, but it doesn't notice me. It doesn't move at all. Cautiously, I approach. It is the Senior that was chasing Lin.

Dead.

Lester will be furious. Scorch marks cover its exoskeleton, but the killing blow is reserved for the Joker jammed in its beak. Lin must have distracted it somehow, gotten in close, and blasted out its inners. Movement catches my eye, a small robotic leg twitching under the tip of one Senior tentacle. I know that leg. Bracing my back against the tentacle, I plant my feet and lift. With a groan, I'm able to get the tentacle a whole twenty centimeters off the ground. It's enough. Aide scrambles out from under the felled Senior.

Its cracked lens zooms in on me, and it shakes his head disapprovingly.

"Good to see you too. Where are the others?"

Aide turns its focus skyward, and I hear it: the *Helios'* whirring engines. Less than a hundred meters away, my ship lifts skyward. An orange light coalesces around the engine vents. It's beautiful against the starless sky. I blink as the ship spins out into the Tetrahedron.

My ship, no more.

We're stranded on Planet Junior.

ACT 4: THE GUTSHOT

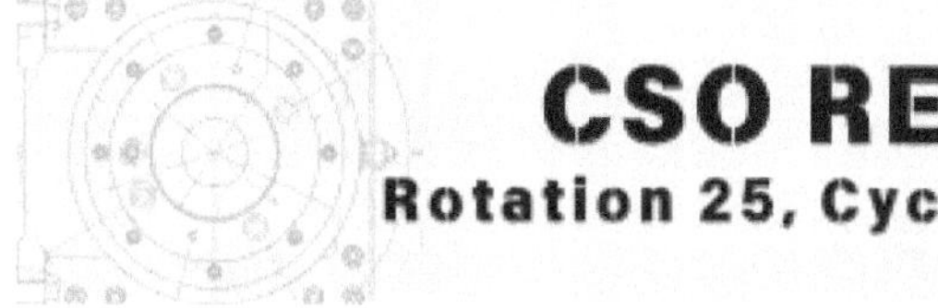

CSO REPORT
Rotation 25, Cycle 11, Orbit 70

SHIP STATUS: STOLEN

STORAGE CONTAINS	STORAGE DISPOSED
[Empty]	1 Slizard assassin, Ms. Honey

CSO SUMMARY

- Mission: A steaming pile of Senior Shit
- Transit: Who knows?
- Notes: CSO storage is empty due to a slizard assassin venting the entire ship into Planet Junior's upper atmosphere. The Helios and crew have been stolen by a murderous psycho, but I can't do anything because I'm marronned on a planet filled with giant hungry Cephalovoidus ... it's going great.

21

— · —

Do Not Get Left Behind

I've decided that common sense only takes you so far in life.

For me, that's a clearing on the outskirts of the bioluminescent forest in the Bermuda Tetrahedron. Here the scorch marks from the *Helios* engine's vents cool. Aide and I wander around the clearing. I'm numb as I find my smiley face stress ball. I nudge it with my foot before picking it up and giving it a squeeze. Is this what shock feels like? I think I'm in shock.

What lie did Lin tell the crew so they'd leave us behind? Lin is identical to Solis. He could easily have impersonated the captain and tricked them into jumping planet. Maybe he told them he'd been too late to save their CSO from being eaten by a slizard. It wouldn't have been a hard sell. Will they be safe with Lin? I don't want to think about that. I can't do anything to help from here. I can't even save myself.

"You don't happen to have a halocom in there do you?"

Aide shakes his head.

"Damn, that would have been useful."

I step away and scream into the void. Flopping back onto some roots beside a boxy IC, I stare at the inkblot sky. My visor's warning has suit lifespan reduced to twelve hours. The whiffs of Planet Junior's rotten egg smell are getting stronger and burn my nose, signaling the auto-repairs continuing to fail. Will my suit fail first? Or maybe a Senior would be so kind as to swallow me whole? Okay good, I feel something again. Too bad its unilateral terror.

Earlier with Lin, I'd felt prepared to accept my fate, but now? Solis needs me.

Slapping my helmet, I try to focus.

There must be something I can do, but where do I go from here? It has been so long since I've been truly alone. The *Helios* always has someone causing mischief. Solis would have some bit of wisdom on how not to give up. Lester would have some crazy idea involving the Seniors, no doubt. Natasha's idea would definitely involve an absurd number of explosives. Certainly, Qual would have unleashed a new invention upon this unsuspecting world.

From atop the IC, Aide leans over me.

"I was so close, Aide. If I'd just noticed the slizard sooner, we'd have been on our way to Roxy as planned. I would have been able to accept the Boss' offer, buy the *Helios*, and find somewhere safe for Lin. Somewhere he could have gotten treatment. But now the crew is … Solis is…" I clench my hands together and give my stress ball a squeeze, before stuffing it into my suit's belt pouch.

Aide pokes me with a metal leg, but I wave it away.

"Don't bother me. I'm busy contemplating the end."

"Contemplating the end," my own voice echoes back. Beastie materializes beside me.

"Beastie!" I throw my arms around his neck. "You're here. Why are you here? Did you get left behind too?"

He chirps as the soulstone on his head glows a brilliant but cold violet. How is he alive without a suit? Not that we had a Beastie-sized suit, but … my mind spins. His ethereal nature or the soulstone itself must be helping him. Either way, if he's fazed by the environment, he's not showing it. I wish I had that level of adaptability. Aide jumps out off the IC and circles Beastie excitedly, no doubt very happy to capture the fact that the special animal from Doomirage is not in enemy hands. So much for my promise to Natasha. After all the life and death situations, I couldn't care less about Aquila's plans.

"Well, any ideas gang?" I ask my fellow marooned companions. Beastie cocks his head to the side, and Aide pauses recording. "We're stuck on this planet. Nobody has a halocom and, while you two are good with this atmosphere, I'm not going to last forever."

Aide raises a metal leg and swivels its eye back and forth.

"What is it?" I'd not been expecting an answer. Aide's bright red light shoots out from the lens and displays a halo recording. Aide's viewpoint on the ground looking up from beneath tree roots. It's the nesting ground, complete with prowling Seniors. The view changes to focus on the egg-covered Astra ziggurat, but from a new angle. Embedded at the top and half-covered in Senior dung, is the metallic sheen of a Resonator.

I suck in a breath. As I learned from Natasha, where there is a Resonator, there is a way to send a universal beacon. That might be the only signal that'll penetrate the Tetrahedron's weirdness. If *Helios'* crew sees it, will they know to come back for me?

How am I going to get to the Resonator? Normally, I'd have my crew and gear at my back. Now all I have to work with is a semi-trustworthy robot and a hungry Spirit Beast ... That's not entirely true. I purse my lips as I look around the crash site. ICs lay scattered across the clearing. If I could harness the dangers inside those containers ... Every instinct screams that this can only end poorly, but what do I have left to lose?

"I think ... we're going to have to get a little creative."

Staring at Seniors moving in the fog, I'm struck by how royally screwed we are. From my hiding place in the roots overhanging the Cephalovoidus nest, I've seen not one, not four, but twelve Seniors wandering in and out of the nesting grounds. Beside me, Beastie chirps and bristles his feathers. He's not a fan of the creatures below. I think his invisibility trick won't work well on them. He clutches the two small ICs in his talons a little tighter. Across the nest, Aide oversees the distraction.

"Get ready." I pat Beastie's side. "It'll be any second now."

It's closer to a minute before an explosion erupts in the forest beyond, flames a brilliant neon blue in the sulfuric atmosphere.

"Thank you, Natasha," I whisper as her smuggled explosives—that I'd confiscated half an orbit ago—brighten the starless sky. I can feel the heat from here, and so can the Seniors. The thermal-sensitive creatures aren't fans. At least ten burst from the fog and weave through the trees toward the perceived danger. The forest trembles with their eerie wails.

It's time. Removing the ICs slung over Beastie's sides, I open the first one. Inside is a collection of Junior's eggs. I stick them in my belt's pouches like an icky bandolier. Opening the second, I retrieve Qual's shrink ray that, occasionally, explodes its target and ready it under my arm.

"No chance you can do this part?" I cast a glance at Beastie.

"You can do this part." He bobs his head.

"Thanks for the vote of confidence."

I head down the hillside in a much more controlled fashion than my last visit. Sneaking is much easier on my ribcage, but nothing is comfortable right now. At the bottom, I hide behind the nest from earlier. It's hard to see here, but I know there should be at most two Seniors remaining. I need to lure them out. Taking several Junior eggs from my belt, I roll the eggs out into the open between me and the egg-coated ziggurat. It doesn't take long for the first Senior to arrive, attracted by the cold oval egg.

As Senior reaches down, I charge Qual's shrink ray. It whirls and the Astra runes on its side alight with a green glow. I cross my supporting hand's fingers, steady my aim, and pull the trigger. One moment, the enormous Senior looms over the egg, and the next it all but disappears with little more than a whisper. Thankfully, it doesn't explode. That would likely have attracted more Seniors, and Lester would be pissed if he ever found out. I should have at least ten minutes before it reverts to its normal size.

Rolling out another egg, I wait.

Precious minutes pass with no sign of the last Senior.

Condensation drips down my visor. I can't wait any longer. Keeping Qual's shrink ray charged, I step into the fog. My breath is deafening as I take sizzling steps across the stones and make my way to the Astra ziggurat pool. The ziggurat must have sunk over time because it's only three stepped pyramid levels to the top where the Resonator sits. An Astra-sized stairwell joins the levels. Eyeballing it, I'd say it's about ten meters to climb. It's only two meters to jump across the pool to the ziggurat's first ledge, but it might as well be kilometers. Considering my alternative plan is to asphyxiate, I guess I'll jump. Leaning over it, I tense as bubbles burble to the surface, but there are no giant Seniors in its depths. Taking a deep breath, I wince as my ribs remind me I'm not allowed to do that. Grinding my teeth, I ignore them and leap across the gap, landing on the ziggurat's eggy base.

My foot slips on the slimy eggs. They don't break, but squish like over-full water balloons before shooting out from beneath my boots. Landing visor-first, I slip down toward the acid pool but dig my free glove between the eggs and catch some ancient ledge underneath. Heart hammering, I drag myself away from the pool which is mere centimeters from my boots. Rolling onto the stairs, I release a shuddering breath and rest the shrink ray by my side.

I'd made it.

An unfamiliar green Junior tentacle clamps onto my visor. It tries pecking me. Screaming, I grab its core with my free hand and throw it from my visor. The Junior flies into the pool below. Scrambling upright, I glance over the edge at the bubbling liquid, the shrink ray in my hands at the whirling ready. Another Junior swims to the surface and snaps its beak at me. I watch in horror as more surface and join it. They begin to climb.

With a renewed adrenaline spike, I follow suit and scramble up the ziggurat. One hand in front of the other I go, not caring if I smash an egg or two. As I do so, the mini creatures tumble down into the pool below, wake, and begin to chase me as well. Not far behind, the first few Juniors swarm up my bumbling path. My hands tremble as I clear the last ziggurat level, and race to the Resonator. It's encased in slime and dung. I can hear the slithering of Juniors approaching as I slam the butt of my weapon into the encasing gunk: once, twice before the Resonator falls free onto the stepped pyramid's surface.

The runic black obelisk absorbs attention alongside light, but it has some stiff competition at the moment. I scoop it up in gloved hands. It's surprisingly warm to the touch but not unbearably so. Without this artifact, we're trapped on this world. I clutch it to my chest as the Juniors begin to creep over the ziggurat's upper ledge.

"Plan B!" I shout skyward. "It's time for plan B!"

Nothing happens. With a gulp, I turn to face the onslaught of Juniors. The green one that first attacked leads the slithering charge, flanked by three more of various sizes. I ready the shrink ray, and they warily encircle me. Then, from a nearby pool—the last Senior arises. It drips with acid and fog as it lumbers toward me.

Well ... this could have gone better.

The Senior wails and the Juniors join its chorus with chittering excitement. They swarm toward me. I fire at the Senior with the shrink ray but the device sputters in my hand. Void! Why can't Qual just build normal inventions? The first few Juniors reach my feet, and I kick them back. A larger one grabs me, and I beat at it with my useless weapon until it wrenches the shrink ray from my hands. I'm done for.

"Time for plan B!" Beastie swoops down and plucks me up in his talons.

My stomach lurches as it tries to catch up to the rest of me. One Junior clings to my boot until I kick it off. It lands with a splash in the pool below. We did it! We have a chance now. I stuff the Resonator under my arm and cling to Beastie as we fly higher.

Below, the crowd of Cephalovoidus disperse in hungry disappointment. I catch a glimpse of a tiny purple form waving goodbye at me. It's hard to tell but I think it might be Lester's Junior. I wave back. This will be the last time I ever see the slippery nuisance. I feel like I should have brought a parting gift, maybe something round ... Slipping my free hand into my pocket, I pull out my stress ball. The yellow face smiles back at me.

"Good luck!" I shout as I drop it below. Junior catches it and waves it above his head. I crack a smile and tighten a grip on the Resonator. It's time for everyone to go home.

Beastie lands in a grove where we'd made camp. It is a modest spot—not too far from the confrontation with Lin—but it has dense trees to provide cover, thick roots to stand on, and several choice ICs for protection. I don't see Aide yet, but I suspect it'll be here soon. The little aracbot is surprisingly fast. I wince as Beastie sets me down. My ribs remind me that I need to stop with all the moving business.

I check on Solis, where IC210 is wedged between some roots. We'd moved him down here earlier before the raid on the nest. Through the small viewport, I catch a glimpse of his face. He looks ... constipated. If Lin had been telling the truth, then Solis can hear me.

"Hey," I shake the Resonator at him. "Good news. We have a way off this rock."

Taking a seat beside his IC, I turn the obelisk's four sides over in my hands. The back of my neck itches fiercely, but I ignore it and focus on the device. When Natasha activated the Doomirage Resonator, she'd had to do two things. First, she'd asked Solis to charge the bugger. Second, she'd aligned the runes by twisting the obelisk like an ancient alien puzzle box.

One of Resonator's sides has a large composite eye at the top. Underneath it are a set of ten Astra runes. If it's not already in alignment, I'll have to brute force it ... Void, I hope it's in the right alignment. It gives me hope to see that the pattern starts and ends with the three-concentric-circles rune. Natasha had used that in the pattern for the Doomirage door.

Well, no use wasting time, I should try to charge it first.

"Here, hold this." I press the Resonator into Beastie's claws and wait for the soulstone in his forehead to react but ... nothing happens. Okay, that would have been too easy, I guess. I scratch the starting combination into a nearby root before trying others. Each time I pass it back to Beastie and it fails, my anxiety grows. Precious minutes tick by as I exhaust each combination. I'm going to be pissed if I spend my last rotation alive messing with this damned thing.

It chooses who it helps and who it harms.

Solis' words bubble up from the back of my exhausted mind. Beastie plops down beside me and puts his very large head on my lap. The violet soulstone in his forehead all but winks at me. My visor had every warning flashing in the peripherals of my vision. I'm not ignorant of what the stone did to Lin but ... Do I have any other option?

I lean into the pressure of Solis' IC at my back. He's counting on me.

I twist the Resonator back to its original pattern before retrieving a vine-like root nearby. Fashioning a torniquet, I wrap it around my left arm. I try not to think too much as my fingers go numb. With an uncertain breath, I remove my left glove. My oxygen levels lower slowly, and I'm certain my skin will sting from the exposure. Grabbing the Resonator with my bare hand, I touch it to Beastie's soulstone. Closing my eyes, I reach out with a pinky and press into the violet Astra soulstone. I wait to feel that blossoming power which allows Solis so many amazing feats of strength.

Any second now.

Aaaany second now.

I crack my eyes and note that nothing much has changed. Glancing down, I watch the soulstone pulse faintly, as if it's giggling at me.

"Why isn't it working?" I ask Beastie but he's started to snooze in my lap.

Forgetting my ribs, I take a deep breath and … it doesn't hurt. There is an easiness that I've missed desperately over the past few hours. My chest tingles like I'd just swallowed some carbonated candy. Under my pinky, Beastie's soulstone begins to glow. Beside it, the Resonator sputters and sparks. It's working!

As the Resonator's runes light up, I know that the universal beacon must be emitting. Anyone listening will race to locate the source before their rivals do. Surely, with the *Helios* so close they will find us first. If nothing else, it'll be a warning to my crew that something isn't right. Warmth fills me, and I start to laugh. I feel so light and strong. Is this how Solis feels all the time? No wonder he's so confident.

The back of my neck itches and the future seems so clear. Visions of landing lights bathing us as the *Helios* comes to pick us up. Recovering from this ordeal in the infirmary with Solis healing in a tank. Why wait though? If the soulstone can heal me, it can heal Solis as well. I just have to open the IC and place it in his hand. Then he'll be all better. Why am I so dense? I should have done this all along. I reach back and…

I don't want to be a monster like him.

That's not right. I'm helping him. Solis will be fine. He'll be safe and whole.

Reaching behind me, I press up on the busted IC lid until Aide jumps on my shoulder. It waves its legs frantically. From its lens, it projects a halo of Beastie and I: Beastie twitches as my sunken face glows in his soulstone's violet hue. A streak of white runs down my once pure brown hair. That's not right, I feel so *good* right now. I try to brush it away. Aide stabs a metal leg through my right hand's glove.

Sealing foam splashes out as I howl and drop the Astra tech. As my connection with the soulstone servers, I'm all too aware of the toxic atmosphere burning my hand.

Gasping, I struggle to reattach my glove as all my visor's sensory alarms flash. My movements feel like I'm trying to swim in IC gel. Every muscle reminds me of how very human I am. What was I thinking? That was dangerous. So dangerous. Once my glove is in place, I remove the tourniquet and feel the painful pins and needles rush in with the blood. My vision blurs, and I close my eyes.

My lightheadedness will surely pass...

I awaken, I don't know how long later. Beastie has wrapped himself around me and snores lightly. I try to sit up but that's painful. Soulstones. Never again. My entire body is one big regret right now. The hand I'd used to hold the Resonator burns. I groan and turn to see Aide watching us from Solis' IC. Beastie stirs and then helps me upright.

"Thanks, you two. I didn't realize that would be so ... all consuming."

Aide bobs as Beastie yawns. If Aide hadn't helped me ... I shudder. I'd almost used the soulstone on Solis. Just like I'd used one on Lin. Crazy as it sounds, the soulstone *wanted* me to use it on him. The back of my neck itches like mad but I can't scratch it in this suit. Who knows what damage I've done to myself.

"Where is the Resonator?" I glance down to see a hole burned through the roots.

A meter down, on the boiling bedrock below, the Resonator steams and glows that eerie green hue. Natasha had said Resonators are intimately connected to the world they're discovered in. The one on Doomirage was connected to the spirit. I suspect Planet Senior's Resonator is thermally inspired. Best to just leave that lie.

Either way, the device is active, and a universal beacon sounds for anyone to hear. Will the others realize that Lin isn't the captain? I should prepare, but I'm so tired; I can hardly lift a finger. Leaning back, I rest my head on IC210 and stare at the empty sky. I need to rest but the countdown on the inside of my visor has reached the one-hour mark. Adjusting the settings, I power down all non-essential systems. It buys me another half-hour. That's all I get.

"Aide, do me a favor?"

In response, the little aracbot skitters up to me.

"Can you take the first watch?"

While I wait for Aide to reply, I close my eyes for just a moment ... and wake up to the sound of engines.

Bright light fills my vision. I raise my hand to block it out. The engine's dull thrum vibrates in my chest. Aide and Beastie are missing from my side as a disc-shaped ship descends. So much for Aide taking first watch! Hot air rushes past me as the ship crushes the spindly trees nearby. Its ramp extends into our camp, and a man's silhouette appears.

"Well, I'll be damned. Ashreal Payne is that you?"

Darius Draco in a white and gold spacesuit steps out from the light, and I don't know whether to be giddily happy or inconsolably frustrated. I settle for bitter laughter. Of all the people in the universe to pick up my distress signal, it had to be him.

22

DO NOT TAKE UNCALCULATED RISKS

"Hey Darius, long time no see." My throat's hoarseness ruins the nonchalance I'd been aiming for. I feel like hell, and the crick in my neck isn't helping. My suit's life support is on its last five minutes. My vision blurs so I can't see the expression on Darius' face, but I hear a sharp intake of breath. Void, I must look worse than I feel.

"What happened to you?" Genuine curiosity twinges his voice.

"Loaded question that one. Too much to tell while sitting on a hostile alien planet. As a CSO, you should know that. How about we discuss it inside the ship?"

The long silence that speaks for itself. It says I'm not here to help you. I just want the Resonator. Void, of all the ships to find us it had to be the *Titan*! Why are they even in the Tetrahedron? My mind races for ideas to escape this mess. None of them are good.

Darius types on his halocom, and the lights dim giving me a good look at the *Titan*. It is a carbon copy of the *Helios* save for the paint job. The *Titan* has jet-black coloring with streaks of gold. The streaks form a crisscrossing pattern on the disc's underside that splinters at its edges. As Darius hops off the ramp, the Evil Co. white crossbones become visible.

My former friend's face doesn't betray much as he walks up. His MOP is in one hand and an orange light cast from his visor scans everything. If he's looking for traps, he'll be disappointed. His gaze rests on the IC containing Solis. He glances past me into IC210's viewport, and his eyes go wide. I can see him putting the pieces together as he stands beside me.

"Is he dead?"

"Not yet. The IC's keeping him stable, but he needs medical attention."

"Where is his soulstone?"

"Safe." I try not to look at my boots as I think of Lin. "Are you going to help us or not?"

Darius doesn't even blink.

"You know Ash, it's kinda funny." His tone is conversational. "You got the ship I wanted, but looking at you, I'd say I dodged a bullet! No offense, but you look like a chewed-up hairball that's been frozen in vacuum."

"Offense taken," I murmur.

"Well, nothing can fix your sense of humor, but I'll take some weight off your hands."

He adjusts his MOP to an extended tong and pushes it between the roots to pluck the Resonator from the mud below. He sets it on the roots between us. Twisting the pattern, he turns off the device and disables my last hope for rescue. The green glow dissipates as he lets the Resonator cool on the roots. Darius glances around with a disappointed turn to his lips as if expecting a ruse any second now. He picks up the Resonator again with his MOP's tongs and walks back to the ramp.

"Wait!" I shout and force my body to lurch forward.

"Give me a reason to." Darius waves a hand.

"Because…" My mind races. Out of the corner of my eye, I see the outline of a certain Spirit Beast hiding in the grove. "Because I know where the Doomirage parrot Spirit Beast is!"

He stops and cranes his neck to look at me. His expression is hidden behind the glare of his ship's lights.

"You must know we took it from Doomirage." I try to sit a little straighter and project confidence … I doubt it works well. "If you ever want to find Beastie, you'll need my help."

Darius' halocom flashes as Erisa's miniature figure appears on his wrist.

"What's the hold-up CSO? Where's my new Resonator?"

"I've got it." Darius takes a deep breath. "It and two more subjects of interest."

I relax with a mixture of relief and surprise.

"Thank you." I hardly believe my own words.

"Don't thank me, Ash." Darius turns off his halocom. "Not yet."

Trust isn't what it used to be.

I've been magcuffed to my bedframe in the *Titan*'s plain white infirmary for the past two rotations with only the burbling tank and a rotating guard to keep me company. This rotation's pick is Oz who sits stiffly, observing me from his seat by the infirmary door. I can't help but compare him to Natasha. They're complete opposites. Where she's chaos incarnate, Oz seems to favor order. Aside from his broken glasses—likely from our Terminal brawl—the man is practically symmetrical. It's unnerving how perfectly his face aligns. His blond hair doesn't have a follicle out of place. I think back to Halley's nickname for him, 'the Bore.'

Being captive has been a fuzzy experience so far. I blame the IV dripping painkillers into my system. Part of me understands the drugs are meant to keep me malleable, but the other part is relieved that I can't feel my body. On the wall beside me is a list of things that have gone wrong with me. Toxic gases damaging my skin and lungs, and Astra runes burning into my hand from the Resonator are at the top of the list, but my ribs are miraculously healed. In theory, I should be much worse off. I guess I can thank the soulstone for that ... I twist a finger in my new white hair streak. Although, if I'd held it much longer, I may have ended up like Junior when he'd first held the soulstone.

At least I know why I've been itchy since the botched jump into the Tetrahedron. A fern-like scar pattern spreads from the back of my neck down my shoulders. The scar's bizarre pattern itches like mad. I guess it was naïve to think that I'd been spared from the Tetrahedron's effects. But it could have been worse, I could have switched bodies with Lester.

Picking up a spoon, I scoop another bite of fabricated green goop from my tray that presumably isn't meant to kill me. After experiencing total exhaustion, there is a ridiculous amount of joy in holding a spoon.

"Lime flavored. You want some?" I offer to my guard. My pain-killer-laced voice sounds slurred. My jaw feels like I'm chewing the biggest piece of gum in the universe.

Oz grimaces like I've just threatened to poison him. Who knows? Maybe it is poisoned, but they don't need to be subtle if they want me dead. His black eye from our Terminal fight has turned green.

"Does anyone really like that stuff?" Oz scoffs.

"Suit yourself." Shrugging, I lean back into the pillow and wave the spoon at him. I try another tactic. "How is the captain?"

"Erisa? Why do you ask?" Oz narrows his eyes.

"Void Oz, no, I mean my Captain Solis. Is he alright?"

Last, I'd seen Solis, Darius used a gravlift to cart his IC away. They'd kept us separate since then. I don't even know if they've given him medical attention yet. It's driving me a bit crazy. There are too many unknowns, and my brain is still fuzzy ... man, this green goop stuff is great. I take another bite.

"How would I know?" Oz shrugs.

"Surely, you have some say in this crew, or are you just the guard dog?"

Oz smirks. "Maybe I won't have to play guard dog much longer?"

Even my fuzzy brain knows that's a threat. Good. Great. I love threats. A power surge racks the Titan, and the lights flash from white to red to white again. A strange sense of déjà vu comes to me. I know a little birdy that has a habit of chewing electrical wires when nervous. That's happened a few times now ... I think. Again, fuzzy. But this is the first time I notice the vent above Oz's chair has a familiar red light in it.

"What was that?" Oz asks. "What are you smiling at?"

I touch my face; I didn't even realize I was smiling.

"Just thinking if you get another black eye, you'll be symmetrical again."

Oz starts to reply, but he doesn't get the chance. Aide tumbles out of the vent above him and hits Oz's head. Hard. The not-so-good doctor's eyes roll back, and he teeters forward, landing face first with his backside in the air. A lump forms on the right side of Oz's head.

"I never thought I'd be so happy to see you." I grin as Aide scrambles over to my bedside. I pull the IV from my arm and hope that's not too important. For the first time since entering the *Titan*, I have a sense of control. Time to find Solis and get out of here. I examine the magcuff that has me linked to the bed.

"Okay Aide, step one: Can you get a keycard for these cuffs?"

The aracbot hops to it, skittering up and down the unconscious Oz before triumphantly returning with the keycard. Taking it, I free my wrist and swing my feet over the side. My legs collapse out from under me, and I nearly faceplant.

"Woah." I catch myself on the bed. What type of pain meds did they give me? The fun kind evidently ... this'll make escaping interesting. Aide circles me, impatiently prodding me to move again. I forgot how much I hated that.

"Okay, okay, I'm getting up."

Aide relents. How do I use legs again? Grabbing the side of the bed, I force myself upright and get my feet under me.

"Okay now for step number two." I take a second step and giggle. Aide pokes me again, urging me forward. I sigh. "Everyone's a critic."

What next? Clothes. Clothes would be good. Flopping beside Oz, I apologize before stealing his lab coat, pants, and halocom. All are too big for me, but I make do. It's better than wandering around the halls in my underwear and white sleeveless shirt. Afterwards, I magcuff him to the bed, stuff one of his own socks into his mouth as a gag and stab the IV into his arm. Why not share my former sedatives? Did I even get a vein? I shrug.

My bigger problem is the lack of shoes. But mine aren't in sight and Oz's are way too big even if I stuff them full of cotton balls. Now that I'm not hooked up to the happy IV, my brain feels less like a pile of mush. I glance at Oz's halocom. No telling when the next shift will arrive, and there's no more time to delay.

"You ready?" I ask my rescuing aracbot.

From Aide's perch on my shoulder, it gives me an approving bob. I open the door, and we sneak into the belly of the *Titan*. I head for the CSO storage. Assuming the *Titan* is a true carbon copy, that's the most secure spot on the ship, and, likely, where they'll be keeping Solis. The cylindrical corridors mimic the *Helios* but there are some differences such as the honeycomb black and white paneling lining the walls. They have a disorienting effect as I slide my way down the hall. Approaching the stairs, I freeze at the sound of voices in the cantina.

"They are so cute!" Halley's nasal tones echo into the hall. "I think I'll call them Voidkrakens. They have completely repurposed the ziggurat structures as their nesting grounds. I just want to dissect them all into little bitty pieces. Why do they keep running away from us?"

"Give it up. We're not staying to chase monsters. Void, we've stayed long enough after that distress beacon was sent out." It's a voice I know but can't quite place. Probably the ship's Engineer who missed the party at Zigs. Inching up to the doorway, I risk a glance inside. The two are sitting with their backs to me.

"Why do you always kill the mood?" Halley's blonde hair is twisted into a couple of tight pigtail buns. She rests her chin in her white-gloved hands as she stares at her companion. I've seen the man sitting next to Halley before, it's the Engineer of Our Destruction from Doomirage, Sven. He's dressed in all black. Though I can't see their faces, from behind they look like salt and pepper shakers.

"I like relaying facts." Sven holds up a finger. "Facts like, 'we're out of here as soon as we're done clearing the ziggurat,' and"—a second finger joins the first—"'I'm happy that this bothers you.'"

Halley sulks. "I hate your facts."

He leans back into his chair. "How about some fun ones then? We have this planet's Resonator and a lead on your missing Spirit Beast."

"My specimen!" Halley inflates once more. She whirls in her chair, and I duck my head back. Did she see me? "I can't wait to work on him again. I've missed our sessions. If only he hadn't been taken ... Oh, I wish Darius would let me at that CSO already. I'm sure I can make her talk. He's, like, wasting all those meds on her."

"True fact. Maybe D has gone soft." There is a hungry edge to Sven's voice, like he's been waiting for a reason to stab Darius in the back. "But she does need to survive you ... at least until she talks."

Welp, that settles any lingering hope of negotiating my way out. Quiet as I can, I slink past them as they chat about different methods of torture. Nothing gives you quite the extra pep in your step like hearing the horrible ways you'll suffer. I make it down the stairs in record time. Down a level, I find the *Titan*'s CSO storage between the hyperdrive room and the life support.

"Okay Aide, think you can unlock this one?" I shift him from my shoulder to the vent above me. He unscrews the lower bolts with his legs and shimmies through it. Hopefully, he can unlock the door. Footfalls catch my attention, and a shadow stretches out from down the hall. I duck into the hyperdrive's open door and press my back against the wall. Erisa strides past the door on her way to the stairs. Pretty sure she must stride everywhere with purpose. Instead of running in her sleep, I imagine she struts. I stifle a giggle. I hear her stop walking for a moment—a long nervous moment—before her footsteps recede fully.

"That was way too close."

"Too close." Beastie peers out from behind the astra-rune-covered engine.

"There you are," I whisper. Happy tears prick at the corners of my eyes. It is so good to see a friendly face, even one with a beak. Stepping around the hyperdrive, I scritch the scruff of his feathery neck. Beastie coos at my touch. "I'm glad you made it. How did you remain hidden?"

He disappears.

"You're right. That was a dumb question."

"Dumb question." Beastie reappears and nods in agreement.

"No need to rub it in." I smile before adding more seriously. "Just stay here. I'll send Aide to come get you once we're ready to leave."

Beastie yawns and returns to his wire nest behind the hyperdrive engine.

Sneaking back to Darius' CSO door, I find it open and Aide in the entrance.

"Good aracbot." I offer it a hand to climb up on my shoulder.

Aide accepts, and we enter. The storage mirrors my own. The only difference is where Darius decided to put his desk, by the entrance, and that gaudy color pallet of black and gold everywhere. Plenty of ICs line the walls here, but there is only one I care about. In a sea of black and gold containers, Starprint's IC210 is closest to the incinerator. Rushing over, I crouch down to check on Solis. Aide jumps onto the IC and joins my examination. There are signs of repair but only to the IC. My heart sinks as I realize they haven't bothered to treat Solis for his injuries. What are they waiting for? Didn't they want him alive?

Beside IC210 is my discarded jacket, a new halocom, and ... is that a navicore? Removing Oz's halocom, I put the new one on before examining the device. No, it's different. Only one side of the device has fluctuating coordinates, the rest are blank.

I shake my head. "How did Darius get this?"

"That's a sincore. Like a navicore, but only good for one jump." I whip around to see Darius walking in. Behind him, the circular doors slide shut. In his hands is an Orion ration bar which he promptly tosses to the desk. So much for going undetected. I—

"The gravlift is in the corner over there," he says, pointing. "If you take a left out of storage, you'll find a fueled shuttle ready for you. It should be enough for you to escape the Tetrahedron."

"What?"

"The gravlift, you know, so you can move his IC." Darius shakes his head before taking a seat in his desk chair. "Come on, we don't have all rotation. Erisa wants the *Titan* to jump out of here in the next hour or so. She hates that we've taken this long after a Resonator's distress call, anyway."

"What are you doing?"

"What does it look like I'm doing?" Darius rubs his temple. He doesn't leap for a duress switch or call for backup on his halocom. Is he just letting me walk out of here?

"Fair enough. Let me rephrase, why are you helping me?"

Dare doesn't say anything at first. Uncertainty tightens his brow before he tentatively says, "Do you remember our bet with Knox?"

"Yeah ... I remember." The three of us had snuck into the *Helios'* hangar as part of a hazing ritual. We'd bet on who'd find Lost Earth first. Knox had joked he wouldn't settle for a constellation prize. Horrible pun. "A lot has happened since then."

"Do you remember what you said before the bet?" Dare sits up a little straighter.

"That we were the only sane people in the universe."

Dare nods. "At the time, I'd thought it true, that I'd finally found rivals worth my time."

He pauses, and I let silence fill the room.

He shakes his head. "Then Knox died and you ...When did you go insane?"

"Excuse me?"

Dare stands up, walking over to me. "On the Terminal, you should have run, but instead you attacked the AWD with hardly a slip of a plan and, for what? An enemy? Or perhaps you'd like to shed some light on how you got stranded in the Tetrahedron?"

"You don't know the circumstances—"

He tosses his hands up. "Okay, let's talk about your latest act of foolishness. Why not escape the Titan while you had the chance? Instead, you endanger yourself to save this clone."

I jolt. How does he know that?

Dare casually waves away my shock. "I was a Starprint Inc. cadet too, remember? You really think I didn't check for more than the *Helios* blueprints when I stole the records?"

He kicks Solis' IC rocking it. Anger, like a live wire, curls and sparks in me.

"Don't touch him." I shove Dare away. He stumbles back but regains his footing. I position myself in between him and Solis.

He shakes his head. "See? You're not acting like a CSO. You're acting like a fool. You were supposed to be my rival after Knox died but ... you're insane. Why go through so much effort to protect a disposable product? So much so that you got trapped in the dark nougaty center of the Tetrahedron?"

"First off, it's not nougaty. Secondly, because we don't leave our crew behind."

"And look where that got you. Do you really not care about your own self-interests?" Dare sighs and takes a step back to his desk's chair. He reverses it so he can sit while resting his arms on the back. Once settled, he holds up a finger. "The way I see it you have two options. Option one: you can take the insane route and escape with captain popsicle and keep doing stupid crap until it eventually kills you." He holds up a second finger. "Option two: ditch the dead weight and join E. Vilco."

"Why would I do that?"

"Because of the Big Three, only E. Vilco is on the rise. You can find a place here. Hell, I'll even help you. Watch your back like old times. All you need to do is give up some Starprint Inc. secrets: location of a certain Spirit Beast? Great! Cloning operations discoveries? Even better! Any Astra artifacts you can share? Perfect. It all gets you perks in Evil Co. What do you say?"

The thinning pain meds wear have me considering his offer. It would be easier, but … The *Titan* might be the same in design as the *Helios*, but the people inside are nothing alike. There is no trust between the crew. I saw it at Ziggie's with the fear Erisa stirred in Halley, I saw it in Oz's suspiciously questioning nature, and I saw it in the cantina with Sven and Halley's conversation about Dare going soft. Does Dare even realize how alone he must be?

I chuckle and shake my head.

"What's so funny?" Dare frowns. "I'm being serious."

"All that talk that I'm insane for helping those I care about, and you're going to tell me that you don't see the irony in what you're doing?"

"That's different—"

"Quit lying to yourself. It's the same damn thing. I'm guilty of acting 'insane' but you're no different. In your own way, you've just offered me protection. If I'm insane, so are you."

"Does that mean you reject my offer?" Dare's confident smile transforms into a hardline grimace. "You won't get a better one."

"Yeah, I'm going to have to say no."

"Why?!"

"It's an uncommon universe. Sometimes you need a little uncommon sense to bet on."

"What does that even mean?"

"It means," I walk up to Dare until we're eye to eye, "that there are some things worth trusting your gut over instead of logic. And my gut? It says take option one. What does yours say?"

Dare looks away first.

Turning my back to him, I slip off Oz's lab coat and don my ragged blue Starprint Inc. jacket. I add the sincore to my other pocket. As I turn to get the gravlift, I hear the telltale whirling of a Joker. I don't bother looking, there is only one person who could be holding the weapon. I sigh. "One minute you're risking your career to help me, and the next you're pointing a blaster at me. Make up your mind."

"Don't do this."

"My choice is made." I slide the gravlift under Solis' IC. There's a satisfying suction sound as the lift adheres to its bottom and the IC begins to float. Facing Dare, I match his gaze. He's afraid. On the Terminal, when he'd asked for help to leave Evil Co., I'd thought it an act, but now?

"It's not too late, you know. You don't have to stay here either. Come with me."

Dare's face twists, and I wonder if he's considering it, but the Joker is still charged. If he shoots me now, he could be the hero that stopped a rival CSO from escaping.

The room rocks as though the ship hit something, nearly knocking me over.

"What in the Void was that?" I cling to the gravlift to stay upright.

"I don't—" Dare starts, as the ship rocks violently again. He flies into the shelves of magnetically locked ICs. The chess board on his desk clatters to the floor as pieces scatter. I'm knocked to my knees. Dare's halocom buzzes to life.

"All hands to your stations," Erisa shouts. "We're under attack!"

23

— • —

DO NOT CARRY DEAD WEIGHT

Another hit rocks the *Titan*.

Red emergency lighting flickers.

"Report in when you've made it to your post. We're out of here!" Erisa's voice demands.

Dare's halocom chimes with each check-in as I scramble to my feet.

"Sven here. I'll prime the engines to get us out of here."

"Halley here, reporting that Oz screwed up."

"Is it my fault that the CSO escaped?" Oz chimes in from the background.

"Dude, it's definitely your fault."

"Chasms of Planet Hell!" Erisa curses. "Get me eyes on her now!"

Dare's face pales as he looks at his halocom. He glances at me, and I feel my heart's pace triple. He reaches over with his free hand and activates the halocom on his wrist. "Darius reporting, I have eyes on the target."

My heart sinks.

"She's headed to the bridge. Sven, intercept at the top, I'll approach from below." Dare disconnects and takes a deep breath. "It's your lucky day, Ashreal."

As he slumps his shoulders, his uniform appears too large for him. Maybe it never really fit quite right. I appeal one more time, not to *Titan* CSO Darius Draco but to Dare. "Come with me."

"Just get out of here," Dare scoffs, but there's a smile on his lips. "Don't make me regret not shooting you."

"It was a good call. My friend wouldn't have liked that very much."

"Who are you—" Dare is interrupted by the appearance of Beastie in the doorway. The Spirit Beast devours the Orion ration pack on his desk. Dare stumbles backward. I take the opportunity to steer the gravlift out the door and Beastie jumps aside. Aide leaps out from behind the shelves and lands on the IC.

"Until the next bet." I mockingly salute as I pass Dare. Behind me, I hear his light laugh. He may not think I'll make it, but he is giving me a chance. I don't intend to waste it. The ship shakes brutally under unseen enemy attacks, but that's an Evil Co. problem. I'm getting out of here.

It's a clear route to the *Titan*'s cargo bay. I burst onto the catwalk. Just as Dare said, the shuttle is in the bay below, hatch open and inviting. Thankfully, it doesn't have its sunroof down and is rigged up for vacuum. It should be able to fit our ragtag group.

Another blast rocks the *Titan*, but this time, three grappling hooks pierce through the cargo doors opposite the shuttle. Void, whoever's attacking aims to board the *Titan*! My escape route is about to be blocked. No time to waste. I go down the fast way. Using the gravlift, I shove Solis' IC over the catwalk's edge. It drifts on antigrav until I jump on top and drive it to the deck below. We land next to the shuttle, but the IC tips over. I catch myself but Aide tumbles off and bumps into the shuttle's side. Beastie alights beside me with a delighted chirp.

"Get Aide into the shuttle!" I shout as I straighten Solis' IC. Beastie, thankfully, listens and scoops up our aracbot in his beak before rushing into the shuttle. I follow suit, shoving Solis' IC into the open hatch and dropping it in the backseat. It's a tight fit and Beastie coos unhappily.

I'm only half in the shuttle, when a deep mechanical groan sounds from behind. I turn in time to see the *Titan*'s cargo door snaps loose.

My feet lose purchase, and my grip slips from the shuttle. For a terrifying second, I'm flying, bodily pulled toward open space—until the *Titan*'s emergency shield barrier kicks in. I drop to my hands and knees, a good six meters from the shuttle. A hooked boarding dock crashes through the shield barrier and digs into the cargo hold. Beastie squawks from the shuttle's open hatch, trapped behind IC210.

"Void it all." I stagger to my feet as the boarding party enters.

Twenty humanoid killbots—just like those that attacked Starprint's hangar—spill into the *Titan*. I hardly have time to raise my hands in surrender before they have Ajax rifles pointed my way. Walking down the boarding ramp's center is a familiar dark armored android with the soundwave mask. Surrounded by minions, he's a far cry from the salesbot I'd first assumed him to be. One of Hijack's Reclaimers has boarded the *Titan*. Another BS2 funded assassin, here to finish the job.

"Witshade," I whisper.

His head snaps in my direction. His facescreen's blue wavelength twists into a horse-shoe shape that I can only interpret as a smile. Honey had said he liked collecting ships, but never mentioned what happens to the crew afterwards. A lump forms in my throat, I'd been so close. He raises his hand. Is he going to attack? I flinch as ... he waves at me. I think shock makes me wave back.

"Told you I'd catch you later, Ashreal." Witshade holds a contemplative hand to his chin. "I'm starry for the wait."

Witshade's light flickers, and his shoulders shake. The terrorist who'd sent a slizard assassin, a murderous AWD, and now has the *Titan* in his grip, laughs at his own terrible puns. Who does that?

"Quit playing." An electronically distorted voice calls out from behind Witshade. He salutes with a fist to his chest and steps aside as an androgenous figure descends the ramp. A stole with Astra runes drapes their spacesuit's neck, the long fabric almost reaching their knees. A wide shark's grin decorates their tinted visor. My eyebrows raise at six astra wings protruding from their back. Those can't be real, can they? No. Astra were huge, this figure is just a human. Just a very intimidating human. I hope.

"That one." Hijack—the Terminal's boogeyman with a 15,000,000 glint reward—cocks their head to the side at me. "Shouldn't be here."

I shiver as their long stole crackles with an Astra aura. It feels wholly unnatural yet familiar, like a song I just can't place. Around their waist is an assortment of spherical grenades … this really isn't my rotation. As their killbots advance, I take a step back.

Shots rain down out from the catwalk. Killbots fall back, fried.

The *Titan*'s crew has arrived. Halley wields dual Jokers from behind a cargo box. Beside her, Sven whips a Blackjack to his shoulder. Even Oz is there with a Joker in his left hand and a bed rail magcuffed to his right. No Erisa. I guess she's busy attempting to free the ship from its chains. Dare arrives last and aims a Joker.

"And the gang's all here," Witshade says, his facemask glowing brighter.

"Sorry, no solicitors." Dare sneers and chaos erupts.

I duck down as Joker blasts meets advancing killbots. Several bots go down. Halley fires at Witshade, but—faster than I can blink—he sidesteps and flicks blades from his arms, slicing through the blaster shots as if they were solid. Steam drifts from the metal and the Astra runes covering them. I'm frozen in place, watching as Witshade eyes the defenders then advances.

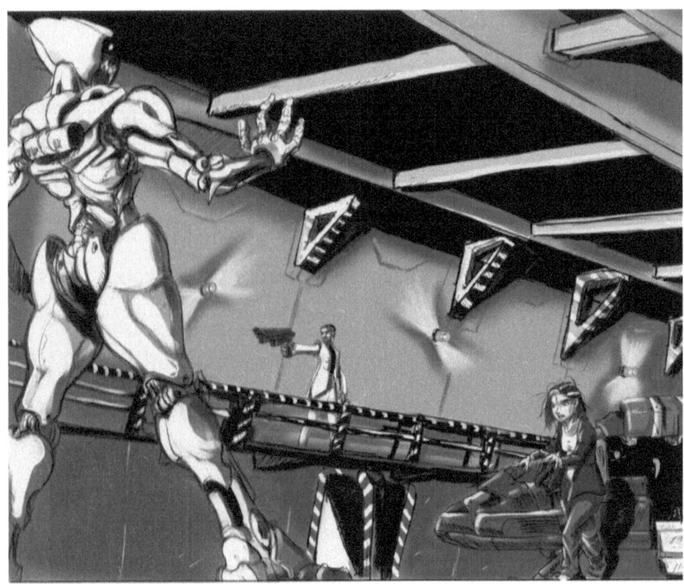

A blast burns just past my ear. The scent of smoldering hair breaks me from my stupor. I glance at the shot's source and see Dare. His mouths the word 'Go.' That's … good advice. Finding my feet, I flee to the shuttle. The firefight rages behind me.

Stumbling inside, I seal the door and slip into the pilot's seat. Aide hops up and down in my copilot seat. Beastie pokes his head between us from his perch half-atop IC210 as the shuttle engines purr to life. Unfortunately, that also makes the shuttle a more interesting target. Blasts pelt the hull. From the catwalk, Sven redirects his Blackjack toward us. The weapon's barrel glows with deadly power. We'll be toast if that hits us, and I don't even like toast!

Out of the corner of my eye, Hijack jumps up. No, not jumps—those Astra wings on their back flicker as fast as a turbine blade and launch Hijack level with the catwalk. I almost miss them ripping a sphere from their belt and tossing it between the *Titan* crew's feet. As the sphere lands, pistons indent in its sides, like a reverse miniature anti-grav engine. I've never seen anything like it.

Dare glances down as an unseen force smashes against everyone on the catwalk, knocking them off their feet. Sven's Blackjack blast goes high, punching a shuttle-sized hole in the hull. Vacuum pulls everyone toward the breach until the *Titan*'s shields flicker into place again, dropping them to the ground. I seize my chance.

I ignore the itching of my neck.

I ignore the approving nod Dare gives me.

I ignore Hijack's Reclaimers and pull up on the controls. Our shuttle scrapes through the jagged hole before bounding out into space. For the first time, I see the enemy's ship. Hijack's ship is a massive X-shaped structure with long chains attaching it to the *Titan*. The Evil Co. ship was reeled in like a fish.

A chained grappling hook fires at our shuttle and just misses us.

"Time to go," I say, and Beastie bobs his head in agreement. "Aide, take the sincore from my pocket and plug it into the shuttle's console. We need to jump ASAP!"

Aide fumbles the sincore as I jink the shuttle, trying to avoid more grappling hooks. It drops between the seats. Beastie's beak shoots past my hip after the sincore. Aide grabs it from Beastie and leaps for the port console. There's a click and a clunk as it locks into place and a green hyperjump light flickers to life on the sincore. All it needs are coordinates.

I take a hard left. Another chain whizzes past. Hooks scratch against our hull but fail to find purchase.

The shuttle's console hyperdrive button flashes green. Jacking in my new halocom provides an array of coordinates and corresponding musical accompaniments. I almost select the first one labeled TERMINAL HYPERRING but stop. There at the bottom is one labeled Roxy ... I'd not known the *Titan*'s crew had dealings with her.

If the *Helios* and its crew are anywhere, it's with her. That was their next destination, and Lin would have a hell of a time convincing Qual to go anywhere else. If I select the Terminal, I'll be able to get myself and Solis to safety, but if I choose Roxy ... I can warn my crew about Lin before it's too late.

There isn't any choice in the end.

I chose Roxy's coordinates and heavy metal music erupts from the console.

"Hit it!" I shout, and Aide jumps on the hyperdrive button.

24

Do Not Venture into Uncharted Territory

Fortunately, when a Tetrahedron hyperjump goes as planned, you don't go hopscotching through space with afterimages trailing you. Unfortunately, a shuttle is more limited than the *Helios* or a hyperring. The turbulent ride through space's pocket is taking forever.

Aide and Beastie do their best to rest while I focus on the shuttle's system health check. Again. And again. And how about one more time? The more I focus on the system's checks, the more I don't think about what just happened. Or the fact that the pain meds have entirely worn off, and I feel way too much with each jostle of the shuttle. But that's the price of being alive.

Dare's face flashes through my mind. Is he still alive? Hijack's forces had the advantage when I'd fled. Hijack's Astra gear is beyond anything I've encountered before, and the thought of Witshade's blades wet with Dare's blood sickens me. But I can't turn back now that the sincore's destination is set—not that I have the firepower to challenge Hijack's reclaimers. Even if I could, Dare might be on my side, but the rest of Evil Co. are far from friends. Logical arguments do little against the guilt that rides on my shoulder and whispers regret into my ear.

"I wish…" I turn to Solis' IC. "I wish I could ask you about it."

Pain in my palms reminds me not to clench my fists so hard. Deep even breaths help me center myself. Is it strange that I haven't cried, despite everything that has happened since being marooned? Maybe there is something broken in me. I thought this moment of solace would be my undoing, but I just feel angry. I scratch the barcode on my neck a little too hard. There's a prick of pain from my Tetrahedron scar that covers the tattoo.

"Hey, Aide?" The aracbot sitting dormant on the co-pilot chair stirs. Seven legs sprout from underneath it, and its lens turns lazily to me. "Think we'll find the others with Roxy?"

It shrugs two legs at me.

There is a beeping from the shuttle's console as the hyperjump begins to wind down. Beastie yawns awake from the backseats and nuzzles my chair, no doubt wanting some snacks. He prods Aide with a claw, and the aracbot smacks angrily at the Spirit Beast.

"No time to squabble, you two. We'll be out of here soon."

We must be close to the exit. If all goes well when we arrive at Roxy's, I'll expose Lin, save the crew, and get Solis medical attention. If not ... well best to approach them cautiously. Closing my eyes, I try to relax, but it's impossible not to feel jumpy. With a final bounce, the shuttle breaks free from the pocket. We're here. I take over the controls from the autopilot. In the distance, the scanners pick up something the size of a hyperring, but it's shaped like an apple with a bite out the top. Is that an asteroid? The shuttle shakes again.

Beastie whines.

"It's okay, boy." Another invisible wave hits us, and the ship strains under the force of it. Aide's body swivels nervously. Metal creaks in a worrisome fashion. My nerves fray as the shuttle's console flashes a gravitational wave warning.

"Brace yourselves!" I cry, but my hands can barely hold onto the controls. A wave hits us, and this one sends us into a flat spin toward the asteroid. My vision goes darker in the corners. I know this sign. I'm going into G-LOC. I'm going to—

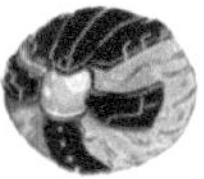

I'm being carried away to somewhere new.

Dragged almost … like how Honey had dragged me.

"NO!" I thrash and knock over several round spaceball-sized robots with a white and black checkered pattern. They've tiny arms, legs, and an AI sphere with blue eyes on top. I get my foot free and kick at the spacebot holding my legs. Its mechanical blue eyes irises wide, and it collapses into a defensive sphere. My bare foot sends it rolling down a hill covered in mechanical parts. My heel flares with pain from kicking the metal bot.

Disoriented, I roll over to get my bearings. I'm in a junkyard on top of a scrap pile under a cavernous dome. Three-fourths of the dome's walls are solid metal, but the last quarter is a shield wall. It gives a view of an inconceivably long net that spans further than my eye can see. I groan. Just my luck. The asteroid I'd seen was a scrapper ship, and I flew right into their gravitational net. I'd been right to fear Roxy's coordinates. She'd sent us into a trap.

About fifteen meters below my junk pile, the *Titan*'s shuttle is wedged between broken infirmary tanks. It's actively being disassembled by an army of the spacebots. More of the robots try to approach me, but I grab the nearest object: a discarded regular old wooden mop.

"Get back!" I shout, swinging at them. They aren't fighters, and it's enough to discourage them. They roll away from me. Still brandishing my makeshift weapon, I navigate to the shuttle. I'm careful not to step on anything sharp. I should have just stolen Oz's shoes when I had the chance. As I approach, I chase away the scavenger spacebots with my new mop. They scatter for the junkyard hills.

"Aide! Beastie!" I call out. No response.

Stepping inside the shuttle's remains, I sigh. It's been picked clean of anything valuable. My heart drops when I see Solis' IC is missing. I don't know who these scavengers are or what they'll do to survivors. I slam a fist into the skeletal frame of the pilot's chair. Why is it always out of the cosmic frying pan and into the fire?!

I must find them.

But first, I peel off the chair's fabric and tie strips around my feet. It takes several tries to assemble something that doesn't fall apart. Hopefully, that'll be enough to get me through this junkpile without slicing my feet open. Maybe if I follow the spacebots I can find where they've taken the others. I grab the mop, a square shuttle panel to use a shield, and depart. I search for the blue mechanical eyes of the spacebots.

"Solis, could you, for once, stop getting kidnapped?" I mutter to myself.

I'm drenched in sweat, and I've started talking to myself. Great. Love this for me. The scrapper ship's junkyard is large, and, in the distance, there is a cylindrical structure in the center. It looks like an elevator. That must be how scavengers transport treasures to the upper floors. I spot a line of blue lights entering its base. Luckily, it's mostly downhill to there. Taking the panel I salvaged from the ship, I hop on top. I've never been sledding before, but I've seen halos. I shove off and go sliding down the junkpile.

Who says rescue missions can't be fun?

I do. After the fifth time sliding downhill, crashing my panel, and scratching myself up, I can attest to the fact that sledding in a junkyard isn't fun. I sneak the rest of the way to a hiding place behind a broken pile of salesbots. Peeking down, I spot hundreds of spacebots marching with various goods into the elevator about thirty meters away. Unfortunately, standing vigil between the elevator and I are six autonomous weapons droids, and I don't have Tim the mechanical shark to throw at them this time.

My breath catches as I see IC210 carried by six spacebots into the elevator.

Solis is down there.

I'll have to sneak in. Maybe there is another way around? Using my mop for support, I circle around a busted shuttle nose. My foot slips. I try to catch myself on a scarlet-colored salesbot, but its face-screen breaks off and tumbles down the junk causing a mini avalanche. Marching spacebots scatter, and the nearest AWD rolls over to investigate.

Oh no.

Scrambling back, I look for somewhere to hide. There! The nose of the old shuttle has enough space. I climb up into the discarded nose and try to make myself inconspicuous. This is fine. Just think happy thoughts: gummy worms, Ziggie's margaritas, an aces high full house, not dying. The rubble shifts as the AWD rolls through and examines where I'd been standing. My pulse dances as it moves closer. It's red laser sight scans just below my hiding place.

Rescue missions are the worst!

The AWD abruptly stops, and I hear a guttural battle cry. The light disappears and there are the sounds of buzz saws, blasters, and ... is that a cheerleading chant? Outside my hiding place, the sounds of combat dwindle and a discarded black AWD AI sphere rolls under me. I debate making myself known to my rescuers. But the decision is made for me as the top of the nose peels away. A robotic arm wraps my shoulders and pulls me up and out. Before I can be afraid, the arm around my shoulder converts to a crushing hug.

"Ash! Y-you're alive! We were told you'd been killed. How are you alive?" Qual is a mess of grease stains, and his robotic arm has recently been repaired using scavenged parts. I'm pretty sure that's a can opener incorporated into his bicep. He releases me to the power of my own feet.

"Ashy? Be that ye? And what happened to yer hair?" Natasha Pollux's face is a picture of surprise. She's changed a fair bit in the last few rotations. Her long hair has been chopped short, her clothes are ratty, and even her tricorn is more tattered than usual. She lowers a makeshift Blackjack 2.0. The weapon is a hodgepodge of a shuttle blaster, exposed rat nest cabling, and scratched Astra runes into its barrel.

"Sugar is here?!" Behind Natasha, the teenage form of Lester appears. Is that war makeup on his face? Lester gazes at me suspiciously. "Are you sure it's not another slizard? Make her say something."

"Something," I reply dumbly. They're here. They're all here. I'd hoped, but after the crash I'd doubted everything. Am I hallucinating? "How are you here?"

Lester clears his throat. "Well, turns out you might have been right about Roxy. Her halocom coordinates lead us straight into a scrapper's net."

"Wait, why are you a teenager?" I touch Lester's face with the tip of my fingers to make sure he's real. "And why are Natasha and Qual back to normal?"

Natasha shrugs. "Me thinks the Tetrahedron's effect wears thin after a while. Though at times, Qual and I be of the same mind."

"She means l-literally. We have a telepathic connection," Qual replies.

He blushes as Natasha winks at him.

"Speak for yourself! I've just hit puberty again," Lester grumbles. He's a little taller than when I last saw him on Planet Junior. There is even a wisp of hair on his upper lip. His voice cracks as he speaks. "How did you get here?"

"It's a long story, but both Solis and I are here. Solis has been taken by the spacebots. Aide and Beastie were with me too, but I don't know where they've gone." I glance between them and a sudden horrible question spawns on my lips. "But where is…"

I almost say Lin, but I can't get the word out. How much did he tell them?

Qual and Lester exchange an uncertain glance, but Natasha isn't one to pull punches.

"Ye mean to ask, where be imposter Solis? He's the reason we be in this mess. We should have trusted Beastie's instincts. The old bird fled at the sight of him. When the *Helios* was captured by the scrapper net, we exited to cut the ship free by damaging the net."

"Cut it free?" I said. "It's a gravitational net, not rope and wire."

Qual raised a mechanical finger, looking both sheepish and proud of himself. "I j-jury-rigged the anti-grav generators from the Helios as grav-net c-cutters, but they had to be uninstalled and attached to the hull to work."

Natasha pets Qual's real arm. "Twas a good plan, but we be too slow. We succeed in damaging the net, making it unstable, but the *Helios* was pulled into the scrapper, and we were shaken off into this here junkyard. And, instead of trying to help us, the Captain's imposter"—Natasha spits—"abandoned us. He stole the *Helios'* shuttle and slipped through the unstable net. All the while spouting lies that ye were dead and that Starprint runs on the blood of clones."

They still don't know. The crew stares at me, and I have a horrible flashback to my Cosmic Fever dream where everyone closes the door as I drown in IC gel. I consider staying silent, but, if I've learned anything from *repeated* near-death experiences, it's that life is too short to live with lies. They deserve the truth.

"Lin wasn't lying. He is the clone from IC210. He's ... not well."

"I-I knew that one was the clone!" Qual replies, but I shake my head.

"It's more complicated than that. I've been lying to you all and sabotaging the bet we made about IC210. But the truth is, none of us have worked with the original Lin Solis. Both men are clones. Starprint Inc. wanted to ensure Solis' ability to handle Astra tech wasn't lost, so they made spares. Lin was once our Captain until the soulstone damaged his mind. It was my fault ... I've been trying to help him but I..."

I choke on the words. Those tears that were so suspiciously absent fall freely now.

"I think we'd recall if he'd been replaced," Lester muses. "How did they even get memories from one clone to the next? They'd have needed to take regular scans."

I shake my head. "Do you remember the decontamination process? The universe's most uncomfortable hats are in the decon chamber for a reason. They're how memories are transferred from one clone to the next. I'm supposed to protect him, so it doesn't happen frequently and become obvious to the rest of the crew. I ... I failed."

"Is this why you've been distant this past orbit?" Natasha's voice is small. "Why didn't you tell us?"

Great questions.

"I couldn't tell you. I didn't know how you'd react … I was scared and once I started lying, I couldn't stop. So, I kept it from you." Wringing my hands to keep them busy, I can't look up to see the judgment on their faces. I try and fail to stop myself from shaking. "But back on Planet Junior, Solis—our Solis—learned the truth and didn't even blink. He even put his life on the line to save mine. It's my fault he is injured and trapped in an IC. You have every right to hate me for my deceit. By the Void, I hate me. But I can't help our captain alone. Please, help me save him."

Silence reigns supreme, and I can't stand it. I close my eyes. They have every right to abandon me, just like Lin left me on Planet Junior. I've been nothing but a liar to them. I've been—

A hug wraps around me, another on my left side, and a third on my right. Cracking open my eyes, I find them all still here, embracing me in the firmest of group hugs.

"Did ye think we be so callous?" Natasha raps a knuckle on my forehead. "Ye've a thick skull but no brain inside it. We don't abandon our own in this crew. We face our fears together."

"D-don't get me wrong," Qual stifles a sniffle, "I'm mad at you. But you did the right thing in the end. Just like with Halcyon. I t-trust you to have good intentions now, too."

"You know," Lester smirks, "for a Common Sense Officer, you're an absolute idiot."

I sob. Waves of incoherent blubbering prevent me from saying all the things I want to. The knot in my gut cuts loose. Floodgates have nothing on the monsoon that pours out from me. I can't believe I have this many tears.

"Thank you," I say when I can finally use words again.

"Don't worry." Lester gives me a side hug. "We got you."

"Thank you, guys, but please stop hugging me." I wave a hand over my face. "You all smell awful."

Natasha scoffs with a half-smile. "Tis what happens after two rotations at sea."

I clear my throat as they let me stand on my own power. In our original bet on IC210, they'd picked tests of spirit, science, and loyalty. Now there is one more test to complete.

"Are you all ready to save Solis?"

"Be that ever in doubt?" Natasha shoulders her makeshift Blackjack.

"We don't l-leave our crew behind," Qual affirms.

"Oh, I love a good rescue mission." Lester grins. Yep, that's him alright.

"Good," I smile and hook a thumb at the broken AWD, "because I have a plan."

From our hiding place in the hollowed-out AWD, I have some regrets.

Uncomfortably crushed together, we cling to the gyroscopic frame. The only light is from Natasha's halocom which projects the exterior as we roll up to the elevator. Qual jury-rigged manual controls for her to drive the AWD, but it's awkward going. Tiny spacebots scurry out of the way as we pass. Scanners buzz as we approach, but nothing stops us as our AWD enters the ten-square-meter elevator. Once inside, the elevator doors close and we ascend.

"Okay Qual, you're up," I say.

Everyone but Natasha climbs out of the crammed AWD. Scavenged scraps surround us, and we scramble over the uneven footing to reach the elevator controls. Qual's robotic arm plugs a hacking probe into its console. He downloads everything he can as I keep watch with Natasha's scrappy Blackjack. My scavenged mop is on my back, slipped through my belt. Precious seconds tick by.

"Got it." Qual grins and projects a 3D map of the scrapper ship from his halocom. The ship is built like a giant spacebot. It is a massive orb with arms and legs holding out the scrapper net. The junkyard we're ascending from is its belly. Qual zooms into the ship's head. There are a series of adjoining rooms that connect to storage, life support systems, shield generators, the bridge, medical, and hangars.

"Do you have any data on where they've taken Solis' IC?" I nervously watch as the elevator rises higher into the ship.

"Give me a m-moment." Qual brings up scrapper manifest.

"Wait! Did you see that?" I point at the hangar's listed assets. "The *Helios* is still here?"

I'd been hoping to steal a ship, but this is perfect. Once we save Solis, we'll have a familiar way to fly out of here.

"Good find, Sugar." Lester peers over my shoulder from his perch on a junk pile.

"Must you call me Sugar?" I ask with a withering glance at him.

"It's part of our tradition."

I shake my head with a smile before returning to the manifest. Aide and Beastie aren't listed. Where could they be? And where is Solis?

"There!" Lester points to the medical lab. "IC210 taken to medical for treatment. Solis must be there."

"Thank goodness," I mutter under my breath. At least the scrapper's forces don't want Solis dead. I hadn't let myself consider the possibility that they might try to help him. "When we got to the top,

Qual and Natasha can two secure the *Helios* while Lester and I will retrieve the captain."

The boys nod and Natasha tosses a thumbs up from inside the AWD. Turning to Qual, I ask, "Do you see any defenses?"

The elevator doors slide open and answer my question. Thirty spacebots and two AWDs turn in unison. All their mechanical eyes narrow their lenses at our gang.

"Y-yeah, I'd say there are some defenses."

"Avast!" Natasha calls before throwing the AWD in gear. She plows into the awaiting robots. She knocks one AWD aside and Qual jumps on it. Ripping away the access panel, he jacks in his hacking probe.

Lester nods to me, and we go racing down the opposite hallway to medical. We pass through patchwork corridors. The ship seems like it's built from salvage. The floor and walls are a multicolor assortment of tiles. Several doors down, we find the infirmary sign and slip inside. Panting, I press my back against the wall and take in the room. It's more of a repair shop than a medical bay. Robotic arms hang on the walls, and parts are strewn about the place. But against the back wall is a healing vat, obviously scavenged from elsewhere.

My breath catches as I see him. Solis, floating in a healing vat not five meters away. His wounds actively stitch together where Lin had shot him. There is more damage than I thought. I'd not noticed the exit wound centered on his spine. Even so, his face is serene as he floats.

"Lester, can you tell if he's safe to travel?"

"Do sulfur-based lifeforms only exist because of anomalies?"

I raise an eyebrow at him.

Lester sighs. "The answer is yes."

He runs over to the console monitoring Solis' health. Fortunately, there don't seem to be any login credentials required. I guess the scrappers didn't expect to have anyone make it this far. Lester checks Solis' status and frowns.

"What is it?"

Lester shakes his head. "The damage he sustained. It's serious … the vat has repaired the life-threatening part but there are some serious issues with his spine. The captain isn't going to be walking out of here."

"Can he survive outside the tank?" My mouth is dry. The sounds of combat outside grow closer. We need to move fast if we're going to escape.

Lester purses his lips before saying, "Yes. Yes, he can."

"Then let's get him out of here," I say. Lester nods and initiates the tank shutdown sequence. I hand him Natasha's pieced together Blackjack and grab a hoverchair from the corner. The liquid in the tank drains, and the tank's seal hisses open. Solis' body is released. I'm there to catch him. It goes about as well as can be expected when a fifty-five kilogram woman catches a soaking wet and slippery one-hundred kilogram man. I nearly drop him before I maneuver him into the waiting hoverchair.

"Solis." I tap his cheek lightly. "Solis, can you hear me?"

The toxin burns on his face are all but healed, and only the thinnest trace of the blaster burns remain on his abdomen. Solis' eyes flutter open and meet mine. He starts to speak, but it ends in a ragged cough. I pat his back.

Once the cough passes, Solis cracks a smile. "It's good to see you, Ash."

I cradle his cheek with my hand. "I never skip out on a bet."

Solis places a hand on mine. "Never doubted you."

"Incoming! We've got—oh, crap!" Lester's shouts as the infirmary door crashes open.

I whip around. Lester is restrained by a couple of spacebots, the scrappy Blackjack discarded. Disarmed and disoriented, Qual and Natasha are in the spacebots swarm as well. There is no sign of their stolen AWD. I pull the mop off my back and place myself between Solis and the bots. They form a semi-circle around us. We're not going anywhere.

"Relax." From behind the mob of spacebots, a giantess steps through. Roxy's appearance in the halo didn't do her justice. It couldn't capture the fact that she is now a good two and a half meters tall, with, not two, not four, but eight arms. Seven are giving the universal 'calm down' gesture while the eighth is hidden, wrapped against her body in a silk sling. Her blood-red sari makes her look regal, the mechanical goddess of the scrapyard. She stares down at us mere mortals and crosses two of her arms. "If I'd wanted you dead, you wouldn't be here."

25

Do Not Destroy the Universe

Roxy's threat settles into the air.

"That's good because I don't think we're going to win this fight," says Lester from under a particularly large spacebot. Beside him, also under a spacebot, Qual lets out a series of hiccupping laughs. Evidently, he is very ticklish. Natasha tries to curse her way out from under a pile of others until one spacebot removes her hat. Then she grows eerily quiet.

"If you don't want to harm us," I lower my mop, "then release everyone."

The gears in Roxy's head spin as she calculates. It's clear from her gaze that she doesn't like to be told what to do, but she waves a third hand at the spacebots. They quickly back off as everyone struggles back to their feet. Natasha trembles until a spacebot returns her hat. She snatches it, plops it on her head, and promptly boots the offending spacebot. It flies past Roxy and out the door.

Roxy uncrosses a pair of arms. "Clearly, we've gotten off on the wrong foot."

"Wrong foot." A voice agrees, and Beastie materializes next to Roxy. He rubs his beak against her mechanical shoulder with a happy coo. She doesn't even flinch but gives the traitor a scritch behind the ears. His back leg flutters with enjoyment.

"Well, Beastie clearly trusts you, but he is a terrible judge of character," I grumble. Beastie chirps indignantly at me, but I ignore him. My focus is on Roxy. "Maybe you can help set us right. Why have you tricked us into coming here? And what were you doing with our captain?"

"Only saving his life," Roxy says as she moves to lean against the wall. "Do you realize the amount of damage that his body took? Between the perpetual Astra soulstone exposure and those blaster holes, he's lucky to be in the land of the living. He probably needs another week in that tank you prematurely removed him from just to get feeling in his toes again. He'll definitely need some cybernetic enhancements after that spinal injury if he ever wants to walk."

Cold settles in my gut as I glance at Solis' stoic face. He doesn't flinch at her diagnosis, only raises his chin to he can better look her in the eye as he says, "You haven't answered my CSO's first question."

"Ye trapped us here," Natasha adds, crossing her own arms. "That doesn't breed trust."

"Yeah." Lester nods in agreement.

"Hey R-Roxy," Qual says, with a little blush and wave, "Good to see you—"

Natasha elbows him in the side.

Roxy turns to face him. Her smile widens as she casts a wink his way. "Hey, Eugene."

Qual blushes as Natasha's frown deepens in a murderous way. This telepathic link isn't going to end well. I shake my head. Good grief.

"Look," Roxy starts again, "was it a trap? Yes. Yes it was. But not a malicious one. If those of you who arrived on the *Helios* had bothered to stay with it, you would have been welcomed with open arms. But you all jumped ship into the scrapyard, and we've been playing cat and murderous mouse ever since. Do you know how many bots I lost trying to find you? All this just to get a message through."

"What message?" Solis asks.

"One that I don't want spies to learn and—believe me—you are crawling with spies. Speaking of." Roxy opens the palm of her upper right hand, and a joker blast hits a vent above the door.

Aide falls from its hiding place. I hadn't even realized it was there. Its lens whirls around in 360-degree rotations until Roxy plucks it up. The lens focuses on her as it squirms, but she simply flips Aide over, opens its belly, and disconnects its power source. Aide's red lens goes dark.

"Finally," Roxy drops Aide onto the desk beside her, "we can talk in private."

"What is it you want?" I ask.

Roxy purses her lips. "How about I just show you? It will be easier than explaining."

She waves a fourth hand, and the spacebots march us out the open door. One even pushes Solis' hoverchair beside me. His hand slips into mine naturally as if we did this all the time, a warm comfort in the sea of spacebots. After a few corridors, we enter the scrapper's bridge. Its halo system is three times the size of the *Helios*', but the console in the center is a familiar design. We're swimming in stars as it displays each quadrant. I flick a finger through a black hole, and it warps at my touch.

Roxy settles in front of the console and brings up a starchart. "It's been over an orbit since we last worked together, but I trust you to recall what I can do?"

Qual jumps in eagerly. "Y-you're a navibot. You are superb at calculating and recalculating space-time coordinates for interstellar travel through abnormalities in space. In real time no less! You're a work of art in the field of probabilities."

"You say the nicest things, Eugene." Roxy smiles.

"Ye also be a treacherous she-devil who attempted to trap us in the Bermuda Tetrahedron," Natasha adds with obvious contempt for Roxy's charade, but the android is unfazed.

"Both of you are correct. I was both a state-of-the-art navigator and a vixen mercenary, but a lot has changed since we last met. Not only do I work for myself now that I've acquired this scrapper station, but I've grown into much more than a navibot." Roxy removes the wrap hiding her one arm. Underneath, built into her arm, is the scarlet soulstone we'd seen in her halocom message. Next to me, Solis' grip on my hand tightens.

"Since arriving in the Tetrahedron, I've been able to take advantage of ... let's call it the Tetrahedron's timelessness and make predictions. Let me show you what I found." Roxy closes her eyes and the gears in her mind spin wildly. The soulstone on her wrist radiates and sparks. When she opens her eyes, they're black with pinpricks of starlight inside. All around us, the bridge's halo projects her vision: a universe of probabilities. It's impossible for me to take it all in, but as I watch, stars start to go dark until entire quadrants disappear from the starchart.

"What is that?" Lester's voice is small.

"That is the death of the universe," Roxy's voice resonates as the last of the stars go dark and the entire bridge is pitch black. I can't even see my hand in front of my face. Everyone's breathing comes in nervous pants. I'm shaking until Solis' hand gently squeezes my own.

"W-what causes it?"

"That is the strange thing." Roxy's voice chimes in the dark. Slowly the universe resets and the process repeats once more. "I've been running simulation after simulation, and there is little to no hint. Until I found the one thing that changes the timing."

The image zooms into the Tetrahedron, onto this scrapper ship, and, finally, the *Helios*.

"This is why I've lured you all here. Your *Helios* and, perhaps your crew, are inexplicably linked to this catastrophic event. But in what way, I haven't been able to fully calculate. I believe it has something to do with your captain's Astra attunement. So, I brought you here to stop this universal Armageddon. But it's not stopping … I need more data."

"Roxy?" My voice echoes through the bridge. "Can you check one more thing?"

"Of course I can." Roxy's omniscient face stares at me.

"Before you captured the *Helios*, there was a shuttle that escaped it. Can you see if that ship is also linked to this event?"

She nods and the halo resets again, possibility after possibility centered on the *Helios'* shuttle. It doesn't matter where the shuttle goes, the simulations all end the same way. The shuttle is the origin for the death of the universe. Lin's shuttle.

"What is this?" Roxy cocks her head.

"That's Lin and his soulstone."

Roxy purses her lips. "But your Captain is right here. I made sure you'd all be here."

"But there is more than one Lin Solis with the Astra's Luck."

"You're right, CSO…" Roxy focuses on me, her star filled eyes wide as her mind's gears turns. "That does change things. We must work quickly. Every second of delay is a second your probability of success decreases. You have unleashed the destruction of the universe. It's up to you stop it."

26

Do Enjoy the Little Things

Roxy allows our crew to return to the *Helios* while we are re-supplied. It's a brief breath before we dive into the journey ahead. A few spacebots roll past the cantina doors on their way to make repairs. Although, one watches us and waits. The *Helios* crew surrounds the cantina's poker table with a thirty-cubic-centimeter IC in the center. Natasha sits backwards and rests her arms on the chair's back. Beside her, Qual fiddles with the AWD's old AI sphere. Lester brushes his stubby beard next to them, and Solis reclines in his hoverchair. Even Beastie has a spot at the table and scratches himself in nervous anticipation.

Or maybe that's just me projecting.

Solis examines each face. "I want to give you an out right now. If you wish to leave, there will be no judgement, and I'll see you safely returned to the Terminal. Our next journey will be the most important one of our lives, and we'll need to be able to act freely. So, I'll ask you all one final time, are you willing to resign from Starprint with me?"

Natasha clears her throat, and all eyes turn to her. She hesitates before reaching up and taking off her tricorn. She holds it in her trembling hands. "Would you look at that? I guess I'm really scared.

I forget what that's like sometimes. But you, Captain, must feel like this all the time and still, you go on. I'll have your back."

"W-we're of the same mind." Qual nods. Natasha and he share a suspiciously similar smile. "Each of us has sacrificed to be here on the *Helios*, but for us, it was a choice. It is w-wrong what Starprint did, cloning you and threatening to replace you if you didn't comply. Choice is key to the philosophy of Qualbotics. I won't represent an organization that doesn't allow it."

"I'm with you too." Lester smiles and strokes his teenage mustache. "I come from a family that demanded my loyalty without earning it. You earned it without demanding. There really isn't any other option as far as I'm concerned. I'm with you till the day I spontaneously combust."

Solis nods. He turns to me with a stoic face, but I know him well. His jaw is too tight and his eyes tired. He's scared about what comes next, just like everyone else. I stare at the IC in the center of the table, a miniature version of the device I'd kept Lin in and take a deep breath.

"Growing up, I wanted to find Lost Earth. I even bet my friends I'd beat them to it. But when Dad died, I felt I needed to follow in his footsteps. I fought tooth and nail to become the *Helios'* CSO. I never imagined I'd choose to step down ... but what happened to Lin is my fault." I meet Solis' eyes. "I can't move on until I make this right. So yeah, I'm with you."

The bend in Solis' shoulder relaxes as if releasing some great weight.

"I'm with you." Beastie chimes in and nuzzles Solis' arm. He brushes Beastie's chest with a smile. The Spirit Beast has been a lot more friendly with Solis lately. I'd bet that his dislike of the captain had to do with Lin's stolen soulstone. I'll have to ask Natasha, but at least they're finally getting along.

Solis faces us and nods to me. "Okay, let's do it."

Standing up, I open the IC and pull out Aide. I reconnect its power supply and set it on the table. It shivers awake and all seven remaining legs twitch under it. I dab off a bit of gel stuck in a leg joint. It took a fair bit of negotiating to get the aracbot back from Roxy, and she only agreed to give it up for this explicit task.

"Aide?" Solis asks, and the aracbot rotates to face him. "We need you to deliver a message to Boss Aquila for us."

Solis tosses his Starprint-issued halocom into the open IC. Aide rotates around, observing everyone in turn as they follow suit and toss their Starprint halocoms in too.

As Qual drops the last one into the gel, Solis says, "We quit."

Aide's lens widens to take everyone in as if gauging how serious we all were.

"Just one more thing we'll need you to tell our former boss." Solis tilts his head at me and the aracbot swivels toward me.

Typing into my new halocom, I forward Aide the signed digital contract with Boss Aquila to purchase the *Helios*, Roxy's not-so-polite declination to partner with Starprint, and a promise of evidence against BS2 for the Terminal attack—so long as our deal is honored. "We're keeping the *Helios*." I straighten as Aide takes that in. "Don't worry, she'll be in great hands."

Aide bobs up and down, evidently unfazed by the bad news. I purse my lips, a little concerned how Aide will fair with the Boss. It helped me on the *Titan*, maybe I can help it. "You sure you want to be our messenger? You could stay with us if you wanted. I could talk to Roxy."

Aide takes in the cantina and with its organized chaos: dirty dishes and robotic parrot newly thrown into the dartboard. It then examines each of us, this ragtag group of survivors. Aide stops on my face, narrows its lens, shakes its head vigorously, and jumps back into the IC.

"I-I guess not everyone is like Halcyon." Qual shrugs.

"Why do I feel insulted?" I close the lid and hand the IC off to a passing spacebot for shipment to the Terminal.

"Good riddance!" Natasha calls after.

"I think this calls for a celebration!" Lester jumps out of his chair and heads to the dartboard. He lifts it and pulls out a rum bottle from Junior's old hiding place. He tosses the bottle to Natasha. She catches it and uses her saber to pop the lid.

"A toast, me hearties! To truly becoming pirates!"

"Pirates?" Qual asks as Natasha fills his glass. "I t-thought we were more of freelance mercenaries at this point."

"Independent agents!" Lester corrects and steals the bottle for a swig.

"Drunkards," I chime in and take my drink as well.

I lose myself to revelry. There is freedom in no longer carrying my dad's legacy, but there is sadness here too. Like I'm giving up on a dream, the same way I'd given up on finding Lost Earth with Dare and Knox. As I take in the smiling faces around me, I wonder if those dreams were ever really the end goal. All I want right now is more time to enjoy these little moments.

Time to make mistakes.

Time to share our stories.

Time to enjoy a warm hand in mine.

Lin's Armageddon may be coming, but this time is ours. Someone suggests we air out all our dirty laundry, and my buzz thinks this is a good idea. I bust out some gummy worm snacks to share. Solis admits he can sing, which I already knew. Natasha admits she can't dance, and Qual tries to teach her the waltz while Solis sings. Qual unveils his work-in-progress AI sphere, a pilotbot like Halcyon's original coding. Lester admits nothing and claims he is an open book, which might just be true. It is my turn, and I admit something I probably should have kept to myself.

"Did you really k-kiss that slizard?"

"One time! And I didn't know she was a slizard."

"Yeah, but did ye slip her the tongue?" Lester asks coarsely.

"You're sick, man," I say, my cheeks burning.

Lester hugs himself and makes kissy noises.

I bury my face in my arms. "I hate you guys."

Solis is subdued with a quiet smile on his lips. Occasionally, I catch him casting lingering glances at the soulstone in Beastie's forehead. I don't doubt he's tempted by the soulstone. Three rotations ago, he was superhuman, now he's like everyone else. Even with Qual and Lester working on his spine implant, it'll take him many rotations to fully recover ... time that the universe may not have.

"Wait, a sec," Lester pauses in making out with himself, "if you didn't think it was a slizard, who did you think it was?"

My face gets redder.

"'Twas Qual, wasn't it?" Natasha raises a sly eyebrow at me.

"What? No!" I shake my head.

"Well, it better not be me." Lester shakes his head. "Sugar, you'll get arrested going after minors."

"You're not a minor!"

"So, it *was* me?"

"NO! Captain, please stop this madness."

"Well, t-tell us then," Qual insists with a hiccup.

I gaze over at Solis and shove my face into my drink.

"I knew it!" Lester cries out and turns to Qual. "I knew she had a thing for the captain. Cough up the glint."

"Cough up!" Beastie agrees.

Qual curses and begins rummaging through his pockets. They took a bet on me?

Solis pats my back in solidarity. I enjoy the proximity of him. I still can't say everything I want to, but I know we have each other's back. This crew is my ship, my responsibility, and my family. I trust them more than I trust myself.

I trust them with the universe.

The End

Acknowledgement

Thank you so much for reading *Gambling on Common Sense: Rationality, Romance, and the Space Between*! I hope you've enjoyed this mad fever dream turned story. I want to take a moment to thank everyone who has helped build me up as a writer. It's been a long journey, but you've all made it so worthwhile. First, I'd like to thank my editor and fellow author, David Hankins, for his professional insights and guidance. You demystified the indie publishing process for me, and I can't thank you enough. A special thanks as well to my artist, Solace Garcia—an incredibly talented Denver artist and maker I was fortunate to meet at the local tavern.

Additionally, thank you so much to my alpha, beta, and ARC readers for their feedback Alissa Olson, Alyssa P, Amanda W., Bill Olson, Casey Creed, Emily D., Eric Bates, Fiona Hall-Zazueta, Jana, J.K., Karyn, Louisa VdB, Nikhil Prabala, Michael, Miranda Chapman, Monica Plumb, Nathan Vaughn, Olivia Lance, Sam Ledel, Tess, Triston (Qwop) Harlin, Ty Melancon, Vasha, Wes Fox, and Zach Palmer. Thank you to the writing communities I've been blessed to have learned from including the Wulf Pack, my Mountain View, and my Denver Writing Group. I'm lucky to have you all in my life.

I'd also like to thank all those who made the Kickstarter a massive success! Your excitement is contagious and I'm so happy to be sending my story your way. Alissa Olson, Allie Quinn, Annette, Casey Creed, Carl Spitzer, Carla Bermudez, Cherelle H., Christina Baclawski, Christy S., Claire Gallant, Clayton Cravath, CLG Porter, Daphne, Dave Holets, David Hankins, David Weintraub, Dead Fish Books, Eli Hawthorne, Elisa Ponsell, Ergo Ojasoo, Erick Bates, F.J. Estrada, Frisky, Gabbie, Glori Medina, Gwen and Stephanie Greeley, Halcyon Gates, Heiko Koenig, inspirnathan, Irinel Finco, Jack Oskay, Jamie, Jenny Perry Carr, Jillian Baker, Joel Singer, John Lucas, John Markley, Judy McClain, Karina Krogh, Karyn, Keric, Linda, Linda Teuschler, Lisa Herrick, Luke Leveque, Melissa Graham, Michelle Tebben Teuschler, Miranda Chapman, Myke Tea, Natalie Fitch, Olivia Lance, Patrick Hay, Peggy Plogman, Rick Hertzberg, Robin Wallace, Royce Roeswood, Ryan P., Sergey Kochergan, Stephen W. Buchanan, Thomas Horne, Tim Anderson, Tracy Popey, Trip Space-Parasite, Triston (Qwop) Harlin, Ty Melancon, Victoria P., Wingnut, Zachary Palmer, and Zander Woolley.

Lastly, I'd like to thank my parents. Mom, you've always encouraged my creative side, and I love you for it every day. Dad, you've instilled in me an appreciation for the hard work it takes to build something of your own and a deep awe for the natural world. I can't thank you both enough for shaping everything that I am.

EXCERPT: THE LOST ORBITS

TURN THE PAGE FOR AN EXCERPT FROM THE LOST ORBITS A SHORT STORY COLLECTION FROM THE UNCOMMON UNIVERSE

The Lost Orbits:

An Uncommon Universe Novella

Coming July 2026

Excerpt:

Love, Loss, & Robots

By L. Briar

LOVE, LOSS, AND ROBOTS

NOTE-TO-SELF: WHO NEEDS FRIENDS WHEN YOU HAVE TREBUCHETS?

CSO Summary: I can't quite put my finger on it, but I think the engineer is out to get me. He's been holed up in his laboratory since I confiscated his unlicensed nanobots and he's tinkering with something. I've tried to bring it up with the captain but … well, let's just say we don't see eye-to-eye on the subject. Requesting additional override permission.

Engineering Officer Eugene Qual trusted humans as far as he could throw them, which, if he had his homemade trebuchet, would be significant, assuming standard Terminal gravity and the person's weight. Unfortunately, throwing a humanoid in the tight, boxy quarters of his engineering lab would break his delicate instruments. Perhaps that wasn't the best solution to his current dilemma. If only threats of trebuchet perils worked on his new colleague, Common Sense Officer Ash Payne. She was being stubborn again about stopping his AI experiment.

"You can't override the control module. It's not safe." Blah. Blah. Blah. Ash yammered from behind him as he hunched over his workbench. At twenty, the newbie was eleven years his younger and fresh out of the academy so, naturally, she knew everything. Qual did his best to ignore her as he worked on the AI sphere in his hands. His goggles' vision filled with the sphere's code, showing the parameters he used to train its module. If he wanted to create an android, he'd need to make this work. Qual pulled the plug that connected his goggles to the eye of the orange AI sphere and reached for it.

Ash beat him to it. She placed her hand over the sphere, preventing him from grasping it. "Did you truly account for all the risks here?"

Qual sighed and twisted from his workbench to face her. He raised his goggles to his forehead to stare her down. Of the *Helios'* five crew members, at 160cm she was the only one short enough to try that on. She returned his glare with blue eyes the same shade as his own, although hers had judgmental green flecks. Her long brown hair was tied in a low bun, and she had a loose set of bangs that he was relatively sure were ill-advised. Qual stroked his black beard. It was tidy and the last remaining vestiges of his own hair after he'd given up on the toupee.

"I-I assure you." He straightened in his chair as he pushed through the words. His stutter made him sound uncertain, which was inaccurate. He knew one thing for sure. "I know what I'm doing."

Ash let go of the sphere and shook her head. "That's the problem. I know you're capable, but you're not careful. You can jailbreak an AI sphere, train it into a full-blown android, but the aftermath?" She paused and let the idea of an android's rogue AI settle in. There'd been horror stories of engineers who had failed to train their spheres properly, and the resulting android laid waste to their creators ... but they were fools and Qual was no fool.

He shook his bald head. "C-can't you just go bother Lester? He's probably hatching some scheme."

Ash snorted. "We both know our biologist is harmless compared to your contraptions." When Qual didn't reply, Ash crossed her arms and made a gimme motion with one hand. "If you can't respect my request, respect the CSO position. Hand it over."

Qual bit his lip in frustration. The CSO was second only to the captain in rank. Not relinquishing the AI sphere would be an act of insubordination, and he'd hate to disappoint the captain with another insubordination case. Qual picked up the orb and tossed it to her.

Ash snatched it out of the air and cradled it to her chest. Her stern, angular face melted in relief. He didn't understand that fear, but this new CSO splashed it across her face like clown makeup. Newbies like her always tried to push their rules onto the *Helios* crew. All that academy learning had rotted away their everyday sense, which—given the name of her position—was ironic. When she first joined, he hadn't expected her to last thirty rotations. The fact that she'd made it to sixty rotations still surprised him.

Ash brushed her bangs out of her face. "I'm taking this one into storage. If you've an issue with it, take it up with the captain." She pocketed the sphere and moved to leave the cramped quarters of his tidy lab. Ash stepped outside, and Qual nearly relaxed before she poked her head back into the lab. "Oh, don't forget our subcontractor with their navibot are meeting us at 17:00:00. Be in the cargo bay by then, okay?"

"N-no, not okay," Qual all but groaned. "We wouldn't need an outsider to guide us if you'd let me w-work."

"The Bermuda Tetrahedron can't be taken lightly. We need an experienced guide to enter such a spatial anomaly." Ash pursed her lips and patted the pants pocket where she'd stuffed the orange AI sphere. It bulged out awkwardly. "Be honest. In your expert opinion, could this AI sphere get us safely into the Tetrahedron?"

"Every n-new advancement requires testing." Qual fidgeted with his left arm and dodged the question. He tried not to show it, but the mention of the Tetrahedron's anomaly made his stomach spin. When he had applied for the *Helios* deep space explorer he'd known there would be risky missions—that's inherent in the Big Three's Terminal space race—and the Tetrahedron would be their most dangerous yet. But that uncharted space was teaming with Ancient Astra artifacts and ignoring that was a fool's errand. The first time an artifact was discovered, it reinvented space travel and enabled the creation of hyperdrives. Since that discovery, every company wanted its own deep space explorer crews searching for Astra artifacts. In Terminal's corporatocracy, whoever held the most artifacts controlled humanity's future.

"Are w-we sure that this subcontractor is up to the task?" Qual asked, adjusting his lab-coat's sleeves. "What did Starprint HQ say?"

He and the rest of the *Helios* crew had cast their lots in with Starprint—the lesser of the Terminal's Big Three evils. Starprint, E. Vilco, and BS2 all owned a third of Terminal Humanity's pulse, and none played nice with the others. At least with Starprint Inc., they cared about their explorer's survival rates. Still, he'd be lying if he said he wasn't nervous. That's why he needed to train his AI sphere into a navibot android. Couldn't Ash see that? They needed to rely on themselves, not to rely on some random human subcontractor. More humans only ever created more errors.

"Starprint HQ is the one pushing their hiring. Even Griz vetted them."

Qual crossed his arms at the mention of their ship's Terminal caretaker. "If th-that know-it-all says it's okay, I'm sure we're headed up a wormhole without a paddle."

Ash shook her head, ignoring his gibe. "Look, I have my reservations as well … there is something more going on here, I think, but let's at least meet them." Ash gave him a teasing smile. "Isn't that better than a fresh and untested AI with a jacked ethics module?"

Qual pursed his lips and didn't reply. That seemed unfair. Maybe he had joined the wrong Big Three company? Would E. Vilco bother with mortality and admonish their engineers in such a way? Surely BS2, with all its robotics focus, wouldn't block his engineering insights. But ... those companies didn't have Captain Lin Solis and, despite his distrust of most humans, Qual did trust his captain.

Ash turned to go.

"Qu-question for you," Qual called out.

"Yeah?" Ash glanced over her shoulder.

"H-how much do you weigh?"

"About 68 kg, why?"

Qual thought through the trebuchet calculations. "No reason."

Ash raised an incredulous eyebrow but left without another word.

Qual waited, counting five heartbeats. Once he was sure she wouldn't return, he pulled out the real AI sphere from his workbench. He'd gotten wise to the new CSO's interventions and had prepared a decoy sphere, just in case Ash tried anything. He rolled the green apple-sized sphere onto the table. The color indicated it to be a pilot sphere, one that could greatly improve the auto-piloting of the *Helios* if he trained it well, but he had bigger ambitions for the AI inside.

(Click here to continue or scan the QR Code below).

ABOUT THE AUTHOR

At 4 years old, Briar's home burned down. Worried for her daughter, her mother began reading to her at night. *The Hobbit*, *Harry Potter*, and a waterfall of other stories gave Briar an appreciation for fiction's escapism. Unfortunately, this led to a terrible affliction called becoming a storyteller. As of writing these words, there is no known cure.

She tried to fight it by studying magic—or as some call it—engineering at The Ohio State University. She even became a productive member of society, hopscotching across the USA in the age-old effort of "making a living." But after settling in the Rocky Mountains of

Colorado, she was forced to face the truth: sometimes, you just have to write things down.

In their free time, Briar enjoys hiking, board gaming with friends, and stabbing people with foam swords. Today, they are the author of over 42 short stories, and their 535%-funded Kickstarter hit, *Gambling on Common Sense: Rationality, Romance, and the Space Between*, is now available on Amazon.

Learn more about the author or get the latest in Gambling on Common Sense news by signing up for their newsletter

Enjoying the Uncommon Universe?
Remember to leave a review. This helps other readers discover Ash's story. Thank you!